PRISM
CLOUD

PRISM CLOUD

the HARBINGER SERIES

JEFF WHEELER

47NORTH

Text copyright © 2019 by Jeff Wheeler
All rights reserved.

No part of this book may be reproduced, or stored in a retrieval system, or transmitted in any form or by any means, electronic, mechanical, photocopying, recording, or otherwise, without express written permission of the publisher.

Published by 47North, Seattle

www.apub.com

Amazon, the Amazon logo, and 47North are trademarks of Amazon.com, Inc., or its affiliates.

ISBN-13: 9781542044134 (paperback)
ISBN-10: 1542044138 (paperback)

Cover design by Mike Heath | Magnus Creative

Printed in the United States of America

To Travis

Lady Corinne of Pavenham Sky is possibly the most dangerous woman in the empire and likely a spy for the court of Kingfountain. While there is but one record of her having visited that foreign power, when she was a young child, I cannot resist the suspicion that she is part of Montpensier's Espion. I believe she has managed, through subtlety and caution, to infiltrate our society and rise to one of the highest levels of power.

My investigation into her dealings has been thwarted at every turn. But I have come to discover that the Lawton family has controlling stakes in nearly every industry in the empire, forming a massive interest of which our empire, at large, is completely ignorant. This extensive enterprise has been forged in secret, but she is at its apex. My officers report that zephyrs go routinely to Pavenham Sky. I have done all that I can to block Lady Corinne's marriage to the emperor, which I cannot in good conscience condone until the investigation is complete. The emperor grows more fractious and impatient by the day.

I must even conceal this record. My chambers are repeatedly rifled through and examined. How, I do not know. But I cannot leave any evidence of my suspicions in plain sight. When I finally bring her to justice, there will be many who fall with her.

—Brant Fitzroy, Prime Minister

CETTIE

CHAPTER ONE

Fog Willows

The young officer of Law with reddish-brown hair described grisly murders with the dispassion of one talking about the weather. Cettie couldn't imagine what unspoken details he was concealing from her. What she was hearing was enough to give her nightmares.

"That makes, by my reckoning," he said in his neutral tone, "another fifteen tenements at risk. The latest deaths were here and here," he said, pointing to a detailed map of the Fells, where circles of red ink had been dabbed within a larger circle. "As you can see, all occurred within this radius."

Cettie felt her gorge rising in her throat. "H-how many were killed?"

"A little girl . . . here," he said pointing to one of the blots. "A young lad . . . here. No one saw them taken. All disappeared after dusk."

Cettie swallowed and tried to calm her nerves. She was the keeper of Fog Willows, the personal estate of the prime minister of the empire. But staring at the map brought back memories of the dark childhood she'd spent in that very slum—days filled with hunger and fear and hopelessness. She steepled her forefingers, intertwining the others, and stared again at the murders marked on the map.

"And so you think the Fear Liath," she said, looking him in the eye and pointing to the center of the ink blots, "is lurking somewhere in these tenements?" Just thinking about the creature made her muscles clench. Memories from the dark grotto, its former lair, began to intrude on her thoughts. She'd had nightmares of the beast's jaws, its feral smell, and the aura of terror it seemed to exude.

"I do, ma'am," said the young lieutenant crisply. "When the murders first began in the Fells, they were haphazard. There was no pattern. But over the last six months, they seem to have clustered in this area. It is the recommendation of the Ministry of Law that we begin a house-to-house investigation for the beast's new lair, and the Ministry of Thought has suggested that Leerings be set up in these locations"—he pointed to street corners in a circumference around the circled area—"to contain the creature and prevent it from escaping us."

A shudder went down Cettie's back. "Is it your goal to merely contain the monster, Lieutenant? Or to kill it?"

"We'd like to destroy it. I came, per the prime minister's request, to ask if you would help us track and trap the beast."

"Me?" Cettie asked in shock. She'd wondered why her father had sent this man to deliver such news, but it hadn't occurred to her that she'd be asked to do such a thing.

"Yes, ma'am. As you know, the prime minister is currently at the court of Kingfountain with Miss Fitzempress. He gave these instructions before he left. He indicated that you are especially . . . attuned to this creature. That you could possibly help us locate its lair. I also understand that Mr. Patchett of Gimmerton Sough helped you and your brother chase the Fear Liath from Dolcoath. His experience with the Fear Liath and his past service in the Ministry of War would make him a great help to us, but he has refused our overtures thus far. We were hoping, ma'am, that you might persuade him to come. I don't mean to pry, but I've heard that the two of you used to be . . . close."

If Cettie hadn't already felt unsettled and wary, this latest request would have shoved her over the line. In the eighteen months since she had rebuffed Rand Patchett, they had hardly spoken, and she could see that his resentment was still festering. They had come into contact more than she would have liked because Cettie's sister Anna had become close friends with Rand's sister, Joanna. Sometimes it felt like Anna spent more time at Gimmerton Sough than at Fog Willows. The thought brought on a familiar twinge of guilt. Her friendship with Anna had become strained. Anna had wished to marry Adam Creigh, only he had asked Cettie to marry him instead. That she and the Fitzroy family were the center of such gossip made her head ache.

Cettie rubbed her temples. "Things between Mr. Patchett and I have been . . . difficult . . . of late, Lieutenant."

"I don't know anything about that, ma'am," he said in his all-business manner. "Yet I feel bound by duty to request you put aside your personal feelings, in the interests of the poor chaps living in the heart of the Fells. If the people knew what we know, there would be a mass panic. They believe a murderer is living among them. They have no idea that a monster is haunting their streets each night. They would leave, but they are too poor to go anywhere else."

"I know," Cettie answered. "Of course I will help. And I will go to Gimmerton Sough and ask Mr. Patchett to join us." She sighed. "Still," she could not help but add, "with all the dragoons in retirement after the war in Kingfountain, I'm surprised we cannot find an able substitute."

The lieutenant did not respond. He was only an officer of Law doing his duty. The relationship between the Ministry of Law and the Ministry of War was always strained. Perhaps they simply did not wish to ask for any favors. Besides which, it occurred to her that this young man had been to many of the places where the victims had been found. He'd seen death in its most gruesome manifestations. If he could bear such a burden, then she could face the discomfort of a conversation with Rand.

"Is there anything else?" she asked him.

"No, ma'am. Send word once you've spoken to Mr. Patchett, if you please."

"I will. Thank you, Lieutenant Fields." Seeing him reminded her of another young lieutenant, from her childhood. That man had dragged her back to the Fells in anticipation of earning a promotion. It had been so many years she could hardly remember his name, but the memory still made her wary at times around officers of Law.

"Thank you, ma'am," he replied with a stiff bow. He planted his officer's hat, which had been cradled under his arm, squarely atop his auburn hair and left the sitting room. The aging butler, Mr. Kinross, was awaiting the visitor in the corridor, and he escorted the man back to his zephyr in the landing yard.

Cettie directed the nearest Leerings to reveal her mother's location within the house, and the magic of the Control Leering showed her Lady Maren writing a letter in her room. Probably to Father.

Cettie walked down a series of corridors and then knocked on the door. Lady Maren invited her inside, and when she opened the door, her mother lowered her pen.

"Was there a visitor?" Lady Maren asked.

"It was Lieutenant Fields."

Lady Maren's countenance fell. "More deaths below?" she asked sadly.

Cettie nodded. "Yes, unfortunately. He came to ask my help in hunting down the Fear Liath. They have narrowed the search to a particular area. They also asked for Rand's help."

Lady Maren's look darkened even more. "Did they? And I assume by your expression they asked you to approach him?"

Cettie nodded, trying not to reveal her conflicted feelings.

"Well, it's brave of you to do this." Lady Maren paused, then added, "Anna spent the night at Gimmerton Sough."

Cettie's eyebrows arched in surprise. That had never happened before.

"She wasn't feeling well. She became sick during her visit yesterday. Joanna sent a note saying she'd sent for a doctor. I was thinking of going there myself to retrieve her, but perhaps you can see if she's well enough to come back with you. I'd rather have her seen by a doctor here."

"Of course," Cettie said, feeling her worry grow. "I'll go at once. I didn't know she was sick."

"I should have told you last night," Lady Maren said, "but I was distracted. You two used to be so close. It pains me to see such conflict between my children."

Cettie couldn't help but purse her lips. The Fitzroys had tried for years to legally adopt her, but until the identity of her birth mother could be discovered, the request would forever be stalled in court. As the family's fortunes had risen, so had the expectations of reward.

"I wish I were your child in truth," Cettie whispered, looking down.

Lady Maren rose from her writing desk and swept Cettie into an embrace. "You *are*, despite everything that has been done to keep us apart." She cupped Cettie's cheek. "I may not have given birth to you, but I love you as much as my other children. You must know that your father and I will not let this rest. We'll see to it that you're adopted, no matter how long it takes. You're entitled to the same rights as the others." She caressed Cettie's cheek. "When the time comes, the maston rites will bind our family together through the next existence. The powers of the *irrevocare sigil* are real, you know. And when you and Adam are married," she said, unable to suppress a joyous smile and a squeeze of her hands, "you and he will also be bound together . . . inexorably."

"Is it inexorable?" Cettie asked. "Don't we both need to live up to our promises?"

"Of course. But can you imagine a man more faithful than Adam Creigh?" She smiled at her own question. "He was meant for you all along, Cettie. I tried to soften the blow for Anna. To her, you stole her dream away, but it was only a dream all along. She'll fall in love again; I know she will. Then things will be better between you."

"I hope so," Cettie said. "Thank you, Mother." Adam had been sent to Kingfountain over a year ago to research the cholera morbus. The separation was painful, but they kept in regular contact. She savored his letters, which always seemed to carry his scent, and they exchanged parcels whenever they could. Once he'd sent her a small brooch he'd fancied made of sea glass, something she wore whenever she needed to feel close to him. Sera had just left for Kingfountain again, and her maid, Becka, had promised to deliver a parcel Cettie had spent weeks preparing for Adam. It was to commemorate the day he had proposed to her, but it had taken Cettie longer than she'd thought to gather everything.

The pain she felt was something her mother understood all too well—the separations from Fitzroy were difficult for Lady Maren. Each letter he'd sent her sat in a stack on her bedside table, and she'd told Cettie in a quiet moment that she read them every night before retiring.

Once Adam returned, Cettie would have to move away. Perhaps her mother would write her letters at this very desk.

"I wish I never had to leave Fog Willows," she said in a gush of words. "But I will someday. I . . . I fear returning to the Fells for good, and yet we both know Adam dreams of being a doctor there."

"All the more reason for you to help the Ministry of Law with their problem. Will you go to Gimmerton Sough this afternoon?"

"I'll leave right away," Cettie said. "I can't say I look forward to speaking with Rand, but I'll get to see Joses while I'm there. It seems he prefers serving their household. Mr. Kinross hasn't been able to persuade him to come back."

"That doesn't surprise me," her mother said. "I think Rand Patchett would be an interesting man to valet for. He did some good with Stephen after all. He's not a bad man."

"No, he's not," Cettie replied. The problem was the complicated—and conflicted—way Rand made her feel. Despite having rejected him, she was still attracted to him, and the very thought of him summoned up a good measure of guilt. Her sudden engagement to Adam had certainly upset him. Still, he was a good man. She believed he'd help her in the Fells because it was the right thing to do.

After finishing her arrangements, Cettie had Mr. Kinross prepare the tempest for the journey to Gimmerton Sough. It was a beautiful late spring day, and the air was finally warm enough that she didn't need a cloak for the journey. Cettie climbed aboard the tempest, and it responded to her thoughts and presence by thrumming to life. At her direction, the floating tempest arced away from the landing yard. She increased the craft's speed, savoring the sensation of soaring through the sky, hands gripping the helm, hair blown back by the wind. The beauty of the enormous clouds on the horizon never failed to move her, and the freedom she felt skimming through them made her grin despite herself. Now and again, she glanced down, taking in the sight of the small villages on the ground beneath her—little more than clusters of cottages with sheep in pens.

From the storm glass, the method she and her father had developed for predicting the weather, she knew the day would continue to be mild and calm. An occasional jolt of bad air rumbled the tempest, but the lurch it made in her stomach only added to the thrill. She was at one with the sky ship, so in tune with its abilities that it was almost an extension of her own thoughts. Time passed quickly in such a transfixed state. The craft would continue to its destination without her active attention, so Cettie allowed herself to close her eyes for a moment, enjoying the feeling of being at one with the world around her—with the tempest, the air, and the ground far, far beneath her.

And that was when the vision came.

Instantly, she was transported far away, almost as if a part of her had left her body behind. She was in a crowd of people walking along a bridge. The thunder of a massive waterfall could be heard all around, adding to the majesty of the enormous sanctuary that rose on the island opposite the bridge. These visions allowed Cettie a kind of omniscient sight—she could observe a dirty brass penny trampled on in the street, or she could rise far enough to see the entire span of the bridge that straddled the waterfall. She recognized this place, the city of Kingfountain, from a previous vision. The sanctuary, Our Lady, was one of the holiest structures in that world. The gates of the sanctuary were bedecked in flowered garlands. There was a celebration underway, she realized. Was it a festival?

There was a disturbance happening in the street. People were carrying on about a wedding, and a few of them started to shove each other roughly. Was this a vision of Sera's wedding to Prince Trevon of Kingfountain? If so, Cettie's heart was glad for her friend. She had met the prince several times on his visits to court. He was warm and kind, and he and Sera seemed quite comfortable with each other. Fond even. They joked and talked with each other as dear friends do, and she'd even caught them admiring each other surreptitiously. She'd asked Sera about it on their last visit, and her friend had actually blushed, which wasn't like Sera at all. The match may have started as a political one, but she knew it had become more for both of them.

But if the marriage was a happy occasion, as it should be, why was there such a commotion?

Then she saw a group of soldiers push through the crowd. Lord Fitzroy, the father figure of her life, was with them. He was wearing his everyday clothes, except the jacket was somewhat finer than what he normally wore. He was talking to some men who were gathered around him. She felt a thrill of pride to see the others listening to him so intently, but something about the scene worried her. His expression was guarded, intense. There were too many people around him.

She watched as he frowned at something and then hobbled a bit in place. He bent down to examine the heel of his boot.

And it was at that exact moment she heard the gunfire, an explosion of black ash that sent an iron bullet into Fitzroy and knocked him down. There were screams and instant pandemonium. Cettie saw Fitzroy lying in the street, clutching his side, his face a mask of pain. The sight of the blood seeping beneath and around him filled her with horror.

The vision pulled back, and she saw a man crouching on the roof of a nearby building, the plume of smoke still jetting from the barrel of his arquebus. Fitzroy's attacker leaned back against the roof, hidden from the sight of those gathered on the bridge below.

She recognized the brooding man with the scar on his face.

The last time she had seen the man who claimed to be her father, she had shot him in the Fear Liath's cave. He was supposed to be dead.

CHAPTER TWO

GIMMERTON SOUGH

Cettie was a harbinger. It was not a gift she had asked for or even one she wanted. Her visions were glimpses of the future—events that *would* happen. As far as she knew, she had no ability to change them, just as she could not control when the visions came or what they entailed. Now, with the vision still vivid in her mind, she experienced the deepest anguish and conflict of her life. She couldn't bear to see it fulfilled. Her father was in Kingfountain at that very moment—the attack could happen at any time.

Her stomach twisted with worry, but her heart stiffened with resolve. She had to try to save him. But how could she return to Fog Willows right away to tell Lady Maren? Surely she deserved to know first.

Conflict and inner turmoil heaved inside her breast, but she forced herself to think the situation through logically. Her visions were usually of the near future. There was probably time to react. She wouldn't do anyone any good if she acted in haste. Besides, she might be able to prevent the Fear Liath from killing again if she secured Rand's agreement to find and fight it. Her father was the one who'd asked her to handle that situation. Then there was Anna to consider . . . she didn't like the thought of leaving her at Gimmerton Sough, especially if she was sick.

She was close enough to the other estate that she might as well finish the task.

Her decision helped calm the turbulence of her thoughts. Perhaps the injury she'd witnessed was not fatal. Adam was in Kingfountain. Surely he would try to help if he could.

The final stretch of the journey to Gimmerton Sough was spent in misery. As she finally guided the sky ship to the landing yard, she stared at the rugged stone mansion and wondered how she was going to face the Patchetts, especially Rand, with such heaviness in her heart.

Another tempest was docked in the yard with the Patchetts' zephyrs. It didn't surprise her to learn they had a visitor—Joanna was very popular and had many friends and visitors. Cettie's goal wasn't to intrude. She only wanted to talk to Rand and then take her sister home.

The thought of talking to anyone about anything was almost too much to bear. She rested her forehead on the helm, trying to gather her strength, summon her courage. She'd always trusted in the Knowing, and that trust had served her well in the past. But in this moment of blackness, she felt she'd been betrayed by the very powers she had always trusted.

Why give her such a vision if she couldn't change it? Or was this a sign the visions had changed somehow? That her intervention was needed?

She squeezed the rungs of the helm and took a steadying breath. Then she lowered the rope ladder and hastened down to the ground. Arms folded, she crossed the gravel yard to the walkway leading to the manor. She'd heard from Anna that the Patchetts had finally hired a keeper of the house, a woman named Mrs. Rosings. Cettie had never met her, but her sister had said she was a stern woman who ran a steady household. As Cettie approached the doors, they opened, and a matronly woman bustled out of them.

The woman's hair was parted in the middle, and pins held back her dark curls. She had a sour expression on her mouth, as if she'd been interrupted in something important. Both her appearance and her demeanor instantly reminded Cettie of Mrs. Pullman, the previous keeper of Fog Willows, who had tormented her and attempted to manipulate and control the entire Fitzroy family.

"And who might you be?" said the prim woman as Cettie approached. Even her voice was hauntingly similar.

For a moment, Cettie gaped at Mrs. Rosings in surprise, feeling as if she were standing before her old enemy.

"I-I'm Cettie, keeper of Fog Willows."

The woman's brow furrowed. "You're rather *young* to be a keeper. You can't be more than twenty."

"I am . . . I am almost twenty-one, Mrs. Rosings. I came to fetch my sister Anna."

"Ah," she said, her look darkening. "Anna is unwell. She's not fit to go anywhere. Doctor Donaldson is still here, tending her fever. Come in." She stood back from the door, holding it open for Cettie.

The keeper's words filled her with unease—was Anna's condition truly so serious?—and that feeling only heightened as she stepped into the hall. She had not been back to Gimmerton Sough after the fateful ball. That night the hall had been decorated festively with flower garlands and music, and happy voices had filled the air. Now it felt strangely empty, and despite the fact that Mr. Batewinch stood farther down the hall with someone, talking softly, everything was eerily quiet.

When the woman with Mr. Batewinch turned toward the door, Mrs. Rosings stepped to the side and gestured for Cettie to do the same. The other guest was a handsome woman in her late thirties, a plumed hat atop her dark hair. Her outfit was the pinnacle of fashion and style—frills at her throat, a tight buttoned vest with stripes, and a teal-colored jacket and skirt. Her eyes met and held Cettie's.

Batewinch, who'd also turned, presumably to escort the guest to the door, paused upon seeing the pair of them. "Ah, Miss Cettie! Welcome back to Gimmerton Sough."

The woman tilted her head and continued to study Cettie. Something glimmered in her eyes, a subtle look of recognition, perhaps?

"Hello, Mr. Batewinch." Cettie dropped a short curtsy.

"This is our landlady, *ahem*, Lady Corinne of Pavenham Sky," he said, smiling broadly and gesturing to his companion.

Yes, Cettie had guessed as much based on Sera's description of the woman. There was a look of cold malice in her eyes, but her expression was carefully guarded. She was the wealthiest person in the empire, and it was said she had her sights set on the emperor. Sera herself thought it to be true.

A shudder went through Cettie's heart, but she offered another low curtsy.

Lady Corinne gazed at her shrewdly, her dark eyes examining her, finding her wanting. "It is nice to meet you at last," she finally said. "Miss Patchett speaks highly of you."

Her words caught Cettie off guard. She hadn't expected to be addressed at all, let alone civilly. After all, she'd been forbidden to communicate with Sera during her friend's tenure in Lady Corinne's household.

"Thank you, ma'am," Cettie mumbled.

Lady Corinne turned back to Mr. Batewinch. "He doesn't have enough funds to run for parliament. See that there are reserves kept aside for the rent obligation, at least three years' worth. Let him find supporters willing to give, not *lend* him money. I will brook no late payments. Not a single one."

"Of course, my lady," Batewinch said, opening the door for her. "The lad will be disappointed, but there is wisdom in your counsel."

"Come with me," Mrs. Rosings said to Cettie and led her down the hall. Cettie followed, but glanced back at the door as the other two were leaving. She met the gaze of Lady Corinne, who had just looked back at her. Something in the woman's eyes filled Cettie with a keen sense of foreboding. She looked away first.

The keeper led her down the hall, past the staircases, and then down another corridor. Cettie rubbed her temples, trying to shake the feelings of unease, but it was impossible.

"This way," Mrs. Rosings said firmly. The corridor was strangely dark. No Leerings were lit, and the dark wood panels on the wall seemed to repel light. The trepidation in Cettie's heart grew.

That was when she heard coughing.

Mrs. Rosings stopped in front of a closed door, knocked briefly, and then opened it, revealing Anna in the midst of a coughing fit.

The extent of her illness shocked Cettie. She wore a nightdress drenched with sweat, and the upper buttons had been tugged open to reveal the maston chain at her throat. Her temples were slick with sweat, and her lips had a grayish cast to them. There were shadow smudges beneath her eyes. She'd been perfectly well the day before. How could such a thing happen?

"Cettie," gasped Anna weakly, trying to reach out a hand.

A doctor with a white-and-blond beard and a black armband stood by the bed, next to an array of medicines on a small table. Rand stood on the other side of the bed, his arms folded, his look one of brooding and worry. He glanced at Cettie as she entered, his lips tightening into a frown.

She paid him no mind. All her attention was for Anna. She rushed to her sister's side and took her extended hand. The skin was wet with perspiration.

"Doctor Donaldson," said Mrs. Rosings, "this is the keeper of Fog Willows. She came to take Miss Anna back, but I told her you didn't advise it."

"You came," Anna gasped.

"I heard you were ill," Cettie answered, kissing her hand. "You look awful."

"I feel awful," Anna said, and then broke into another violent fit of coughs.

Doctor Donaldson sat down in a nearby chair. He looked exhausted, as if he'd been there all night and hadn't slept himself. "I cannot recommend removing her," he said to Cettie with conviction. "She is very weak."

"What is it?" Cettie asked. She took a deep breath before she spoke her fear aloud. "Is it the cholera morbus?" She knew a bit about the disease from Adam's work, and it terrified her how quickly its victims succumbed to it. Though he had made some progress in treating the disease, he still had not determined how the infection spread.

"No, I don't think so. The symptoms aren't remotely the same. To be honest, I don't know what it is." He took a small cup of water off the table and handed it to Anna, who'd finally stopped coughing. She sipped it greedily and then lay back on her damp pillows. Rand shook his head slowly, worry creasing his brow.

"I fell sick after lunch yesterday," Anna whispered, her voice hoarse from coughing.

"If any of the food had spoiled," Doctor Donaldson said, "then the rest of the family would be sick as well. She's the only one. None of the servants are sick either. It doesn't make sense to me, but as you can see, she is very ill." He looked at Cettie again and then pulled her aside to speak more privately. "I am concerned. Her mother should be advised of the seriousness of this illness."

"She's the one who asked me to check on Anna," Cettie said.

The doctor's face turned grim. "I know. But she needs to be told that she's getting *worse*. I've not seen such a dramatic illness before. It is unlike anything I've experienced."

Cettie's heart was already burdened with the secrets from her vision. Now this. Fear filled her heart as she took in Anna's frailty, her flushed cheeks from the burning fever, the listlessness as she writhed on the pillow.

"Have you sent for a vicar?" Cettie asked the doctor. "To give her a Gift of Healing?"

"I'll summon one straightaway," Rand said. He nodded to Cettie and departed the room.

"We'll take good care of her, Miss Cettie," said Mrs. Rosings, putting a hand on her shoulder. The words were kind, yet they didn't *feel* kind. Even the weight of the woman's hand reminded her of Mrs. Pullman and made her want to shrink away.

"May I have a moment alone with her?" Cettie asked, looking at the doctor. Mrs. Rosings slowly lowered her hand and then nodded. As soon as she and her sister were alone, Cettie squeezed Anna's hand.

"I'm worried about you," she said, feeling miserable.

"I don't know what happened," Anna gasped. "I feel so weak. I've had terrible nightmares. Like when I was a child. I want to go home, but it hurts to move."

"I want to stay with you." Cettie bit her lip as she pressed her palm to her sister's forehead. It was burning hot and dripping with sweat.

"I don't want you to get sick too," Anna said with a sigh. "I'm so hot. Every part of my skin is burning."

Cettie questioned her about her symptoms, trying to understand what had happened, but though she had studied the Mysteries of Wind, she'd never trained as a doctor. Shortly thereafter, Doctor Donaldson returned to care for Anna, and Cettie had no choice but to give way. She felt utterly helpless in the face of her sister's illness.

At long last, Anna stopped coughing and then fell into a fitful sleep.

Cettie retreated from the room. Not knowing what else to do, she stood in the silent corridor, her back to the wall, her emotions wrecked. After a few moments, she heard the sound of two people approaching. When she opened her eyes, she saw it was Rand and Joses.

It was a relief seeing her childhood friend again, although he looked nothing like the street urchin he had once been. He was a man grown now and wore the uniform of a valet. He gave her an eager smile, but his eyes looked worried.

"Hello, Cettie," Joses said.

"It's good to see you," she answered with a smile. That smile faded as she turned to Rand.

"I've sent word for a vicar," Rand said, coming up to Cettie. "I should have thought of that sooner. Her illness came on so suddenly, we all began to panic."

"Thank you for caring for my sister," she said.

Rand seemed to be struggling with what to say next. She saw him flex his fists. "It's difficult to be patient when patience is probably the best remedy of all. I would hate it if . . . anything happened to her. She's a dear friend now. To both Joanna and me."

Cettie nodded, feeling the awkwardness yawning between them. She was determined to bridge it. "I came for another reason, Rand."

His eyebrows lifted in surprise. "And what is that?" Joses shot her a surprised look too. He knew about the awkwardness between them, and the reason for it.

"Earlier this afternoon, I met with a lieutenant from the Ministry of Law. They think they know where the Fear Liath is skulking in the Fells. It's killed again."

Rand's face turned hard. "And?"

Cettie didn't let his expression daunt her. "They need help hunting it down, Rand. I'm going to help them find it and set some Leerings to prevent it from escaping. But they could use a good dragoon . . . to see this thing destroyed."

"We should go!" Joses said excitedly.

Rand smirked. "Hunting things with antlers isn't enough for you now, is it? A Fear Liath is a very different beast."

"I know," Joses said without a trace of fear, "but we can't let the Law have all the glory, can we? They're sniveling cowards. They *need* us!"

"They are not cowards," Cettie said, trying to rein him in with a glare. "They asked for you, Rand. And I told them I'd deliver the message myself."

There was a conflicted look in Rand's eyes, but at least he hadn't rejected the request offhand. "We're very busy. I don't know."

"We are *not* busy!" Joses interjected.

Rand shot him a warning look. "Anna?" he reminded him.

Joses's countenance fell. "Yes. That. Well, *you're* busy, sir. I've been rather idle since yesterday. But you do have a sister who could watch over Anna . . ."

Rand sighed as he shifted his gaze back to Cettie. "I don't know why I ever let you convince me to take him on. He's been nothing but a bother since the day he came." He tempered the insult with a teasing grin. "I do feel rather useless here. I'm no doctor. All I can do is twiddle my thumbs and worry. Where in the Fells did they find it?"

"I saw the map," Cettie said. "But I no longer know the area like I did."

"I do," Joses said proudly. "If I saw the map, I could tell you. So we're going?"

Cettie looked at Rand hopefully.

"With both of you needling me, the odds are stacked against me, I'm afraid," Rand said, holding up his hands. "I'm uncomfortable leaving Anna so sick, but I don't know what else I can do. Doctor Donaldson is capable. And if a vicar can't heal her, then we can only cling to hope. I assume the good lieutenant wanted to handle this matter immediately? We'd need to get ready."

"I can handle the preparations, sir," Joses promised.

"Can I persuade you to stay the night?" Rand asked Cettie.

The thought of the delay filled her with dread. She needed to speak with Lady Maren at once, both about Fitzroy and about Anna. "I have to get back. I can send a zephyr for you in the morning if you like."

Rand shook his head. "I think Joses is overeager enough to gather our things quickly. Perhaps we can go back to Fog Willows . . . with you?"

His request made her slightly uneasy, but there was no rational reason to refuse it.

She nodded to him, and Joses grinned and hurried away.

"Well, at least something good has come from this misfortune," Rand said, his eyes looking intently into hers. "We're talking again."

CHAPTER THREE
FATAL DECISIONS

How was it possible that she felt even worse leaving Gimmerton Sough than she had upon arriving? Troubles truly did seem to come in pairs, like one storm that followed in the wake of another. The tempest cruised at a steady pace back toward Fog Willows, Cettie at the helm. Rand and Joses were below.

What was she to say to Lady Maren? Anna was deathly sick, the cause unknown. Cettie knew her mother would want to go to Gimmerton Sough and see Anna for herself. Could she really add to her burden by revealing the vision she'd had of Father being ambushed? Cettie was still resolved to try to do something about it, but what if she didn't succeed in preventing the attack? She loved Father so much. The thought of losing him was excruciating.

"You seem very far away," Rand said, startling her. She had not heard him approach, but the wind was blowing against them after all. "I'm sorry, I didn't mean to frighten you."

"I was lost in my thoughts," she replied, gripping the helm more tightly. He walked around and leaned against the railing, folding his arms.

"You're worried about your sister." He nodded sympathetically. "Part of me is grateful to be doing something. I hate being idle, and I'm a terrible nurse. But I'm worried about her too. She's become . . . a dear friend." He gave her a wary look, as if preparing to receive bad news.

"She is the sweetest girl in the world," Cettie said.

"That is true," he said with a rueful chuckle. Then he sighed. "Must we keep dancing around this shadow between us? No man relishes being thwarted, least of all to a rival. Your devotion to the good doctor is admirable, truly, but I had the sense that you and I were forming a . . . connection. Was I wrong? Was I deluding myself?"

Perhaps she ought to give him an explanation. But she didn't feel capable of having this conversation at such a moment.

"Where is Joses?" she asked, glancing back toward the lower deck.

"He's being a good valet and polishing my boots," Rand said. "I see you're discomfited by my probing question."

"No, it's just that I am engaged to be married, and I'm not sure I should be having such an intimate conversation with another man."

"Intimate?" he scoffed. "Hardly. We haven't had a real conversation since you abandoned me the night of the ball." He winced. "Sorry, that was too strong a word. When you *unceremoniously* departed. But I hope you recognize that we never shunned you. Even though you breached protocol in an egregious manner, neither my sister nor I took revenge. The shunning has all been on your side."

Cettie bit her lip, but she managed to keep her outward appearance calm. If Joses were on deck with them, she'd feel much more comfortable. "I humiliated you, and I'm sorry for that," she said after a lengthy pause.

"Apology accepted," he said, unfolding his arms and clenching the railing behind him. "That is out of the way now. The next time I visit Fog Willows, I hope you will at least be civil enough to greet me. I don't hate you, Cettie. You hurt me, but I have tried to move onward."

He gave her a pointed look. "I was tempted to drown my hurt another way, but I did not."

He spoke of poppy, an addiction he'd finally broken.

"My sister helped preserve my sanity," he continued. "And your sister has been kind and encouraging as well. But it is you who changed my course, you who helped me leave that habit behind. If you bid me go to the moon with you in this ship, I daresay I would."

"I don't deserve such devotion," Cettie said, shaking her head.

He shrugged and looked away. "We can disagree and still be friends. We *have* to be neighbors, though."

That won a smile from her, which made him grin in turn.

The clatter of quickly moving feet met her ears, and Joses burst up onto the deck. "The boots are polished, sir!"

"Good, now clean my arquebus as I've trained you. I'm not done talking to her yet."

Joses's shoulders sagged, but he turned obediently and went back.

"I saw Lady Corinne with Mr. Batewinch when I arrived," Cettie said.

His mood altered noticeably. His nostrils seemed to flare with resentment. "Did you?"

"I'd never met her before."

"That isn't a surprise. I think Lord Fitzroy is the only person in the empire who doesn't owe her money. She came to deliver her rejection in person. How considerate."

"Rejection?"

"That was too cryptic, I'll admit." He gazed at the horizon a moment, then folded his arms again and faced her. "It's likely the war between us and Kingfountain is over. From what I've heard, the emperor is pushing for a marriage to seal the peace permanently. That means officers, such as myself, will be out of work. What good is a dragoon anyway, except for chasing deadly monsters?" He winked at her. "I've decided I need to be useful. I can't sit in Gimmerton Sough day and night and watch the clouds go by. Even hunting and hawking is not satisfying me anymore. And I think I'd be lousy at growing cabbages."

His choice of vegetable made her laugh.

"I amuse you still? Good. So I've decided to run for a seat in parliament. Maybe someday, when my hair is snow white, I'll earn a seat on the privy council. But unlikely. At least I can do some good in parliament. I approve of the measures Lord Fitzroy is taking. He needs more support, people who will fight the corruption in the government with him. I need a good fight. I also need, it turns out, a great deal of money, for getting a seat is costly. So of course I asked the wealthiest woman in the empire for a . . . contribution. Well, she said no. I think it's apparent she doesn't approve of my political leanings."

Cettie felt another pang at the mention of her father. He'd done so much good in his short time as prime minister. The government had increased its allocations to feed and shelter the poor, and more money was being spent on fixing dilapidated buildings, bridges, and roads in the cities on the surface. Those projects, in turn, generated more work for the poor. Of course, as Rand had mentioned, there were those who didn't approve.

The memory of what Lady Corinne had said about Rand's rent, how she wished to strangle his income to preserve it, made Cettie like the woman even less.

"Well, I do," she answered, nodding at him. "I oversee Lord Fitzroy's contributions. I think something can be arranged to help you."

His eyes brightened, and he leaned forward. "You'd do that for me?"

She nodded.

The smile he gave her made her heart lurch despite herself. "Well," he said in a surprised tone, "I am not too proud to refuse aid from my foes." He paused. "That was a poor joke. I'm still astonished. Thank you, Cettie. I never would have thought, or dared, to ask."

She saw her home in the sky. Still a good distance, but the sight came as a relief.

"Can I ask you a question, Rand?"

"Of course. You can ask me anything."

She wasn't sure she should bring this up, but it had been weighing on her. "Remember the man we killed in the grotto at the end of the river walk? The one who freed the Fear Liath?"

"Why yes, I do recall the man. He tried to drown me, and moments like those tend to be permanent in the memory."

"Are you certain he was dead? Is it possible he might have recovered?"

There was a look of confusion on his face, but also something else. The "something else" was gone too soon for her to interpret it. "What a peculiar question to ask, Cettie. I saw his body go into a box. He'd been shot multiple times, including by you. Without a doctor tending to his wounds . . . I just don't see how it makes sense that he *could* have survived." He looked genuinely perplexed. "Why do you ask this?"

It was exactly what she'd feared he would ask. She hesitated.

Rand leaned forward. "I know you're not just making conversation. You said before that the man claimed to be your father."

"I did," she answered, watching her manor as they neared it. "*He* did."

"Cettie?"

She felt the intensity of his gaze before she turned to look at him.

"Have you . . . had another vision?" he asked softly.

He was one of the few who knew about her power, that she was the first harbinger in more than a generation.

She nodded, and then immediately wished that she hadn't. How could she tell him something that she hadn't yet shared with her own family? It didn't seem right. But she yearned to tell someone, to seek advice from someone she trusted.

"And your vision involved . . . him?" he pressed. "I'm just deducing here. Your reticence is alarming me."

She closed her eyes, wavering even more.

"Did you see him kill someone?" Rand asked pointedly.

She squeezed her eyes, and then something within her broke. The weight on her shoulders felt impossible for her to bear alone. "Yes," she answered, opening her eyes and looking at him in anguish. "I saw him in Kingfountain. He shot . . . he shot Lord Fitzroy."

Rand looked absolutely stunned. He stared at her incredulously for a moment, then his look transformed into one of horror. "By the Mysteries, that would lead to war. All-out war. When? When did you have this vision, Cettie?"

"On my way to see you," she said. "I felt the Mysteries strongly, and then the vision opened up. There were decorations on the street, some sort of festival or . . ."

"A wedding," Rand said, nodding.

"It was on the bridge by the sanctuary of Our Lady. I heard the gunshot, saw the smoke. I saw Father . . ." Her voice started to tremble, and then tears came gushing out of her eyes. She hung her head and sobbed.

Suddenly, Rand was holding her. She pressed her face into her hands, trembling violently. In her grief, she smelled him, that curious heady smell that she'd almost forgotten about.

It was a relief to share the burden with someone else, but it felt wrong to be comforted by him in such a way. She looked up, tear-stricken, and saw his look of compassion.

"You haven't told anyone else, have you?" he asked. "You haven't had the time."

"Shouldn't I tell Mother?"

His lips pressed firmly. "No, I don't think so. It would only cause unneeded pain. You need to tell someone in the government, but who can be trusted with such a secret? I mean, the prime minister is already over there! Lord Welles? I think not. There's no zephyr to deliver such a message." He put his hands on her shoulders and squeezed. "I know others in the admiralty. My father was one of them. I think Admiral

Hatch could get a message to your father quickly. Surely we must warn him."

"If you think Admiral Hatch *could* get a warning to him in time?"

"I'll write the message immediately. We can send a zephyr as soon as we land."

"There's also Sir Jordan," Cettie said, her worries starting to ebb now that she was taking action.

"He's only a vice admiral," Rand said, shaking his head. "I think Admiral Hatch is a better choice." He started rubbing her shoulders. "He can arrange to have someone cross the mirror gate straightaway. You did right to tell me, Cettie. I'm proud of you."

It did feel better. But there was still a part of her, a nagging part, that wondered if she should have confided in him.

The emperor wishes his daughter to marry the Prince of Kingfountain so he can bar her from the line of succession. I have interviewed him many times to try to understand his hostility toward his own flesh. I've read reports from investigations that were undertaken by members of the privy council to corroborate his notion that Sera is illegitimate. No evidence exists for this claim, yet the emperor is convinced, beyond reason, that it is true.

Sera has told me that it has something to do with a visit Lady Corinne made to their family manor many years ago. That visit altered the relationship between father and daughter and led to their bitter rivalry. What was said in that meeting remains a mystery. But what was felt after it has become a troubling link in a tangled chain of events.

—Brant Fitzroy, Prime Minister

SERA

CHAPTER FOUR

GLASS BEACH

It was a fair trade, a term of the deal Sera and Prince Trevon had negotiated after four long years of war between the empires. He would spend three months of each year visiting the empire of Comoros; she would spend an equal amount of time visiting the court of Kingfountain. The armistice had been signed eighteen months ago and would expire in another six. Many men and women from the empire had come to visit or live in Kingfountain since the armistice, most of them intent on exploring business interests. There was a little bubble of hope spreading that peace might prevail. But what would the conclusion actually bring? War? Marriage?

Maybe both.

What Sera hadn't expected, what had surprised her, was how much she enjoyed the freedom of Trevon's court. Had that been his plan all along? Take, for example, the style of dress worn in his court. There were no tight bodices, no corsets that clenched at her stomach and ribs. No gloves or hats or hoods. There were no rules about being alone with young men, none of the restrictive protocols that had always made her chafe.

She was back in Kingfountain again, in the same suite she had stayed in on her other visits. While her maid, Becka Monstrum, unpacked her trunks, Sera doffed the constrictive gown she'd traveled in and changed into one of her Occitanian ones. The silk-and-velvet gown felt deliciously comfortable in comparison.

"That's one of my favorites," Becka said as Sera admired it in the full-length mirror.

"It's one of Trevon's favorites too," Sera said, meeting her maid's gaze. In the year and a half Becka had been in her service, the girl had blossomed. Sera had inherited her from Lady Corinne's service, where the young girl had witnessed the murder of a young advocate, an old schoolmate of Sera's. It was a secret known only by the two of them, the prime minister, and the lead investigator he had chosen. They were now bound together by fate, and Sera was determined to see Becka's old mistress brought to justice for her crimes and intrigues.

Sera put on a pair of earrings Trevon had given her during his last visit. Each one dangled a bead of smooth glass from the famous beach in Brythonica. She was tired from the voyage, because the two worlds operated on opposite schedules—it was always day in Kingfountain when it was night in Comoros.

On this visit, Lord Fitzroy had come along to begin preliminary peace overtures to extend the armistice into something longer lasting. There would be several long, drawn-out meetings, many of which would be dreadfully boring, but Sera wanted the mission to be a success.

"He can't help but like it," Becka said, before returning to her work. "But I think he likes the woman wearing it even better."

"Unload the chests and trunks later," Sera said, turning around so abruptly the skirts swished around her legs. Becka's words had given a rush of pleasure, and she didn't want the younger girl to see the blush on her cheeks. "Why don't you see what the prince's sisters have been up to? It would be helpful to learn something before dinner with his family this evening." Always so conscientious and hardworking, Becka was also Sera's eyes and ears with the palace staff.

The younger girl nodded and promptly obeyed, leaving Sera by herself. Sera looked at herself in the mirror once again. She'd made herself as pretty as possible and was anxious to see Trevon again. Three months had passed since they'd last parted, each longer than the last, and she often thought of the look of regret he'd given her as he took his leave. When she'd asked him what was wrong, he'd said that he didn't mind leaving the smoky City, but he did mind leaving her in it. Normally, he awaited her on the palace steps, but he hadn't done so today. No doubt some pressing business of state had called him away. He had taken on more and more responsibilities from his father in expectation of ruling someday. She was eager to see him again and felt a giddy, fluttering sensation in her stomach.

A solemn click sounded, and the wainscoting on one of the walls opened on quiet hinges. Trevon appeared in her room a moment later. His decorative tunic and jacket befit his noble heritage. His hair was a little longer than she remembered, and she noticed the now-familiar scar on his chin. Just looking at it made her want to kiss it, a thought that made her immediately flush.

"You came in through the spy door like an Espion?" Sera asked, tilting her head.

"I had to," he answered gravely, although his eyes were twinkling. "I've come to abduct you."

She sauntered away from the mirror, keeping her head at an angle. "This sounds serious."

"It is very serious, Your Highness," he said with a playful tone. "In abductions, there is a long tradition involved. Secret plans. A bounty." He met her in the middle of the room and then took her hand and kissed her knuckles. "As long as we are back in time for dinner with my family, I think we can avoid causing unnecessary consternation. If you are game?" He brought his other arm from behind his back, and she saw the brass cylinder he held.

The Tay al-Ard.

"So you truly are abducting me," Sera said, arching her eyebrows. "Where were you planning to imprison me, cruel Espion?"

A smile flickered on Trevon's mouth. "Actually, the hostage will decide that. As long as it is a place that you have already been in this world, this clever device will take you there."

He offered it to her.

Sera took the cylinder in her hand, savoring the warmth his hand had left on it. There were jewels embedded into the caps on each end. It looked like some sort of ancient scroll case. It carried a powerful magic that had no equivalent in her world.

"Are you sure you want to give this to me?" she asked slyly. "I may not want to give it back."

"I trust you," he said, his eyes gazing into hers. He held out his arm.

"So in reality, *I* am abducting *you*," Sera said, grinning.

"Whatever will I do?" he said with a sigh.

"Come willingly, of course," Sera said, hooking her arm with his. She examined the jewels on the rim of the device he'd given her. "I don't press anything. I just *think* of the place."

"Indeed," he answered, standing very near her.

Sera imagined the beach of sea glass in Brythonica. She loved the sound of the ocean crashing against the surf and the ancient beads of glass that, with each year, became fewer and more valuable. As she fixed the image in her mind, a trickle of trepidation went through her. Could she truly control such powerful magic? But it responded to her will, and the power of the Tay al-Ard yanked them from the suite.

In the next instant, she was standing in the sand, her knees wobbling so much she thought she'd faint. Trevon held her upright, his hands on her waist. The air smelled wonderful, the salty flavor of the sea rich in every breath she took, and the sun was warm and radiant.

She noticed she was clutching Trevon's tunic to steady herself and slowly released him, giving him a shy smile as she did so.

"I see you're wearing the earrings I gave you," he said, sounding pleased.

She started to step away from him, but he caught her arm and extended his palm. He wanted the Tay al-Ard back. She was tempted to run and make him chase her, but she was still too dizzy to risk it, afraid she'd flop down in the sand after only a few steps. She placed it back in his palm, and he pocketed it.

Guardians protected the beach from those who might steal the precious bits of polished glass, and the glorious stretch of sand and colored pebbles was empty more often than not. Here she felt gloriously free— away from court, away from the uncertainties of her life. She reached out her hand to Trevon, inviting him to walk with her, and they strolled hand in hand. Within moments, sand had crept into her shoes, and so she stopped and pulled them off, one at a time, enjoying the feel of the fine sand beneath and between her toes. She scooped up her shoes with her free hand, and they walked toward the crashing surf.

A few seabirds appeared to be congregating in the sand near the edge of the surf. There was something there, a blanket and a wicker basket?

"What is that?" Sera asked, tugging Trevon after her.

"Let's go see," he said. As they drew nearer, the gulls began to squawk in protest and flutter away. Her eyes had not deceived her. There was a blanket and basket, abandoned on the beach.

"This is curious," Sera said, looking at him. "I thought you said that this beach was private to the duke's family."

"It is," he said, nodding. When they reached the basket, she set down her shoes and knelt on the blanket. There was a little hasp that kept the basket closed, and she opened it and lifted the lid, finding a collection of berries, some pears, some Occitanian cheeses wrapped in wax, and a bottle of wine and two goblets.

She looked at Trevon over her shoulder and found him smiling as if caught.

"You knew I'd choose this place," she said accusingly.

"More like I *hoped* you would."

"Are there other baskets with berries sitting idly elsewhere?"

He shook his head and dropped down on his knees. "I was fairly confident you'd pick this place."

"Fairly confident? Am I becoming too predictable?"

He began rummaging through the basket. His body emanated a heat that made her want to nestle closer, but she couldn't be the one to do so. Instead, she turned toward the hiss of the surf. The sight of the green-gray waters lapping against the sand and glass pebbles filled her with awe. There was magic in the ocean, a power both relentless and fierce, only barely tethered. Those in Trevon's world called it the Fountain. She could appreciate the strength of the legends behind it, though she knew in her heart it was the same power her world knew as the Mysteries. All power came from the same source, the Knowing.

"Good, no sand in the berries," he declared after a short investigation.

"Thank you for thinking of this, Trevon," she said, turning to look at him. His eyes were peering directly into hers. He moved nearer, just as she had longed to do.

"What?" she asked, feeling her heart start to race. They had known each other for a year and a half. They had walked hand in hand. He had lightly caressed her sleeve now and then. They had danced at state balls. But they had never kissed. As she stared at him, she realized she wanted him to kiss her.

There was a warning in her mind, a danger that once they crossed that bridge, there would be no going back.

He put a hand on her hip, and his touch made her heart pound like the waves on the beach. A feeling of dizziness swept through her. He leaned closer, their faces so near she had to shut her eyes. The aching inside her heart made the distance between them painful. She wanted him too. Without warning, her mind flashed to a memory of kissing Will Russell in the darkness of an abandoned house, the act that had very nearly ruined her. This situation could not be more different. She knew Trevon well, and they'd built to this moment for months and months. Why would that memory intrude on her now?

She gripped the front of his tunic, closing her fingers around the fabric. Then they were kissing, their lips finding each other at last, and she nearly choked on the jolt of emotions that came from it. Sera released his tunic and cupped his face between her palms, kissing him back with passion and wonder. Every part of her came alive at his touch. They parted, gazing at each other in surprise, and then he kissed her again.

She didn't know how long it lasted, only that it filled something inside her soul that had been missing. Her breath came fast, and she blinked rapidly, her eyes burning.

"I was afraid," Trevon said, a crooked smile on his mouth.

"What were you afraid of? That . . . that was wonderful."

"I was afraid you'd push me away." He shook his head. His hand found hers, and he brought her knuckles to his lips again. "I was afraid you wouldn't want it."

"I'm sorry, Trevon. The problem is more likely that I will want it *too* much. Have you been . . . planning this moment?"

He shrugged but offered a conspiratorial smile.

"Well done," she said, laughing softly. She scooped up a handful of colorful glass beads and stared at them, feeling the grit of the sand on her palm. "But I have to wonder at your sense of timing. Why now? Why today?"

"I am more than happy to explain," he answered, shifting closer. She shook loose the pebbles of glass and cocked her head to one side, looking at him curiously.

"What is that chain?" he asked, looking at her neck. His brows knit in confusion. "You normally don't wear necklaces."

Sera hadn't intended for him to notice it, but it had slipped free of her dress. She was instantly a little embarrassed. "It is new."

"Can I see it?" he asked her.

She shook her head.

Then his eyes widened with realization. "It's a maston necklace. I thought they only gave one to those . . . who passed." He recoiled slightly. "You took the Test, didn't you?"

"I did," she answered truthfully. "A few weeks ago. I took it at Muirwood with the younger students."

Trevon closed his eyes, his shoulders sagging.

"What's wrong?" Sera asked, placing her hand on his.

"You didn't tell me," he said, his eyes still closed.

"I was planning to," she said. "I wasn't even sure I *would* pass."

He opened his eyes, and she saw hurt there. Indecision.

She reached out and smoothed the hair by his ear. "Tell me."

"It would have been easier if you hadn't," he said with an anguished voice.

"I don't understand."

"Sera," he said, taking her hands in his and squeezing them. "I brought you here not just because I hoped to kiss you. I wanted to convince you to marry me. Now. This very week."

CHAPTER FIVE

CONFLICTS OF LOYALTY

She felt as if she were at the edge of a cliff, arms wheeling to try to keep from falling. Certainly they had discussed marriage before. He cared for her, and she cared for him, but there was so much at stake, not the least of which was her future in the empire. And yet . . . if she became his wife, she would someday become the Queen of Kingfountain. There was much she admired about the way of life in her adopted world.

"You could have warned me," Sera said, feeling the urge to scuttle back from him. His visceral reaction to seeing the maston chain around her neck couldn't be forgotten so quickly. He was troubled by her devotion to her culture and beliefs. Her confusion, his nearness, the smell of the sea, and her longing to be kissed again . . . it all created a writhing conflict within her.

"Must everything be so scripted?" he asked, cocking his head. "It torments me when we're apart, Sera. When I returned from my last visit to your world, I could hardly bear to wait three months to see you again. I've been asking myself over and over, why are we torturing ourselves? Why wait until the armistice is about to end to come to terms? I want you *now*. I want you to be my wife. This isn't political anymore." He leaned forward until their foreheads touched. "We have not been impetuous. Give me a good reason why we should wait." His hand snaked over and caught hold of hers in the sand.

"The problem is I can think of several reasons," she said breathlessly.

He leaned back, looking at her in concern.

"Lord Fitzroy and I have been making progress on some of the social changes in Comoros. We are seeing results. Repairs are finally happening in some of the more broken-down parts of the City. Orphans are being cared for better. They're no longer starving."

His brow wrinkled. "I don't think your prime minister plans to halt any of those efforts."

"It's not just that," Sera said, shaking her head. She wanted to throw her arms around his neck and agree to marry him. But she wouldn't surrender her own ambitions so easily.

"Tell me," he asked softly. There was pain in his eyes.

"It will not be easy bridging our differences," Sera said. "I saw your reaction when you noticed this, Trevon." She tugged at the chain around her neck. "I cannot deny this part of myself. In my world, when a man and woman marry, the rite is meant to last forever."

Trevon shrugged. "As it is here. I don't just want you for a lifetime, Sera. I want you in the Deep Fathoms as well."

"Won't we get a little wet?" she asked, then regretted it. She had been tutored in their beliefs, which no longer seemed so strange.

Trevon gave her a reluctant smile. "There is more that binds our worlds than separates them. You taught me that. Having you here would only help break down the walls. I think our people would grow to love you as much as I have. Many have already started."

It made her ache to hear him say it. She closed her eyes, groaning inwardly.

"Sera, hear me out. I've given this a great deal of thought. I know one of your chief concerns is the succession. You *want* to become the Empress of Comoros. I don't fault you for that."

"But you do fault me for something?"

"Stubbornness and pride?" he offered with a tender smile.

"We both have those in abundance."

"Agreed. But listen, I beg you. I know your father is not in the best of health, but he could live another twenty years. Your grandfather lived to be seventy-four, I think, and that was after a long illness. Do you intend to live alone until he dies? If we were to marry now, we could have several children before he dies. An heir for Kingfountain. An heir for Comoros, if needed. With you to raise them, they will be smart and cunning and wise. But let us say your father dies sooner. Would that not give your privy council an opportunity to unite both of our worlds under our leadership? Think of it, Sera! A lasting peace between our worlds. A full exchange of ideas, of belief." He reached out and traced her jaw with his finger. "I'll admit, I was startled by your confession about taking the Maston Test. I'm sorry I couldn't conceal my reaction. I see why you did it. You want to be eligible to rule your people, and you must be a maston to do so. I would also consider . . . someday . . . taking the Maston Test if that's what it takes for both of us to be eligible to rule your people . . . and mine. So I ask you once again, why should we wait a moment longer?"

Sera looked down at her lap and then back into his eyes. They brimmed with conviction and purpose. His thoughts were bludgeoning hers, but in a sweet and tender way. This wasn't a political gambit. He loved her, and he wanted her.

Oh, Cettie, how I wish you were here to advise me!

"It's a bold plan, Trevon. I would adore being your wife, but I don't think my father would agree to this," Sera said, shaking her head. "He wouldn't allow me to marry you unless I abdicate my claim to the throne." Her smile began to droop. "My father hates me. He still doesn't believe I'm his true daughter."

She watched Trevon's eyes tighten with anger. "He's weak-willed and venal. But your system of government keeps his power in check. Without you, we never would have formed this armistice. You've more than proven yourself to the privy council. If he tries to sabotage this alliance, I think they would overrule him. He may want us to get married to be rid of you as a rival"—Trevon smirked—"but I think we can outmaneuver him. We are both far better at Wizr than he is."

Sera looked down again. The berries caught her eye, and she reached into the basket and pulled out a large, ripe thimbleberry. She held it for Trevon and then pressed it into his mouth. As he ate it, a smile playing upon his lips, he reached into the basket and withdrew one for her. He teased her with it, holding it back and making her lean for it before he finally fed it to her. The flavor exploded on her tongue, but there was another hunger that pressed even more.

"Do you want to walk along the beach for a while?" he asked her.

"No," she whispered. "I'd like to kiss you again first." Then she wrapped her arms around his neck and sought his mouth with hers.

~

Trevon lay on his back on the blanket as she fed him the final berries from the basket. The sun was warm, but the wind was just cool enough to keep it from growing too hot. It had been a languid and pleasurable day, and she was drowsy from having stayed awake so long.

"You still haven't given me your answer," he observed, looking up at her.

"So impatient, Prince Trevon?" she answered, teasing him with another berry.

"I think I've been remarkably patient. I've been waiting for you for years."

She stretched out next to him, propping her head on her hand. Such a pose in her world would have caused an enormous scandal, and yet here they were, all alone on the beach. Guards roamed the perimeter, whom she could occasionally see in the distance, but no one had intruded on their private interlude.

"And I've rewarded you with berries," Sera said impishly. "You should be satisfied."

"I don't want berries," he said. "I want Miss Fitzempress."

"Well, Miss Fitzempress is going to discuss your proposal with the prime minister first. Even if I promised you here and now on this beautiful shore, it would not be binding without being sanctioned. I can't exactly give myself away."

He sighed, looking up at the brilliant blue sky. "I suppose that makes sense, but I thought I'd have an answer from you, one way or the other."

She touched his nose. "Don't pout, Trevon. It's unbecoming."

He claimed her fingers and kissed them. "Your neck is looking a bit pink. Perhaps we should return to the palace? You must be tired."

"I am weary, but can we walk along the shore first?"

"If you like." He rose and then reached down to help her stand, which was very gallant. She left her shoes in the sandy pile, and they walked, hand in hand, along the smooth pebbles of glass and sand. It struck her again that the feelings in her heart were so different from the ones she'd entertained for Will Russell. There was no artifice between her and Trevon. She felt he was acting according to the dictates of his heart. And he had mostly persuaded her. If Lord Fitzroy agreed that the marriage was a sound idea and that her father would not be allowed to disinherit her, then she was ready to concede. She could not imagine anyone else being her husband.

As they strolled along the beach, they came to the edge of the cliffs that jutted into the waters. The setting reminded her slightly of the beaches beneath Pavenham Sky, though there was less fog and mist in Brythonica.

"Have you had any success in learning more about Lady Sinia's disappearance?" Trevon asked.

The shared history between their worlds contained an overabundance of controversy. One of them, which they'd discussed in the past, was that a previous duchess of Brythonica—the powerful Wizr Lady Sinia—had never returned from a visit she'd made to the empire. It was presumed that she'd been abducted and concealed.

"None whatsoever," she answered, knowing it would disappoint him. "Whatever happened, it was done in secret. I spoke to the Aldermaston of Muirwood personally not long ago, and he consulted the records of his predecessors. There are many records to search, you see. Even the Minister of Thought had not heard of Lady Sinia's visit."

Trevon pursed his lips, but he nodded in understanding. "You would tell me, though, if you discovered something? Even if the news was bad? I wish I could search the records myself, although I imagine that particular ministry wouldn't permit access to a nonbeliever."

She squeezed his hand. "Of course I would tell you. And no, I don't think the Ministry of Thought would divulge its secrets to you." She noticed a cave in the wall of the cliff. The outgoing tide had exposed it. "What is that?" she asked, pointing.

Trevon looked and shrugged. "A sea cave. The waters carve them out of the rocks. They don't go anywhere."

Perhaps not, but there was something special about this sea cave. Something powerful. She'd walked on the beach before, but she'd never noticed this feeling before. "Can we look?"

"They are pretty dark, but if it pleases you." He tugged her after him, and they approached it together. As they drew near, a guard wearing the badge of the Raven emerged from inside. Trevon looked taken aback.

"Can I help you, Prince Trevon?" the guard asked, his eyes shifting warily to Sera.

"What were you doing in that cave?" Trevon asked.

"I patrol the beach, my lord," he answered.

"We were just going to go inside a moment," Trevon said.

The guard frowned, and Sera could see the indecision in his eyes. "The tide is about to return. I would advise against it."

His reticence intrigued Sera even more. She waited to see how Trevon would handle the situation.

"We won't be long."

The guard looked uncomfortable, as if he wanted to forbid them but dared not. He grimaced and then stepped aside. "Very well, Your Grace."

After they passed the guard, Trevon cast a wary glance back at him and then escorted Sera to the opening.

"That was odd," Sera said in a low voice.

"I know. I'll have to ask the duchess about it." Trevon had to stoop to enter. Sera did not, which made her inwardly groan. Her lack of height ever seemed to undermine her authority. The cave was dark, even more so since their eyes were so accustomed to the sunny beach outside. They stumbled a bit, and the wet sand clung to her bare feet. The misshapen, jagged walls put her in mind of the Fear Liath's lair, which Cettie had described to her at length, but she sensed the protective presence of Leerings. Could it be? A giddiness swelled inside her at the thought. Yes, the feeling was unmistakable, but what were Leerings doing here?

"I imagine this cave fills up with seawater," Trevon said, looking around. They still held hands to steady each other.

Sera touched one of the walls emanating power, and her fingers sank into a spongy layer of moss. She scraped some of it away, trying to feel for the carved face that must be hidden beneath it, and she activated the Leering with her mind.

Immediately, the cave began to glow.

"What on earth?" Trevon gasped in surprise as several Leerings illuminated their surroundings.

Sera felt a giddy rush of power in her heart. She had activated the Leerings without any trouble at all. All of the practice she'd done over the past year and a half had made her adept with them.

"There are Leerings," Sera said, looking at him, "hidden beneath the moss."

"Did you know they were here?" Trevon asked, reaching out and touching the one they stood near.

"I think I sensed them from the beach," she answered. "It was very faint. Leerings have a purpose. They were put here to do something, and I don't think it was simply to illuminate a cave." She gazed up at the craggy ceiling, the broken edges where rock had been shattered loose by the relentless pounding of waves.

"These have been here for a long time," Trevon said. "The moss is thick." He broke a clump of it off and smelled it. "It's sweet." He offered it to her, and she sniffed at it too. It did indeed have a pleasant aroma.

"The guards are protecting this cave," Sera said, looking back at the opening. "The question is from what?"

"Or whom," Trevon answered. "He was very reluctant to let us in."

"I know," Sera said. She touched the Leering they'd partially cleaned again, wishing she understood its purpose. It was doing *something*, but she felt it would be wrong to try to invoke it. "If Cettie were here, she could tell us. She has a gift for controlling them. But why are there Leerings *here*? And why keep them hidden? Is this not evidence that our worlds are more connected than we understand?" They had discussed, on many occasions, the similarities between their respective faiths. The Knowing was interpreted differently in both worlds—it even empowered people in different ways—but it was in essence the same.

"It does seem so," Trevon answered. "I have an uneasy feeling."

"So do I," Sera said. "You still have the Tay al-Ard?"

"In my pocket," he answered. "Let's go back to the palace. There are some questions I would like answered." He fished it out.

Sera stepped close to him, putting one hand over his heart. Her other slid around his back. Before the tug of magic twisted them both away, she stared at the glowing moss and wondered at the mystery of the cave.

Why would Kingfountain want to keep such a secret? What were they hiding?

CHAPTER SIX

FATE'S HARBINGER

Not only was Becka deft with braiding and arranging Sera's hair, but her quiet ways made her a natural gatherer of gossip and current news. It was almost time for the state dinner with Trevon's parents and siblings, and Sera wanted to look like she belonged at court. She'd changed to a different gown—a design from Marq that she hoped would appeal to the queen.

"So all the servants are talking about a wedding, even though I haven't said yes?" Sera asked, looking over her shoulder at the young woman, who had just added a lace collar to Sera's outfit. The lace chafed against Sera's sunburned skin, making her wince.

"I'm sorry, Sera," Becka apologized, noticing her reaction.

"I spent too much time in the sun. It's my fault, not yours."

"The wedding is the *only* thing they're talking about," Becka said, squinting and leaning in close to fix the hook and eye of the collar. "I even saw an enormous cake being prepared in the kitchen. The prince's sisters both pressed me, asking if I thought you'd like living here. They're anxious to have another sister. Even Trevon's brother said he wouldn't mind, so long as it was you."

"Which one?" Sera demanded, feeling a flush of gladness that she'd managed to win some of them over. Trevon's parents were a different story. The queen was especially aloof, no matter how Sera tried to please her.

"Prince Kasdan," Becka answered.

"Really? He's the next oldest. He's hardly said more than hello to me."

"Well, he's not as talkative as Prince Lucas, for certain," Becka said, smiling. "But I overheard him talking to his sisters, and that's what he said."

The collar was done, and Sera planted her palms on the dressing table in front of her and let out a pent-up breath. "They're not making it easy for me to say no." Not that she wanted to.

"No, I suppose not. But not all the talk is pleasant, Sera. You should know the bad as well as the good." Becka's look darkened. "I heard an undercook complain about the wedding. She fussed about going to so much effort for a heretic."

Sera frowned at that comment. "She'd likely think it a wedding of two heretics had she seen the prince talking with the Aldermaston of Muirwood Abbey." The word "heretic" still chafed. At least Trevon's study of her world had helped him realize their differences were not as keen as he'd once thought. He was coming around to the idea that the Fountain and the Mysteries were two different aspects of the Knowing. The meeting with the Aldermaston had broadened Trevon's views. Made him less distrustful. She considered it progress.

"I've also heard," Becka went on cautiously, her nose wrinkling, "that there have been some protests about it. Some of the people feel that the prince shouldn't marry someone who hasn't had the water rite. There are even whispers you're a water sprite come to deceive them."

"A water sprite?" Sera said with a little laugh. "Something tells me they don't get burned by the sun." She breathed out her nose, feeling the conflict of the decision she faced. "Why is Lord Fitzroy delayed?"

"That I do not know," Becka answered. "I did see Adam Creigh, though. I won't give him Cettie's parcel until later, of course, but he

51

was pleasant and asked how you were doing. He'd like to come by the palace now that you've returned."

"I would like that very much."

They had nearly finished their preparations when a knock landed on the door. Becka answered it, and invited Lord Fitzroy to enter. He wore the fashions of Comoros, which made him stand out in the society of Kingfountain. He dressed in the same understated manner everywhere, and often looked more like a butler than the second-most powerful man in Comoros.

"I was hoping we could speak before dinner, Lord Fitzroy," Sera said.

"I'm sorry I could not come sooner, Sera. There is a lot of commotion at court right now. I'm assuming the prince has already proposed?"

"He did earlier today," Sera answered. "Which is why I wanted to speak to you."

Fitzroy's short tenure as prime minister had put more gray in his hair. It was probably her father's fault. They were constantly at odds, but the contentious relationship hadn't stopped Fitzroy.

"I must confess I'm not surprised that he did," Fitzroy said. "Only the urgency troubles me. There were preparations underway before we even arrived. I don't like the haste."

"I'm glad I'm not the only one who feels that way. Have you spoken to the king or queen about it? How do they feel?"

"The king is very pragmatic. He sees it as an obvious solution to forming a more permanent peace accord. General Montpensier, as you can imagine, thinks you are evil incarnate. I've heard he's been whispering in the queen's ear, trying to persuade her that you aren't a suitable match for her son. Maybe one of the younger ones, but not the crown prince."

"Has he now?" Sera said with indignation.

"That can hardly surprise you. If the war with our empire ends permanently, his role as general will mean much less. Some believe he has too much power already, that no one man should command the army *and* the Espion. Your marriage would benefit the royal family by reining him in. Still, the queen may be against it."

"Then I suppose this dinner is another opportunity to win her over," Sera said, frowning.

"I wouldn't fix your hopes on that," Fitzroy said, scratching his ear. "I've seen enough marriages in my day. If you do wed Trevon, seek to please your husband more than his parents. Some people will never be content because they've determined not to be. The queen, I fear, is one of them."

"Sage advice, Lord Fitzroy. So what would you advise me to do? This whole affair does seem rather rushed. Should I marry Prince Trevon so that we may establish peace between our peoples? I don't want to abdicate the possibility of becoming empress. In fact, Trevon wonders if we might be able to jointly rule both."

The suggestion seemed to take him by surprise. He thought a moment before responding. "Your people love you, Sera. There is no denying it. But there would be many obstacles against this path. It would require a great deal of mutual goodwill that doesn't presently exist. While I know Richard—your father—wants you barred from inheriting at all, the people would revolt if he made it a condition of your marriage. He also wishes to marry Lady Corinne, and this wedding would give him a good pretext to fulfill his desires."

Sera couldn't help but give him an angry look. "Haven't you told him about her machinations?"

"Not yet," Fitzroy said, giving her a warning look. "I've been assembling the evidence discreetly. I even have a spy in her household, one we recruited to the cause."

"Who?" Sera pressed. She'd been almost fond of Lady Corinne's butler, but surely it couldn't be someone so close to her.

He shook his head. "It's best if I don't tell you. You have already provided the most important witness," he said, flashing a smile at Becka, who flushed at his praise. "I have a writ prepared for Lady Corinne's arrest that only needs to be signed. No doubt she has an army of loyal advocates who will try to confound the case."

"Then you must confound *them*," Sera said, feeling frustrated that her nemesis was still exercising power in the realm.

"I am very methodical, I assure you," Fitzroy said. "She is being watched closely, especially when she visits Lockhaven. She has beguiled your father, but the infatuation is clearly one-sided."

Sera nodded curtly. "So what do you advise, Lord Fitzroy? Should I accept Trevon's proposal?"

"It's your decision, of course."

"Yes, but I want your advice. I depend on it. Trevon raised some articulate points. And I have no doubt about his affections." Her memories from the beach brought a flush of pleasure and warmth. "Part of me is not ready to risk my ambitions for our world. I wonder why we cannot wait until the end of the treaty to finalize our agreement. But my heart tells me that waiting will only make it more . . . difficult if I decide not to marry him. I do care for Trevon. Deeply. There is much to admire in such a man."

"There is also much to admire in such a woman," Fitzroy said, nodding to her. "I've seen you together in our world and this one. You make a striking couple. He's intelligent, deliberate, and honorable. As long as our people could call on you, should the need arise, I do not think they would violently oppose the match. That must be a term or precondition."

"I agree," Sera said, wringing her hands. "Shall we away to dinner, then?"

"Of course."

Sera had been to the dining hall in Kingfountain so many times it felt as familiar as any such room in Lockhaven. Indeed, she preferred the hall's intimate arrangement of round tables to the long, formal tables that decorated the manors back home.

The king and queen sat at the head table, and the queen's only comment to Sera was that she looked a bit weather-beaten, followed by a sniff of disdain. Trevon flashed his mother an angry look and then offered an apologetic one to Sera as he escorted her to their table. Luckily, General Montpensier and his alluring wife, their usual dinner companions, were seated elsewhere this eve. Prince Trevon had arranged for Lord Fitzroy to be at their table as well as his two younger sisters, Princess Lyneah and Princess Elaine.

The dinner conversation was pleasant, but they all felt the underlying tension. The sisters kept exchanging knowing looks and bursting into giggles. Trevon tried to silence them, but Sera found their antics amusing. Lord Fitzroy was a good dinner companion and engaged the young princesses in a discussion about the weather and some of the Mysteries of Wind.

At one point, Trevon reached for Sera's hand under the tablecloth and squeezed it. She squeezed back, savoring the feel of his warm, rough hand. Is this what it would be like if they were wed? His thumb was caressing her hand when a man approached their table. He wore the military uniform of the admiralty of Comoros, and his hat was tucked under the crook of his arm. He came up behind Lord Fitzroy, who was in the midst of a story about Cettie, and coughed into his fist to gain the prime minister's attention.

Fitzroy turned at once, and seemed startled to see the man. "Admiral Hatch. This is a surprise."

"I crossed the mirror gate several hours ago," he said and withdrew a sealed letter. "I've read the contents of this letter first, as it was addressed to me, but I thought it best to come straightaway."

Fitzroy looked worried. "Why didn't this come through the ambassador?"

"It will," Admiral Hatch said. "My understanding is the privy council is meeting with the emperor this evening, and the ambassador will receive a dispatch in the morning. I came to you as quickly as I could."

Lord Fitzroy, still looking concerned, quickly examined the letter after the admiral excused himself. Trevon squeezed Sera's hand, and when she glanced at him, she saw he, too, looked troubled by the admiral's sudden arrival. Did this have something to do with their possible marriage?

"What do you think it is?" he whispered in her ear.

"I don't know," she answered, studying Fitzroy's face as he scanned the missive. A subtle smile crossed his face, but he pursed his lips to conceal it. Good news, then. He folded the letter and stuffed it into his jacket pocket.

"What was that about?" Sera asked in an undertone.

"If we can speak privately, I will tell you."

Sera pushed away from the table, offering Trevon an apologetic smile, and rose and followed Fitzroy to one of the curtained alcoves embedded in the wall. Her prince was burning with curiosity by the look he gave her as they left. Some of the other guests noticed their abrupt departure, but the conversation and tinkling of silverware on plates showed that most had not. When they reached the shallow alcove, Fitzroy gestured for her to enter first. She knew why without asking—with his back to the diners, no one could read his lips.

"Well?" Sera asked, feeling her insides twist with eagerness.

"Cettie had another vision," Fitzroy said, his smile returning. "She didn't know how to get the news to me quickly, so she entrusted the message to Rand Patchett, who knows Admiral Hatch. He came straightaway."

"Rand? That's odd." Things were quite awkward between them, last she'd heard. That tended to happen when a woman rejected a man.

"True, but the message is valuable. Cettie has had a vision of your marriage to Prince Trevon here in Kingfountain." His smile broadened. "I think this addresses both of our concerns. You are meant to marry him. You have your answer."

Sera felt a little prickle of doubt, but it was quickly washed away when she looked back at the table and saw Trevon gazing at her, clearly worried about the news and what it might mean. The devotion in his eyes was unquestionable. Besides, she trusted Cettie implicitly, and her visions had never been wrong before. The weight of her decision no longer felt so heavy. Yes, their differences would create challenges, but they would also bring opportunities. Perhaps the Knowing was trying to heal the breach between its warring children at last.

"That is not news I was expecting," Sera said. "Maybe Trevon's desire to hasten the marriage is just another indication that we're supposed to do this. Well," she added with a hopeful smile, "I suppose I should give him an answer, then."

"I think you ought to," Fitzroy said, smiling broadly.

"I'm so grateful for Cettie's vision. I would love for her to come and visit." The thought of Cettie reminded her of the Leerings she'd seen earlier. Perhaps Cettie would be able to divine their purpose if she ever visited Kingfountain. Arranging such a thing would be much easier once she and Trevon were married. "Fitzroy, I discovered Leerings in one of the beach caves in Brythonica. Did you know of them?"

"I did not," Fitzroy said. "That is fascinating."

"It is. Did the letter say anything else? Anything we should be concerned about?"

"Nothing," Fitzroy said, shaking his head no. "All is well at home."

"What a relief to get good news only," Sera said, touching his arm. "I dreaded what the letter might say."

"So did I," he confessed. He turned and looked back at the table. "After you."

Sera returned to the table, but instead of taking her seat, she stood by Trevon's chair so that she would be, for once, taller than him.

Trevon gazed up at her face, his look suddenly hopeful. Sera's heart felt ready to burst. She put her hand on his shoulder, partially to steady herself, partially to reassure him.

"I wonder if there is any cake in the kitchen?" she asked impishly. "I'm feeling hungry for some at present." Then she leaned down and kissed his cheek. "Tell the cook it is time to finish it. I will have you, Trevon." She smiled at the two young princesses, who stared at her in shocked surprise. "I've never had any siblings before. It is about time to change that."

The look of joy on the prince's face made her throat catch. He rose from his chair and embraced her in front of the entire gathering. And then he kissed her.

There is a saying here in Kingfountain that I much admire. You cannot step twice in the same river. Change is inevitable and relentless, and I have found that it does not matter how slowly progress happens so long as it does happen. I think our persistence in treating peacefully with our enemies will yield, in the end, a lasting result. The Aldermaston I studied under taught me that people change for two reasons. Either they have learned much, or they've been hurt much.

People fear change, however, and it requires much coaxing. Not because it is difficult, but because the future is uncertain. I am grateful for Cettie and her wondrous Gift from the Medium. It has made it much easier to face the future with courage. When she was a child, she was afraid of the dark and the ghosts she could see. It is easy to forgive a child for being afraid of the dark. The real tragedy of life is when one is afraid of the light.

—Brant Fitzroy, Prime Minister

CETTIE

CHAPTER SEVEN

THE FELLS

So many years had passed since Cettie had lived in the Fells. Yet seeing the ramshackle tenements, the suffering looks and gaunt cheeks of the hungry and impoverished, made her heart respond with pangs of memory. Her father's bodyguard, Raj Sarin, had dubbed her Cettie Saeed, "Cettie of the Clouds," a moniker that fit the young woman she'd become. But as she navigated her zephyr to the center of the earth-bound city, she was reduced to her earlier nickname—Cettie of the Fells. No amount of soap, no comfortable gown, no hard-earned confidence could purge the inner child that had felt trapped by this teeming city.

"I don't see how people can live like this," Rand said, his voice betraying the pity he felt for those forced to endure it. "There's nothing like this in Pry-Ree."

"Most of them don't have a choice," Joses said. He gave Cettie a solemn look from his seat across from Rand. They sat on opposing benches on the deck of the sky ship. No doubt Joses was thinking of the past too, of the days when they had scurried through the streets below trying to find food for the other children they lived with.

At least they had not been hunted by a beast like the Fear Liath.

It was excessively windy that day, and strong gusts had rattled the sky ship off and on throughout their flight. Debris from the streets flitted like ash in the air, working up clouds of dust. The tempest was a hardier ship, but it would have been too cumbersome to maneuver through the winding streets of the Fells.

"It has gotten better, but not much," Cettie said, bringing the zephyr lower to avoid another ship as it raced toward its destination. As a child, she used to stare up at the ships floating above the buildings. She'd never have imagined that she'd be piloting one someday. It felt as if a shadow had crossed over her heart. In one of her Mysteries of Wind classes at Muirwood, they'd studied prisms. Light carried every shade of color within it, and a prism could show different dazzling arrays of colors depending on how it was looked at. At some point in the class, a cloud had covered the sun, ending the experiment. Without light, a prism was nothing but clear glass. That was the way the Fells felt to her. They blotted out everything that was good.

"Thanks to the prime minister," Rand offered encouragingly, "that is changing. If slowly."

"He started charities in the Fells long before he became prime minister," Joses said. He looked over at Cettie. "Where are we meeting the lieutenant? The ministry building?"

"Yes, but I need to stop at Sloan and Teitelbaum first," Cettie said.

"Your advocates?" Rand asked.

Cettie nodded. It was near enough to the ministry buildings that it would not delay their meeting. Light was the monster's greatest weakness. The goal was to locate the Fear Liath's lair before noon, when the sun would be at its brightest.

She lowered the zephyr and dropped the rope ladder over the side.

"Would you like us to come with you?" Rand asked.

She shook her head. "If you'd wait here, I would be obliged. I won't be long."

When she climbed down the ladder, she was met by a small group of urchins who'd gathered beneath the zephyr. How she longed to wipe clean their sooty faces and bring them all back to Fog Willows with her. Seeing them brought back memories of her own hunger and desperation. She opened her purse and began dispensing coins to each of them, earning words of "thank you, ma'am" and "bless you, mum" from them. On her rare visits to the Fells, she usually brought a purse of coins from her own private funds.

She hastened to the law offices, knowing that even more children would be gathered around the zephyr upon her return. When she entered the building, she breathed in the familiar scents of old papers, wax, and aged timbers. There was a subtle edge of mildew to it. Various clerks sat at their desks, scribbling furiously. The desk that had belonged to Mr. Skrelling, her old classmate and admirer, was now occupied by a replacement. The reminder of his accident caused her pain, but she squelched it as she made her way toward the lawyers' private chambers. She'd sent a zephyr post, so they should be expecting her.

Mr. Sloan greeted her at the door and apologized that Mr. Teitelbaum was off on private business for Fitzroy.

"Do you have way of communicating with Father?" Cettie asked, feeling again unsettled by her earlier vision.

"We do, if it's an emergency," he answered. "It takes several days, but our messages do arrive in his correspondence parcel. Is there something you'd like to send to him?"

She thought again of the vision. Rand had assured her the message he'd sent to Admiral Hatch was already speeding its way there. Part of her questioned whether she'd done the right thing. Though she'd always shared her visions with Fitzroy first, this one felt different. In the past, they'd never tried to prevent something from coming to pass. They'd always reacted to the information as if it were unassailable. But this one couldn't be . . .

Why would she receive a vision of something that would affect her so painfully if it were unavoidable? It jarred with her sense of fairness, rattled her faith.

"I will send it to you later."

He beckoned for her to join him in his private study, and she did so, taking the proffered chair as he went around the desk, scratching his snow-white hair. He had been the family's advocate for many years. There was a friendly manner about him, which set him apart from the normally stern Mr. Teitelbaum.

"Have you an update on the state of Stephen's debts?" Cettie asked him after he sat down. Stephen was the Fitzroy's oldest offspring and only son. He'd accumulated excessive debt while working at the family mine. Though he was a changed man, the shackles of the past still had hold of him.

Cettie hoped more than anything that her father would survive, but she thought it best to prepare for the worst.

Mr. Sloan pursed his lips and tapped his fingers together. "Since we last spoke on this matter, well over a year ago, he has not taken on any more debt and has worked out payments with his creditors. It will take him roughly four more years to settle them all, assuming he does not fall back into his spendthrift ways." He smiled at her. "He's quite changed since the incident at the mines. He looks more and more like his father every day. Thank the Mysteries, he's begun to act like him too."

"Four more years," Cettie said, sighing regretfully. "How much would it take to eliminate the debt altogether?"

"The interest is the problem," Mr. Sloan said. "We have renegotiated some of the rates of interest on his behalf, as you requested, but the obligation was sizable. We did our best."

"I know you did, Mr. Sloan, but he cannot inherit Fog Willows with this debt."

"No, he cannot," Mr. Sloan said. "Lord Fitzroy's instructions were explicit. Phinia cannot inherit either, as she is not a maston. That means Lady Anna would likely inherit."

Cettie felt her pangs of worry increase. Anna was so ill . . .

"Is something wrong?" Mr. Sloan asked. "You look troubled."

"Anna is very sick," she answered. "I'm worried about her . . . and Fog Willows. Lady Maren would not inherit?"

"No," said Mr. Sloan. "The estate must be passed from father to child. Upon Lord Fitzroy's death, which will not happen for quite some time, Lady Maren would be entitled to a stipend, but it will not be within her power to control the destiny of the manor. Lord Fitzroy has no siblings. He has three children and has sought, as you well know, the right to adopt *you*, which would also make you a possible heir to the estate. But there is still time. Four years really isn't very long for Stephen to pay off his debts. When your hair is as silver as mine, you'll understand what I mean."

Cettie closed her eyes, debating whether she should tell him. She hadn't told Mother, even though she'd longed to share the burden. But the news of Anna's illness had deeply affected Lady Maren. Her skin had taken on a pale cast that had put Cettie in mind of her mother's former illness, the one Mrs. Pullman had instigated. She'd decided it would be better to stay silent and hope for the best. Rand's idea *should* work.

"Mr. Sloan, I would like to pay off Stephen's debt."

The advocate's brow wrinkled. He gave her a solemn look. "Did he ask you to?"

"No, of course not," she answered hastily. "He would never do that."

"He might have not that long ago," Mr. Sloan pointed out.

"True, but he never did."

"I don't think this would be wise, Miss Cettie," he said, rubbing his earlobe. "Nor do I think your father would approve."

"Here is my intention," Cettie said. "I have, as you know, saved a sizable amount of my salary as the keeper of Fog Willows. I want to use my savings to do away with the prohibition against him inheriting. Stephen's payments can come to me until he has paid off the full amount, without interest."

Mr. Sloan leaned farther back in his chair. "Why?"

"I can't tell you my reasons, Mr. Sloan. I believe I have sufficient funds."

"You do," he agreed. "I'm assuming you don't want him to know that you are helping him?"

"I don't," she answered. "I would prefer if Father didn't know either."

Mr. Sloan inhaled slowly, looking troubled. "I can arrange the papers, of course. It will take several days, maybe longer, but I would have to advise you against this. You earned your money through hard work, and you've saved much of it. Stephen made entirely different decisions and has justly earned the consequences he now bears."

"I understand," Cettie said, leaning forward and putting her hand on his desk. "But my funds are mine and can be spent as I see fit. I know you have a duty to Father that supersedes your duty to me. Can you see your way toward helping me?"

Mr. Sloan shrugged. "It is your money, as you said, Miss Cettie. I do not see how Lord Fitzroy's interests would be *harmed* by this arrangement. No, if anything, it provides more flexibility. If this is your wish, I will see it done. I'll come by Fog Willows when I am ready for your signature on the deed." He folded his arms and gazed at her. "I'm not usually surprised, Miss Cettie, but your generosity has taken me aback. It's no secret that Stephen once disdained you. I could not be so forgiving."

Cettie rose from the chair. "Thank you, Mr. Sloan. I didn't deserve Father's mercy in bringing me away from the Fells. Yet I am grateful, every day, that he did. I will do anything for the Fitzroys."

Mr. Sloan rose from his chair. "I hope your purpose in coming is fulfilled. It is good to see you once again, Miss Cettie."

"Thank you for helping me," Cettie said, feeling good about her decision to help Stephen anonymously. It was the sort of thing Fitzroy would have done . . . and did . . . for someone else's child.

They rendezvoused with Lieutenant Fields at the Ministry of Law building, which had a solemn gray stone facade and grimy windows. The young lieutenant greeted Rand with a grin of relief and thanked him for joining the party.

"Don't thank me," Rand said offhandedly. "Thank *her*."

One thing she'd always respected about Rand was his outspokenness, his sometimes brutal honesty.

The assemblage was impressive. Some of the officers carried Leerings the size of bread loaves, which they brought aboard zephyrs that had been prepared for the mission. There were a few sharpshooters as well, but it was clear they were looking to Rand to take down the beast. He was a dragoon, after all, trained in the Ministry of War. All in all, about two dozen people had been gathered for the mission—a bigger and better-armed group than the miners she and Stephen and Rand had led to the beast's old lair in the grotto. After the entire group had gathered, Lieutenant Fields ordered them to board the zephyrs and make way for the area they intended to investigate.

Cettie rode in a zephyr with Fields, and she wrapped her arms around herself as she gazed down at the broken streets, teeming with wagons and small carriages. The place looked familiar, yet all streets in the Fells, save for in the nicer neighborhoods, were full of broken crates, trash, and useless debris. Smoke billowed from the various factories' smoke stacks, obscuring the view at times, and a few shrill bursts of whistles reached them above the billowing wind.

When the zephyrs arrived, she had an uncanny sense that she'd been there before. Could it be true? Or did all the streets look this similar? A queer, uneasy feeling made her hold her stomach.

There were skylights in many of the roofs beneath them, offering the sky ships easier docking since the streets below were crowded and unsafe.

"We'll go down below, ma'am," Lieutenant Fields said. "The map I showed you earlier featured this general area. If you can sense the monster, let us know, for we can impose the boundaries before luring it out of its lair."

She nodded and watched as he threw the rope ladder over the edge of the craft and then climbed down to the roof below. She saw Joses and Rand climb down from their zephyr too. Joses glanced her way, giving her a reluctant smile. It would seem the adventure suited him less than he'd thought it would, and no wonder. The memories were heavier down here in the thick of the Fells.

Cettie took a deep breath and climbed down to join them.

The building's attic was musty and dank, and they had to make their way down several flights of stairs to reach the street. People stared at them, and Cettie reassured herself that no one could possibly recognize her for the urchin she'd been. Not now that she was dressed properly and had tidy hair. They couldn't know who she really was. It was a warm day, so no cloak or veil was needed, but she suddenly wished she had one, if only to conceal her twisting emotions.

She felt a hand grip her arm. "Are you all right?" Rand asked worriedly.

The answer was no, absolutely not, but she nodded anyway, her throat too swollen to speak. A feeling of uneasiness permeated the air, making each step feel like it required extra effort.

"This way," Lieutenant Fields called out, waving them to follow him. He had an arquebus slung over his shoulder. The Leerings had been stowed in packs and were being carried by four different men.

They turned at the street corner, and she stopped short, recognizing the small market she'd passed hundreds of times as a little girl.

"I know this place," Joses whispered in recognition. He looked at her in surprise. "I used to steal from that fruit cart."

"I know," she answered, emotion clutching at her heart. She gripped his hand in hers, and they walked forward hand in hand, two old friends returned to the nightmares of their youth.

Lieutenant Fields was walking directly toward the tenement where Miss Charlotte had once lived. The one where she and Joses had taken care of the smaller children in the attic.

"It can't be," Joses said, shaking his head. And yet it was. The two of them trailed the band of officers, falling in just behind Rand at the back.

But as they drew closer to that awful building, Cettie felt a blast of icy fear that had nothing to do with the past. She could sense the Fear Liath in that tenement. There was no doubt in her mind.

She squeezed Joses's hand harder as the next wave of awareness struck her mind. The beast sensed her as well.

And it was angry.

CHAPTER EIGHT

FEAR

"Now Miss Cettie, if you get a sense of where the beast's lair is," said Lieutenant Fields as he and the others continued to walk toward the dilapidated building, "will you—?" He turned to look at her, and his voice cut off abruptly.

"You sense it already?" he asked.

Cettie raised her arm and pointed at the building in front of them. "It's in there."

His bafflement was evident. He'd heard she could sense the beast, but he hadn't truly believed. "How can you be sure?"

"I can feel it, Lieutenant." How had the Fear Liath ended up at Miss Charlotte's? Surely there had been enough suffering in that abode to attract such a creature, but the coincidence seemed too great. Could it have been drawn to this place because Cettie had once lived there? Had it been pulled in by the darkness of *her* past?

Rand had turned back toward her, and he came up and took her by the shoulders. "Do you want to go back to the zephyr?"

The compassion she saw in his eyes did something to her. The old feelings started to return, welling up from where she'd buried them deep inside after her engagement to Adam.

"I'll be all right," she stammered. "It's in there. Probably the cesspit." That was the place she had feared most while living in that foul house.

Rand nodded firmly and then swung his arquebus off his shoulder. "Get those Leerings set up on each adjacent street. When you're done, call Cettie to invoke them. Lieutenant, how many of us are going in to drive the beast out?"

"I thought ten suitable. What do you advise?"

Rand pursed his lips and nodded. "Pick your men and have them assemble at the door. Is anyone in that place?"

"Who knows?" the lieutenant said, gazing up at the ramshackle building with a sour expression.

"There may be children inside," Joses said, his brow pinched with worry.

"There probably are," Cettie agreed. She wondered at the desolate streets, but it was still early, and most of the people who lived in the area worked at the factories.

"Let's get them out, then. Move!"

Joses let go of Cettie's hand and brought his own weapon off his shoulder.

"Don't go, Joses," Cettie said, shaking her head.

His usual smile now looked more like a baring of teeth. "Oh, I'm going. I'd like a shot at that thing."

Cettie stood in the middle of the street, feeling an overwhelming urge to run far away. The Fear Liath's emotions spilled from Miss Charlotte's house, reaching in and clutching her heart, making her dizzy with fear and doubt. The officers moved quickly, surrounding the building with Leerings. Even if they failed to slay the beast, they wanted to contain it, to prevent it from continuing to wreak havoc.

Cettie couldn't shake the thought that this was somehow her fault. That the beast was some sort of strange message to her. She thought again of her vision. Of the man who'd claimed to be her father hiding on the roof of that building in Kingfountain. Had he truly died at the grotto? Or had he been healed somehow? She had learned from Sera that the people in Kingfountain held magic dissimilar to theirs. Maybe it had brought him back to life . . . and empowered him to summon and control the Fear Liath. Her thoughts continued to buzz with agitation until one of the officers called her over to secure the first of the Leerings.

The officer, a younger man with a thick mustache, had positioned it against the side of a building in an iron box equipped with a padlock.

"We'll chain them up, otherwise they'll be stolen," he said, rising and dusting his gloved hands. "I've never been very good with Leerings. Glad you're here."

Cettie sensed the Leering in the iron box and reached out to it with her mind. Normally, invoking Leerings came as naturally as taking a breath of air. This time, although she sensed it, it wouldn't respond to her thoughts. Another spasm of fear went through her. She bit her lip, trying to calm herself. Her turbulent emotions were blocking her natural ability with Leerings.

"What's wrong, miss?" the officer asked.

"Give me a moment," she said.

He nodded and walked off, leaving Cettie by herself, crouched by the box tarnished with rust spots. She closed her eyes, trying to worm her way past the awful feelings. A little light emanated from the box as the Leering's eyes started to glow. Its reactions felt sluggish, but it did obey at last, and she felt the first part of the web of protection extend from the mouth of the alley. She didn't know how long she had crouched there, and judging by the sweat dampening her skin, she was drained by the experience. Rising, she walked back toward Miss Charlotte's building.

A strange mist spilled into the street in thick, curling wisps, rising up from the gutters that dumped into the sewers. She'd never seen mist in daylight before, so she could only gape at the otherworldly sight.

Looking around, she saw only a handful of officers. There was no sign of Rand, Joses, or Lieutenant Fields. She hurried over to one of them.

"Where did the others go?"

"Some of them went inside to clear the tenement," he answered, "and the rest are waiting for you at the other Leerings, miss."

Cettie walked hastily to the next alley entrance. The Leering had been hidden in the sludgy waters near the base of a fountain.

The officer who awaited her pointed it out. "It's right there."

Cettie glanced back at the tenement, feeling another throb of worry and fear.

She struggled to invoke this Leering too. The response was again sluggish and fitful, although it did finally begin to glow. Normally, she sensed the magic of the Leerings as soft, soothing sounds—as music—but this time it sounded discordant and jarring. The magic was rebelling against her. And it was because of *her* fear, *her* worries.

The vision she'd had of Fitzroy being shot had totally jarred her. Why would the Mysteries have shown her such a thing if she wasn't supposed to do anything about it? And if the attack were unavoidable, why would the Mysteries allow such a thing to happen? Fitzroy was such a good man, such a good maston. Her implicit trust in the Mysteries was wavering, and because of that, the tokens of its power were no longer heeding her.

Understanding what was happening wasn't keeping it from happening.

A few children were starting to emerge from the tenement, all of them with mussy hair and smudged faces. They looked terrified and clung to the hands of the officers escorting them. There was Joses, coaxing along two at once, reminding her vividly of the times they'd both tried to calm children who were starving and afraid while their guardian, Miss Charlotte, raged below.

She felt the Leering shudder.

The mist had risen higher, and it swirled down the street, obscuring her vision. A woman was shouting at the officers, demanding to know why they were being evicted. Her screams reminded Cettie of Miss Charlotte, although the voice was quite different. She felt the Fear Liath's glee, its power growing as the fog began to shield the light of the sun.

It would try to escape. She could sense its intention.

There wasn't time to dither. Cettie called to one of the officers nearby and asked where the other two Leerings had been concealed.

"There and there," said the officer, pointing at the two other alleyways.

"Lieutenant!" Cettie cried out, and Fields turned sharply to look at her. She met his gaze. "It's coming."

"Get them out, now!" shouted Fields. The children were picked up and carried away, the older woman shrieking at the officers as she followed them. She even started to pummel one of them with her fists, spewing hatred at him.

Cettie rushed to the next Leering and hurriedly knelt beside it. Her arms shook as she tried to summon the Leering's power. Maybe it was because she was desperate to save the children, but this one responded more quickly. The eyes began to glow immediately, and she felt it connect with the other two, forming a barrier that would prevent the monster from passing.

The cold that settled upon her was so severe mist rose from her mouth. It was too late in the spring for that. Those who dwelled in the tenements were coming out into the streets to see what was happening. The officers barked at them to go back inside, that there was danger, but many didn't listen. Cettie felt the Fear Liath begin to move through the bowels of the tenement.

Chaos and commotion were like sugar to it.

"Rand!" Cettie shouted in worry, unable to see him. "Rand, it's coming!"

She hurried to the next Leering, but bystanders had filled up the streets surrounding the tenement. Fog in the midst of the wrong season was a spectacle to behold, and a seemingly safe one. And it was unnaturally cold too.

Then the Fear Liath roared.

The sound was familiar and terrifying. She'd heard it in Dolcoath, but hearing it in the broken streets of the Fells was a thousand times worse. She covered her ears as the people around her started to scream and flee. Someone bumped into Cettie, spinning her around, and she lost her bearings.

Cettie couldn't see well and stumbled toward where she thought the Leering was. The hiss of an arquebus sounded from the mist behind her.

"It's out! It's—!" yelled one of the officers before his voice was cut off by a scream. There was a pattering sound of wetness on stones that made Cettie shrivel inside. Where was the last Leering? She could barely sense the others, their sound a scratching, discordant wail in her mind.

Then she heard Rand's voice. "On my mark. Ready, aim, now!"

Multiple arquebus shots sounded at once, and she heard the bullets thud into something solid, something impossibly firm. Before she could even think to hope, she saw the Fear Liath's shadowy bulk in the mist. Saw one man soar through the air before crashing onto the cobblestones.

Children screamed in horror as the monster attacked the officers. She saw claws. She heard snuffling grunts, and her mind went black with fear and despair. The Fear Liath was the master of the moment, not them. Where was the final Leering?

Cettie realized she was on her knees, crawling, weeping, unable to master herself enough to stand. *Where is it? Where is it?*

"Back, you devil!" she heard Rand shout, and she feared for him. Would they all be killed?

Then she sensed the Leering right in front of her.

A spark of hope lit inside her.

Cettie's dress tore at her knees, but she pulled herself forward. Her mind was blank with fear, her fingers hardly more than crooked roots, unable to unclench. But she reached the Leering and pleaded with the Mysteries that the monster's threat might be contained within the boundary she'd created. They could come back with more soldiers, with Aldermastons and dragoons, and . . .

She heard the soft padding of the monster, its claws ticking against the stones.

Cettie flung herself onto her back and saw its shadow rise up over her. It was everything dark and savage. Its power was primal and ancient. It felt oddly familiar to her, as if she were somehow a part of its magic. She'd felt this way before with dark things, with the Myriad Ones who'd clung to her when she was a child and on her other encounters with the Fear Liath. It alarmed her that the old, shameful feelings were still rooted inside her.

The beast lowered its massive snout, snuffling at her. One bite of its awful teeth or swipe of its razor-sharp claws would end her life. It reeked of blood. Her mind was a clot of darkness, and she shuddered as it smelled her. She had never been so close to death, not even when she'd dangled from the roof at Fog Willows in her attempt to escape Mrs. Pullman.

She sensed the Fear Liath liked her scent. It raised a massive paw, and she shut her eyes, knowing she was about to die.

It flicked the Leering near her away, shattering it against the wall opposite. Then it breathed into her face with its horrid, noxious breath, and bounded down the fog-shrouded street, seeking other victims.

The strain had been too much. Cettie fainted.

~

She didn't know how long she'd lain in the street, but most of the mist had vanished by the time she roused, save for a few stray wisps.

Struggling to sit up, she gazed at the scene on the street full of tenements. Several bodies lay still. A few officers had survived and walked in confusion from one body to the next. Then she saw Rand crouching over one of the bodies, one hand holding his arquebus, the other covering his face.

Cettie blinked, trying to see, trying to understand, and then realized that he was hovering over Joses.

A groan escaped her mouth as she got up, her legs trembling, and hurried over to them.

Rand looked at her, and there was no hope in his expression. She saw the pain twisting his features. But he had the hardened look of a soldier who had seen many previous deaths.

Cettie knelt beside Joses, her eyes wide and burning with tears. Her friend's jacket and shirt were soaked in blood, and more of it trickled from his mouth as he gurgled for air. His eyes were wide with panic.

"Joses," Cettie croaked in misery, touching his cheek, smearing his blood with her fingers.

He nodded at her eagerly, still fighting for breath. Cettie was a maston. She had always been strong in the Mysteries. If she believed, she could heal him. Doubts swarmed her mind like ash-colored moths, but she laid her hand on the crown of his head, willing the Medium to heal her childhood friend. Its power over life and death was immutable. It *could* heal his wounds. It could grant him his breath.

It had done so once before. Fitzroy had saved Joses's life years ago, in a tenement in the Fells.

She bowed her head and tried to utter the words of a Gifting. Her throat clenched. She was unable to speak.

She tried again, tried to use her will to *force* the Mysteries to obey her. Her intention only made the power flinch away, moving totally out of her grasp.

Her friend was dying in front of her. Was there nothing she could do to save him?

Please, let me heal him. Joses, why didn't you stay behind?

Hot tears seeped past her lashes and scalded her cheeks. Her shoulders shook violently. She willed the Mysteries to heed her plea, to save her friend's life, but nothing happened.

A being of evil had spared her. Why wouldn't the Mysteries spare Joses?

She felt fingers grab her wrist and opened her eyes, her blurry vision seeing Joses staring at her in desperation. He was trying to say something, but he couldn't speak. She leaned closer, her tears splashing against his chin.

She would have done anything to save him, but she could only watch as her friend's life force ebbed away, his grip on her wrist going slack. Then his head lolled to one side, his eyes still open. The battle was over. He had died in the Fells after all, on the very street he had always tried to escape.

Cettie's grief came out in a pent-up flood. She sobbed and sobbed, clinging to Joses's bloody jacket with her fingers, mourning a life extinguished so young. A life snuffed out because of her lack of faith. The agony of her loss was unbearable, especially since Fitzroy might yet be taken from her. How could she even breathe with so much pain in her heart? A dagger plunged into her chest could not have hurt more. Tears wrenched from her eyes as she began to wail. The sounds that came from her seemed to come from a stranger. She had never felt such misery before, such loss. She couldn't endure it. Rand enfolded Cettie in his arms, pulling her to him, but she struggled away, wanting, begging, to die on the street next to Joses.

CHAPTER NINE
LADY CORINNE

Cettie sat on the sturdy plank seat of her zephyr, exhausted from weeping, yet still unable to doze, as Rand piloted her back to Fog Willows. She felt drained, so utterly spent that she lacked the strength to sweep the hair from her eyes. Night had fallen. The monster was still a threat to the Fells. She had failed—not only Joses, but everyone who lived below. She doubted she could make a Leering glow to the brightness of a candle. She worried she might never be able to use them again.

The Mysteries had forsaken her. There was no beauty in the music she heard emanating from the zephyr. It was an eerie sound to her now, the discordant hum of a machine.

She was alone with Rand on the zephyr, but the impropriety of that—she, a woman engaged to another man; he, a man who'd once courted her—felt flat and hollow. She didn't care about customs or propriety now. Her friend lay dead along with many officers, including Lieutenant Fields. So much death . . . so quickly. The corpses were being examined by a doctor in the Fells, and then Joses's body would be sent home for the rites. He had no other family. But she would mourn him the rest of her life.

She had also failed her father, who had sent her on this task. He'd trusted her to defeat the Fear Liath, but she'd made everything worse.

"We are almost there," Rand called to her from the helm.

Cettie's eyes felt like leaden balls. Her neck muscles ached from her rigid posture. It was still early in the evening. She saw the manor in the distance, the radiance of the Leerings illuminating the sculpted grounds. The lights within the manor would still be aglow. Cettie longed to see Lady Maren, longed for a mothering embrace. She wanted to be coddled like a child, comforted and kissed and told that her heart would heal, that the pain of losing a dear friend would eventually ebb.

"Thank you for piloting us home," Cettie said. Even to her own ears, her voice sounded weak.

He came away from the helm, paused to stare at the manor for a moment, and then leaped down to the main deck. Rand heaved out a sigh as he slumped next to her. His look was dark and brooding, and she could tell he, too, was struggling with the events of the day.

He put his arm around her and squeezed her shoulders. "When my father died, I was bereft," he said stonily. "It's difficult to describe. Words are inadequate." He gazed off to the side, tilting his face away from her. "I'm not made of the same stuff as you. The poppy oil didn't ease my pain, but it helped bury it." He pulled her closer and kissed the top of her head. "I wouldn't recommend it."

The gesture was tender, but her heart felt nothing. The zephyr dipped abruptly, and she felt his control of the craft weakening. He grunted, slapped his thighs, and then stood and went back to the helm. He cast her a backward glance, a small smile on his mouth. "You make piloting seem so easy."

Cettie appreciated the praise, but if it were not for him, they'd both plummet to their deaths like poor Mr. Skrelling had the night of a terrible storm.

After Rand resumed his spot at the helm, the zephyr's movement became smooth again. She shivered, the warmth he'd temporarily brought her seeping away. She gazed over the side, watching the manor become larger, noticing the breeze on her face. This was the very zephyr she and Fitzroy had used to test the properties of the storm glass—her greatest accomplishment—but even that memory had burned to ashes. There wasn't even a spark of pleasure to be had from it. Her heart was a void.

She must have noticed the tempest in the landing yard at the same moment as Rand, for he leaned forward and called out, "There's a tempest there."

Cettie didn't remember anyone announcing they planned on visiting. Poor Lady Maren was all alone too. For a moment, she dreaded it was the accursed Captain Francis again. The last time he had chosen to disgrace Fog Willows with his presence, Raj Sarin had beaten him into submission and sent him skulking away.

As they drew closer, Cettie got a better look at the ship. She didn't recognize it. But Rand did.

"That's Lady Corinne's tempest," he said in a surprised tone. He cast a sidelong look at Cettie, his eyes registering confusion, his voice betraying resentment.

Cettie rose from the bench, swayed slightly, and had to grip the railing. She gazed down as Rand maneuvered the zephyr and set it down near the tempest. His brows knit in consternation as he tossed the rope ladder over the railing.

"I thought your family was estranged from her?" he said.

"We are," Cettie answered. Although her heart felt dead, a toxic brew of wariness, distrust, and fatigue formed inside her.

Rand climbed down first and then waited for her at the bottom, seeing her safely down.

"I don't have a way to get back to Gimmerton Sough," he said. "I can take the zephyr post tomorrow if you'll let me stay the night."

Cettie nodded to him. "I'll have Mr. Kinross prepare a guest room for you."

"Thank you," he said, and together they walked to the main doors. She felt the magic of the manor respond to her presence, recognizing the key she wore, which gave her the authority to command it. But her home no longer felt peaceful.

When they reached the doors, she opened them, finding no butler or servants in the main hall. She tried reaching out to the Control Leering and felt its sluggish response. The key granted her certain abilities, regardless of her own worthiness or capability, but the power she accessed felt wrong . . . ugly. In a moment, Mr. Kinross appeared down the corridor, hastening to reach her.

"The Leerings just alerted me to your arrival," he said to her, noticing with a small frown that she was alone with Rand. Her heart seemed to grow even heavier. He didn't know about Joses yet. "We have a visitor. Lady Corinne is talking to Lady Maren." He puffed out his cheeks as if trying to describe the moon growing flowers spontaneously.

"Would you tell Mother I've returned?" Cettie asked him, touching Kinross's sleeve.

"She told me to watch for you," Kinross said. "She wants you to join them."

That was odd. But perhaps it was best for her to keep an eye on Lady Corinne. What she'd heard of Sera's experience at Pavenham Sky had put her on her guard.

"Would you prepare a room for Mr. Patchett, please?" Cettie said.

"Of course. If you'll follow me." He gestured to Rand, who looked at Cettie in concern and then nodded. His expression told her to be wary, as if she needed any further coaxing.

Mother and Lady Corinne were in the sitting room. Cettie knocked softly before entering. It would appear the day's surprises were not over. The two ladies sat on adjacent stuffed chairs. Lady Maren's face looked flushed and strained, and upon seeing Cettie, she jumped up from her chair and hastened to embrace her. Lady Corinne slowly stood, giving Cettie a dignified look, but one that showed some strain.

Cettie didn't think she could bear any further news. She wanted to flee from the room, to hide somewhere and cover her ears.

"I'm so glad you are back," Lady Maren said, swallowing as if to master herself. There were tears in her eyes. This was clearly news of the worst sort.

"What is it?"

"Can I tell her?" Lady Corinne asked, looking to the lady of the house for permission.

Maren gripped Cettie's arm and led her back to the stuffed chair. There was just enough room for them to sit side by side. Lady Corinne seated herself again as well, her eyes still fixed on Maren, seeking permission.

"Yes," Maren stammered. "Yes, it should be you." Her mother's voice, her gaze—all spoke of disappointment and sadness. What had happened? She squeezed Maren's hands, as if clinging to a rope.

Lady Corinne was beautiful, but it was a cold, stately sort of beauty. Her posture was rigid and proper, her gloves edged just so with lace. Her hat, a confection of feathers and lace, had been placed on a nearby table. Cettie stared at Lady Corinne expectantly, daring her to do her worst. No news could be as awful as what had already happened.

She was wrong.

"Cettie, I came to Fog Willows tonight because I am finally at liberty to speak. What I have told Lady Maren, what I now tell you, will soon become public knowledge now that the binding sigil has been lifted. Do you know what a binding sigil is?"

Cettie nodded. Mrs. Pullman had used one against her as a child, preventing her from speaking about the former keeper's abuse and the crimes she committed.

"I thought as much. What I tell you has been a secret since before you were born. It is a shameful secret, but it can be kept silent no longer, for it affects the government of this world and worlds beyond. Lord Fitzroy, before he was prime minister, had long searched for the identity of your mother in order that he and Lady Maren may adopt you. It was not until he became prime minister, however, that he was able to discover the truth, which has been deliberately concealed." Lady Corinne paused, her lips pressed firmly together.

Before she could say any more, Cettie knew. It struck her like a lightning bolt. "It's you," she whispered.

Lady Corinne looked down a moment, her emotions under firm control, then gazed up at Cettie and nodded. "Yes. I was very young when I had you. Because of the scandal it would have caused, a binding sigil was performed to prevent me from speaking of it. I assure you, I could not have told you even if I had desperately wanted to. And I did not. I was young and naïve. And I gave in to the advances of Willard Richard Fitzempress, who is your natural father."

At the words, Cettie felt a sudden surge of heat inside her heart. It shocked her, made her squirm. She stared at Lady Corinne in disbelief.

"You are a Fitzempress," Lady Corinne said.

The news shocked her, overwhelmed her, overturned her self-identity. She and Sera were . . . were sisters?

"B-but Mr. Pratt," Cettie said, shaking her head.

Lady Maren began stroking Cettie's arm. "He is Sera's father," she said, her voice quavering. "That, too, has been kept a secret. He has no authority over you. He never has."

Cettie was in a whirl of confusion. "I-I don't understand." She had been told that her father was the kishion.

"Has it not seemed strange to you," Lady Corinne said, "why your birth mother never came forward? I could not. Nor did I want to bring shame on myself . . . or Richard. I was unable to do so."

Cettie stared at her, unable to cry, but feeling like she wanted to. "You left me in the Fells?"

Lady Corinne looked down. "You were taken from me at birth," she said huskily. "I didn't know you'd been sent there. There was no doctor when you came. My parents wanted to be rid of you. To purge the stain of my shame. They signed the deed under an assumed name and did it in the Fells where it wouldn't be questioned or researched. Illegitimate children are not rare down there. I didn't even know what they had named you."

Cettie stared at the floor, unable to cope with the tumult the news had unleashed inside her. Suddenly, it struck her that this would not just affect her. It would affect Sera as well.

"So Sera is illegitimate as well? She has gone to Kingfountain in the hopes of marrying Prince Trevon someday."

"I know," said Lady Corinne dispassionately. "When the emperor found out, he was willing to let the marriage happen to be rid of her forever. But Lord Fitzroy discovered the binding sigil and had it removed. If he tells the truth, it will destroy the peace treaty between our worlds. The emperor . . . Richard wants the marriage to proceed, but he does not want to grant Sera the right to inherit when he knows she cannot." There was a little pause. "There may be another way to solve this problem. That is why I came here. You could take Seraphin's place in the marriage contract. The peace treaty will not expire for another six months. Perhaps you can set things right. You are a Fitzempress, no matter that you were born out of wedlock, and thus of a rank to appease the court of Kingfountain. You have the power over Leerings that Sera has always lacked. When she was living at Pavenham Sky, I saw that she was no true heir. Now I know it is you. As I have no other children, Cettie, *you* will inherit Pavenham Sky and all that I possess."

Cettie felt herself swooning beneath the weight of this new information. The dramatic change in her fortunes was completely unexpected. But a feeling in Cettie's heart assured her that Lady Corinne was being truthful.

"What . . . what happened to Mr. Skrelling?" Cettie demanded. "He went to Pavenham Sky before he died. Did he know?"

Lady Corinne looked at her fixedly. "He stole the Cruciger orb. And yes, he discovered the truth. It was his work that led the prime minister to the binding sigil. The orb was lost at sea when his zephyr went down. His death was a tragic accident."

Cettie gazed at Lady Corinne, feeling a mixture of horror and respect to learn this woman was her natural mother. The lack of emotion in Lady Corinne's face showed that she had long ago mastered any feelings she might have about the matter. Cettie was jealous of that. She hated being so distraught.

"I cannot imagine Father countenancing such deception," Cettie said, shaking her head. "Even if it meant securing permanent peace with Kingfountain."

"I came here tonight to persuade Lady Maren to let me bring you to him. I do not know the outcome," Lady Corinne said, a small smile curling her mouth. "The emperor would never permit it, so I risk his wrath and displeasure. If the truth is exposed, I will lose my reputation and my position on the privy council, but I will not lose my wealth. Perhaps a change of worlds would be best for me at this time. Either way, I suggested to Lady Maren that you should no longer be the keeper of Fog Willows. You cannot take your key to another world, and it would be best if it were kept by someone she trusts while you are gone and this . . . affair . . . is settled. Now that I *can* speak the truth, I have options that I did not have before."

Lady Corinne stood abruptly. "I will leave you both to discuss what you will do. My understanding is that the wedding will happen in three days unless it is prevented. I suggest you decide quickly. I can arrange for passage through a mirror gate. It is up to you."

The lady of Pavenham Sky turned to leave but paused. Cettie saw only her profile as she said, "I should like to get to know you better, Daughter. You may bring your answer to my estate."

The privy council is at loggerheads with Richard Fitzempress over the terms of the marriage contract. He has offered to triple Sera's dowry in exchange for forfeiting her right of succession. His persistence is a nuisance, but I know something he does not—he will yield, and the marriage will, indeed, happen this week as Cettie foresaw.

Without a strong supporter, Richard lacks the discipline and persistence to see his aims through. And with the government officers tightening the net around Lady Corinne's interests, his last key supporter will be hobbled. I've instructed my private secretary to reveal Corinne's duplicity to him following the wedding. Even Richard Fitzempress will cringe at a charge of murder, and his office will not allow him to stop the wheels of justice once the case is passed along to the Ministry of Law. I plan to have her arrested upon my return from Kingfountain. It will be a lengthy and complex legal battle, but I have arranged the case against her meticulously.

The court in this world is sparing no expense for the prince's nuptials. They have already hung garlands on the bridges, and arrangements are being made for the celebrations.

There is a real chance that permanent change is near. I want to hope that it can happen. But there is a part of me that says something isn't quite right.

—Brant Fitzroy, Prime Minister

SERA

CHAPTER TEN

VANISHED

The evening had turned out to be much more enjoyable than Sera had anticipated. Trevon had assembled a small string quartet in one of the palace's many sitting rooms, and they'd invited his siblings for a dancing lesson to prepare them for the celebratory ball following the wedding. Trevon and Sera had taught his brothers and sisters several of the popular dances from Comoros with the aim of surprising the guests at the ball with a display of cultural solidarity. Sera had already learned the court dances from Trevon's world. It was something she had relished. The two styles of dance were very different, the one in Kingfountain less scripted, more intimate.

Trevon's sisters, Lyneah and Elaine, had taken to the idea with great enthusiasm. Sera and Trevon were the teachers, and they demonstrated the sets together before pairing off with the different siblings individually to help. After the quartet finished an impressive rendition of "Sky Ship's Cook," she and Prince Kasdan applauded the musicians while Elaine insisted that everyone do that one again.

"Thank you for being patient with my clumsiness," Kasdan said, nodding to Sera. He was several years younger than Trevon, the next in line to the throne, and had always been on the quiet side.

"You did quite well, Kasdan. It's your misfortune that you had to stoop so low to dance with me." Sera flashed him a self-deprecating smile.

Kasdan was not one for bantering, though, and he did not take the opportunity to tease her as Trevon would have. "I'm grateful for the influence you've had on my brother," he said in a serious tone. "I've always looked up to him, and I think the two of you will make a strong couple."

"Thank you for your support," Sera said. The music did not start up again. Kasdan offered his arm, which she accepted, and they began to walk slowly toward Trevon and Lyneah.

"Well, I wanted you to know that you had it," he said, his tone and the arch of his brows implying something she didn't understand.

"What do you mean?" she asked.

He pursed his lips. "Not all quarters are pleased at the match."

"Oh?"

His brow furrowed further. "It's no secret that General Montpensier has made efforts to discredit you with my parents. They've made it clear to me, privately, that they oppose your marriage to Trevon for personal reasons. They trust neither your empire nor your father. I think they believe that the emperor will not yield in the negotiations and that the wedding will be scuttled."

She intended to marry Trevon in just a few days. Why was she only now learning that his parents opposed the match this vehemently? Her stomach became queasy.

"That is why I wanted you to know," Kasdan said in a low voice, "how I feel. I think my parents are wrong to oppose it. In fact, I've spoken to each of my siblings privately, and they all think the world of you. As do I." His smile was sincere. "Weddings can be rather political among our class. But a marriage doesn't have to be. I hope you and Trevon will come visit me in Ploemeur."

"In Brythonica?" Sera asked in surprise.

He nodded, a little smile starting on his mouth. "Now that Trevon has chosen you, I'm free to marry. One of the possibilities is the heiress of Brythonica. Within a year or so, I hope to become betrothed to her. If she'll have me." His cheeks turned a shade of pink. He had never been so talkative with her before, but she appreciated his candor and, even more importantly, his support.

"Brythonica is probably my favorite place in this world," Sera said. "That means we would see you quite often."

"I would like that," Kasdan said. "After our older brother drowned . . . Trevon has been a strength to all of us. Did he tell you what happened?"

"He did. And I'm surprised you're not afraid of the sea because of it."

He shrugged slightly, for they had finally reached Trevon and Lyneah. "I've learned to overcome my fears."

Trevon raised his eyebrow at the last comment. He reached out to take Sera's hand, but Lyneah had already enfolded her in a hug. Sera returned the embrace, feeling a rush of warmth at the generous affection bestowed by her intended's siblings.

Elaine and Lucas approached, their cheeks still flushed from the dance. "I could do that all night," the youngest princess said with a grin.

"You crushed my foot," Lucas complained. "I hope it's better by the wedding."

"You all did very well," Sera complimented. "There are dozens more dances like these in Comoros and new ones invented each year. One day, wouldn't it be grand if we all attended a ball in Lockhaven?"

"I don't know," Trevon said doubtfully. "I suspect Lucas is afraid of heights."

"I am not!" the younger brother spluttered, before realizing he was being teased. "Well, not overly afraid. I'd like to ride a hurricane, though. That would be more fun than attending a ball."

"Let's keep this secret," Trevon said. "When the quartet begins to play, we will assemble as we practiced."

"I can't wait to see the looks on Mother's and Father's faces," said Renowen, the middle brother, slyly.

"Here they come now," said Lucas.

"You're such a—"

"No, seriously!" Lucas affirmed, gesturing, and Sera saw he was right. The King and Queen of Kingfountain had just entered with Lord Fitzroy. Sera wondered if one of Montpensier's Espion had tipped them off.

Trevon looked wary, but he took Sera's hand, and they walked toward his parents.

The queen saw the musicians and arched an eyebrow at her son. "Having a little private concert, were we?"

Trevon shrugged. "I saw no harm in it. Hello, Mother." He bent and kissed the queen on her cheek. She was a stately woman, but the antipathy in her eyes was unmistakable. It added to Sera's disquiet. She was used to brooking her own parents' disapproval, but she'd hoped that might change with her husband's family.

Lord Fitzroy was looking at her, and she could tell that he wanted to speak with her.

"Prime Minister, is there any word from Comoros?" she asked.

"There is, Your Majesty," he said. He turned to the king and queen. "If I may speak with her privately for a moment?"

"Of course," said the king. Having dismissed them, he took Trevon aside to speak to him alone as well.

"I'm worried by the look in your eye, Lord Fitzroy," Sera said after they'd walked a few paces away from the others and secluded themselves by a window.

He clasped his hands behind his back, a nervous gesture typical of him, and started to pace. "I received word this evening that Lady Corinne has asked permission to cross a mirror gate and come here."

Sera's eyes widened. "Before the wedding? That is highly unusual."

"Indeed, and highly suspicious. I have no doubt that she's feeling the pressure from my investigation. I haven't dared to send officers to

Pavenham Sky to search for evidence yet. But if one of the younger officers let it slip . . ." He frowned and shook his head. "An investigation such as this requires so much trust. And I've come to learn that her sphere of influence is deep and shadowed."

"Did you grant her permission?" Sera asked.

He looked at her. "I did not. In fact, I expressly forbade it. Her movements are being watched and monitored. She was recently with your father in Lockhaven. Then she left to return to her estate. I've heard nothing else about her until now. I don't know why she asked to come here."

"Maybe she wants to strike a deal," she said.

He snorted through his nose. "I doubt it. I don't know what she could possibly offer to turn my investigation from its course. It's like that game they play in this world. Wizr. I see her move, but I can't understand what prompted it."

"I think she's desperate," Sera said. "She knows she's about to lose power. Permanently."

Fitzroy shook his head. "She's far too shrewd for desperation. I wanted to tell you what I've learned. The privy council has rejected your father's bribery attempt. They control the purse strings of the empire, and they need a legitimate successor should anything happen to your father. We're at odds, but I anticipate this resolving in the next day or two. The marriage will then proceed at week's end."

Sera sighed. "Part of me just wants it to be over," she admitted. "I learned this evening that the King and Queen of Kingfountain hope our negotiations will fail." Sera tried to mask her disappointment. "They have given their son the freedom to decide, but he does not have their support. I feel sorry for him."

Lord Fitzroy gave her a sympathetic look. "I understand the position he is in, having been in a similar one myself. I did not see eye to eye with my parents, especially my father."

"I hope you don't mind, but Cettie told me about what happened when you were a young man. How the young woman you loved was sent away. You never found her, did you?"

He shook his head no. "But I never would have met Maren had Christina and I married. Never would have had the children or found Cettie."

"I miss her. I wish she could be here for my wedding."

"If we'd had more time to *plan* it," he said, smiling. He paused, the smile slipping, then added, "I'm afraid neither of your parents has chosen to come. The emperor doesn't care to, and your mother is fearful about traveling through a mirror gate. I'm sorry."

"I am too," Sera agreed. "But I'm not surprised. Neither of them appreciate being inconvenienced." She choked back the feelings of insult that had suddenly flared. Determined to change the subject, she asked, "Has your investigation determined why Mr. Skrelling went to Pavenham Sky that night?"

Fitzroy gave her an enigmatic look. "I have no direct evidence, but I do have suspicions. I've asked myself that question over and over. I think I know why he did. After she's been arrested, she'll be interrogated in front of a Leering that prevents a lie from being spoken. Then we will finally come to learn the truth."

"I wish I could be there when it happens," Sera said.

"You will probably be touring the realms here with your husband," he said. "A much better way to spend your first days of marriage."

"Thank you, Lord Fitzroy." She reached out and squeezed his hand. "The people of the empire are fortunate to have you in their service."

"I will continue to do my best," he answered. "Good night."

She rejoined the Argentine siblings, who were still dancing, and enjoyed the rest of the evening. The austere presence of the king and queen dampened the merriment, but only slightly. When it started to get late, Trevon offered to walk her back to her rooms, and she accepted. They walked hand in hand down the corridor, which was now empty of servants. "Tomorrow, I thought we might visit Leoneyis," he said. "I don't believe I have taken you there yet."

"That is the land that used to be underwater, correct?" she asked. "The source of the glass pebbles on our beach?"

"The very one. Leoneyis was brought back by Lady Sinia, following our war with Gahalatine centuries ago. A variety of cultures live there now. Many of Gahalatine's people flocked there following the fall of his empire. I believe all we are waiting for, as my parents said just now, is your privy council's final agreement of the terms. Did Lord Fitzroy seem optimistic?"

"He is always optimistic," Sera said with a small smile. They reached her door, but she didn't want to part from him yet. Standing in front of him, she took his hands in hers. "Are you sure you still want me? Even if your parents don't?"

His eyes narrowed. "Who told you this? Renowen?"

"Kasdan."

Trevon scowled. "He shouldn't have."

"Well, you *should* have," she said, squeezing his hands. "I'd rather know the worst than be kept in the dark."

He stepped closer to her, and she stepped back, only to feel the door blocking her. "Sometimes the dark can be nice."

"Prince Trevon," she said, giving him a look and speaking in a tone that said not to trifle with her.

"I'm answering your first question before you forget it," he said. Pulling his hands away from hers, he cupped her cheeks and kissed her. Her heart pounded in her chest as she dug her fingers into his hair and kissed him back, feeling sweet and sad at the same time.

Trevon pulled away, giving her a pointed look. "That is my answer, my princess. You are worth the wait, however long it takes." He kissed her cheek. "Would it were tomorrow."

She felt a similar feeling of restless impatience as she felt his kiss linger on her cheek. Part of her wished he'd start on her neck.

"We can wait three more days," she said with a sigh.

"I will try," he said, then gently pinched her earlobe between his lips. "Good night."

"Good night, Trevon."

She watched him walk down the hall before she opened the door to her rooms. Once inside, she leaned back against it, trying to let the tension ebb from her body. She pressed her fingers against her nose and cheeks, savoring the bittersweet feelings. The bed had been turned down in preparation for her.

"Becka?" Sera called, imagining her maid would be in the next room.

There was no answer, which was odd because Becka usually came straightaway when Sera returned. She looked around the room and went to the area with the tub and towels. Her maid normally prepared a bath for her at night, but the bathing area was empty. Sera turned around quizzically, then began searching the room in earnest.

"Becka?" she called again. Silence was her only response.

This was entirely unexpected and panic-inducing. Becka had always been there when Sera returned to her rooms at night, for she slept there as well. It was late, and no errand had been assigned to justify her absence at this hour. A dagger of worry and fear hit her stomach.

Becka was missing.

And Lady Corinne wanted to come to Kingfountain.

CHAPTER ELEVEN
THE GENERAL'S GUEST

Sera stormed out of her state room and marched down the hall, seeking anyone she could find, guard or servant—she didn't care. The night watchmen were already on duty, and they greeted her with concerned eyes, which became even more concerned when she demanded they take her to Prince Trevon's rooms immediately.

"Is something the matter, my lady?" one of them asked her.

"Indeed, there is, but I would address it with the prince himself. Please take me to him at once."

"Of course." The officer in charge gave orders for the others to continue their patrol while he and another man escorted Sera upstairs. The hall was eerily quiet save for the tramping of their steps, and her worry and concern bloomed into a frantic need to find her maid.

Sera had been to the upper levels of the palace before, so the path was familiar, but she had never been to Trevon's rooms. Her insides twisted into concerned knots, and she fidgeted with her hands, trying to remain calm despite her anxiety. Lady Corinne was always so unflappable. Even after years of observing the woman, Sera didn't understand how she could maintain such a facade.

After a brief walk down another corridor, they arrived at the chamber, and the officer rapped on the door. It was answered by Trevon's valet, an older man named Kemp. When he saw her standing behind the officers, he turned his head quickly and spoke into the room, but she didn't hear what he said. Trevon appeared moments later, his formal jerkin removed, his collar open—he'd obviously been preparing for bed.

"Something's wrong?" he said worriedly.

"Becka is missing," Sera answered. "She wasn't in my rooms when I returned. There is no note, no trace of her. She's never been away at such an hour."

His brow wrinkled in concern. He hesitated a moment, then nodded. "Come with me." He gave a small jerk of his head to the officers, indicating he wanted them to follow.

"When was the last time you saw her?" Trevon asked in an undertone as they hastened down the corridor.

"Before dinner, hours ago."

"Was she feeling ill? Is there anything you can remember that wasn't right?"

"Nothing at all," Sera said. Was Lady Corinne behind this? She didn't think it wise to speculate out loud, not with so many bystanders.

They went back down the stairs to the main level and down a corridor that Sera didn't recognize. It led to a sturdy wooden door, battered by age but unmarked by sign or sigil. Trevon approached it and knocked firmly, frowning as he waited.

The door opened, and a man stood in the gap. He had long hair and a fancy jerkin with little studs. Sera noticed the Espion ring on his hand and a pistol and dagger in his belt. Though she didn't recognize him, there was a deadly glimmer in his eyes, and the sight of him immediately brought a chill to her heart.

"Prince Trevon," the man said in surprise.

"I need to see the general," the prince answered.

"Let him in," said Montpensier from inside the room.

"And Miss Fitzempress?" the man asked.

There was a pause.

"Very well, let them both in."

Trevon entered first, but Sera was right on his heels. The two guards from the night watch remained outside as the door shut.

General Montpensier sat at a wide desk stacked with papers, scrolls, stubs of wax, and other arrangements all organized and situated perfectly. A man wearing thin-rimmed glasses sat in front of a sheaf of papers and a pen and ink at a little desk behind the general. A secretary, it would seem.

"Ah, Princess," Montpensier said with a yawn. He gave her a cunning look. "It is a little late for a social call. Do you not think so?"

"This isn't one." Trevon's voice was hard.

"My maid has disappeared," Sera said forcefully, wanting to smack the smug look from the general's face.

"And the lost lamb has been found," Montpensier said, his eyes twinkling.

"Where is she?" Sera asked, trying to curb her anger but also feeling a little flicker of relief. It soon wavered when presented with the smug look on the general's face.

"More importantly," Montpensier said, "is *where* she was found. She was caught sneaking through the Espion tunnels, Prince Trevon. She was promptly arrested and is now under confinement."

"Arrested?" Sera gasped, and Trevon held up his hand to forestall her from speaking more.

"Release her at once," the prince said.

The general had clearly been expecting this line of attack. "I'm afraid I can't do that, my prince. There are questions we must ask her. I have to perform my duty as head of the Espion, of course. There is evidence to suggest that Miss Fitzempress's maid is . . . in fact . . . a spy of the empire."

Sera wanted to say that his words were utterly ridiculous, but she realized he wanted such a reaction from her. She remained silent, trying to understand the motives behind his accusation, all while her stomach throbbed with worry.

"She's fourteen years old," Trevon said incredulously.

"Spies younger than that have been secured, my prince," he said with a nasty smile. "I should know."

"I don't understand why we must play this game, General," Trevon said, coming forward and planting his hands on the desk. He nudged one of the stacks askew, and Sera noticed Montpensier frown as he glanced at the pile. "Release her at once. She's not going anywhere. She's already confined to the castle."

Montpensier folded his arms. "Naturally you seek to please your future wife," he said. "But I'm afraid I must insist that she be held until the investigation is complete." The words made the pit in Sera's stomach sink deeper. "Why was she scuttling about in the tunnels? I'm afraid your negligence of Espion procedures, Prince, has opened up a breach in our defenses. You use the tunnels too often to see Miss Fitzempress, and it would seem you made the girl aware of them. I'm afraid I can no longer turn a blind eye to your misconduct."

"My misconduct?" Trevon said in outrage. "I order you to release the girl at once."

"I serve the man who wears the hollow crown," Montpensier said coldly. "Not you."

"Then I will go tell my father," Trevon said, straightening.

"Really, Prince Trevon. He's already abed, and I have much work to do still. I am quite tired, as you can tell." He feigned another yawn. "Surely this can wait until morning. Would you prove your insecurity to him by acting with such impatience? I tell you the girl is safe and sound. In fact, she's sleeping."

"I want to see her," Sera said in a low, measured voice.

Montpensier gave her a look of annoyance. "Do you not believe me, Your Highness?"

"Not particularly," Sera replied.

"What are you playing at?" Trevon asked warily.

"Playing, sir? You think this is a game?" The general rose from his chair, his eyes glittering with animosity. "You think I am slack in my duties? That I would arrest Miss Fitzempress's maid on a whim? Believe me, sir, that I would not have done so without believing the king would fully support me in this. This is not some petty vengeance for Miss Fitzempress's personal slights to me. The investigation will happen, as it should, and there will be consequences if the lass is a spy. You should thank me for doing my duty."

"Thank you?" Trevon asked in amazement.

"You're welcome," Montpensier replied.

An idea sparked in Sera's mind. A Tay al-Ard would only take someone to a place they had been before, a place that was fixed in their memory. She had used it to take Trevon to the beach in Ploemeur. If she could convince the general to bring them to the cell where Becka was being kept, then she would be able to return later if need be. She would be able to question the girl without being observed.

"General, I understand that you believe you are doing your duty," she said. "But surely my concern for my handmaiden is also understandable. I would like to see her and verify that she has not been mistreated or abused."

"Miss Fitzempress!" the general said with exaggerated offense. "That you would—"

"Then put my mind to rest, General, and take us to her now. You cannot convince me that it would be counter to your duty to bring me to her. She's probably terrified."

"It is more than a fair request," Trevon added, folding his arms. He gave Sera a confirming nod.

Montpensier threw up his hands. "Hours more work to perform, and now I must deal with children. You both tax my patience. But I will concede, as the request is not beyond reason, although it *is* against civility."

"Thank you for your understanding," Sera said, not believing his theatrics in the least.

Sera had visited the Espion tunnels before, but in the past she had not understood the extent to which they infiltrated the palace. A person could likely travel from one end of the castle to another without using the normal hallways. The man equipped with the pistol and dagger had remained behind, and the general acted as their guide. The secret corridors were cramped, at odd angles, and incredibly narrow at some points. A musty smell permeated the air, and the sound of whistling wind came from both ahead and behind. General Montpensier chattered along as he walked ahead of them with the single lamp, bragging about the trust that had been placed in him and his connections, both in this world and in others. He even made a snide comment, which seemed to be addressed to Sera, that he expected an Espion caught in Comoros would receive harsh punishment.

Was that a veiled implication that Lady Corinne was part of the Espion? Had they plotted this ruse together to get Becka out of the way and defame Sera?

"Ah, we are almost there," Montpensier said.

Sera wished that the two night watchmen had come with them. She realized, with growing concern, that they were deep within Montpensier's domain. He was someone who opposed the marriage. Someone versed in acting covertly. She had been holding Trevon's hand as they walked through the tunnels and squeezed it harder out of worry. He gave her a reassuring look.

They reached an iron door, guarded by two men who were dozing until Montpensier arrived. They quickly shuffled to their feet.

"Good evening, General," one of them said, saluting.

He saluted in reply without speaking, and they unlocked the iron door. Beyond it was a stairwell leading down. As before, Montpensier led the way. The stairs were too narrow for Sera and the prince to travel side by side, so she followed the general, nearly hugging the wall, and Trevon fell in behind her. She smelled dampness and heard drips of water somewhere. Her skin crawled at the thought of rats scurrying in the dark. The area below, lit by flaming torches, was lined with about twenty cells on either side. Iron doors were embedded with small, barred windows. A warden with a disfiguring scar from his eyebrow to his nose sat in the midst of them. The man didn't seem to be relishing his assignment.

Sera worried how Becka was handling imprisonment in such a wretched place.

"Which one?" Trevon asked gruffly.

"Open the cell the maid was brought to earlier," the general said to the warden, setting his lamp down on a nearby table covered with scraps from dinner.

The warden grunted, then unlocked the door and opened it. Sera gestured for Trevon to remain behind as she crept into the dark opening. She saw a small cot and a figure lying on it, covered by a blanket. There were no windows in the cell, no source of light save the torches in the hall. Sera's stomach clenched with worry. Biting her lip, she approached the bedside and knelt by it, recognizing Becka's dark hair. She gently shook her awake.

The face that turned to her was her maid's, and she felt a spasm of relief.

"S-Sera?"

"I'm here."

Becka sat up quickly, rubbing sleep from her eyes, and then hugged Sera in a frightened embrace. "Can I go now? I've been here for hours. Is it morning?"

It pained Sera's heart to see the hopeful look on the girl's face. She shook her head no. "It's not morning yet. I'm going to get you out of here, Becka. I'll find a way. How did this happen?"

"I don't know. My head still hurts. Something happened, and I woke up in a dark tunnel." Her voice quavered with tears. "I cried out for help and tried feeling my way along the wall. Some men with torches found me, and they brought me to the general, who accused me of being a spy. I'm not a spy, Sera. I swear I'm not!"

"I know," Sera said, stroking her hair. "I think they're doing this for another reason."

"Are you satisfied?" Montpensier asked abruptly from the door, holding up his lamp. The sudden light made Becka wince and shield her eyes, which Sera imagined he'd intended. "Do you see any marks on her? We are not so savage toward our women in this world, Miss Fitzempress."

Sera felt her anger stir again, and she stood up and turned to face him. "She is the handmaid of the daughter of the Emperor of Comoros," she said with indignation. "And this is a dungeon."

Montpensier shrugged. "I'm sure your prison spoons are all made of silver too."

There he was, goading her again. He'd always said impertinent things to her whenever they were seated together at state dinners. It struck her again that he held too much power for one man. Trevon's father had erred in putting him in charge of both the army and his spy service. It was clear he did not intend to make friends with Trevon, who would someday be king, and she suspected she knew why. There was a strange look in his eyes, an edginess that she'd not seen before. This was a man who made calculations in his sleep. What was he calculating now?

"I would like my doctor to examine her tomorrow," Sera said firmly. "I cannot see any injuries, but I don't know what to look for." She remained quiet about Becka's mention of hurting her head and awakening in the tunnel. No doubt, Becka had already told the same to Montpensier. There was a good chance he was behind whatever had happened.

"Your doctor? And who is that?" he asked disdainfully.

"Doctor Creigh, who has been treating the victims of the cholera morbus. I'd like his opinion on the matter first thing in the morning."

The general sighed. "Another missive to write. You have no compassion for me."

"I will write it," Sera said. "Don't trouble yourself. Trevon, if you could have it delivered?"

"Of course," he said, appearing in the light next to Montpensier. He looked infuriated by the whole affair. Sera kept her upset concealed. As well as her strategy to rescue Becka.

"I'll not forget this insult, General. But I think that was your intent all along."

CHAPTER TWELVE
THE DUKE'S POISONER

Sera's agitation had not decreased in the least by the following morning. The absence of her companion was pronounced, and it forced Sera to recognize how much she had grown to depend on the girl. It also quickened her resolve to get Becka back. If the abduction was Lady Corinne's doing, Sera vowed to repay the woman with stark consequences.

Although she preferred the comfort and style of her Kingfountain wardrobe, she donned something from her own realm as a statement of her disapproval and set off to find Lord Fitzroy. When she was brought to him, he was enjoying a private breakfast in his own chamber, but he put it aside as soon as he saw her worried look.

"Becka has been imprisoned," she told him and quickly related the events of the previous evening. She could not disguise the contempt in her voice when she spoke of General Montpensier, and before the end of her tale, she'd started pacing restlessly.

Lord Fitzroy pulled the napkin from his lap and wiped his hands and mouth with it before setting it down on the table. "Have you told the prince about my investigation into Lady Corinne?"

"No, not directly," Sera answered, coming to a stop across from him. "You counseled me not to."

"Not everyone heeds my counsel," he replied with a sad smile. "This situation with Becka is highly unusual. Why create a diplomatic controversy before such a momentous alliance?"

"Because the king and queen are against the match," Sera answered hotly.

Fitzroy gave her a shrewd look. "While I, too, have seen some evidence of their apathy toward the match, I've spoken to both of them, and their reasons are understandable, albeit not commendable. I think they had hoped for more of a figurehead princess for their son, not a strong woman who knows her own will. And it is difficult for any ruler to give up a portion of their power. No, this situation feels like it's the general's doing. I've not been told this, but I suspect the king and queen are planning to retire him from service following the wedding. He's a man desperately trying to cling to his power. And desperate men do desperate—and dangerous—things."

Lord Fitzroy rose from the table. "This may be a last-ditch effort to scuttle the union. But we both know that it won't work. Cettie's vision gives us a view of the end. I am expecting to receive the latest word on the privy council's negotiations. They were due to meet while we slept last night."

Sera nodded in agreement. "You're right, of course. I'd almost forgotten Cettie's vision. If what you predict does come to pass, and the general is relieved of his duties following the wedding, then Becka will be freed. I just can't abide the thought of Lady Corinne coming anywhere near her. Montpensier's gambit has struck me in the heart."

Lord Fitzroy smiled. "Remember, I've forbidden Lady Corinne to enter a mirror gate. Once the marriage is done, I will go back and deal with her. Her treachery will be revealed at last."

Sera took in a deep breath, trying to steady herself.

A knock sounded at the door, and Lord Fitzroy went to answer it. He opened it wider, and Prince Trevon entered. By the glum expression on his face, she knew the news wasn't good.

"I spoke to my parents just now," he said, turning to watch Lord Fitzroy shut the door. "They've ordered Montpensier to finish his investigation in three days. They won't let your maid be released until then."

"Why?" Sera said, her frustration spilling out again.

"Because the general is very persuasive. He pointed to the fact that she was a servant in Lady Corinne's household before she became your servant."

Lady Corinne again. It only heightened her suspicion that the deceitful woman and Montpensier were in this together.

His brow wrinkled. "You flinched when I said her name. I know she mistreated you, but I didn't realize you still felt such an aversion to her. I'm sorry."

"It's not your fault, Trevon. I'm sorry, do go on."

"It's not just Becka's past that was used as evidence but her actions here at the palace. She talks to the servants. She's known and doted on by my two sisters. She has been observed listening in on conversations."

"She's following *my* instructions," Sera said in a tone of exasperation. "She tells me things I could not otherwise learn for myself. She is my friend and confidante. Do not your sisters do the same for you?"

Trevon glanced down at the floor and back at her. "And the general swears that she was discovered by the Espion inside the tunnels. He said it convincingly enough that my parents believed him. I don't doubt that she *was* found there, but the question remains how she got there." He started to pace. "That is what concerns me the most. Remember that night you left your room with Becka and found me talking to my father about the cholera morbus? You mentioned that someone had followed you down the hall, but no one could find any sign of the intruder. Do you recall this?"

"Of course I do," she said hotly. "Are you going to accuse me of being a spy now?"

"Goodness no, Sera! I trust you implicitly, and I hope you trust me." He took a step closer. "What I want to say is that I took your words seriously. I believe someone *did* follow you down that hall." He lowered his voice and gestured for Fitzroy to come closer. When the three were standing in a tight cluster, he continued. "The castle is protected by the Espion, who roam inside these walls, and the guards, who patrol the main corridors. The captain of the guard has expressed concerns to my parents about General Montpensier's ambition. He has been conducting an investigation into the general's activities and believes a faction within the Espion is more loyal to the general than to my father. There are rumors that Montpensier hired a poisoner years ago, and this poisoner has helped in his rise to power." Trevon wiped his mouth and then grimaced. "The captain is taking precautions for the wedding. As you can imagine, there will be quite a crowd. People have already started arriving from all over the realm. Montpensier is not the only one opposed to our marriage. There are those who say that you won't do the water rite because you aren't even mortal." He chuckled. "I've tried to reassure everyone to the contrary, but these are dangerous times, Sera. There may even be a faction that tries to prevent the marriage."

He reached for her hand, and she took it and felt his thumb rub against her glove. How she wished her hands were unfettered . . .

"We cannot let anyone stop it," he continued.

He had probably said more than he should have and revealed information that was considered highly secret. Sera was grateful for it. She would rather know what she faced than not, even if the truth was uncomfortable. Should she not treat her intended with the same respect? Biting her lip, she glanced at Lord Fitzroy. Sometimes there was no need to speak. It was like their minds touched, and they understood each other.

"Prince Trevon," Fitzroy said in an equally subdued voice. "Thank you for divulging that information. We are still committed to the marriage and hope to receive word shortly that approval of the terms has arrived from the privy council. You likewise should know that I have also been conducting an investigation."

Prince Trevon's eyebrows lifted.

Lord Fitzroy continued. "It is regarding Lady Corinne and her apparent murder of a young advocate to conceal evidence that might discredit or betray her. It is our understanding that she has a man in her employ, a man from this world. A kishion."

The prince's eyes narrowed. "Could it be this secret poisoner? I think they are called that in your world."

"Quite possibly. Or the poisoner might be Lady Corinne herself. In my investigation, I have learned that she visited the court of Kingfountain as a young woman, around the age of twelve, on a business contract with her parents. It took many months for me to discover this, but it appears the trip was a long one. Several months. I have personally seen the record of her travels. It is my suspicion that Lady Corinne may have been approached by the Espion. That she has, through sheer cunning and duplicity, infiltrated the highest ranks of privilege in our society. We've long known that the general has spies in Lockhaven, and she may be one who has not yet been unmasked. Perhaps I should not have told you, but I think being candid in this perilous moment will prevent disaster. Do you agree?"

"You never told me," Sera said, reeling from the news. And yet, in some ways it did not surprise her. She could definitely believe that Lady Corinne was a spy. And she'd married the most powerful man in the empire, one with contacts and connections and information that would have proven invaluable to Montpensier. Now, if they did not succeed in stopping her, she was poised to marry another such man.

Her father. The emperor himself.

"I was going to in due time," Lord Fitzroy said. His gaze shifted back to Trevon. "Becka witnessed the murder I spoke of. Can you see why her imprisonment by the Espion is doubly concerning? And we received word yesterday that Lady Corinne has asked permission to cross a mirror gate and come here. I won't grant it."

Trevon started. "Yes, by all means, she should be kept away."

Sera touched Trevon's arm. "You must get Becka released, Trevon. I don't want her involved as a pawn in this Wizr game."

He nodded. "I will speak to the captain of the guard. Perhaps I can have her transferred to his custody. I believe we can trust him."

"If you can, I would be most grateful," Sera said. She looked at Fitzroy and saw the determination in his eyes. It was a determination she shared.

Lady Corinne and General Montpensier must be defeated.

The day crawled by with agonizing slowness. Word arrived that morning, as promised, that the privy council had ratified the marriage treaty between Comoros and Kingfountain on the terms stipulated by Lord Fitzroy. Sera's father, the emperor, had finally dropped his insistence that she be disinherited, allowing her and her offspring the potential of being chosen as successors. He still did not know that his aspiration to wed Lady Corinne was soon to be thwarted.

Sera spent hours in fittings for her wedding dress. There were also practices for the ceremony as she was taught the customs of her new people. Through it all, her mind brooded on the situation—on the Espion and Montpensier and Lady Corinne's spiderlike ability to deceive and control. She was given some time to rest in the middle of the afternoon and went back to her rooms, to find Adam Creigh pacing the corridor.

She gasped in relief when she saw him.

"How long have you been waiting for me?" she asked worriedly.

He shrugged and gestured with a wave of his hand that he wouldn't answer the question. "I did have an opportunity to examine your maid.

I thought I should report my findings in person instead of leaving a note."

"I am grateful you did, Adam. Thank you for coming." She noticed the lines around his eyes. He had worked tirelessly to serve the people of Kingfountain. After over a year of research, the cause of the cholera morbus still eluded him, as did the disease's uncanny ability to spread. Quarantining victims was still the best recourse. But Adam was determined to unravel its mysteries.

"I am yours to command, Miss Fitzempress."

"Please, we have been friends for many years, Adam. You've earned the right to call me by my name."

He shrugged again. "Would you like to hear my report?"

"Yes, please come in." She went to the door and opened it, nearly calling out to Becka out of habit.

Adam followed her into the room, leaving the door open. He glanced out into the hall.

"Are you worried that no one is here with us to chaperone?"

He smiled. "I know the customs here are quite different than on our home world, but I still try to honor them. For courtesy's sake."

"You are an admirable man," Sera said. "Let's walk the corridor, but we had best speak quietly. These walls have ears."

They headed out into the corridor, and Adam was quick to relate his news. "She is frightened but unhurt, save for a head injury. She still has no memory of how she arrived in the tunnels. That may be a result of a fall. If she struck the floor hard enough, she could have been dizzy and confused for hours. I've seen similar cases over the years. She had a knob on the back of her skull, but it was not broken. I examined her for other signs of injury or mistreatment and found none. They feed her regularly and let her walk outside this morning to get some sunlight."

"How do you know they didn't tell her what to say?" Sera asked angrily. Anger wouldn't help anything, of course, so she tried to focus on her gratitude that at least Adam had been allowed to see Becka.

"I interviewed her alone. She acted as I would have expected someone in her situation to act. She answered my questions promptly and without hesitation or glancing at the door."

A little private chapel was tucked into the bend at the end of the corridor, complete with a water fountain splashing inside. A guard stood just inside it, wearing the tunic and badge of the royal family. Why was a guard stationed at a fountain?

Sera paused to gaze at it, and Adam stopped alongside her.

"So you can tell if a patient is trying to mislead you?"

"I usually can. It happens frequently," Adam said with a sigh.

Sera looked at him, confused. "How so?"

"A woman arrives with bruises, a swollen cheek, and split lip. Her husband says that she is clumsy and injured herself. It doesn't require a gifting to realize the truth of the matter. People say much even when they don't speak at all."

Sera pursed her lips and nodded. "Wiser words were never spoken. So you think her lapse in memory may be a result of hitting her head on the floor?"

"Or she may have been struck from behind," Adam said. "Either method of injury would produce the same result. Then she could have been carried into the dark corridor and abandoned on the floor. It would take an unscrupulous man to do such a thing."

"Indeed," Sera said, frowning. "Thank you, Adam."

She gazed back at the bubbling fountain. The guard had noticed them, but he did nothing to acknowledge them. The pattering sound of the fountain was soothing. The fountains were another thing she enjoyed about the realm that was to be her new home. She still hoped Trevon was right, and they could persuade both of their worlds to unite, but it would be foolish to count on such an implausible outcome.

"I will check on her tomorrow and make sure nothing has changed. In the meantime, there are other patients who need my help in the city."

Sera felt a throb of warning in her heart. It was sudden, immediate, and pressing.

As Adam offered a little bow to her, she caught his arm, which startled him.

"What is it?" he asked in concern.

She felt the gooseflesh rush up her arms. "I don't think you should go back," she said. "Could you stay? I'm worried about Becka. And I . . . I just have a feeling that you shouldn't go."

Adam looked at her, studying her face. "I have a lot of work still to do."

Sera felt the throb of warning again. "Please, Adam. I'd like you to stay."

From the way he pursed his lips, she could tell he was struggling with his feelings, but he merely said, "If you say so, Miss Fitzempress."

I have a great deal of apprehension concerning General Montpensier. Some say he is Fountain-blessed, that he is another incarnation of the legendary Owen Kiskaddon of centuries ago. It is difficult, so many years later, to parse the man from the myth. But the chief difference, from what I have learned, is that Owen eschewed power, although power was thrust on him. Montpensier seems to crave it, and his ambition is, from my observation, without limit.

One of the Aldermastons of the past said there is no evil that does not promise inducements. Vices tempt you by the rewards they offer. Avarice promises money; luxury, an assortment of pleasures; ambition, a purple robe and applause.

What reward is Montpensier seeking? He does not seem content with what he was freely given.

—Brant Fitzroy, Prime Minister

CETTIE

CHAPTER THIRTEEN
MIRROR GATE

As Cettie walked toward the tempest moored in the landing yard, she paused to glance backward at the home she had lived in for almost half of her life. The sunlight was dazzling against the silver roof tiles and glass. Though she had not yet left, a pang in her heart whispered of homesickness. In one of the upper windows, the one belonging to Fitzroy's study, she imagined him as she'd seen him as a child, working to solve the Mysteries of Wind, using the elements as instruments to unveil secrets. She could almost smell the metallic tang that always filled that room.

Then she turned back and kept walking.

Cettie and Lady Maren had talked for hours the previous day. There was a heaviness in the young woman's heart that would not be dispelled no matter how bright the sunshine. Joses was dead. Father would almost certainly be shot. Cettie had almost revealed her vision, but she'd decided that perhaps her interpretation of it might be incorrect. At first she had believed Fitzroy would certainly die. And yet, he had stopped to bend down and fix his boot just before it happened. Did that mean the Mysteries would protect him? The Aldermaston had survived his wound. And wasn't Adam at the court of Kingfountain? The years he'd spent as a doctor in the Ministry of War must have given him the knowledge he'd need to save her father's life.

Another cloud passed over her heart. Not her true father.

And now he never would be. There could be no adoption now.

Of all the things she'd learned last night, Cettie was perhaps most troubled by the news about her true father's identity. Of course her opinions about Willard Richard Fitzempress were tainted by Sera's experiences with him. She also had no desire to disrupt Sera's wedding. No desire to be dragged through the muck of a dynastic power struggle, especially one fated to harm her closest friend. It was impossible to discern the right thing to do. If only she could see Fitzroy in person. She trusted her father's judgment and wisdom. And she also wanted to forewarn him about her vision. Yes, he'd likely received Rand's message already, but what if something had prevented him from receiving the message. She didn't trust it completely. If she could take his hands in hers, she could convey the depths of her troubles, the sorrows of her heart.

Cettie had not gone to sleep that night, choosing instead to hold vigil and try to regain her connection with the Mysteries. The sacrifice of sleep brought her no peace, no revelations, which only increased her uneasiness. She had relinquished her key of authority to Lady Maren before leaving, and doing so had made her feel even more bereft. Lady Maren would keep the key herself for now, at least until she found a suitable replacement. She had also signed the papers that Mr. Sloan had left for her and given instructions to Kinross to see them delivered by zephyr post.

Her identity had been settled these last few years. She had been proud to be the keeper of Fog Willows. Now she was the illegitimate daughter of the wealthiest woman in the empire. While she'd always wanted to see Pavenham Sky for herself, she wasn't looking forward to the visit.

After reaching the tempest, she climbed up the rope ladder. The weariness caused by her vigil was taking a toll on her. She did feel more at peace than she had the previous day, but the pain of losing Joses was always near, ready to stab her heart with agony. And no matter how hard she tried to force the sadness away, it was like pushing a boulder. It just wouldn't budge. She had already parted ways with Rand, who had promised to update the family on Anna regularly. He was hopeful she would be cured.

Cettie gazed back at the manor, hoping the tempest would respond to her. She was afraid it wouldn't, and that fear would only hinder her power. Cettie climbed up to the helm and grasped it firmly.

She had piloted this sky ship so many times it was part of her now. Surely it would recognize her.

Bowing her head, Cettie invoked the Leerings that controlled it. Nothing happened, which made her heart wilt. Screwing up her face, she tried again, remembering how difficult it had been for Sera to control Leerings back when they were in school together. How confident Cettie had been back then. She regretted it now.

Please, Cettie thought, squeezing the helm tightly. *I need to see Father. Without Lady Corinne, I won't have any way to get to Kingfountain.*

She tried again, using her will and her need to amplify her petition. There was a stirring belowdecks, a throb of connection. Her heart sped with hope.

Please, she repeated, knowing that she could not force the Mysteries to obey her. She had to submit to them. At that moment, she wasn't sure that she could. She was still so hurt and angry.

The tempest thrummed to life, and she felt and heard the chords of power. Again she noticed that the sound was off, jarring. She had always been soothed by the magic. Now it grated on her. Why was that? But she knew the answer. A damaged violin could still play music, but it wasn't as sweet. The problem lay in her brokenness, not the Mysteries.

The tempest lurched up, giving her that giddy feeling in her stomach that she so loved. She watched the manor fall away, and the grief of seeing it diminish brought a swell of sadness.

Was she seeing Fog Willows for the last time?

The thought had flashed through her mind unbidden. Was it a premonition? Or just her deepest fear? She'd kissed Lady Maren goodbye. Would that be the end of their connection as mother and daughter?

Tears spilled down her cheeks at that thought, and she wiped them away on the back of her wrist. Cettie had always wondered how she would feel if she discovered the identity of her real mother. She had given Brant and Maren Fitzroy that place of prominence in her heart, and they still held it. The Mysteries had confirmed Lady Corinne was her natural mother, but she had felt no warmth from the woman, no regret. Cettie had been unwanted from the start. She'd been abandoned because her birth had brought such shame.

As the tempest zoomed toward Pavenham Sky, Cettie's thoughts turned to Adam. How would he take the news? No matter what happened, Cettie would not abandon her love of him. Adam's father's speculation had left him penniless, and though Fitzroy had ensured he received an education, his salary as a doctor would never make him rich. It didn't matter to Cettie. She knew better than to think wealth brought joy.

The prospect of seeing him was another reason she'd decided to go to Lady Corinne. Her love was in the world of Kingfountain. She needed to see him, needed to hear his words of reassurance. Being with him would bring such sweet relief.

Pavenham Sky was situated on the coast. As her tempest approached the beautiful manor, Cettie stared at it in shock. It exceeded the size of Fog

Willows. There were multiple gardens on other massive broken mountains that orbited the estate at different levels. The gardens were famous, and Sera had told Cettie all about them. A private beach stretched out on the ground beneath the main estate, inaccessible because of cliffs on either side. There were a few small islands off the coast as well, mostly just crags of rock that jutted out of the waters. Some had tall trees growing on them. It was a picturesque scene, one that few had the luxury of beholding. Cettie had longed to visit Sera here, but every single letter she'd sent had been returned, unopened. Perhaps Lady Corinne had forbidden her from visiting because she knew the truth and the truth caused her pain, even if she didn't express it.

There were other tempests and zephyrs gathered in the landing yard, and Cettie steered hers down amidst the others. Although she was still weary from the journey and her vigil, she was determined to plod on and get to Kingfountain as quickly as possible. After settling the sky ship, she climbed down the ladder and quickly approached the massive manor. Though the weather was pleasant, the noonday sun high overhead and the lawn grass fluttering mildly in the breeze, she couldn't help but think about poor Mr. Skrelling's doomed visit. He had done it in attempt to help her, which made her feel even worse.

Cettie mounted the steps to the front door, but she did not knock. From experience, she knew the keeper of the manor had already been alerted to her arrival. She waited, and her patience was rewarded when a man opened the door. He was a handsome fellow and matched the description Sera had given of Master Sewell. While Sera had not liked being held prisoner in Pavenham Sky, she did have positive feelings for the butler, who was constantly attentive to Lady Corinne's moods and wishes.

"Ah, Miss Cettie," he greeted her, flashing a broad smile. "Her Ladyship is expecting you. Please come in."

"Thank you, Master Sewell," Cettie said, nodding to him as she approached.

"You know my name?" he said with a surprised chuckle. "How is Miss Fitzempress?"

"I saw her a few days before she left for Kingfountain," Cettie replied. The steward gestured in the direction they would go, and she fell in next to him. "She is doing quite well."

"I'm glad to hear it," Sewell said, taking her down a corridor. "If truth be told, I still miss her. She always spoke fondly of you."

Cettie was not in the mood for small talk, but his friendliness did help ease her discomfort somewhat, if only for the moment. They reached a door at the end of the corridor, and Master Sewell knocked and then introduced her.

Lady Corinne was waiting for her in a sitting room of sorts. The wood paneling was much darker than that in Fog Willows, and a set of glass doors opened to a veranda. The curtains were open, revealing a view of the gardens beyond. Lady Corinne had changed costumes from her visit the previous day. She now wore a dark red jacket and a skirt lined with pearls and small decorative flourishes.

"So you came," Lady Corinne said, eyeing her.

Cettie nodded, not sure how to address her. "How long will it take for us to reach Lord Fitzroy?"

"There is a mirror gate southwest of here at Hawkington," Corinne replied. "The contracts and covenants have already been arranged. You know about the arrangements that must be made for a person to travel in such a way?"

"I do," Cettie said, "though I have never traveled there before."

"I imagine not," Corinne answered, a little smile on her mouth. Then she approached and stood before Cettie. They were the same height, although they looked nothing alike. Lady Corinne was wearing black silk gloves—Cettie was not—and she reached out and took the young woman's hands. The silence between them grew painful. What could she say to her natural mother that didn't sound like an accusation?

Nothing. So Cettie said nothing, though it felt as if a stranger held her hands. There was no familiarity in the gesture.

Lady Corinne squeezed her hands and then let them go. "I have a zephyr waiting to take us. I suggest you leave your tempest here. When we return, you can take it back to Fog Willows . . . or Lockhaven, depending on what happens next. I'm sure the emperor will wish to meet you eventually. It will be quite a shock for him to finally see you."

"I can imagine," Cettie said blandly. It was not an interview she looked forward to. She knew he had always held her in disdain.

Lady Corinne then brought her to the glass doors leading to the garden. She opened one of them, gesturing for Cettie to exit first, and then shut the door behind them once they were both outside.

"We will not be gone long," Corinne said. "I imagine only a day or two at the most. The privy council will want to see you, naturally. An investigation will undoubtedly be done to validate the claim. The evidence is there, however, and the truth *will* come to light. Your life is about to alter rather dramatically. But then again, change is usually unexpected."

There was something in her words and the look in her eye that made Cettie uncomfortable. A zephyr hovered at the end of the garden path. A pilot stood in it, ready to take them away. He wore a similar uniform to the one Master Sewell wore, showing him to be an employee of the estate. They walked up a short gangway to board the zephyr, and the two of them took a seat—Lady Corinne on one side of the aisle and Cettie opposite her.

The zephyr lifted and banked away from the estate, steadily increasing in velocity. When it was a small distance away, it dropped suddenly and swiftly, making Cettie grasp onto the bench beneath her as her heart raced. She cast a worried look at Lady Corinne, who seemed completely unperturbed by the speed of the zephyr.

The sky ship maneuvered around some of the floating gardens, providing a splendid but brief view of them. Cettie craned her neck, trying to catch sight of everything. They shot into the shadow beneath the floating manor. Little trickles of water rained down on them from the hulking edifice of rock above their heads. The zephyr shot free of the shadow, accelerating as the pilot guided it along the coast.

Two tempests come into view behind them bearing the sigils of the Ministry of War.

"We're being followed?" Cettie asked, looking back at Corinne.

She glanced at the sky ships in unconcern. "No, my dear. Those are our escorts. They'll make sure we get to the garrison safely."

A throb struck Cettie's heart at the words. It seemed odd that the ships had appeared after they exited the manor out of the back, so to speak. But the garden had been the nearest to Lady Corinne's rooms, and she could come and go as she pleased. Obviously, she preferred her pilots to be daring.

Cettie watched the two tempests come into formation and tail the zephyr. They did not speed up or slow down, keeping a measured distance behind the craft. Something felt a little off, but the Mysteries had confirmed Corinne's words.

They reached the garrison of Hawkington a few hours later. It was a coastal town, a military town, on the western shores. Huge hurricanes were perched in the sky overhead, and Cettie could see people walking the squat streets beneath them. There were sea ships in the harbor and soldiers patrolling the streets. It was a pretty little town with a church in the midst of a small center square. The zephyr, however, passed over all of this, floating just higher than the steeple of the church, and went to the wharves.

"My late husband and I used this port for trade with Kingfountain," Lady Corinne said as the zephyr slowed and began to lower. "I own the warehouses you see on either side."

Cettie had lost sight of the two tempests that had escorted them. The zephyr landed, and the pilot put down the gangplank again and waited as both women exited the craft. There was a lot of commotion on the docks as ships were loaded and unloaded.

"Where is the mirror gate?" Cettie asked.

Lady Corinne walked slightly ahead of her. "At the cliffs over there," she said, not pointing but inclining her head. "This mirror gate is rather tall, which makes it good for trade. I have a ship ready to go as soon as we receive the signed contracts allowing us to use the mirror gate."

Cettie had to move abruptly to avoid getting hit by a cart. Her senses were overloaded, and she distantly noticed some children playing with a stray dog by one of the buildings and the smell of fresh-baked bread wafting from a bakery. Her stomach rumbled with hunger. Lady Corinne escorted her to the ministry office and entered first. There were many crew members inside, arguing about getting this signature or that seal, growling at the people working at the desks to hurry along. Lady Corinne bypassed the line and went straight to the back room, where a man sat behind a desk covered in layers of papers.

"Ah, my lady," he said, rising instantly from the desk, his annoyed look transforming to one of pleasure. He was an older man, and he mopped his nearly bald dome with a handkerchief.

"I've brought the young lady with me. We need to depart within the hour," Lady Corinne said. "Do you have the contracts written up as I instructed?"

He winced. "I would, under any normal circumstance," he said with an apologetic grimace. "But I cannot permit you both to cross."

"Explain yourself, please," Lady Corinne said, her voice firm but calm.

"I have orders from the prime minister himself," said the man helplessly.

"Orders for what?" Lady Corinne asked. "Can no one use this mirror gate?"

The man shook his head. "Oh no, plenty are coming to and from Kingfountain and other worlds. The orders specifically bar the two of you from crossing."

Cettie looked at the man in concern. "Do you know who I am?" she asked.

"Yes, you are Miss Cettie from Fog Willows, as Lady Corinne said, are you not?"

"I am," Cettie answered, her worry intensifying.

The man shrugged. "The prime minister has specifically said that the two of you cannot pass. He said he would address you both when he returns. *After* the wedding." He held up his hands. "There's really nothing I can do about it. Good day."

CHAPTER FOURTEEN

PERSUASION

Crestfallen at the rebuff, Cettie looked at Lady Corinne in concern. She could understand why Lady Corinne might have been forestalled, but why would Father forbid her from crossing a mirror gate? Was this because of the warning that Rand had sent through Admiral Hatch? Was Father trying to protect her, or was it something more? She felt a strong compulsion to see him, one that made her willing to disobey him, even though she normally never would. The news was too important. And perhaps he had some mistaken information as well?

Lady Corinne stepped closer to the desk. "You must understand that it is imperative for us to cross the mirror gate. We bear news that the prime minister must be informed about at once. Where are the contracts?"

The official winced, but his eyes darted to the left quarter of his desk. "I can't help you, Lady Lawton. I wish that I could! I would lose my position if I obeyed you."

"But why would the prime minister bar his own keeper from coming to him?" Lady Corinne said. "You must admit this is highly unusual."

"Indeed. I wasn't given the particulars, ma'am. I had already prepared the contracts in anticipation of your arrival, but I am afraid I cannot give them to you."

Lady Corinne turned to Cettie, her face betraying a look of concern. "Can you think of a reason why he would bar you from coming?"

Cettie already felt rattled, and seeing the worry in Lady Corinne's eyes made it worse. "I . . . can't be sure," she stammered in reply.

"I can think of a reason," Lady Corinne said. "Perhaps he's decided to allow the marriage to proceed in order to secure a lasting peace with Kingfountain."

Cettie frowned. "He would not do that."

"I did not think him capable of such subterfuge either, but what other reason could he have for preventing us *both* from going there? If we do not go immediately, we will be too late to stop it." Lady Corinne's eyes narrowed, and she looked at Cettie closely. "You are who I said you were. And you have the authority to cross a mirror gate on your own right."

The official looked at them both with a perplexed expression. "I don't understand what this is about. But I will not go against the prime minister's orders."

Lady Corinne did not look at him. Her eyes were fixed on Cettie. "Tell him," she said. "Order him to give us the passage contracts."

"But he doesn't know," Cettie said, her anguish growing.

"Then make him believe. You *are* a true Fitzempress. You always have been. These portals were created to obey you."

As Lady Corinne spoke, a feeling of energy and power began to churn within Cettie. A conviction began to build, a certainty that surpassed reason alone. Her natural mother's words made her realize that she had long lived beneath her potential. *You are a Fitzempress.* The assurance came as a whispering thought. In some ways, she felt she'd always known. Sera had struggled with the Mysteries for years because of who she really was . . . or rather wasn't.

Trust your feelings. You must make him understand.

Cettie turned and faced the official. The feeling of strength and conviction grew inside her, and she saw him flinch in his seat, leaning back in his chair. Sweat dribbled down the side of his face.

"You must give us the passage contracts," Cettie said, extending her hand.

A throb of power jolted through the room.

The man shuddered in his seat, looking as if he'd been running for a long time. He panted with effort and shook his head.

"I c-cannot!" he said in a strangled tone.

"I am the emperor's daughter," Cettie said firmly, feeling the truth of it ignite her veins with heat. "And you will."

The feeling in the room was palpable. Cettie recognized it as the Mysteries and could not remember a time when she had felt it so powerfully. In the last few days, she had been beset by such weakness and darkness—such doubt. But this power was real, and she felt it wriggle into the mind of the official, overcoming his resistance and composure. He started to weep as he reached for a set of folded papers on his desk. His arm shook as he tried to hand them to her, his throat making choking noises. As soon as the papers were in Cettie's hand, the man slumped onto the desk, sniveling and weeping.

Cettie felt a rhythm inside her. This time there was no discordance. It was powerful and it was strong and it vibrated within her core. But it left her feeling a little uneasy. She'd always been able to control Leerings, but this power felt different. Had it always lain dormant within her?

"Well done," Lady Corinne said approvingly, and Cettie felt her cheeks flush with the praise.

Lady Corinne turned and left the room, leaving behind the weeping official. Cettie followed, savoring a renewed feeling of vigor. As they left the building, they started back to the zephyr and found the pilot engaged in conversation with four dragoons. Cettie recognized the uniforms as the kind Rand wore. The pilot was arguing with them somewhat heatedly.

"More problems to overcome," Lady Corinne said, glancing over her shoulder at Cettie.

As they approached, the pilot saw them and folded his arms defiantly. "Here she is now."

"Lady Corinne," one of them said, turning to face her. "I have orders to escort you back to Pavenham Sky."

"On whose authority?" Lady Corinne said mildly.

"The prime minister," he replied angrily.

"We are going to see the prime minister," Lady Corinne answered. "He can arrest us himself if he desires. Now stand aside."

"My lady, if you resist, we will take you into cus—"

His words stopped suddenly. In response to a subtle nod from Lady Corinne, the pilot had struck the edge of his hand into the man's throat, choking off his words. The man sagged to his knees, and the pilot stepped forward and punched the next man in the ribs, so hard that Cettie heard a little cracking sound. The pilot did not even break a sweat as he incapacitated the third and fourth soldiers. When all the men lay groaning on the ground, contorted in their misery, he nodded to his mistress and gestured for them both to board the zephyr.

Cettie walked past the recumbent soldiers, completely disregarding them.

"I will take responsibility for disobeying your guardian," Lady Corinne said to Cettie as they mounted the deck of the sky ship. "Whatever consequence that falls will fall solely on me. We must get to Kingfountain before the wedding happens."

Cettie felt pity for the soldiers who had stopped them, but the conviction that they were doing the right thing, the *only* thing, still burned inside her. Once they were both seated in the zephyr, the pilot jumped on board and readied the sky ship, which rose quickly and headed toward the shore.

A shadow fell from overhead as a tempest maneuvered down from above to block their path.

"This is getting tiresome," Lady Corinne said with a sigh. "Can you outrun it?"

"Of course, my lady," said the pilot, gritting his teeth. "Hold fast."

Cettie gripped one of the railing bars, as did Lady Corinne. The zephyr increased speed and banked away from the tempest, but Cettie saw another one lowering farther ahead. Her stomach lurched as the pilot angled the zephyr sharply, cutting around the first tempest toward the cliffs along the shore.

Then the mirror gate came into view. It was a high, narrow arch of rock, the apex so thin that if the zephyr had struck it, the whole thing would have collapsed. It looked like a giant bridge, though it was overgrown with greenery and made of broken stone rather than brick. It was tall enough for a ship to pass through, but the patch of water before it was empty. The only thing stopping them from entering was the tempest that had lowered to block the space.

The zephyr suddenly dropped, making Cettie gasp with fright. The pilot continued to increase his speed, and it seemed he would try to steer the zephyr through the gap beneath the tempest. If they struck the water at this speed, it would surely rip the zephyr apart. Fear and exhilaration battled within her.

"Can you make it?" Lady Corinne asked, her voice betraying concern.

"It will be close, ma'am," said the pilot.

The other tempest had swung around to chase them, but it was hopeless. Zephyrs were naturally faster, and indeed, Cettie had never flown one this fast before. There was a groan from the timbers as the Leering within the craft compelled it to fly faster and faster.

Then Cettie had an idea of how she could help. As they approached the blockading tempest, she reached out with her thoughts and ordered its Control Leering to rise. Instantly, the captain of the sky ship countermanded her, determined to hold the ship's position.

"Ma'am," their pilot said worriedly.

"Their ship will move," Corinne insisted. "I feel you trying, Cettie. Harder."

Cettie gritted her teeth and increased her pressure to wrest control from the captain. Her power flared and the captain's will crumpled beneath hers. Suddenly the tempest vaulted straight up, and she heard the cries of panic from the crew as their zephyr raced beneath it and plunged into the mirror gate.

Then Cettie went blind.

Cettie gripped the railing in terror as the zephyr bucked and bounced through some dark vortex. The explosion of magic that ripped her from one reality to another was cataclysmic and impossibly loud, and it so overwhelmed her senses that she couldn't even scream in terror. It was no small feat of power that brought Cettie from her world to that of Kingfountain. She felt as puny as a ladybug crawling on the hand of a picnicker, suddenly aware it could be crushed by a mere flexing of the hand.

The darkness remained, but Cettie realized it wasn't blindness. Her eyes were simply responding to the sudden absence of the sun. She felt wind on her face and could smell the conspicuous tang of sea air. The whorl of magic was over. They had crossed between the worlds.

Cettie hesitantly looked up and found the sky glittering with unknown stars and constellations, baffling in their unfamiliarity. She had always found comfort in the orderly march of the celestial lights in her world. But this was new and different. Excitement began to replace the throbbing fear in her gut.

The pilot maneuvered the craft steadily, seemingly comfortable with his knowledge of their destination. Lady Corinne sat with her hands folded in her lap, gazing overboard as if their escape had been of little significance.

"I didn't think we'd cross in a zephyr," Cettie said to her, brushing away some stray hairs that were bothering her nose.

"It's preferred to cross in a regular boat," came the reply. "Neither side wants to share their secrets with the other. But there is no way we would have made it through on a rowboat. Sometimes we're forced to . . . improvise."

"We are going to Kingfountain?" Cettie asked hopefully. "How far is it?"

"Not very far in a sky ship," said Lady Corinne, giving her a fleeting smile. "You should rest. You look exhausted. I'll wake you when we arrive."

"I want to see Father as soon as possible."

A peculiar look crossed Lady Corinne's face. "You call him . . . Father?"

"That is what he means to me," Cettie said, wondering about that look. It had been a rare show of emotion for Lady Corinne. Was it envy? Was it disdain? It was so hard to read her, especially in the dark. The breeze was cool, and she felt herself starting to shiver now that the warmth from the noon sun—and the chase—had drained away.

"And you would do anything for him?" Lady Corinne asked softly.

"I would," Cettie answered. "And there must be some other explanation for that official's orders. I don't believe my father would conceal the truth from Sera. Even if she were illegitimate, she would want to know the truth about her parentage."

"Are you sure?"

"I am." Cettie could feel the doubt in her voice. But she knew her friend. And she knew the emperor had been trying to get Sera declared illegitimate for years. Her friend had never believed it. It would be painful for her to learn the truth.

"That makes her very different than most people. Most would rather conceal a scandal, at any cost. So much happens in the dark corners of our world, driven by shame or by guilt. People will willingly deceive others to save their reputation, which they esteem higher than their integrity."

Cettie did not appreciate the cynical comment. *You would know,* she wanted to say, but she was always too kind to let her lesser thoughts spill out. She rubbed her hands together for warmth.

"Try and rest," said Lady Corinne, reaching over and touching Cettie's leg. "Tomorrow will be a difficult day. But it will come. The sun always rises just as the darkness falls."

Cettie remembered how eager she'd been the first time she traveled by zephyr. She'd stayed awake and watched the scenery. But there was not much to look at here, just the undulating waves of the sea and some dark cliffs in the distance. There were no lights to show if any houses or dwellings were nearby.

"I'd rather stay alert. Where are we?" Cettie asked, digging her hands under her arms and squeezing down on them.

"Somewhere off the coast of Legault. Mirror gates can be anywhere the sea has carved away a natural bridge. Some of them are in the middle of nowhere. Like this one."

Cettie's eyes were getting heavier and heavier. She wished to stay awake for the journey, however, and she pinched herself. She wanted to complete her vigil before talking to Father.

"How long will we stay before we have to return through that mirror gate?" Cettie asked.

"The passage contract is for only a week. I don't think our business will take that long. I hope your meeting with . . . your father goes well."

"So do I," Cettie replied.

There was a pause, and the silence made Cettie's head swim with fatigue. She was so weary.

"Would you like something to drink?" Lady Corinne asked. "It might help you stay awake."

"What do you have?" Cettie asked gratefully.

"Just a little tea. Valerianum tea. I think it will help."

It didn't. Shortly after sipping from the cup, she felt her eyelids grow even heavier. The last thing that passed through her mind before her eyes closed was the image of her father's bleeding body from her vision.

Then a fog of sleep came over her, as unavoidable as the fog of the Fear Liath, and she remembered nothing else.

CHAPTER FIFTEEN
THE EDGE OF GENEVAR

Cettie's eyes slowly fluttered open, her lids feeling heavy. She could tell she was still in the zephyr because of the feeling of motion, but it was day now, and she'd fallen asleep despite her goal of maintaining the vigil. There was a foul taste in her mouth, the residue of some tea she barely remembered drinking.

She was lying on the bench seat, her hip cramping due to the awkward angle of her legs. She tried to sit up. The effort was difficult, but she forced herself to do it. Memories from the previous day were slow in coming, but she did recall journeying through the mirror gate and ending up in the pitch-black night of a different world. She blinked, her eyes having difficulty focusing. She saw Lady Corinne at the helm, her head bent low in conversation with the pilot who had incapacitated several officers the previous day in an impressive display of martial ability.

Cettie gripped the railing of the zephyr and looked overboard. Their speed had much decreased, and they were gliding over a vast city made of interconnected wharves teeming with ships. She blinked in surprise at the vast congregation, the towering cranes lifting cargo from holds, the sailors and workers thronging the decks below. A massive wall, at least fifty feet thick and arranged in a star-shaped pattern, surrounded the city. The barricades were impressive, and the towers were equipped with a variety of cannons. She had seen Kingfountain in her visions, and this looked nothing like it. Where was the enormous waterfall and the river that split around the ancient sanctuary of Our Lady? Where was the castle on the nearby hills that had stood for generations?

Where was she?

Lady Corinne touched the pilot on the shoulder, nodding to him, and then came back down the short ladder.

"We'll be arriving soon," Lady Corinne said as she approached her. "Are you hungry?"

Cettie was famished, but a wary feeling had unfolded in her stomach, one that made her not want to eat.

"Is this Kingfountain?"

Lady Corinne tilted her head slightly, looking at Cettie in confusion. "Isn't that where I told you we were going?"

"You did," Cettie answered, feeling the worry grow deeper. "It doesn't look . . ."

Lady Corinne raised her eyebrows.

Cettie didn't want to tell this woman about her visions. Not yet, not when there was no connection between them. "It's not like the stories I've heard."

Lady Corinne smiled at the statement. "The real world is never like the stories," she said. "We will be landing very soon."

As Cettie looked down at the building tops, the crooked shingles, and the ancient streets below, her feelings of unease began to flare into a seething panic. This was not Kingfountain. She was certain of that. Where had Lady Corinne taken her? Why was the woman deceiving her? Deep inside, she had the budding knowledge that all was not as it seemed. They were not on their way to see Father. She had been tricked or duped into a scheme of some sort.

Lady Corinne watched her closely, her own expression neutral. Cettie felt like crying, like begging to be brought back to Fog Willows, but she did her best to look as untroubled as the woman opposite her.

The buildings gave way to sculpted parks and hills, all within the walled boundary of the city. They weren't parks, she quickly realized, but secluded estates. Each was beautifully constructed, and each looked centuries old. But these estates had not been left to molder—they had all been maintained and improved upon. The zephyr continued to lower until it arrived at one particular estate, nestled in a small valley surrounded by vineyards and short green trees. Several stone buildings with clay-shingled roofs surrounded a central courtyard. Small covered walkways connected the buildings, and there were exterior stairs, also made of stone, connecting the different levels. The courtyard hosted a lush herb garden with rows of bushes of varying sizes. A few stone urns decorated it, along with skinny trunked trees with perfectly rounded tops. Everything was meticulously maintained. There were small clusters of tables and chairs arranged around the garden. Some of the doors leading inside were glass, some were of a heavier wood, and the windows all had iron shutters. On some of the walls, ivy crept up.

This was as regal an estate as Pavenham Sky, but it was a mansion, not a palace.

It was not Kingfountain.

The zephyr landed within the courtyard, just above a gravel path on the far side of the herb garden. The pilot came down from the helm and fixed the plank on its hooks so they could walk down. He stood at the top of it and gestured for them to go.

Lady Corinne walked down first, looking completely at ease. She even gave a hint of a smile as she gazed at the garden. Her shoes crunched in the small-pebbled gravel, each crunch inflaming Cettie's instinct to flee. She couldn't, of course—she'd only be running into her enemy's stronghold. Her only hope was to overpower the pilot. If she struck him by surprise, perhaps she could knock him off the edge of the zephyr. She could find a way to get to Kingfountain on her own.

Part of her thought the plan was ludicrous, but she was so certain now that she'd been deceived. Her insides quivered as she stood from the bench and slowly shuffled along the aisle leading to the plank. She kept her eyes on Lady Corinne, but watched the pilot in her peripheral vision. As she arrived at the edge of the ship, she took a deep breath.

Instead of stepping onto the plank, she planted her foot near the pilot's boots. She used the *butterfly hands* technique Raj Sarin had taught her and struck him in the chest, using all her weight to unbalance him and send him toppling over the edge.

It would have worked if he hadn't been expecting it.

His hands gripped her wrists, and he countered her push by leaning forward. She was the one off balance now. She could see in his eyes that he had suspected she would do something rash. In fact, he seemed pleased by it.

Cettie had to fight. Perhaps she could use the sky ship to her advantage. In her mind, she tried to invoke its Leering and bring the zephyr hurtling into the air. But the Leering on board refused to obey. The pilot's eyes started to glow silver, something she had not seen in years. Something she had not seen since . . .

His disguise melted away, and Cettie found herself grappling with the man who had claimed to be her father. He was the one who had shot Fitzroy in her vision.

And she was the one who had brought him there.

A groan of despair escaped her mouth, but she would fight him still. She brought her knee to his groin, but he outmaneuvered her again and shifted his body so that she struck his hip instead.

He spun her around in his powerful arm, folding his forearm over her throat. His other hand jerked one of her arms behind her back, and as she struggled against him, she found herself being marched off the plank. He then dumped her unceremoniously onto the gravel path at Lady Corinne's feet.

"She has spirit. I've always liked that about her," said the man, the kishion, to Lady Corinne.

"Where am I?" Cettie demanded, hot tears burning in her eyes.

Lady Corinne gazed down at her. "You are at one of the poisoner schools."

"What?" Cettie said. "This is Pisan?" She'd learned of the island kingdom from one of her history classes and from conversations with Sera, who was fascinated with the history of Kingfountain.

Lady Corinne smirked. "No, my dear. There has not been a true poisoner school there in a long time. Welcome to Genevar."

Cettie knew the rudimentary geography of the world of Kingfountain and had discussed it on occasion with Sera, who'd traveled to many of the different places with Prince Trevon. Genevar was a trading nation on the edge of the continent. It was very, very far from Kingfountain.

Her hopes began to wilt.

"What do you want from me?" Cettie whispered as she trembled.

"What we've wanted from the start," Lady Corinne said. "We want you to come back home."

Yes, it had all been a trap, and Cettie had blundered into it with blindness and naivete. They intended to murder her true father, the man who had loved her and taught her and befriended her.

A blinding rage filled Cettie's heart. She would not join them. She would not be part of their society of killers. More than anything else she wanted to hurt Lady Corinne. To smack that smug smile right off her face.

The instinct made Cettie lunge for the woman. She could not hold herself back.

But while Lady Corinne had long acted the part of a defenseless lady, she was not. A dagger appeared in Corinne's hand as if from nowhere, and she whirled to the side, leaving Cettie nothing but air to grasp. She stumbled again into the gravel, the stones gouging her palms. Corinne grabbed Cettie's hand, contorting her fingers into a position of utter agony, and then pressed the blade to her throat.

"Kill me, then," Cettie said angrily, gasping. Her voice cut off as Corinne torqued her fingers more, shooting pain up her entire arm.

"Why would I do that when I've spent so long preparing you?" came the woman's inscrutable answer.

"You don't *own* me," Cettie muttered, moaning in agony.

"There is so much you don't understand, Daughter. But you will learn. You will be taught." Corinne shoved Cettie face-first into the gravel. The torture in her shoulder and wrist came to an end, flooding her with relief. She scooted back a little, looking at the two people towering over her. Mother and father. Her insides quailed with horror.

Could she be anything but a monster with such parents?

"Take the zephyr to court," Lady Corinne said to the man. "I will join you this evening through the ley lines to make sure all is in place."

Cettie had no idea what those words meant.

"Tonight," confirmed the kishion. Then he bent and kissed Corinne on her neck. Before he left, he gazed down at Cettie without compassion. "You should have come when I came for you the first time. It would have hurt less than it will now. But every pain can be taken away. Remember that."

"He's right," said Corinne. There was a feeling in the air, a ripple of the Mysteries. For a moment, Cettie thought, *hoped*, it had come from within her, but then she sensed the true origin—Corinne. The fear and confusion, the feeling of betrayal slipped out of Cettie's heart. Those words held meaning still, but only as an abstract concept. It happened quickly, like medicine relieving pain from a wound. Cettie felt her heart slowing. The sense of panic was gone too. There were no feelings of desperation, no pressing urge to save her true father. Her emotions were placid.

"What are you doing to me?" Cettie asked Corinne.

"Just giving you a taste of the power that is your birthright. But you've already tasted it, haven't you?"

She found herself thinking of the man at the wharf, the one she'd forced to relinquish the documents. That sense of power that had felt wrong somehow.

The kishion smiled at the statement and then leaped up onto the zephyr in a fluid movement. He drew up the plank, and Cettie watched as his eyes turned silver again. The ship's Leering thrummed with power, but while Cettie could sense it, she could not tap into it. It was shielded from her in a way she didn't understand. The zephyr and its pilot lifted silently and streaked off into the sky eastward.

"Stand up, Cettie. There's no need to lie on a stretch of rocks."

Cettie rose, feeling throbs of pain in her arms and hands, but even those feelings were barely noticeable. Though she understood the concept of distrust, she no longer felt it. Lady Corinne was an enigma. If Cettie felt anything at all, she felt curious.

"Why don't your eyes glow like his do?" Cettie asked.

"Because I choose not to let them," came the reply. Corinne sized her up. "I am your true mother, Cettie. I am the woman who gave birth to you. Notice that you do not feel any tingling in your heart when I say it. For too long you've been blinded by what you think to be the Mysteries. Now you will begin to see the truth. I made you have those feelings earlier. Just as others have made you feel things in their own way. Your strongly held beliefs are things you have been manipulated to hold dear. And you *have* been manipulated, by both sides."

Cettie gave her a hard look. "If you think I will join you willingly, you are mistaken. You may have given birth to me, but you are not my true mother. And I will do whatever I must to stop you. To save them." Her voice trembled with anger. As emotion flared inside her, she felt the grip on her thoughts weaken slightly.

"Oh, I know," Lady Corinne answered with a pleasing smile. "If you had joined us when you were younger, then you'd see things differently. I understand that. Believe me, I do. I also know the power of leverage. Wanting a zephyr won't grant you one. It requires money. I can't bribe you to obey me, but I can tilt you another way. In fact, you've taught me how to move you, Cettie. I read every one of those letters you wrote to Sera Fitzempress and resealed them before returning them to you. I can say that I know your heart, and I know your goodness, and I know how much your almost-family means to you. So let me be clear. Anna Fitzroy was poisoned, and she will die if you attempt to thwart me. Your cooperation will keep her alive . . . healthy even. But my leverage over you doesn't end with her. If she dies, the estate of Fog Willows will then be left without an heir. Maren is not nearly strong enough to keep it afloat on her own."

Cettie tried to feel anger, but none came. She stared at Corinne helplessly.

"I know you'll likely lay your hopes on Stephen, but really . . . his debts are my doing in the first place. He'll be safe in Dolcoath when the estate comes crashing down, killing everyone living in it. You must know I am capable of this, Cettie. If I let your childhood friend get killed by a beast I helped set loose . . . you know I am willing to do what I must, even to my own daughter, to see my plans accomplished. This school has Leerings that will bar you from leaving until you, too, wear the hetaera brand on your shoulder." She stepped closer to Cettie. "I know about your visions. I know that you are the harbinger. If you wish for your family to stay alive, then you will do as I tell you."

Cettie felt as if walls were closing in around her, forming a prison that she could not escape. The hetaera. What little she knew about them she had learned from Caulton Forshee at Billerbeck Abbey. He'd claimed they were evil and manipulative. That they used kystrels to subvert others' will, to subvert, even, the Mysteries themselves.

And now she was to become one of them.

Thoughts ran wild through her head, but she found herself saying, "So you lied about Mr. Skrelling as well. You killed him."

"Of course," said Lady Corinne dispassionately. "As I will do to anyone who stands in the way of my plans." Then she smiled again. "So near is falsehood to truth that a wise person would do well not to trust themselves on the edge."

The wedding will happen tomorrow, but something is wrong. There is some variety of cunning at work that I cannot see, like a cloud that blocks the light of a prism. Like that piece of cut glass, I feel we are dangling, waiting for the sun to burst through and reveal the patterns of red, orange, blue, and violet. Even though the cloud is there, I know the sun is beyond it. I do not doubt that whatever will happen will be for the ultimate good of us all.

It is what is not said that worries me the most. I have observed several covert glances shared by the King and Queen of Kingfountain. I see worry in their eyes, although they speak nothing about their concerns. More than ever I must rely on the instincts that the Mysteries have given me, for I cannot see what lies beyond my next step.

Into the darkness. Into the cloud.

—*Brant Fitzroy, Prime Minister*

SERA

CHAPTER SIXTEEN

TRUST

The dark Espion tunnels filled Sera with a sense of dread and unease. The general had permitted this second visit with Becka only after much haranguing. There was no doubt in Sera's mind that Montpensier delighted in goading her, testing her limits, and trying to crack her composure. But Sera was stronger than he thought, and she refused to be cowed or ignored. The dank smell in the corridor was unpleasant—all dust and dirt and pulverized stone—but she would not let him know it discomfited her.

By the time she and her Espion guide finally reached the double row of cells, Sera was impatient to be let through the door. The warden muttered under his breath, looking fatigued by his dismal days underground, and unlocked it. There was already a lamp burning inside, and she found Adam Creigh sitting on a small stool beside Becka's bed.

When Sera entered, the girl's smile was enough to brighten the room. She bounded up off the bed and rushed up and hugged her.

"Am I to be set free?" she implored.

Adam gave Sera a weary smile. How long had he been down here with Becka? He was such a kind man to keep her company, to share a dungeon cell for several hours was a sacrifice for anyone.

Sera kissed Becka's hair and pulled back a bit. It hurt to speak the truth, but Becka could already see it for herself, and her countenance fell.

"Not today?"

"I'm afraid not," Sera answered. "Would it were otherwise."

Becka's disappointment showed in the sag of her shoulders. "I don't know what else they want from me," she said in despair. "I've answered all of their questions. I don't know how I came to be in the tunnel. I don't remember."

Sera took her hands and held them firmly. "I know, Becka. This isn't fair."

"I'll be all right," Becka said. "I was just hoping not to miss the wedding."

"I'm disappointed as well," Sera replied. "I need to ask you something. Can we sit for a moment?"

"Of course," Becka said, though her voice sounded a little uncertain. She returned to the little cot.

"Should I go?" Adam asked, rising from the stool.

"No, please stay." Sera beckoned for him to sit back down, then knelt in front of Becka, looking up into her face.

"What is it?" the younger girl asked.

Sera took a deep breath and steadied her emotions. If Becka was the innocent she thought her to be, she would do anything to save her. But to judge that, she had to call upon a wisdom beyond her own. A wisdom that only the Knowing possessed. Sera took up Becka's hands from the girl's lap, laying one of her hands atop them. She gazed up into her eyes.

"Tell me that you are not an agent of Lady Corinne. Or, if you are, tell me the truth once and for all. If you have deceived me in any way, admit it now, and all will be forgiven. I have trusted you with my heart. But I need to hear it from your own lips if you are loyal to me."

Becka's eyes widened with bewilderment and then filled with tears. Her shoulders hunched, and she began to cry softly. "I would never betray you, mistress," she choked. "I've n-never spoken a falsehood to you. Not even once. That you could think . . ." She cried in earnest.

Sera was relieved to see such a gush of emotion from her. It was how she imagined an innocent person would react to being falsely accused. Becka was hurt by the words, but it would only be a momentary pain. She gazed into the girl's eyes, reaching for the Mysteries, and the power assured her the girl had spoken truthfully. The small mothlike doubts that had been whispering near her ears after Montpensier's accusations were gone now. Sera trusted her instincts, but she trusted the Mysteries even more.

She felt her own throat thicken with tears as hot relief surged through her. "I know, Becka," she said, hooking her hand around the young woman's neck. She pulled her closer, embracing her. "I know you're faithful. I just had to be sure."

Becka nodded, her face buried in Sera's shoulder. She pulled up, looking fierce and even wounded. "I meant it, Miss Sera. I'd never betray you. You've been nothing but good to me."

Sera felt the power of those words. "I will get you out of here," she whispered in promise. "Whatever it takes, I will. Do you believe me?"

Becka nodded, a small smile brightening her face. The two embraced again, and then Sera rose. She hated every moment that Becka spent confined. But she would not let Montpensier use the girl's imprisonment as a ploy to stop the wedding.

Hoping to distract Becka with more pleasant thoughts, Sera sat with her for a while longer, telling her about how she'd spent the previous day—the endless alterations of the dress and the practice for the ceremony. When she noticed Adam nodding off on the stool, she suggested that they both needed to leave. Adam rose in agreement, and they left Becka in her prison for another day.

As Sera and Adam followed their Espion guide back through the corridors, she turned and said, "Thank you for staying with her so long. You don't know how much I appreciate it."

He shrugged. "It's important to keep her spirits up." He was too polite to mention that she'd ordered him not to leave the castle.

"You are a good man, Adam Creigh," Sera said. "Cettie is lucky to have you."

He smiled at the compliment. "Well, permit me to feel that *I* am the lucky one. I miss her excessively. Perhaps, with your permission, I could fetch her to visit you following the wedding?"

"I would be most pleased," Sera answered. She had so much to share with Cettie, and would dearly like her advice. They rounded a corner in the corridor, which was wide enough to permit them to walk side by side. "I'm grateful you were there when I spoke to Becka. Did her words ring true to you as well?"

"I have no doubt of her sincerity," he answered straightaway. "Someone who is guilty tends to get immediately defensive, argumentative. They'll try to persuade you why you're wrong. Her words ring true."

Sera nodded. She had seen that sort of behavior before. "You are wise, Mr. Creigh."

"Thank you, Miss Fitzempress. It's a high compliment."

They reached an exit from the Espion tunnels, and the fellow let them out. "Now let me be the doctor and send you to bed."

"If you insist," he replied, rubbing his eyes.

⌒

"You looked preoccupied during the practice," Trevon said. He took Sera's hand, massaging her knuckles with his thumb. The night's formal

PRISM CLOUD

dinner had just wrapped up, and they'd retired to a sitting room with the rest of his family. A couple of Trevon's siblings were deep into a game of Wizr, while the others chatted and played simpler games of chance. Trevon and Sera had nestled into a nook where they could finally speak openly with each other. And yet, Sera felt too exhausted to do so. Her head throbbed with a persistent headache, and she'd been tempted to use it as an excuse not to attend the dinner.

A sarcastic retort nearly slipped out, but she managed to catch it just in time. She gazed up at Trevon, saw the concern and worry in his eyes. He was a kind, thoughtful man, an excellent conversationalist, and there was no doubt that he adored her. Part of her wished the formalities were all finished, and they were simply husband and wife.

"You are dear for noticing," she said. "I am tired."

"I can tell it's more than that," he said, standing closer. He stopped rubbing her hand and traced the edge of her eyebrow with his finger. Then he sighed.

"What is it?" she asked.

"There was a protest today outside the sanctuary. A rabble, really. They were shouting that the sanctuary would be corrupted if we were married there. The crowd was dispersed, but unkind words are being spoken about us in the taverns this evening." He shook his head at the news.

"You heard this from Montpensier?"

"No, Captain Remmer. His resources are stretched right now, but he assures me the streets will be safe for the wedding procession."

"Why not go by river?" Sera asked in concern.

"We just may," Trevon said. "The guard will choose the best path, but both must be prepared. It is better if people don't know what the real one will be. It is the captain's decision to make, depending on which avenue he deems safest. I trust his judgment."

That made sense to Sera. "I see you're disappointed by the mob."

Trevon looked at her and nodded. "The problem with a crowd is there are no leaders. At least, none that we can see. If the Espion knows who arranged it, they aren't telling."

"Maybe the Espion was behind the disruption."

"To what end?" Trevon wondered. He leaned back against the wall next to her so that they both could look at those assembled in the sitting room, which included Trevon's parents and siblings and a host of servants. "The general cannot prevent us from marrying. Is he just spitting on the cake to be spiteful?"

"I wouldn't put it past him," Sera answered. "And how would you know if he did arrange it? We will be blind to what he's doing until he's no longer the head of the Espion."

"And that, my dear, cannot happen soon enough." Trevon chuckled, then his gaze drifted off to the left. "Oh, it's Lord Fitzroy. It seems he is looking for you."

Sera noticed him as well, standing in the doorway and gazing over people's heads in an attempt to find someone. Trevon gave a short wave, and Fitzroy nodded and crossed the room to reach them, stopping to greet the queen, who intercepted him.

When he arrived a few moments later, he looked concerned and grave. His countenance sent a jolt of apprehension through Sera.

"Judging by your expression, Prime Minister," she said, "you are either very tired or you have concerning news."

"On this evening, it happens to be both."

"Is this news from Lockhaven?" Trevon asked. He looked uncertain, as if he thought he should beg their leave and depart but did not wish to do so.

"You can stay," Fitzroy said, putting a hand on the younger man's shoulder.

"Tell me," Sera said.

"I don't know what to make of it," Fitzroy said in a worried manner. "I only just found out." He tried to control a frown and failed. "I just learned that Lady Corinne crossed a mirror gate in a zephyr."

"Lady Corinne?" Trevon said in baffled surprise.

"I thought you'd given orders preventing it," Sera said, her stomach plunging.

"I did. I assure you, there was no miscommunication of my orders."

"When did this happen?" Sera demanded.

"They arrived during the night. Efforts were made to hunt them, but they went by zephyr and it was dark. There was no way to track them. The Ministry of War feared the court of Kingfountain might take any maneuvers on their part as an act of war, and were hesitant to plunge in after them. There has been much confusion."

"Including in your choice of words," Sera said. "What did you mean by *them*?"

Fitzroy's look darkened further. "The report I had from my chief investigator is that Cettie crossed the mirror gate with Lady Corinne. That she . . . coerced the ministry official into letting them pass."

"She has no authority to do that," Sera said, her concern growing faster and faster. In that instant, she was reminded of her conversation earlier that morning with Adam, who had volunteered to bring Cettie to Kingfountain for a visit. What was going on?

"Clearly," said Fitzroy. "I'm as bewildered as you are at this moment. Why would Cettie put herself in the power of such a person? I have only suspicions. Perhaps we have found the identity of Cettie's mother at long last."

"Lady Corinne?" Trevon said, his voice low and guarded.

Fitzroy gave him a curt nod. "That is the only explanation that I can deduce following my investigation into the death of a young man who met his fate after visiting Pavenham Sky. Perhaps they are coming here. Or perhaps Corinne plans to use her as a hostage to hinder my investigation."

Sera's insides were roiling. Was Cettie the natural daughter of Corinne Lawton? What a scandal that would be. Sera's heart hurt for her friend.

"If they came to this world," Sera said softly, "then we are in no position to find them unaided. But I don't trust the Espion to perform the search."

"Neither do I," said Fitzroy.

CHAPTER SEVENTEEN
VOWS

Trevon and his father left the sitting room to discuss the matter privately. The prince had felt, and Sera and Fitzroy had both agreed, that this new information warranted him sharing the details with the king and queen. She waited nervously for Trevon to reappear, but several hours passed with no sign of him. When the servants began clearing away the refreshments, she bid Lord Fitzroy good night and walked alone back to her rooms. The empty hall felt oppressive that night. Would she ever feel truly comfortable living at the court of Kingfountain? Even if they did oust Montpensier, would she always sense his followers lurking in the shadows? She felt as if she were being watched. She probably was. Maybe the feeling would abate as soon as Montpensier was replaced.

Just as she was about to reach for the door handle, she heard the sound of rapid footsteps and spied Trevon as he turned the corner. Relief swept through her, and she waited at the threshold.

He arrived, still winded from his haste. "I'm glad I caught you before you were abed. Not that I would have minded seeing you again in your dressing gown, but we'll save that for tomorrow night . . . after the wedding."

His flattery almost made her smile. "You have news?"

"I do." He withdrew the Tay al-Ard and offered his arm.

"Where are we going?" she asked.

"You will see," he replied, arching his eyebrows. "A place where we can speak privately."

"The news isn't good, then?" Sera said.

"Let's just say that I don't trust we're the only ones in this corridor."

She laid her hand on his arm, and the magic immediately wrenched them away. They had not gone far this time. They were in the gardens of the palace, near the gurgling fountain where they had spoken on her first day in Kingfountain. The moon was out, a pale silver orb in the sky, but it provided sufficient light. All the colors were muted, and the trees cast dark shadows on the lawns. The castle rose steeply to one side. She had traveled by Tay al-Ard many times, but it still made her dizzy, and looking up at the castle made her off-balanced.

He sat down on the edge of the fountain. "Here, sit down to steady yourself."

When she tried to sit next to him, he encircled her waist and brought her down on his lap instead.

"So this is how you prepare me for your ill tidings?"

Trevon smirked and shook his head. "No, this is to remind us both that tomorrow night, we will be husband and wife. I brought us here so that we wouldn't be overheard by the Espion, but I also wanted to give you a proper kiss good night without being watched."

"How proper?" she asked, feeling a little daring.

"First the news," he said. "My father was surprised to hear about the investigation into Lady Corinne. He only knew her as a powerful woman with interests tied to Kingfountain. This was the first he'd heard that she might be affiliated with the Espion. Father told me that he remembers the visit she and her family made to court. He was a young man himself at the time, but the memory stuck with him because she disappeared. She couldn't be found, and her parents were worried sick. But they ultimately found her the next day, and it turned out she had gotten lost in the palace and fallen asleep. It was odd enough that he's always remembered it, especially since she eventually married Lord Lawton." He paused. "The circumstances are strange, I'll grant you, but this happened before Montpensier led the Espion. Father says he confronted the general this evening and demanded to know if Corinne was a spy. Such a secret should not have been kept from him."

Sera frowned. "Why would the general admit to such a thing?"

"Hear me out. My father is wary of the general and has been for some time. But he's very powerful and runs one of the largest duchies in the realm. He gave my father a ring that prevents someone from hearing a lie. I believe there are similar powers in your empire under the Ministry of Law?"

"There are," Sera said.

"Father put on the ring and asked several questions to test it. Then he asked the general again and again if she was a spy, and Montpensier still denied that Lady Corinne is part of the Espion. Montpensier admitted he has another spy at court, one who has risen very high up. He said this person's identity must remain concealed, and so he told my father but said I could not know."

That answer did not satisfy her. Not at all.

"And there has been no attempt by her to come to court? Would the Espion even tell us if she appealed to them?"

"Montpensier told my father that if she did make contact, we would be told at once. I've informed Captain Remmer of the situation. In fact, he went with Father and some guardsmen to interview the general. I also requested that guardsmen be stationed outside your maid's cell. If I had to pick who to trust, I would put my life in the hands of Captain Remmer and his men." He gave her an imploring look and pulled her closer. "Sera, Father told me he would talk to Mother tonight about relieving Montpensier of his duties. It will probably cause a rift with the man. But he needs to be taught who wears the hollow crown, and he will bend to it or . . . Father is prepared to humble him with an army if necessary."

That was a relief to hear. The king was taking the situation seriously, and although it would be difficult to rein in such a wily and strong-willed man, it was better to do it now than to let the situation fester. She wrapped her arms around Trevon's neck.

"Is there more news, or can we get to the kissing?" she whispered.

"A proper kiss," he said wryly, bending his head and nuzzling her neck with his nose. It sent a shiver down her back. Tomorrow, she reminded herself. Tomorrow they would be wed. Cettie's vision would be fulfilled.

She felt an overpowering feeling fill her heart. With her hands, she cupped his face and made him look at her. He was so dear to her, so very dear.

"I love you, Trevon Argentine," she told him. It was the first time she had told him.

There was a shocked look in his eyes. He hadn't expected such a declaration. But the shock quickly transformed into an expression so tender it made her ache. "I wasn't sure if I'd ever hear you say it. The only reason I haven't is because I feared it would frighten you."

"Your love doesn't scare me," she said, rising higher and kissing him lightly on the mouth. "But say it anyway."

He squeezed her to him. "I love *you*, Sera Fitzempress. My treasure. My true queen."

He kissed her back, and it was heavenly.

⌐◞

Though Sera did not have Becka's assistance, Trevon's two sisters and their maids helped her prepare for the wedding ceremony. Sera had seen parts of the gown in the fittings over the last few days, but now that it was together, she admired the workmanship and craft of the Occitanian seamstress who had created it. The light purple dress was trimmed with silver, and its bodice was covered in beads and seed pearls. Once they were done, Sera stared at herself in the mirror for a long moment. Princesses Elaine and Lyneah had given direction on Sera's hair, and the young maids had done their work well. The neckline of the dress concealed the maston chain she still wore beneath the gown.

Sera's stomach fluttered like caged butterflies. She wanted the ceremony to be done.

A knock landed on the door, and Princess Elaine opened it to a guardsman wearing a formal uniform and plumed hat of ceremony. His bearded face looked somewhat familiar.

"Captain Remmer," the man said by way of introduction. "It's time, Your Majesty."

Lyneah squeezed Sera's hand and looked fit to burst with excitement.

Sera thanked the girls who had helped her and then followed Captain Remmer to the door. "Have you decided which way we are taking?" she asked.

He nodded. "We are taking the street. The procession has assembled. You will ride by carriage with the royal family. The guests will line the streets, and guardsmen have been posted to hold the crowds back. There's a mob down there, Your Highness. Some aren't happy with the wedding, but they will be kept at bay."

His words were not very comforting. "I know you will do your best, Captain."

He looked like a man under a great deal of pressure, which was not very comforting either.

She walked with him and the princesses down the main corridor of the palace, past more guards who fell in behind them.

"There might be some fighting," said Elaine mischievously. "That would be exciting, wouldn't it?"

"Hush," warned Lyneah, but she, too, looked intrigued by the drama unfolding.

JEFF WHEELER

When they reached the front hall of the castle, the rest of the royal family was waiting for them. Everyone was dressed for the ceremony in their fanciest and most elegant attire. Kingfountain held a splendid court, and the brightly dressed guards were arranged in orderly rows, wielding flags and swords and arquebuses, wearing either metal helmets or plumed hats. Sera looked at Trevon, who wore a cream-colored tunic and a purple sash, and thought how handsome he was to her. The memory of their lingering kiss by the fountain the night before made her cheeks burn a little. He smiled at her, and she smiled nervously back before shifting her gaze to the rest of the family. The king looked gruff and guarded, the queen distant and aloof. Perhaps those expressions were the best they could do under the circumstances.

Trevon came forward and held out his arm. She put her hand atop it, and he led her out into the dazzling sunshine. Trevon helped her up into the rig, a polished carriage of purple and gold with wheels nearly as tall as Sera herself, enclosed with a sturdy roof and door. It was heavy enough to support two footmen standing on the back and the driver on the top bench. She sat down on one of the cushioned seats. After the king and queen had also ascended into the carriage, Trevon joined them, and a footman shut the door. The horses began to move forward.

Sera breathed in deeply through her nose and out her mouth, unable to describe the surreal feelings in her heart. Neither her mother nor father had come—but she hadn't expected them to suddenly change their minds. With the added danger, they probably would have demanded it be canceled anyway. But their absence still pained her.

"Do you know why the captain chose this way to the sanctuary?" Sera asked Trevon softly as the carriage jostled on the planks of the drawbridge.

"I can answer that," said the king in a surly tone. "Captain Remmer felt the river was the way that most would have expected us to take because it would be the safest and most direct. He chose the unexpected

168

route." He sniffed and then looked to one side. "The river would have been faster, though."

That was the extent of their conversation for some time. Both the king and queen were stiff and uncomfortable. It made for an awkward and uneasy ride down to the bridge, but Trevon held her hand in his and kept giving her reassuring squeezes. She knew what the silent message meant. Soon this would all be over. Once the marriage was done, the tension would ebb.

There were guardsmen posted ahead with poleaxes crossed to keep the public away. Cheers rose the moment their carriage was seen.

"Driver, go faster," the king ordered sharply.

The order was obeyed. At the faster pace, Sera felt herself bouncing on the seat, the movement and haste further agitating her nerves. Sera found the queen staring hard at her, and she met the woman's gaze without looking away.

The queen finally spoke. "You have no compunctions about any aspects of the ceremony?" she asked. "Including the water rite at the beginning?" Why was there so much doubt in her voice?

"None at all, Your Majesty," Sera answered. "My understanding is the water rite functions as a test to ensure I'm not a water sprite. As I am *not*, why should it bother me?"

"Would it not be a form of sacrilege according to your maston customs?"

"Dear," the king said worriedly, putting his hand on his wife's.

"If it were, would I be here right now?" Sera asked, meeting the queen's steely gaze with her own. The older woman eventually looked away, but Sera noticed she had tugged her hand away from her husband's. She sat there silently fuming.

"Have we offended in some way, Mother?" Trevon asked, his voice betraying a throb of anger.

"Not now, Trevon," said the queen curtly.

They were approaching the gate that opened to the bridge, and the carriage had not slowed. Sera felt a sense of dread as they passed under the shadow of the gate. A sickly feeling had passed into her stomach. Something was wrong. She couldn't understand what, but she felt it viscerally. Even so, she knew this was right—that she both wanted and *needed* to marry Trevon.

The roar from the crowd would have made any further conversation impossible. Just as the captain had explained to her, the bridge was lined with wedding guests who stood by the guards holding back the crowds. The curtains on the sides of the carriage were open, so she had a good view through the window. She saw Lord Fitzroy among the guests, and he nodded to her as the carriage passed. It was plain to see that he wasn't comfortable either, but Sera smiled at him. People were waving from windows in the buildings lining the bridge. A few cries could be heard above the general roar of approval and clapping, but nothing distinct. She knew some of the people witnessing the procession hated her, and she felt very vulnerable as they continued down the bridge, moving ever closer to the gates to the island sanctuary. The grounds had been secured and the pathway cleared. Only those permitted to attend the wedding would be allowed inside the sanctuary during the service.

The carriage slowed as it reached the sanctuary gates, and the commotion grew louder yet, blocking out even the noise of the rushing waterfall. Sera's ears were ringing. With an expert hand, the driver of the carriage made the sharp turn. Sera felt a strong reassurance as soon as they'd entered the holy grounds, as if she'd finally exhaled her breath after holding it. The path ahead was lined with soldiers at attention. The carriage came to rest at the base of the steps leading up to the sanctuary, and a footman appeared to jostle open the door. Trevon left first and helped Sera down. He then extended a hand to his mother, showing courtesy in spite of her lack thereof, and then finally the king left the carriage.

The royal company, flanked by guards, marched up the steps to the sanctuary where the deconeus awaited them. He did not look happy to be performing the rites that day. Why was everyone so glum?

Even so, Sera felt an overwhelming feeling of peace surge inside her the moment they entered the majestic sanctuary.

And that was when she heard the explosion of a gunshot outside.

CHAPTER EIGHTEEN
RUNNING RIOT

The sound startled everyone inside the sanctuary. Eyes darted with panic, murmurs began to echo off the stone walls. The king jerked his head, issuing a silent order to Captain Remmer, who strode out quickly, accompanied by several men with arquebuses.

A nervous sweat began to well up on Sera's body. Her stomach had shriveled to the size of a walnut, and she felt tense and uneasy, yet the strange feeling of calm she'd felt upon entering the sanctuary still lingered inside her. Part of her worried that a frenzied mob would rush into the sanctuary to drag her out and hurl her into the river. But another, deeper part of her knew it wouldn't happen. Her senses were acute to every sound, every shriek from the mob outside, and yet she remained preternaturally calm.

"Should we abandon the ceremony?" the queen asked worriedly.

"Wait for Captain Remmer to return," said the king. Sera saw his jaw muscles clenching. A sheen of sweat glistened on his face.

It took several minutes, but the captain of the guard strode back into the sanctuary, pausing only to order his men to shut the massive doors, and joined the royal family. The captain was grim-faced.

"Fitzroy's been shot," he said.

"What?" demanded the king in surprise.

"Several of my men saw a plume of smoke coming from a roof across the street. They're battling through the crowds to get to the house and find out who did it."

"I thought you had secured the rooftops," the king said.

"I did, to the best of my ability," said Captain Remmer in obvious distress.

"Is he dead?" Sera asked in growing dread.

"No, but he's losing blood quickly. He needs a surgeon."

The news had made Sera begin to tremble, but she knew at once what must be done. "Adam Creigh. I don't want anyone else to administer to him." She looked at the king as she said it. *This* was why she'd had the intuition to keep Adam from leaving the castle.

The king nodded and gestured curtly. "We'll postpone the wedding until he—"

"No!" Sera and Trevon said in unison, surprising each other.

Whoever had done this had clearly done it with the intent of forestalling the alliance, but she still felt it was just and right. So did he. She reached out and squeezed Trevon's hand.

"Son," the king said, shaking his head.

"We proceed," said Trevon. "Captain, put the prime minister in our carriage and get him back to the palace. Have Doctor Creigh, and only Creigh, attend him unless the doctor asks for help. Get this done. See to it yourself."

The captain shook his head. "It is my duty to protect the royal family. I'll have Fitzroy taken back to the palace, but I will not leave you. I have a vessel waiting for us outside the sanctuary. We will return to the castle up the river."

"Son," the king said imploringly.

"This is *our* decision, Father," Trevon said, holding up Sera's hand.

The king glanced once at his wife, the two of them sharing a look of concern and worry. Then the king turned and faced the deconeus.

"Continue with the ceremony."

"But, my lord," the deconeus said hesitantly.

"Do it!" the king ordered.

The deconeus, despite his reservations, acknowledged that he would with a curt nod. He motioned for the sextant to bring the dish of water.

"Please kneel before me, Your Majesty," said the deconeus to Sera. His voice was trembling.

Sera, still surrounded by the family, knelt before him. Her heart was pounding in her ears as she bowed her head until she was eye level with the bowl. Traces of the smoke had drifted in from outside, along with sounds of yelling. Sera itched to look toward the doors, but they had been closed long ago. She wouldn't have been able to see anything.

The deconeus came closer. "If you are a water sprite, I abjure thee!" he said in a firm, clear voice. She felt the water strike her hair and run down her neck and chin. He'd not poured very much, but it dribbled on the floor by her knees.

There was a collective sigh from the people who'd gathered to watch the rite. The sound reminded her of waves receding off a beach.

"She is not waterborn," said the deconeus. "We can proceed. Please rise."

Two servants quickly approached with towels—one mopped the floor while the other helped dry off Sera's face and neck. The commotion from outside was increasing. The gunshot had clearly set off a larger demonstration. Another shot was fired, making Sera gasp in fright, but she clenched her jaw. They would finish this.

"Promptly, Deconeus," said the king, wiping sweat from his cheek. He cast a nervous look outside. The queen's face was ashen. Trevon's siblings equally looked concerned and worried, each one glancing at the now-closed sanctuary doors. They did little to suppress the noise.

The deconeus nodded, looking nervous. "Prince Trevon Argentine," he said in a voice more confident than his demeanor, "do you desire Sera Fitzempress as your wedded wife?"

Trevon, his mouth in a frown, answered forcefully, "Yes."

The deconeus coughed. "Sera Fitzempress, do you desire Trevon Argentine as your wedded husband?"

Sera felt like she needed to cough, but she managed a firm "yes" in response to the question.

"The rings," said the deconeus nervously. Trevon, who had both prepared and fitted them, produced them from his jacket pocket. He handed Sera the one for him and took hers himself.

"If you please," said the deconeus, gesturing for them to hurry.

Trevon kissed her ring and put it on her ring finger. She likewise kissed his and put it on his finger, struggling a little to get it past his knuckle. They hadn't practiced that part earlier. After it was in place, they joined their right hands.

The deconeus put his hand on top of theirs. "What the Fountain has joined together, let no man—"

A loud crash sounded outside the sanctuary.

"Sounds like they're breaking the gates!" someone gasped in fear.

The deconeus, blinking and frazzled, repeated, "What the Fountain has joined together, let no man put asunder." He lifted his hand from theirs and muttered in relief, "It is done. Now hurry, Your Highnesses!"

Another crashing sound happened at the gates.

"Bar those doors!" ordered Captain Remmer. "Drag anything heavy in front of them. Hold them until we are gone!"

"Aye, Captain," answered one of his men.

Trevon gripped Sera's hand, his face flushed with concern but still smiling. "Well, it's an unusual way to start a marriage. More excitement than I'd hoped for, I'll admit."

"Come on!" barked the king, and the whole royal family began marching to the rear of the sanctuary. As the family left through the rear alcove, they emerged into a garden and hurried across the lawn to the docks behind the building, shouts and screams filling their ears. Sera felt Trevon tug on her hand as they hastened away from the scene of violence. Now that the marriage was done, she fretted about Lord Fitzroy and hoped his carriage had made it back to the castle.

At the docks, they began to descend the steps, the rushing noise of the river drowning out the worst of the tumult from behind them. Just as the captain had said, a vessel was ready and waiting, guarded by several of his men, who opened the hatch of the ship when they saw the royal party approaching.

One of the soldiers asked the captain about the noise as they came near, and the captain shouted his response. "A riot has broken out. Get everyone on board. We need to subdue the streets. This isn't over yet."

The family had begun to board the sea vessel when Lyneah cried out, "Where is Kasdan? He's not here."

Everyone stopped and looked around, but the princess had spoken the truth. There was no sign of him. Sera's chest constricted with worry. She'd seen him during the marriage ceremony. He was one of the brothers who'd stood witness. In all the uproar, he must have become separated from the group.

Captain Remmer scowled. "Into the vessel," he barked. "We must get to the safety of the palace."

"Where is my son, Captain?" the queen demanded.

"I don't know, ma'am. I thought he was with us. I will send men to fetch him, but everyone must get inside. Quickly!"

The queen and the rest of the siblings were escorted into the vessel. Sera studied the strange vessel as she watched them board it. The rushing waters lapped fiercely against the hull, but it did not budge or strain. No mooring ropes held it in. The Kingfountain navy had many sea crafts like this one, ones that could stand still in inclement waters and travel beneath the waves. It was one reason the war had gone on so long.

Trevon helped Sera enter, but he remained on the pier, looking back toward the sanctuary in confusion and agitation. The two brothers were close, and it did not surprise her that he hesitated to leave Kasdan behind.

"Trevon, get down here!" the queen commanded.

The king had also remained behind, and he and Trevon looked at each other in alarm.

"Your Highness," Captain Remmer said forcefully. "You must board the vessel."

"What about Prince Kasdan?" the king asked coldly.

"I don't know why he didn't come. But he'll be found. It will be our first priority."

The king's face showed deep consternation. His brows were forked, his expression grim and worried. "Madness," he muttered. "It is all madness!" Then he gave Trevon an accusatory look, as if the rabble and riot were his fault for marrying Sera.

Sera could not help but resent the implication. Part of her suspected that General Montpensier and his Espion were responsible for the riot.

"Please!" Captain Remmer said forcefully. He looked about ready to seize both men and drag them on board.

The king finally acquiesced and nodded for Trevon to do the same. He followed, and the captain unclenched his fist and pointed a finger at the two guards who had been left to guard the ship.

"Go back to the sanctuary and find Prince Kasdan. See that he's brought safely back to the palace."

"Yes, Captain," they said and marched away. The captain himself closed the hatch as everyone settled onto the benches. The ship lurched and began to plow upstream against the massive force of the river with ease. As they moved away from the conflict, Sera's fears began to subside, but not entirely. How many guards had been sent to secure the streets for the wedding? That left the Espion primarily in control of the palace. She pursed her lips, not wanting to voice her fear, especially since Kasdan had not yet been found. Instead, she merely squeezed closer to Trevon, who sat beside her on the bench. Her husband. He was her husband. Her mind was still reeling from the chaotic ceremony.

What a frightful day it had become.

After several minutes in the water, the vessel reached the docks on the palace side of the surging river and came to rest in the quay. The men who'd come to greet them were not wearing the uniforms of the guard, Sera noticed at once, and they all wore Espion rings.

"I don't like this," Sera said darkly.

"It's not how I intended our wedding to go either," Trevon replied.

"Not that. Them." She nodded to the Espion on the deck as the Argentine siblings began to climb out of the ship and up onto the pier.

"Where's Montpensier?" the king asked one of the Espion.

"He's attending to the carriage, which just arrived. There was an accident of some sort down there?"

"It was no accident," said the king disdainfully. "Tell him I want to see him at once."

"Of course, my lord," said one of the men. Sera noticed the man didn't look worried or concerned. He wasn't asking questions about what sort of violence had unfolded on the bridge. Why would a spy remain quiet? Unless they already knew?

After they emerged from the sea vessel, they mounted the steps from the docks and entered the castle through the royal dock gate. The servants inside were in various stages of worry. There weren't any guardsmen, but there seemed to be Espion rings everywhere.

Sera frowned again, her suspicions deepening. Had Montpensier staged the riot to stay in power? To show that Captain Remmer wasn't capable of restoring order or protecting the family? It was like Wizr again. Trevon had taught her how to play the ancient game, and she felt as if the general was about to murmur the word "threat."

"I'd like to see Lord Fitzroy," she told Trevon.

"Captain Remmer," said the king, "I want you there when I find Montpensier. Bring some of your guards."

"I will bring as many as I can find," said the captain uneasily. "This way."

"Go to the sitting room," the queen said to the rest of her children. "Wait for us there."

"But mother—" complained Lucas.

She cut him off with a glare. All the Argentine children obeyed the missive, save for Trevon. He took Sera down a side corridor. With all the chaos unfolding around her, she was so turned around, she had no idea where he was taking her. But it ended up being the physician's wing of the castle, where the injured and sick were cared for. This corridor was crowded with guards *and* Espion, as well as servants trying to get in and out of the crush.

Trevon gripped Sera's hand to keep her close. He clamped his other hand on the shoulder of a guardsman and told him that Captain Remmer needed some men to attend to the king at once. The soldier, who didn't have any orders, obeyed without question, taking several of the others with him.

"Get back! Back, all of you!" Trevon barked.

The crowd began to shove against them. Sera felt as if she'd drown in the crush of bodies, but Trevon cleared a path for them. They eventually reached the closed door, which was guarded by four men wearing the colors of the king's guard. The officer standing closest to the door looked rattled and worried. Bloodstains marred the yellow stripes of his tunic, but he did not look injured.

"Where's Remmer?" asked the officer worriedly.

"With the king," Trevon said. "We made it back safely."

The officer nodded in relief. "Good. It's pandemonium out there, Prince."

"We want to go in. My wife would like to see the prime minister."

The officer glanced at Sera in surprise. "The ceremony is over?"

Trevon held up her hand to display the ring.

The officer chuckled and then nodded for the door to be opened. Groans, terrible groans, filtered out to them. Sera had never heard a person make sounds like that. Montpensier stood just inside the door, staring feverishly at the table against the far wall. He glanced back at them and scowled.

The smell in the room was awful, but Sera braved it. Trevon followed her inside and shut the door behind them.

The room brimmed with people. There were soldiers there, two guardsmen, and several court doctors, but Adam was the one giving orders. Blood was on his shirt, his sleeves. He worked quickly, but the worried look on his face showed his desperation. Another groan of agony revealed the bitter truth.

Fitzroy might die.

CHAPTER NINETEEN

REVOLUTION

Sera could do little to assist Adam in saving Fitzroy's life. With all the blood and sounds of agony, she was surprised she hadn't fainted. But she had an inner steel that served her in moments of crisis. She did the only thing she could—she supplicated the Knowing that he would recover.

Eventually Captain Remmer arrived, seeking Prince Trevon and General Montpensier. An assemblage of nobles had been gathered in the council room, and the king wished them to come immediately. Sera accompanied them, but when they reached the door of the sickchamber, Captain Remmer caught her arm and shook his head. She was not invited to the gathering.

Sera bristled with anger at the exclusion. "Am I part of this realm now or not, Captain?" she said.

"It's not my decision, Your Highness," he answered. "The king forbade it."

Trevon scowled. "Let me talk to my father," he said. "Sera . . . perhaps you could wait in my room for a moment?"

Well, at least he wasn't sending her back to her chamber. She still didn't like being left out, but under the circumstances, it would be a poor idea to openly defy the king. Captain Remmer offered to escort her to the prince's chamber, and she acquiesced. Grudgingly.

As they walked down the corridor together, she asked him, "Did you catch the man who shot the prime minister?"

"We did not, unfortunately. I'm sorry I have no further news to share."

"I'm assuming you've already reported your findings to the king?"

"I have, and he is discussing the situation with his council. I think there is some concern as to how the emperor will react to the news."

"All the more reason for me to be there," Sera said in an undertone.

"I don't disagree with you, Your Highness," Remmer said, giving her a sidelong look. "It begs the question of where the Espion were during all of this tumult. The general has much to answer for."

"Indeed, Captain," Sera said. They reached Trevon's chamber, which had several guardsmen posted outside. As they approached, the men opened the door and let her in.

"The council may take several hours," Remmer said, his expression brooding. "I'm sure your husband will come as soon as he can." With that, he bowed to her and then whispered something to one of the guards and left. She burned to know what he had said.

Breathing in through her nose, she savored the cedar smell that reminded her of him. The room was immaculate, but too dark for her taste. The thick curtains blocked out the sun, so she pulled them aside to let in the brightness. They had covered glass doors leading to a balcony. She twisted the handle and stepped out onto it. It provided a panoramic view of the city below, a city that roiled with smoke and the press of people. A shiver went down her spine at the sight of the sanctuary grounds, completely overrun by the crowd. The family had left not a moment too soon. She wondered what had happened to Kasdan and if the guards had found him before the mob arrived. The streets were crowded with people, and she could hear the distant ping of firearms. All was in chaos.

Sera frowned as she leaned forward and gripped the railing. There was a garden below, and she saw guardsmen wearing Remmer's uniform walking along the path. Then her gaze shifted to the river and the gushing waterfall. The thunder caused by the tumbling cascade was plenty loud from the castle on the hill. She felt a certain aloofness from the river. The waters would come and come, regardless of what happened to the city. How many such scenes of discord had the falls witnessed? Had they gone on since time immemorial?

After sating herself with the view of the city, she went back to the room and wandered around, unable to sit still or read. She fondled the Wizr board, examined the closets and trunks, and even drew Trevon's ceremonial sword from its scabbard. Servants came with food and worried faces but no news. After asking them a few questions, she realized she knew more than they did. The time dragged on and on. She was still wearing her wedding dress, fidgeting with the unfamiliar ring that felt so strange on her finger.

How much time had passed, she didn't know, but a knock finally sounded on the door. She rushed forward even as a guardsman opened it and beckoned for her to come.

"What is it?" she asked.

"Lord Fitzroy has just been carried up to his chamber, down the hall. He and the doctor have asked to see you."

She sent a silent prayer of thanks to the Knowing. Fitzroy still lived. Hastening to follow the guard, she walked down the corridor. Guards stood outside Fitzroy's chamber, but they allowed her to enter. Inside, she saw an exhausted Adam Creigh and Fitzroy's bodyguard, Raj Sarin. The look of suppressed anger and regret on the Bhikhu's face was formidable.

Fitzroy lay on his bed, as pale as a sheet of paper. Half of his jacket had been cut away, and his collar was open at his throat. Perspiration glistened on his brow. He looked to be in a great deal of pain still, but he was conscious. There were no other servants or people in the room.

"Shut the door behind you," Adam said to Sera, who nodded and closed it, leaving the guardsmen outside. She then approached the bedstead, her heart twisting in pain.

"Hello, Sera," said Fitzroy in a weak, strained voice. One of his arms was covered in bandages and wraps. He reached for her with his other hand, but it felt limp and practically lifeless under hers.

She pressed a kiss to it, then looked at Adam worriedly.

"He's lost a lot of blood," Adam said with a sigh. She could see the evidence of his statement splattered on his shirt, which he still had not changed.

"How bad is it?" Sera asked.

"Tell her," Fitzroy croaked.

"The ball shattered his elbow, went down his arm, and tore off several fingers. I did my best to heal him, but if the wound gets infected, he will lose his arm. With all the blood he's lost, his system is very weak and susceptible. He may recover from the injury, but there is no guarantee. I can't promise anything."

"Captain Remmer said they couldn't find the man who shot him," Sera said, trying not to sob.

"I went after him," said Raj Sarin, stepping forward. His dark eyes flashed with fury. "The plume of smoke made it easy to spot where the gunman had hidden himself. As you know, we Bhikhu can leap great distances. I was there before any of the guards crossed the street. I saw a man crouching there. A man with a scar and a smoking arquebus. As soon as I arrived, he vanished." Raj Sarin snapped his fingers. "Gone, like a puff of smoke. I know some people in this world can travel long distances in an instant, but this man had made himself invisible. I went to where he'd been crouching and heard something crash on the next roof over. Although I couldn't see him, I tried to catch him. He evaded me, and we exchanged blows." The Bhikhu scowled. "We fought on the rooftop until he threw some dust into my face. It made my eyes burn, but I still fought him until the commotion from the riot made it impossible to hear him. He escaped." A look of terrible vengeance crossed Raj Sarin's face.

"Sera," Fitzroy whispered.

She gazed back down at him, struggling to keep calm. The look on the prime minister's face was oddly tranquil.

"Give her the book," Fitzroy said, grunting with pain.

Adam nodded and reached behind his jacket, retrieving a small, leather-bound book. It was a hand-sized thing, made of hide instead of a formal binding, with the pages sewn into it. The light brown leather was splotched with red stains. He cradled it in his hands and held it out to her. "He wanted to be sure I gave this to you to safeguard. It's his private journal. He keeps it on his person at all times."

"Why give it to me?" Sera asked.

"He's in so much pain, it's better if he doesn't speak. He's concerned he won't survive," Adam answered. "There is information there he says you must have."

A tear trickled down her cheek, and she scrubbed it away furiously. "You cannot die, my lord," she choked.

A little smile came through the mask of pain on Fitzroy's mouth.

Adam's eyes darted toward the door. "He wanted you to come for another reason as well. He asked for a Gift of Healing. I didn't dare perform one in front of the Kingfountain people for fear they'd drag me to the river. We've been given some privacy. I'd like you to help me."

Sera sniffed and nodded. "I don't know what to do."

"I will help you. Raj Sarin, if you'd guard the door, please?"

"Of course," answered the Bhikhu, stationing himself there.

Adam joined Sera at the prime minister's bedside. "I've never performed one myself, but I've seen them done. They're normally the purview of the Ministry of Thought. I'll put my hand on his head and make the maston sign. Put your hand on top of mine, then repeat what you hear me say. Join your conviction with mine."

Sera nodded. She did as he had asked and placed her free hand over her heart, over the maston chain she wore. Closing her eyes, she bowed her head and summoned her inner strength.

"Brant Fitzroy," said Adam solemnly. There was a quivering pulse in the air, the whisper of an unspoken sigh. Sera felt the presence of the Mysteries thicken the air. Her fingertips were tingling. Adam's voice became softer, more intimate. "We are wearers of the maston chain, and we invoke upon you a Gift of H—" he stopped, his voice suddenly broken. He cleared his throat. "We grant you a Gift of H—" Again, he was unable to speak. Silence fell over the room. The tingling sensation grew warmer, shooting up the hand that lay atop Adam's and then down into her heart. She felt Adam trembling next to her. Then she heard him crying.

The words came to Sera's mind unbidden. Not precise words, more like sentiments. And she felt herself begin to say them as the power of the Mysteries coursed through her. "You have been a faithful steward of the Medium's will, Brant Fitzroy. The Gift of Meekness you received in your youth has been a blessing to you and to your family." She tried to speak through her tears. "I Gift you with courage to face the dangers that lie ahead. I Gift you with confidence to know that your deeds will be remembered for generations to come. That your strength and your compassion will inspire the hearts of many yet to be born. Your time in the second life is nearly over." She swallowed. "Well done, faithful servant. Trust that your offerings have been acceptable. You will see her face before the end. We invoke this Gifting upon you, Brant Fitzroy. Be at peace."

The flow of words abruptly stopped, but the feeling of warmth lingered in her heart, even as she realized what this meant. Brant Fitzroy was going to die. Her hand dropped away from Adam's. When she opened her eyes and looked at the doctor's face, she saw tears coursing down his cheeks. Her gaze shifted to Fitzroy, who was, in contrast, in a peaceful repose. He blinked at her, barely able to nod.

"Thank you," he whispered.

Some time after the Gifting, Trevon knocked on the door and entered the room. Adam had changed his clothes, but Sera had refused to leave Fitzroy's bedside. The prime minister was resting, each shallow breath reminding her of what was to come. The pain bore down on her, especially when she thought of Fitzroy's family. Of Cettie. Where was she? Why had she come to Kingfountain with Lady Corinne? What would she do when she learned of this?

Raj Sarin stood at the balcony, watching the sun go down. The breeze brought up sweet fragrances from the gardens below.

"How is he?" asked her husband. He crossed the room to her and leaned down to brush a kiss in her hair.

"Resting," she said.

He tenderly touched her shoulder. "Which is what you should be doing as well. Adam will watch over him for now. Come back to our room." He sighed. "You need to know what was decided."

Sera rose to join him. She had already strapped Fitzroy's little journal to her leg with her garter bands. Her gown covered it completely, but she felt its pressure against her skin as they walked. Before leaving the room, she touched Adam's arm, giving him a look of sympathy. He pursed his lips and nodded at her. Already, he was mourning. And so was she.

When they reached Trevon's rooms—it felt strange thinking of it as *their* room—he unbuttoned his jacket and slumped into a chair facing the balcony. He looked exhausted . . . and troubled. She walked around behind him and massaged his shoulders. "You don't like the decision your father made."

"I don't . . . not at all," he said huskily. "I have an awful premonition, but I lack the authority to do anything about it. He is my father, and he's the king. The choice was his to make."

"What can you tell me?" Sera asked, her own worries growing.

"The city is rioting," Trevon said. "It must be quelled. Some of the nobles suggested that it will burn out in a few days. That the people will return to their homes after growing weary of smashing windows and lighting things on fire. But Montpensier thinks the riot will only grow worse—and that it may even spread to other realms if my father does not act quickly and decisively. There are not enough members of the king's guard to put down the trouble. His advice is for my father to summon the army to restore order. The closest garrison is Beestone Castle, and if word is sent soon, they can be here in one day."

"Montpensier is willing to fire on the king's people?" Sera asked in alarm.

"He is. And ultimately, he persuaded my father to pursue that course of action. If the populace doesn't settle by tomorrow, they'll impose order with cannon and sword. A writ is being sent to summon the garrison."

"Has Montpensier left the city?"

Trevon shook his head no. "The king wants to keep an eye on him. He'll send Captain Remmer to command the garrison."

She breathed out in relief. "That's good news, at least. What caused the rioting? Was it the gunshot?"

"It may have started before that," he said blackly. "The Espion is saying it's too dangerous to go out right now and investigate. They'll interrogate prisoners after the garrison has subdued the riot." He shook his head and looked down over the balcony. "With the sun going down, you can see some of the fires burning. I've never seen it this lawless before."

Sera stopped massaging him and walked around. "I don't trust Montpensier."

"Neither do I," he said. Then he rose and squeezed her shoulders. "Would you like something to eat, my love?" He bent down and kissed her forehead.

"I'm not very hungry."

"But you do look tired," he said. "Why don't you rest? I have some correspondence I can read at the desk. I'll wake you in a little while. Maybe things will calm down tonight, and there will be no need for the garrison."

Sera hadn't slept much the night before, in anticipation of the wedding, and she couldn't deny that she was exhausted. "A little rest would be good. But don't let me sleep for too long, Husband." She leaned up and kissed his mouth.

"The risk is in letting you sleep too little," he said wryly. "I'm sorry for Lord Fitzroy. I'm sorry our wedding caused a riot." He chuckled softly. "Hopefully, the worst is behind us."

She went over to one of the couches, one that had a small blanket resting along the top, and covered herself before snuggling into the cushions. A little quiet, a little rest would do her wonders.

After closing her eyes, she fell asleep almost instantly.

What awoke her was a sound ensuring that Trevon's words had been merely wishful thinking. There was a cry of warning, then a pistol discharged, and something—someone—slumped against the door. The sound jarred Sera awake, and as she jumped to sitting, she saw Trevon walking toward the door with an unsheathed sword in his hand.

"Trevon!" Sera gasped as the doors shuddered. They were battered open, and several men entered the room. Not guardsmen. They closed the distance quickly, separating her from her husband.

"What's the meaning of this?" Trevon demanded hotly.

"You're under arrest, Your Highness," said one of the men with a sneering voice. He was the one she had seen before in Montpensier's office. Sera saw a flash of metal on the man's hand. An Espion ring.

When sleep decided to evade me last night, the eve of the wedding, I held a vigil. It is a blessing from the Knowing that when one focuses on experiences from the past, the memories may bring us new insights. My thoughts kept returning to Cettie. Why did she pass through the mirror gate with Lady Corinne? I sense something is deeply wrong. That she feels lost and confused. Perhaps Lady Corinne intends to use her against me, to thwart my investigation. Would I sacrifice the child I rescued from the Fells to fulfill my duty? Is that the price I'll be forced to pay?

One cannot bargain with the Mysteries, although many try. The power is not a fickle friend to be wooed with fair words when the storms of life crash upon us. No, it is a faithful confidant, a wise companion, a harbinger of all that is good. I cannot pit my wisdom against its knowledge and foresight. And so I did not try. I merely offered that if giving my life to save Cettie's would bring her to a good end, I would do so without hesitation. I would do the same for any of my children. For Stephen, for Phinia, or for Anna. How I love each one of them. And while I hope to endure to a full head of white hairs and to dandle grandchildren on my knee, I would sacrifice myself to see them safe. I would suffer any privation to help them. To see them living up to their individual potentials. My hand trembles writing these words. My heart is full. This, I realized, is how the Knowing feels about each one of us.

—Brant Fitzroy, Prime Minister

CETTIE

CHAPTER TWENTY

THE POISONER'S GARDEN

Cettie awoke in the sparse but dignified cell she had been furnished with upon her arrival at the poisoner school in Genevar. In her disorientation, she'd supposed it to be the keeper's room in Fog Willows, but as the muddle of sleep lifted, her heart constricted with dread and despair. It was just before dawn, a pale glimmer touching the room through a single shuttered window. No magic interfered with her emotions now, and she experienced the full brunt of them. She'd been deceived, and not only by Lady Corinne. Her whole life was a deception. Her reality was nothing more than a glass mirror, now shattered by the truth of her parentage. She'd been afraid to believe that she was a true Fitzempress. Yet hadn't that thought appealed to her vanity? Had she not secretly *wanted* it? Yet the truth was different. Her real father was a kishion. Her mother, a poisoner.

Cettie felt her insides twist, and she gripped her middle tightly. Though her stomach felt sour from hunger, she feared she would be sick. Casting her eyes around the room for a basin or something similar, she first saw a glass mirror, which seemed to mock her thoughts, and then a small dresser. Atop the dresser stood a wash basin and a small pitcher of water. Standing up, still holding her stomach, she set her feet down on a reed mat on the floor. The quailing of her insides subsided, so she instead walked to the window and opened the shutters, looking down on the courtyard she'd arrived in with the kishion and Lady Corinne. Her room was on the upper level. A few birds trilled sweetly, greeting the dawn with their discordantly cheerful songs. The patio below was empty of people.

She found her shoes where she'd discarded them before going to sleep and quickly put them on. Testing the door handle, she discovered it was unlocked. In fact, there was no locking mechanism at all on either side. A quick glance down either side of the shadow-filled corridor revealed it was empty. She'd been told the night before that when a gong sounded, she was to arise and go to the common room for food. Uncertain when that would happen, she decided to explore the grounds.

And find a way to escape.

A stone-paved staircase led to the garden, and she took it, feeling the crisp air on her face as she opened the door at the bottom and stepped outside. She was used to cold climates from living in the sky, so the morning breeze didn't bother her. As she had noticed the day before, there were long rectangular garden boxes filled with small plants and herbs growing in meticulous rows. Potted trees loomed in the center of each box, but none were any taller than her. There were a variety of plants in each of the planters. The smells coming from them were interesting, very unlike the gardens she had walked through in Muirwood. She did not recognize more than two or three varieties from the book Adam had given her. Just the memory of it, the memory of *him*, caused a spasm of guilt and pain. She stopped, an overpowering feeling of wretchedness consuming her. His little book—the little gift he had given her before departing for war—had been lost.

Breathing in through her nose, she knelt at the edge of one of the stone borders to study the plants more closely. That was when she heard a man's voice come from the shadows.

"I wouldn't recommend touching any of the plants yet," he said, startling her. "Not until you know how to do so safely."

He had a quiet way of speaking—there was no harshness at all in his voice. It surprised her that he spoke her language fluently, but she attributed his ability to a form of magic Sera had told her about, one that could allow someone to speak and understand any language. Turning her head, she peered into the shadows and realized he'd been there the whole time, sitting in a small wrought-iron chair at one of the patio tables. He wore a very simple black cassock with large buttons on the front and a small white collar protruding from the neck. He had a sparse frame, a trimmed beard, thick hair combed forward in the front, and very deep, penetrating eyes. A small ledger or book sat on the table in front of him, and he had a white feather gripped in one hand. Had he been studying her, writing his observations? Judging by his face, she guessed he was less than forty years old.

"I didn't intend to touch them," Cettie answered. She did not feel threatened by him, but neither did she feel safe.

"Good," he said, then looked down at the book again and made a few more scratching sounds with the quill as he wrote. He offered no introduction.

Cettie continued her circuit around the planter boxes. Occasionally, she'd glance back at the corner table where the strange man sat to see if he'd moved. He remained where she'd left him. Was he a student? A teacher? His cassock reminded her of the outfit of an Aldermaston.

More memories of home began to torment her.

After finishing her exploration of the garden, she extended her search until she reached the nearest part of the high stone wall surrounding the estate. Some ivy decorated the wall, but it did not look sturdy enough to support a person's weight. Jumping wouldn't help either. But as she walked along the boundary, she sensed there were protective Leerings set into the wall. They were in the form of serpents, coiled into a twisted pattern, and the magic radiating from them was powerful. Threatening, even. She avoided the first few, continuing along the wall until she reached a small postern door. It was made of iron and had a small window set at eye level. Another serpent Leering was set into the archway around the door, and she felt it flare with angry, assertive power as she drew closer, almost as if there were a true serpent coiled there waiting to strike. She pressed forward anyway. Fear slithered down her legs and made them start to tremble. Her heart pounded frantically in her chest, but still she approached the door. The eyes on the stone Leering glowed dangerously, brightening with each step she took.

And then she did see serpents—sleek black-scaled creatures—emerging from gutters built into the floor directly beneath the wall. They hissed and writhed as they emerged, coming to heed the call of the Leering. Cettie's mind went black with terror, and she froze, watching the undulating bodies. One of the serpents hissed at her and started to slither toward her, and she took a hasty step back. She tried to swallow, but a knot in her throat prevented it. The snakes kept coming, probably a dozen or more. The Leering seemed to mock her cowardice as she retreated.

Then she heard the sweet tones of a hautboie behind her. It was a haunting melody, and Cettie turned back toward the man at the corner table. He held a long, pipelike instrument with a fluted end, his dexterous fingers maneuvering the stops while he blew into it. Music was one of the Mysteries of Wind. She recognized the instrument and felt her fear begin to fade as he played. The serpents retreated into the stone gutter from which they'd emerged. The energy from the Leering began to ebb.

The rhythm of the piece lasted for a while, the sweet notes rising and falling, striking chords within her heart. He was an expert musician. But he was also probably a murderer, a poisoner, just like her natural mother and father. She steeled her heart against being taken in.

Turning back, she looked at the doorway again, focusing on the Leering that had summoned the snakes. Intuition told her it would react with hostility to anyone who wasn't part of the school. There was no surprise in that. Cettie reached out to the Leering with her mind. In the past, she had always been confident with them. Her strength of will had tamed any that she'd come across. But the power she had once wielded effortlessly had withered, and this was a very different kind of Leering. She felt a haughtiness about it, a vindictive pride. It would not obey her. She wished she could *force* it to obey her.

That thought brought another memory with it. Rand had retrieved a small, whorl-like medallion from the corpse of the kishion. The kishion, her father, who had helped abduct her once again. Yes, if she had a medallion like that, she could force the Leering to obey her. She knew it instinctively. If only she'd kept it instead of giving it to Caulton Forshee. If only she could find another one. The first had come from these people, and surely they had more. Maybe she could use one to get to Kingfountain and find Father.

She would do anything to save him and Anna. Even if she herself was lost.

The music from the hautboie trailed off in a final, achingly sweet note. Cettie approached the man, crossing the garden again to reach him. He set the instrument down on the table and folded his arms.

"That was beautiful," Cettie complimented, wary and distrustful.

"Thank you," he answered. "You rise early as well?"

"It's my first day here," Cettie said.

"Well, you've slept an entire day away," he answered. "You are not used to the routine. The rhythm of life here. You will be soon." Now Cettie understood her hunger and why she'd woken so early.

"What is your name, sir?" Cettie asked.

"Jevin of Toussan," he replied, bowing his head.

"I don't know where that is."

"I imagine your grasp of our geography is limited," he said, giving her what looked to be a genuine smile. "I am an instructor here at the poisoner school. The gardener, if you will."

"You play beautifully. Where did you study?"

"I grew up in the sanctuary of Our Lady in Toussan. Brythonica. I sang in the choir when I was a little boy." His eyes narrowed, but the smile did not leave his face.

Cettie glanced around the courtyard. "Is the garden where you grow the poisons?"

"You're very astute. And to answer you, yes. All of the learners help tend my garden. I will teach you how to care for the plants. How to nourish them. How to extract tears from them. How to dry them and grind them into powders. Which ones can only be harvested under moonlight, and which can only be dug up in winter. And you will taste them to learn how to tell if you've been poisoned. Of course, you'll also learn the remedies. Not all poisons grow here, so we will go outside the walls—eventually—where you'll learn how they can be gathered and what they do."

"What if I don't want to learn these things?" Cettie asked, holding her head high.

He shrugged and then wagged his finger at the nearest garden box. "Put the purple flower on your tongue, and you'll be dead in a few agonizing minutes. That is the fastest way to leave. Join your ancestors in the mythical portal beyond." He snorted at the end, waving his hand dismissively. "If you believe in those lies. I used to. Or you will continue, in the Deep Fathoms, as a shadow of your former self. Bah! That's a lie too. Life is a contest for power. The sooner you recognize this, the better you will come to grips with your fate."

Cettie pressed her lips together.

"Well, at least you know how to end it if you so desire," he said. "The choice is yours. You were chosen for your particular aptitude. Your mother is the finest poisoner this school has produced in hundreds of years. To be taught in this school is the highest privilege."

A loud, heavy note clanged from an ancient gong. The sun had just risen, although the shade in the courtyard still lingered.

Jevin cocked his head, listening as the sound reverberated. Cettie felt it thrum in her chest bones. The gong sounded again. And again, before the vibrations finally stilled.

"Time to eat," he said, rising from the table and gathering his quill, book, and hautboie.

"How many more students are here?" Cettie asked.

"Students?" said Jevin with a smile. "You are looking at it in the wrong way. You are to become a hetaera! I cannot convey with words what that means. Do you realize what your mother is doing? She has subverted an entire nation . . . nay, an empire! . . . because of what she discovered here. My purpose is simply to help you learn what you seek to learn. All of us teachers are here to share our knowledge with you so that you, too, can achieve great things." He bowed his head slightly. "Realize that I serve *you*. It will be my honor and privilege to share what I know of plants and poisons, of the workings of the body, and how it can best serve as a vessel for the ancient ones. You will have *knowledge*, my young friend. There is no greater fruit."

As he said those words, a shuddering feeling came into her heart.

The Myriad Ones were here at the school. In Muirwood they had been locked out. But here, they were locked *in*.

CHAPTER TWENTY-ONE

Choices

It was like a nightmare that she couldn't wake up from. Cettie had gone from being a beloved and respected member of a world she knew and understood to being a victim in a training school for the deadly arts. Her mind was baffled by the rapidity of the change, yet it also felt as if her entire life had been preparing her for this moment. Beings of darkness had always been attracted to her, like flies to honey. She had thought she'd grown beyond the feeling that something was wrong with her, but it had been lurking in the back of her mind all these years. What made it worse was knowing that if she did not cooperate, those she loved would be harmed. Or killed.

The meal at daybreak was eaten in silence. There were five other girls in the school, all younger than her, and the youngest was probably twelve. That alone was enough to horrify Cettie. They were served their food on elegant plates, but no one ate until they received a nod from the headmistress, a woman of at least fifty with crow's-feet and a taciturn mouth. The girls ate in silence, but the food was excellent and designed for good health, a savory mix of fruits and vegetables, seasoned porridge, and crumbled nuts. Cettie spent most of the meal studying her surroundings. Some of the other girls gave her surreptitious looks, but these were not the disdainful kind she had endured at Muirwood. These girls seemed more curious, more interested.

Following the meal, servants who did not speak to them led the way to a training room that had weapons of all varieties mounted on the walls. Swords, chains, whips, daggers, spears, staves. Mirrors lined the walls as well, revealing their reflections to them. The girls lined up in prearranged positions. Cettie was directed to join the end of one of the lines as the others began stretching techniques. The room was mostly silent, although some of the girls whispered to each other in a language she didn't understand.

After a while, the door opened again. The burly man who entered had a menacing look, a scraggly beard, and scars across his temple, cheek, and bearded chin. He wore a padded leather jacket and pants, making him even bigger in appearance. The feeling in the room changed as he strode into the center of the room and stood before them. The feeling of unease rippled across all the girls, Cettie included.

"*Vut,*" he said in a clipped, strange tongue. The girls all immediately made a move, as if cupping a giant sphere between their hands, one curved hand on top, the other beneath. Cettie quickly imitated them, feeling lost and confused. The instructor scowled at her and came forward, adjusting her hands to make the invisible sphere larger. He pushed on her arms, forcing her to resist him, and when she applied enough force, he nodded and backed away.

"*Jit,*" he said next, and the girls all assumed another stance. Again he corrected Cettie's posture and position as she tried to emulate the others. This went on for some time. Sometimes he'd start at "*vut*" again and repeat the sequence, and he'd scowl if Cettie got it wrong. After he finished the drill, he barked another command, and the girls retreated to one end of the wall and stood waiting.

He pointed at one of the girls with his finger. She then went to the center of the room with him and lowered into a defensive stance. The bearded instructor proceeded to attack her. Cettie watched in shock as he kicked her, threw her down. The girl fought back, of course, but was no match for his skill and reflexes and size. She cried out in pain a few times, but eventually lay still, trembling in pain. Cettie longed to go to her, but the teacher finally stood, folding his arms imperiously, and two servants entered and carried her out.

He pointed at a different girl, one who was closer to Cettie's age. The girl strode forward with confidence. The master stood his ground, arms flexed, and nodded to her. She then launched into an attack, sending high kicks straight for his head. One of them actually connected, rocking the man's head back. He caught the next one, hooking his foot behind the girl's ankle and cutting her down, but she landed smoothly and flipped back onto her feet. Cettie watched in amazement as the two traded blows—arms, elbows, fists, knees. Back and forth they struck at each other, but the master eventually won the match, landing a blow to the girl's stomach that winded her. He then torqued her arm behind her back, leaving her facedown on the floor, hissing in pain as he wrenched harder and harder. Cettie saw her eyes squeeze shut against the pain, and then her shoulder popped out of socket with a sickening sound. It made Cettie clench her own stomach. Was she supposed to do this as well?

The girl collapsed, unconscious and silent, and then the same servants came in and carried her away.

The master folded his arms again, scanning the group. Then he motioned for the youngest girl to approach. To Cettie's amazement, she did so without any apparent fear. The master adjusted his technique with this one. He showed her a series of blocks, then began to throw a punch along with each block. Each time it went faster and faster until the young girl wasn't able to react quickly enough, and the master punched her hard on the shoulder. The girl grimaced in pain but quickly raised her guard again. They exchanged blows until another punch made it through. Tears began to trickle down the girl's cheeks, but she didn't openly sob. They kept at the blocking drills until she could hardly lift her arms. Then the master nodded, and the girl walked toward the doors on her own, rubbing her bruised arms.

Then the master turned and nodded for Cettie to approach.

That surprised her. She'd thought she would be chosen at the end. Cettie wasn't sure what to do, but she didn't want to fight the man. She shook her head no, her insides twisting with dread. The master scowled at her and repeated his gesture, his lips pressed in a firm, hard line. A dangerous warning flashed in his eyes.

The girl next to her gave Cettie a nod.

She felt completely unprepared and vulnerable as she stepped into the middle of the room. The master appraised her and then dropped into a stance she recognized. He performed a movement from the Way of Ice and Shadows, a series of Bhikhu fighting techniques Raj Sarin had taught her. He then nodded for her to mimic him. She did, because she knew the move. As she held the stance, he pushed on her hand and arm, trying to shove her off balance, but her legs were strong from the practice. Was it coincidence that he faced her in a style she knew? She doubted it.

The master pursed his lips and adopted another stance, the next one in the sequence. Cettie copied it. The master nodded for her to go on. She did, performing the rest of the set from memory as he observed her. When she was finished, he made her repeat a certain section. Then he made her do it again. She did. He adjusted her arm positions slightly, applying pressure to her wrist to make sure she was holding it right. He nodded again, stepping back from her. And then he attacked.

Cettie responded on instinct. She'd performed the moves before but never against a man twice her weight and strength. Blocking the kick coming at her ribs hurt her forearms, but it was better taking the pain there. The master wheeled around to strike her from the other side, and Cettie found herself scrambling to counter his move. He was fast and didn't follow the prescribed routine of the set. He kicked her thigh, and it hurt, but she fought on. Then he kicked her in the stomach and knocked her down. She scrambled back to her feet as the final kick struck her chest. Her ribs cracked, and she flew backward, landing so hard she couldn't breathe. Pain ripped through her, and still her lungs wouldn't expand. Cettie clawed on the ground in panic, struggling, and then felt arms grip her and bring her to her feet. She wheezed and choked as the familiar helpers walked her out of the room. Her eyes were misty with tears of pain.

She finally managed to take a breath, and then another, but they were accompanied by painful jabs in her side. Her ribs were undoubtedly broken. It would take weeks to heal. Anger and resentment grew inside her. How could she be expected to fight like this regularly? Why would they maim and injure the girls sent to the school? She was escorted to a door and down the dark staircase beyond it, which was illuminated only by a few Light Leerings embedded in the wall.

At the bottom of the stairs, the helpers led her through another door. Gathered inside the room was a small group of healers and the girls who had preceded her in the training. A few benches and tables had been set up around an enormous, moss-covered Leering that dripped water from where the mouth would have been. The carving was ancient, the face hardly more than a few craggy lines, but the eyes burned a dull orange.

The two helpers set Cettie down on the bench, which she sat on gingerly, holding her side where the pain was the greatest. Just breathing made her flinch. The other girls looked cheerful and well, even the one who'd had her arm dislocated. They looked at her with knowing smiles. One said something in a language Cettie didn't understand to the other girl, who nodded in agreement.

One of the healers walked to the mossy Leering and peeled away a strip of the green vegetation. It had little flowers on it and exuded a sweet-smelling odor. The healer approached Cettie with it and gestured for her to hold the moss in her hands. Confused, Cettie obeyed. As soon as she touched it, she heard and felt the power of the Mysteries ignite in her skin. The strains engulfed her body, and she literally felt her cracked bones mend, pulling back into their proper places, becoming firm once more. The aches and bruises faded as the magic rushed through her, restoring her energy and her health. She stared at the little bit of moss in her hands and watched it shrivel as it yielded its power to her, trading its energy for her health. Watching it die filled her with compassion, but she sensed the magic was given willingly.

The moss in her hand shriveled down to a tiny little stub, which the healer then took from her and returned to the boulder with the Leering. As she watched, it connected its fibers with the other moss growing there, which made it revive and flourish. She had never encountered such a plant before, one that could heal wounds. What would Adam think about such a thing? She stared at the Leering in surprise, and then heard the two other girls laughing at her.

It was not a mocking laughter, but a knowing one. They nodded at Cettie, and the girl whose arm had been devastated stood and demonstrated that she was hale again. While Cettie could still remember the pain she'd endured at the master's hands, it was only that . . . a memory. Her body was perfectly whole again. What sort of plant was it? How had it healed her?

She knew someone who had the answer.

⌐⌐

The girls returned to the training room, where the master continued to practice with them. Sometimes sparring, sometimes teaching them weapons. He paired up the girls, and they practiced drills and forms. The older helped teach the younger while the master walked around, offering refinements to their technique. Cettie was famished by the time the midday gong sounded and they were ushered back to the eating hall. The portions were small, and Cettie ate hers with relish, her body craving food. The meal was eaten in silence, and then the girls were dismissed to the courtyard.

The other girls seemed to know what to do, just like before, and they set to work on the garden beds, each one being assigned by Jevin. It appeared they were allowed to talk and converse with each other, but they communicated in a language Cettie didn't understand. She found Jevin there with his hautboie, playing a whimsical tune, but he set the instrument aside to instruct her. He showed her which of the rectangles was hers and began teaching her about the various plants and how to care for them.

He was very knowledgeable and friendly, and after he had explained the basics of what she'd be doing, she felt comfortable enough to ask him about the moss.

"What is the plant that grows on the Leering in the healing room? The one they used to help us recover from the fighting?"

"It is called Everoot," answered Jevin simply, using a small spade to dig into the rich, dark earth. Then he pursed his lips and gave her a cynical smile. "There are legends about it, of course, but I don't believe them. Not anymore."

"What do you mean?"

"They say it grew in the First Garden, the one that the First Parents came from, beneath the sea. The First Mother smuggled some of it out, keeping it wet in seaweed, and hid it from the First Father. She was the *first* hetaera. The one who got them expelled from the Deep Fathoms and nearly drowned them both before they reached shore."

"I have no idea what you're talking about," Cettie said, shaking her head.

"And why should you bother?" Jevin answered with a shrug. "Every world has its own creation myths. It is strange how similar they are. Yours . . . from Muirwood's garden of Leerings . . . and ours from the gardens of the Deep Fathoms. Almost as if we shared the same origin. But as I said, it's nonsense and foolishness. The myths are meant to control us. To make us act a certain way. Perhaps the purpose of the Everoot story is simply to remind us that the Everoot needs to be kept damp. You see, if it is not, it becomes the most deadly of poisons. The story reinforces a practice, nothing more. It's just a means to an end." He sniffed and dug around the dirt some more, then withdrew a small set of shears and carefully trimmed one of the leaves. "This one only kills you if brewed into a tea. It's called deadlock. Quick and silent."

"What language do the other girls speak?" Cettie asked.

"Genevese is the common tongue here. That girl is from Occitania," he said, pointing to the twelve-year-old. Pointing to a few of the others in turn, he said, "She is from Atabyrion. She is from Pisan. She is from Leoneyis. She's quite good and will be graduating soon. She's needed to seduce the new emperor."

Cettie raised her eyebrows. "The *new* emperor? She'll be sent to Lockhaven?"

"No, not that empire. The new one. The one rising *here*."

Cettie gave him a confused look, her heart bubbling with worry. "What do you mean?"

He set down the shears and picked up the trowel again. "Leon Montpensier's empire. The sun has risen on his new dominion. This has all been underway for many years, you know. The rise of the new empire. The rebirth of the hetaera."

CHAPTER TWENTY-TWO

PERCEPTIONS

Not all the classes of the poisoner's school were equally dangerous. After studying the poisonous herbs in the courtyard, they practiced musical instruments—for finger dexterity, sophistication, and so they might understand the musical culture of other realms. At least, that is what she was told. Then they were brought to their most traditional class yet: mathematics. Cettie quickly proved her capability to the teacher, who then presented her with harder assignments that went beyond what she had studied at Muirwood. The other girls, who were all younger than her, gave her looks of surprise and respect. But the next task they were given put her back out of her comfort zone.

They'd been asked to climb part of the high outer wall surrounding the villa. It loomed up beyond a small pond and was accessible only by hopping from one rock to another across the water. The goal was to reach the top of the wall without falling back down into the pond, a challenging task, and not just because certain rocks protruded more than others. Partway up, a series of Water Leerings would activate, drenching the handholds as well as the climber. As soon as one girl fell into the pond, the Leerings would shut off, and the next girl would get a chance to start working her way up.

The youngest girl had gotten the highest so far that day, an impressive feat for one so small. As Cettie waited for her turn, she thought about all she had learned on her first day and resisted the urge to be charmed by the school and its practitioners. The villa itself was scenic and lovely, and it matched what she'd seen of Genevar. This place wasn't a hodgepodge of buildings and crumbling tenements like the landbound cities at home. It also struck her that the girls here were not imprisoned against their will—at least, it didn't seem that way. She was probably the only one who wished she could voluntarily leave. And had she been brought from the Fells to this place, instead of being discovered by Lord Fitzroy, it would have likely won her over on the first day.

The knowledge that she would be helping General Montpensier, her father's enemy in the war, caused her distress. She'd learned from Sera that he was a vain and ambitious man, not a desirable leader by any means. What was more, she couldn't stop thinking of what Caulton Forshee had told her about the hetaera. In the past, they had persecuted and even murdered the mastons. But was the reverse now true? Were not they the hunted ones?

Was there an inherent right and wrong way to use the Mysteries? She could sense the power in the poisoner school just as she had at Muirwood. It was a different kind of song, but music nonetheless. Was there room enough in the world for both kinds, or must one always be in conflict with the other, just as she was in conflict with herself?

She remembered the look in Caulton's eyes as she showed him the kystrel. Perhaps her father had purposefully arranged for her to have it, hoping to educate her in another point of view. Why had she been so quick to hand it over? She could have used it to escape the poisoner school. She did not see any chains around the necks of the other girls in training. Did that mean the kystrels were only awarded at the end?

Cettie felt a touch at her elbow and turned to find the Leoneyis girl at her side, gesturing for her to go to the wall. Cettie apologized for being lost in her thoughts, but she could see her apology meant nothing to the other girl. The language barrier stood between them. Still, the Leoneyis girl's expression was encouraging. So different from the girls she'd known in Muirwood, who'd despised her because of her origins. The difference made her insides twist. Why was she *enjoying* these challenges so much?

Cettie bounded from one rock to the next, but her balance was not quite as firm as she'd wish. She dreaded embarrassing herself by falling into the pond before reaching the wall.

After crossing the rocks safely, she gazed up at the wall, which seemed much taller now that she stood at the base. There were small ferns and shrubs around the edges, and the stones were still a little damp from the previous climber. All the girls wore dresses and shoes—no climbing gear was allowed or provided. It was a test of physical strength and endurance. Unsure of herself, Cettie studied the edge of the wall, knowing the other girls were watching her. Being alone would have made it easier. But how different was this from memorizing and performing a dance at a ball?

She took a steadying breath, judging the various handholds, and started up the face of the wall. It was not long before the burn in her muscles became distracting. She had not conditioned herself for this kind of effort. Her strength was in her self-control—she refused to quit, pushing herself to climb higher. The strength in her fingers flagged, and her discomfort grew more acute. She hadn't even climbed high enough to trigger the Water Leering yet. But she didn't let her slowness distract her from her goal. Patiently and painstakingly, she ascended, one stone at a time. Even when her legs began to tremble and quiver with the exertion, she summoned the will to move just one stone higher. And then one more.

From a distance, she heard the trilling notes of Jevin's hautboie. The sun was sinking rapidly, making the shadows grow thick and inky. The notes of the music caught her off guard, but they were soothing, and it helped her to think about something other than the pain in her forearms and knees. She was sweating profusely now, hugging the wall, trying to find the strength to keep going. Concentration became difficult. She'd never felt so exhausted, but she clung to the gentle melody of the instrument as she reached for another handhold, her neck muscles so tight and pinched she couldn't even look up. She pulled herself up, her arms shaking.

And then the water started to fall. She sensed the Leering activate, just as she'd always sensed them, and knew it would happen before the first blasts of water struck the crown of her head. The shock of the water and the additional weight of her wet clothes made the agony even more unbearable. Water continued to streak down her face, and she shook her head, dislodging droplets, fearing she might drown in the deluge. Yet still she pulled herself up another piece, unwilling to submit to the fatigue and strain. She couldn't hear Jevin's music anymore, but somehow felt it vibrating in the stone. Another handhold.

And then her foot slipped on the next wet stone, and Cettie found herself being pushed away from the wall by the force of the water. She tried to recover, tried to cling to anything, but it felt as if the entire wall had been rubbed smooth. Her arms began pinwheeling, and she tottered backward, unable to think. She fell down, down, down. Pain exploded in her right elbow as it struck one of the pond rocks, and then she was completely submerged underwater. The pain made her involuntarily yell, which sucked in a mouthful of brackish water. She floundered in the murk, choking and gagging, trying to find her way up. Then she felt a hand grip her wrist and realized the other girls were helping her.

They hoisted her up, and although she was blinded from the water in her eyes, and her elbow throbbed in agony, she let them. They offered foreign words in encouraging tones. She felt hands around her waist and realized more than one was helping her. Clumsily, she reached the edge of the pond, her arm afire with pain, and then knelt on the bank, spluttering and coughing. One of them struck her back between the shoulder blades to help. Her ears were clogged with water as well, but as they drained, she could hear the garbled tunes from the hautboie again.

Although the sun had set, it was still light enough to see. The gong sounded, announcing the call to come back to the villa. Cettie would have preferred to lie on the cobblestones and sleep there for the night. Her arms and legs were still trembling from her effort. At least she'd climbed high enough to trigger the water. That was good.

One of the girls said something, and Cettie felt them grab her elbow to help her stand. The pain made her cry out and jerk her arm away. Some of them exchanged words, and then the Leoneyis girl draped Cettie's good arm around her neck and helped her hobble back to the villa. She brought her directly to the Everoot room.

Fatigued, sodden, and hungry, Cettie waited on the same bench she'd sat on earlier. One of the healers approached with a clump of Everoot and put it in her hands. The reinvigorating magic immediately took hold, repairing the cracked bones in her arm and filling her with strength and comfort. Even pleasure. Her fatigue was forgotten. She could have gone back to the wall and ascended it easily. Cettie straightened her arm, gazing at it wonderingly, then rubbed her hand against the area. There was no pain at all.

The Leoneyis girl smiled at her, motioning with her hands as if she were eating from a bowl with a spoon, and then gestured for Cettie to follow her.

Cettie was ravenous. But she didn't have a change of clothes, and it would take time for her gown to dry. The Leoneyis girl motioned again for her to follow, and so she did. Instead of bringing Cettie back to the common room where the meals had been served, she led her upstairs to the dormitory area. She then guided Cettie to a door and opened it. It was another room, full of dresses of every style, fabric, and fit imaginable. Some were hanging on racks. Others were spread out on flat surfaces. There was easily two hundred different patterns, fabrics, and styles. The other young woman took her to a section that had designs from the empire of Comoros, dresses that would have suited a serving maid or an elegant lady. In fact, Cettie recognized the livery of the servants of Pavenham Sky.

"These . . . these are all for us?" Cettie asked, staring in amazement.

The girl didn't understand her question, but there was no mistaking the tone of her voice. The girl nodded and pulled a dress out from the rack—one that reminded her of her favorite keeper's gown. The girl gestured for her to undo the buttons on her dress and then walked over to a wicker hamper near the door. She bent down and opened it, showing Cettie that it already contained dresses that had been worn by the other girls earlier in the day. She'd noticed the others had changed clothes throughout the day but hadn't thought anything of it. The room was communal, then, and all the girls could wear anything they wanted from whatever style or fashion they preferred.

It was like being an empress.

Cettie gazed around at the selection, feeling overwhelmed by the choices. She finally took the dress the Leoneyis girl had selected, feeling it suited her best. Cettie wasn't ready to try adopting a new style yet. She was afraid if she did, she would begin to lose all sense of herself and her past life. Perhaps that was what she dreaded most.

After unfastening the buttons with her fingers, Cettie began to strip away the damp gown. The Leoneyis girl's eyes widened with shock and alarm. She was staring at Cettie's chest, staring at the maston symbol dangling from her neck. The girl backed away from her, just a step, staring at her with unconcealed fear. She quickly mastered herself again, but Cettie felt utterly self-conscious. Why had the Leoneyis girl been taught to fear the chain?

Cettie quickly changed dresses and hurriedly buttoned up the new one, once again hiding the medallion she wore. Why did she feel ashamed to be wearing it now? The thought of losing the other girls' friendship over it made her sorry.

The Leoneyis girl led Cettie over to a dressing table where there was an assortment of brushes and embellishments. Cettie liked to wear her hair up in the proper and staid fashion of a typical keeper of a manor. It was dignified and respectable. But this new girl styled it a little differently, letting certain tresses hang longer. Some embellishment followed, just a little to accentuate her eyes and to subtly alter the color of her lips. The Leoneyis girl looked at her and nodded in approval. Looking at herself in the mirror, Cettie evaluated the reflection. It wasn't much, but the results were striking, and that made her feel guilty. Had Adam ever seen her like this? What would he think of her now?

The thought made her ashamed, and she pushed it away. The other girl tugged at her arm, smiling at her, and they went down to join the others for the meal. This one was not held in silence as the previous two had been. The girls were talking and laughing, and they waved in greeting when Cettie and the girl from Leoneyis arrived.

Cettie joined the others, and although she did not understand their language, she still felt included. The meal was communal, and the others offered her food from trays of broiled fish, bread covered in cheese, and cut and arranged vegetables—some of which she didn't even recognize from her world, like the ones shaped like green arrows. A sweet-tasting cider that danced on Cettie's tongue was served as the drink. It was so delicious she poured herself a second gobletful.

The meal was excellent, but the fatigue she'd felt earlier was beginning to return. She had no doubt she'd sleep well that night—if she allowed herself to do so. Was there a way to escape this place? She wondered if she should try to find a way out while everyone slept.

Cettie noticed the door open, and Jevin walked in with Lady Corinne, whom she hadn't seen since the day they'd arrived. The two were in conversation, but Jevin made a short gesture and pointed to where Cettie was sitting. She swallowed the food in her mouth, her appetite suddenly vanishing.

Lady Corinne thanked Jevin and then approached the table. The other girls, taking notice, fell silent, their looks revealing deep respect tempered by a touch of wariness.

"Come with me, Daughter," Lady Corinne said to Cettie.

Cettie obeyed and rose from the table. Her stomach felt as if it leaped to her throat in nervous agitation. Corinne led her back into the hallway, where they could be alone. It was dark now, the corridor lit by flickering torches.

They stopped just past the doorway, and Corinne turned to face her with a look that was cold and calculating.

"What is it?" Cettie asked in dread.

"I thought I should be the one to tell you. Brant Fitzroy is dead. I thought you might prefer to know in private. So you may grieve alone."

A jolt, a shudder, a shock—all struck Cettie at the same instant. Disbelief collided with the raw certainty that Lady Corinne would not lie about something so dreadful. This was the woman who'd had Mr. Skrelling thrown from her manor. "D-dead?"

"I assure you. Quite dead. And then his body was thrown into the river for good measure along with those of hundreds of other residents of Comoros. The war has begun, Cettie. There is no stopping it this time. I will return to Lockhaven soon to finish my business before the mirror gates begin crashing down. When you grow weary of feeling grief and despair and want to feel more useful emotions, let your *true* father know. He will give you another kystrel. Yes, he will be continuing your training now. As he tried when he came to fetch you from Muirwood. Be ready when I come for you. If you don't, remember that Anna's life dangles by a thread. One more dose could kill her. Or cure her."

⌐◡

As Cettie wept in her room—huddled on the floor, choking on her sobs—she felt as if she would die from her grief. First Joses. Now Father.

Anna had poison flowing through her veins. The cure depended on Cettie, and the rest of her family could also fall victim to Lady Corinne's wicked schemes. No one was safe. No one was protected. Not even Adam. Had he been killed along with the rest? Was Sera dead? There was nothing she could do to save any of them. She felt lost, abandoned, betrayed.

Was there no justice in the universe? No compassion? Was it all a game of power, a struggle between equals, each side using trickery and deceit to achieve their ends?

In her misery and rage, she tugged the chain loose from her collar and stared at it, her eyes swollen with tears. The pale metal glinted in the moonlight coming from the window.

She threw it violently away and then buried her face on her forearms and sobbed.

Officers from the Ministry of War arrived at my home in the early afternoon. I was quite shaken by their abrupt visit and then shocked to be taken immediately into custody. I demanded to know for what crime, but they refused to answer. Threats of legal repercussions did nothing as I was hoisted onto a zephyr. We shot like a cannon ball up to Lockhaven, a place I had been banned from by the emperor.

One cannot exaggerate, at least I cannot exaggerate, the depths of my trepidation as I was brought to the court for an interview with Willard Richard Fitzempress, the emperor himself. One cannot express the horror I felt to find him at death's door. His doctor said he had been poisoned, and they were struggling to find a cure. His face was ashen. His lips were black. But he gestured to me furiously to attend his bedside and croaked in a strangled, wheezy voice, to review the alteration he had made to his final will and testament. He could barely breathe, let alone speak, but his eyes were fierce, as if he were forestalling death by his will alone. I read the change. He had named Seraphin his heir. Sera, who is by now a married woman in the court of Kingfountain. Were the emperor's wits addled? No, more likely his change of heart was the result of his imminent death. I watched him strangle, watched his eyes roll back in his head as he perished in an agonizing manner. I'm jotting these notes now, while my memory is fresh, as I wait for the privy council to gather and discuss how we might possibly get our new empress home.

—Asriel Durrant, Private Secretary of Sera Fitzempress

SERA

CHAPTER TWENTY-THREE

DYING BREATH

The Espion had taken her husband away hours ago. They had spotted Sera on the couch, still in her rumpled wedding dress, but had left her behind and locked her inside the room. Soon afterward, noises of violence had filtered in from the corridor beyond, the sounds filling her with fear and concern. Afraid for her own safety, she had pushed the couch and some chests to barricade the door. She'd paced the room for a while, her nerves fraught with fear, and then eventually she returned to the desk where her husband Trevon had been working. Perhaps she could find a weapon or something she could use to defend herself.

The papers were written in a language she didn't understand and could not read, and she quickly moved the stacks aside. As she nudged one pile over, a glint of brass caught her eye, and she quickly lifted it. Trevon's Tay al-Ard lay beneath it. She blinked, both in surprise and in relief.

With it, she could escape. And hopefully rescue others as well.

The sound of arquebus shots beyond the window abruptly claimed her attention, followed by someone crying out her name. It sounded like Adam. She slipped the device into her pocket, hastened to the curtain, and parted it to reveal the darkness beyond. When she opened the door, the acrid smell of smoke assailed her, but she cautiously stepped out onto the balcony.

Soldiers wearing the uniform of the king's guard had assembled below. The torches they held revealed each of them wore a white armband bearing the fleur-de-lis symbol. A crowd had gathered beneath one of the balcony windows. They were hoisting something—a body, she discovered—up and carrying it toward the gates. The body wasn't moving.

"Sera," she heard a man croak.

Another gunshot sounded, adding to the smoke, and the bullet struck the wall near her balcony. She cried out in fear as a spray of stone rubble spattered against her. At first, she thought the men were shooting at her, then she saw the man edging along the thin ledge connecting her balcony to the others. It was Adam Creigh, and his arm and the back of his jacket were stained with blood. She saw the fear in his eyes, the pain twisting his mouth into a scowl.

"Shoot him again!" she heard a man say from far below. If Adam fell, he was a dead man.

Sera sprang into action. She rushed to the edge of the balcony and leaned over, reaching her fingers for him. He was out of reach.

Another shot sounded, and she saw it hit the stone just to the left of his head. He winced, the fragments of rock slicing into his ear and scalp. Every moment might be his last as he inched his way closer, hugging the face of the castle, hands splayed to find a grip.

"Did you get him? Did you get him?"

"I can't see him through all the blasted smoke!" someone complained.

"He isn't falling," another said. "Curse his luck!"

Adam's eyes fixed on hers as he shuffled along. The soldiers below started to reload their weapons.

"Hurry, Adam," she urged. "You have to hurry."

His lips pressed into a firm line. Sera reached as far as she could, unafraid that the bullets might aim for her next. If she could only touch him, she could use the Tay al-Ard to take them both away. But she wouldn't leave without Becka. Not without Becka. Or Trevon. If they'd taken him to the same dungeon, she could rescue them both.

"*I* see him," one of the soldiers called. "He's almost to the next balcony. Fire, you fool!"

"Adam!" Sera pleaded, straining.

Another shot sounded, and this time it struck him. She didn't see where, but she saw him rock with the impact. His body began to tilt as he lost his grip.

"Jump!" she pleaded.

Adam flung himself toward her, bringing one arm up over the balcony wall. His legs dangled below, struggling and failing to find traction. He would have plummeted if Sera hadn't been there to grab his arm. She dug her fingers into his jacket, his shirt, anything she could grip, and helped pull him onto the balcony. He flopped onto the ground just as another shot rang out and pulverized the stone where he had been.

An angry voice shouted from below, "Get into the castle and take him! He's going into the river with Fitzroy. Now!"

Clutching Adam's arms, she dragged him into Trevon's rooms, smearing blood on the floor.

"Adam, what happened?" she gasped, winded by the effort to move him.

"The prime minister has been murdered," Adam said with grief. "Raj Sarin too. They're going to kill all of us. *All* of us from the empire. They plan to massacre us and then throw our bodies into the river."

"No," Sera breathed out in despair.

"Lady Corinne is behind it. She came right after Fitzroy and Raj Sarin were killed. I had already made it out to the balcony when I heard her voice from the room. They're going to come for us next."

Sera's mind whirled with panic.

Adam groaned in pain from his wounds, gritting his teeth as he looked down at the blood soaking his shirt. "I may be dead . . . before they get here."

"You will not die," Sera promised. She heard noises from just outside the room. The whole castle was in an uproar. "Where is Captain Remmer?"

"I d-don't know," Adam said, wincing. "I'm sorry, Sera. I'm sorry."

"Shhh," she soothed, smoothing his damp hair.

"I can't . . . protect you," he said, lying prone on the ground.

"No, you can't. So I must protect you."

The door handle jiggled, and she heard something shove against it. She was grateful she'd blocked it earlier. More men joined the effort, and the furniture blockade began to screech against the floor. Sera knelt by Adam's side and fished the Tay al-Ard from her pocket.

"What is that?" Adam asked, staring at it in confusion.

She gripped his arm with her free hand and pictured the dank cell in her mind.

The magic yanked them both out of the room just as the doors crashed open. The familiar nauseating feeling wrenched at her gut, and then they appeared in the small room that held her maid. Becka was standing on a stool, her back to them, looking through the bars. She fidgeted from foot to foot.

"Becka," Sera whispered, and the girl shrieked with fright. She stumbled and fell off the stool and then recovered slightly when she saw Sera on the floor, Adam prostrate beside her.

Becka knew about the Tay al-Ard and had seen Sera suddenly disappear and appear before. "What's happening, Sera?" she said, her eyes tear-stricken. "Some soldiers tried to come down here, and there was a fight."

"Have you seen Prince Trevon?" Sera asked, beckoning for her maid to come near.

"No. The bodies are still in the hall. Some are moaning. What's happening?"

"General Montpensier is seizing power," Sera said, convinced it was true. "I think he started abducting the royal family yesterday." She remembered how Prince Kasdan had never reached the boat yesterday. And then the rest of the family had fled back to the palace where the Espion was the strongest. The Espion had no doubt caused the rioting, forcing Captain Remmer to use the majority of his force to try to quell it. And, of course, the army was coming to Kingfountain. An army, she no longer doubted, whose loyalty was to the general, not the king.

It was a disaster of catastrophic proportions.

Becka huddled next to them. She looked worriedly at Adam, who was writhing in pain and trying to stifle his moans. Sera knew he needed a healer immediately. And they all needed to get away from Kingfountain.

Trevon had been taken away. She'd hoped she would find him in the dungeon. Where was he? Could she afford to look for him?

"What do we do?" Becka whispered.

The need to decide—and quickly—was paramount. She had to focus. She realized, with growing anger, that she couldn't save Trevon's life. For all she knew, he may have already been killed and thrown into the river, making her a widow after only a few hours of marriage. She could only save her own life—and Becka's and Adam's. All of Comoros's people in Kingfountain would be murdered. The thought made her sick to her stomach and angrier than she'd ever been in her life, and yet she was but one person. She could not stop an army.

She could use the Tay al-Ard to go anywhere she had already been. Well, she had been to many places in this world. But she did not speak their language, and without the magic of Trevon's people, it would be difficult to be understood. She also suspected that the Espion would be looking for her, and it would be impossible to successfully disguise herself, let alone a bleeding man and a girl.

Trevon had a ring that could alter his appearance. Maybe he would use that to free himself.

But she had to act now if she hoped to get Adam to a place of safety. Sanctuaries were supposed to offer succor to those who needed it, but could they really trust Montpensier to honor the old rules?

The mirror gate.

She blinked quickly. The Tay al-Ard would not allow her to cross back to her world, but it could take them to a place where the transfer was possible. Trevon had used it that way for years. She had only ever used one mirror gate to enter and exit Kingfountain. Of course, she'd always been in a boat. But if the Tay al-Ard brought them to the gate, they could swim through it. Once they were back in her world, she could use the Tay al-Ard to transport them back to Lockhaven.

Perhaps then they could summon help for Trevon and the Argentines. Or were the king and queen part of this mess? There was so much she didn't know.

Noise came from outside the iron door.

"Becka, go see what's happening," Sera whispered, and the girl immediately obeyed.

Sera shifted and felt something pinch against her skin. Fitzroy's journal. If they went into the water, it would be ruined. How could she protect it?

"What do you see?" she asked Becka.

"There are men coming down the hall." Then she gasped. "Lady Corinne!" She turned, her face suddenly white as milk.

"Adam, I need your jacket. I'm sorry. Becka, give me your dress." She had to protect the journal, which meant covering it with as many layers as possible. Sera reached under her skirts and pulled the journal free. Becka was hastening to obey, although she looked confused. "Wrap this in your dress. Wrap it up tight." She handed the journal to Becka.

Then, bending low, she began to remove Adam's jacket as the sound of steps approached their cell. He tried to help her, but he was too weak. Powerless.

"Hurry," Becka whimpered.

Sera freed one of Adam's arms, then the other.

"I'm sorry," she told Adam as he collapsed back onto the ground, writhing again in pain. There was a bloody smear on the floor beneath him. "Wrap this over the dress and hold the package tight, Becka. You have to hold it tight."

A key rattled in the lock, and the door began to open. Sera gestured frantically for Becka to come close. The girl cowered on the floor next to her.

"She's in this one, my lady," said a man's voice. "The general said you'd come for her."

The door swung open, bringing a slice of light to blind their eyes, which had grown accustomed to the dark. Becka hugged the bundle to her bosom, wearing only a thin slip now. Adam propped himself up on one arm, gazing at the light.

Lady Corinne stood in the doorway.

Sera looked at her, waited until their eyes met, waited for the spark of recognition. It came, and the murderess's eyes widened in surprise.

Sera smiled, a triumphant smile, and invoked the Tay al-Ard once more and watched the anger bloom on Corinne's usually aloof face as they vanished right in front of her.

CHAPTER TWENTY-FOUR

THE DEEP FATHOMS

The Tay al-Ard wrenched them away from the palace dungeons and deposited them on an outcropping of rock just as a spray of water drenched it. It was the dead of night, and after being exposed to the burst of light in Becka's cell, Sera felt as if she'd suddenly gone blind. Adam began spluttering from the sudden intake of salt water, and Becka shrieked in fear.

It took a moment for Sera to regain her bearings. A mountain of stone rose next to them, forming the natural archway that led back to their world. It wasn't a long swim, maybe forty paces, but it would be difficult in the churning water. It felt like an eternity since she had passed through this very portal on a boat. So much had changed in such a short time. Some of it irrevocable.

"Becka, help me pull him higher," Sera pleaded, gripping one of Adam's arms. Becka slipped on the jagged stone, and Sera could hear her teeth chattering with the cold. She clutched the bundle with Fitzroy's journal under one arm and clambered over the rocks to get on the other side.

"Why aren't we back home yet?" Becka asked worriedly. Another wave came up and lifted Adam, threatening to drag him out to sea. It took both of them yanking hard to prevent it. Adam tried to help, but he was only so much dead weight.

"We have to cross the portal," Sera said, grunting with the effort. She gazed up at the distant stars overhead. The moon was nearly gone from the sky, providing barely enough light to see.

"But there's no boat," Becka said, her voice thick with fear.

"I know there isn't. We don't have a choice. This is the only way back to our world that I know of. We have to swim."

"I don't know how," Becka said in sudden panic.

"Neither do I," Sera said with a sigh. She had tried swimming once with Trevon at the beach in Ploemeur, but it had terrified her, and she'd not wanted to repeat the experience. "But we don't have to go very far. Just enough to cross the mirror gate. Once we're on the other side, I can use the magic to get us back to Lockhaven."

"I don't think I can do this, Sera," Becka whimpered.

"I'm not leaving you here," Sera answered sternly. "If we take a big enough breath, we'll float. I'll need your help to pull Adam through."

"I know how to swim," Adam said through clenched teeth. He was in utter agony, and his voice throbbed with it. "If I don't black out."

"Watch out!" Becka said, and then another wave crashed against the rocks, soaking them anew.

A light suddenly shone from beneath the waters, and one of Kingfountain's undersea ships emerged from its lair. It was positioned near the maw of the mirror gate, obviously there to prevent trespassers from crossing. Had it been alerted to their presence? Sera stared at it, feeling a visceral anger. Their escape would not be thwarted.

Becka gasped in worry.

"We don't have time to delay," Sera said. "Adam, you need to do the best you can. Becka, just hold on to him. No matter what, do not let go."

The light from the vessel began to sweep across the mirror gate. It would find them in moments.

"We need to jump in," Sera said. "Help him stand."

Together, they pulled Adam to his feet. Sera was starting to tremble now as she watched the waves smash against the rocks beneath her. They could all drown. They could smother in—

She forced the thought out of her head with a surge of sheer will-power. The light reached them and held fast, exposing them and making them blind at the same time.

"Ready?" Sera yelled, squinting, tasting the salty water on her lips.

"I don't think I can," Becka wailed. The sea looked like it was boiling.

"This is our last chance," Sera said. "Ready . . . jump!"

Adam hooked his hand around Becka's arm, pulling her with him as they leaped into the waters. Becka screamed again, which would make buoyancy that much more difficult. When the water plunged over her head, Sera had a momentary feeling of panic, of fear that they'd all plummet to the bottom of the sea, but the principles of the Mysteries of Wind prevailed. Suddenly, her head popped over the surface, and she gasped in air. Adam's head bobbed up next, and he grunted as he pulled Becka up. The girl was crying, but at least she was with them.

"It's coming after us," Sera said. The light was already shifting, try-ing to find them.

"Kick," Adam said. "I've got her. You stay close to me." He clutched Becka around the waist and stroked toward the open water at the edge of the mirror gate.

The vessel was coming toward them.

Sera kicked as hard as she could, wishing she'd doffed her gown now that it was pulling her down. Her heart skipped wildly in her breast as she tried to propel herself toward the arch. The vessel moved sleekly toward them, coming too fast. It would reach them before they arrived at the portal.

Adam never looked back. He strained against the pain, weak from loss of blood, no doubt, but his grimace showed he was up to the task.

A wave slapped at Sera from behind. Clearing the surface again, she spluttered and found the ship's light in her face. She could hear the hull cutting through the water. Twisting around, she saw Adam and Becka farther ahead, almost at the brink of the mirror gate. How was she ever going to catch up with them?

She stared at the vessel as it closed in on her. Was it going to crash into her? One hand still gripped the Tay al-Ard, but where could she go? Where could she hide? She had to get back to her people.

Suddenly, the watercraft was thrown off course, as if something had collided with it from beneath. The vessel rocked violently, its light jerking in another direction. There was something in the water, something huge. Sera couldn't see it; her eyes were still recovering from too much exposure to the light. She had only a moment to take a breath before she was struck by the thing too and pushed underwater.

The thing that had hit her wasn't made of stone. It had a rubbery surface—not a ship, then, but a sea creature so enormous it rivaled the size of a tempest. Whatever it was shoved Sera toward the mirror gate, and although she couldn't breathe, she felt something hit her middle, a fin maybe? She grabbed at it as it pushed her toward Adam and Becka. The rush of the water in her ears made her deaf, and her lungs craved air, but she was almost there and could sense the Leering at the mirror gate. Sera pushed at it with her mind, demanding that it open for them, that it send them home . . .

And then the magic of the portal seized her. It was a familiar feeling, one that brought a spasm of relief to her frantic mind. She'd never crossed a mirror gate underwater before, but it was thrilling. The water was impossibly warm now, like a bath, and the vortex sucked her in so rapidly she would have screamed if she could. There was light from some unknown source, and despite the strange sensation of having her eyes open underwater, she could see. She could see everything. The marbled skin of the sea beast that was moving her. One of its eyes stared at her, and she felt the beast's intelligence and raw power. In that moment, she felt the power of the Mysteries, a power that connected her to all living things. A power that transcended worlds, that connected them to one another and her to them. An awareness of infinity exploded in her mind. She was at once part of the universe and an insignificant speck, a mote of dust amidst trillions. Yet she had value, she had a purpose. The Knowing was aware of her and her need. And it had brought a giant whale to save her in her moment of terror and confusion. She had learned about the massive creatures in Muirwood, but she'd never thought to see one in her lifetime.

The light swelled around her, and she could see even deeper into the sea. At the edge of her vision was an underwater city cocooned in magic. She saw buildings made of white stone, terraced temples and lush gardens, strange trees she had never seen before in any world. Her heart nearly burst with longing to go there, to see it, to meet its people and share in the feelings she sensed coming from it. It was the Deep Fathoms. The conviction of that knowledge burst inside her mind.

And then it was gone.

The whale breached the waters, and the sudden exposure to sunlight left her dazed. Her hair was plastered across her face, and when she wiped it aside, she saw Adam and Becka had surfaced close to her. They'd made it through too.

The whale ducked back under the water, and then its massive tail emerged just past them, so large it could smash them, but instead it merely slapped the waters as it submerged. Sera stared at it in awe, realizing that the creature had traveled through the mirror gate with them.

The sun beat down on them, warming the waters and driving away the chill. In the distance, she saw the hull of a hurricane sky ship. They were *home*.

Her gaze shifted back to Adam, who continued to stare as the whale lumbered once more into view before dipping away and disappearing. He turned his head, looking for her, and his face split into a relieved smile.

"We made it," he gasped. Becka clung to his arm, her breath coming too fast and quick. She was terrified but safe.

As Sera paddled toward them, emotion swelled in her chest—relief, yes, but also a feeling of loss and fear for Trevon. Sera had upended Lady Corinne's plans by escaping. And like in any game, what happened next could not be predicted.

Worrying wouldn't do her any good now. She needed to do something. Sera reached her companions and wrapped her arms around them. Then she squeezed the Tay al-Ard firmly, using it to bring them all back to Lockhaven.

⸻

To say that their sudden arrival in the privy council chamber, dripping wet and panting for breath, caused widespread astonishment was indeed an understatement. The council was in the middle of a session, and the exclamations of surprise and confusion sent the entire room into an uproar.

Adam was still suffering greatly from his wounds and was too weak to stand. Becka shivered in her underclothes, still gripping the parcel containing the journal.

Sera realized she must look like an otherworldly creature—one of the water sprites the people of Kingfountain so feared—but she needed to take charge of the situation at once. Her gaze found the Minister of Wind, and she addressed him with a command. "Doctor Creigh has been mortally injured. Get him to a surgeon immediately and get him a Gift of Healing at once." She then shifted her attention to one of the matronly members of the privy council. "Lady Jane, please see my maid is properly clothed and taken to a place of shelter."

Both agreed and immediately began to act, but the commotion intensified again until a voice rang out in the throng.

"Sera!"

It was Mr. Durrant, staring at her with a mixture of surprise and impossible joy. He looked about to burst as he pressed through the crowd to come to her side. She was surprised to see him in the privy council chamber since he was exactly the person whose guidance she needed. Her father had exiled him from Lockhaven previously, but that decision had been overturned under the new prime minister.

"I apologize for interrupting the meeting," Sera said, hearing the noise of water pattering on the floor from her soaked dress and hair.

"You are not interrupting," Durrant said with wonderment. "You couldn't have come at a better time."

"I came to save our lives," Sera said, addressing the gathering. "Lord Fitzroy is dead . . . murdered. We only just escaped the same fate ourselves."

Gasps of shock and outrage followed her comment. Several members of the council spoke at once, demanding to know more. It was all in tumult.

"What about the wedding?" Durrant asked. "Was it interrupted?"

"No, it is done," she said, feeling another pang at the thought of the separation from her husband. "The violence began during it. I will explain all if you'll let me change into some dry clothes first." She looked around the room again. "Where is my father?"

Durrant's look altered at her request. His eyes grew very serious and earnest. "I'll take you to him. But first, you are right, you should change. Much has happened here since you left. Almost too much to tell. Come, Sera. Let's get you in a better state." He waved his hand to those in the room. "Miss Fitzempress will be back shortly. Calm yourselves. A little more decorum if you please."

"Has something happened to my father?" Sera pressed, dropping her voice lower. Her stomach clenched with dread, and she realized the answer before he told her. It opened in her mind, like flower petals kissed by the morning sun. Her father was dead.

"Yes, my dear," he said softly, taking her arm, ignoring the wet fabric of her dress. He pitched his voice even lower. "He died this morning. And he named you empress. Unequivocally. I heard him command it myself and saw the will and testament. You've saved yourself. Now you need to save the rest of us."

It was hard to conceive that earlier that day, she had stood in the sanctuary of Our Lady, accepted a ring, and promised to be Trevon's wife.

As the pain erupted in her heart, she realized she might never be able to go back to Kingfountain again.

CHAPTER TWENTY-FIVE

UNFORGIVEN

A change of dress. Becka's careful hands combing her hair. The smell of lavender lotion. She was used to living in her house on Kelper Street in the City, but she had a room in the royal manor in Lockhaven as well. It was a place to sleep, equipped with an assortment of formal clothing and jewelry, all befitting an emperor's daughter. She caught a flash of light from the mirror across from her, and her eyes landed on the wedding band on her finger. A shiver traveled down her back. Sera was exhausted, and she felt out of place in Lockhaven. The surreal nature of all that had happened made her want to pinch herself. Her father had been poisoned, by Lady Corinne, no doubt, but he had named her empress before the poison could kill him.

He had named *her*.

When Becka finished with her hair, Sera rose from the padded bench. The corset pinched her sides as she straightened, still gazing at herself in the mirror. She looked as she always did. Short. A roundish face. Lips that hovered near a smirk whenever she smiled. Her husband was on another world . . .

Thinking of Trevon only worsened the ache. She hadn't cried yet. She would. But that could wait. That had to wait.

"You look so lovely," said Becka softly, admiringly. The younger girl was still pale from the ordeal she'd undergone. It was such a comfort to have her back, to know she was safe from the Espion. Sera had strapped the Tay al-Ard to her forearm beneath the tight cuff of the gown. She would not let it out of her possession.

"Thank you," Sera answered, gazing at her maid in the mirror. The girl tried to conceal a yawn. "Get some sleep. I'll be meeting with the privy council for a while. I'll come back here when I'm done."

"We won't be going back to your house on Kelper Street, will we?"

Just thinking about her little house made her heart ache. There were so many memories of Trevon's visits there, their walks and conversations and the impertinent comments that Mr. Durrant had made to him—all given and received in good humor while Becka watched from a nearby divan, trying not to smile and often failing. Good memories. Painful reminders.

Sera shook her head no, feeling a weariness that went down to her bones. "I don't imagine we will. Get some rest."

Becka nodded. Then she flung her arms around Sera's neck and hugged her. "Thank you."

"I wasn't going to leave without you," she answered, squeezing her back. "And I'll need you now more than ever, Becka. Everything has turned upside down. I need a friend."

Becka pulled away, nodding vigorously. "You'll always have one."

Sera smiled at her and then walked out the door. Mr. Durrant was pacing outside, and his mouth quirked into a smile when he caught sight of her.

"Ah, now you look like an empress-to-be. Not a *Kingfountian* siren."

"Is that even a word, Mr. Durrant? Kingfountian?"

"I just invented it." He gave her an appraising look. "You look tired, which is understandable. How are you holding up?"

"As well as can be expected under the circumstances, Mr. Durrant."

"Decisive. Good. You'll need to be. Lord Welles was just here trying to push three of the admirals as possible contenders for the role of prime minister."

"Three? I'm surprised he didn't suggest himself." Sera said these words with a tone of disdain.

"He'd be the puppet master regardless. The privy council is anxious to see you again. Shall we go?"

"I'd like to see my father first."

Mr. Durrant's brows knit together. "He's going to be embalmed, Sera. Why not wait until afterward, when he looks more . . . presentable?"

She gave him an arch look and said nothing more.

"I see I've trained you *too* well," said Durrant, heaving a sigh. "Follow me, Your Majesty."

Sera was not very familiar with the intricacies of the palace. She knew Trevon's home better than her own. Her father had changed the place, and in a way she couldn't abide. The flaunting displays of wealth—in the gilded mirrors, the polished marble, and the paintings exquisitely done by master artists—all conspired to make her feel she had inherited an empire diseased by its own riches.

She had wanted to become the empress. But she'd never imagined all that she would have to sacrifice to achieve it. The victory was bittersweet.

Durrant led her to the doorway of the state room where her father had died. Two footmen guarded it, but upon seeing her, they opened the doors immediately.

A sour smell abruptly filled her nose as she entered. Bouquets of flowers had been brought into the room in an attempt to overpower it, though they'd only done half the job. This wasn't the rotting smell of death she'd experienced when she'd discovered Mr. Skrelling on the beach beneath Pavenham Sky. Sera felt her courage begin to wilt, but she pressed on, determined to face her father's corpse before she ascended his throne.

Mr. Durrant made a coughing-choking sound in the back of his throat as he followed her in. She could see he was struggling to prevent his disgust from showing. He gave her a nauseated smile and gestured to the bed. Despite his lack of composure, Sera was grateful he had entered with her. She didn't want to be left alone with her father's ghost.

Sera strode to the bed. A sheet covered her father's face. Judging from the size of the body beneath the sheet, he'd shrunk since she'd last seen him. In life, he'd been a corpulent man. Her courage nearly fled from the room. Mr. Durrant remained behind a pace, letting her have a private moment with her father's remains. In all her imaginings, she'd not thought he would die so young. He could have had the throne another twenty years. Maybe more. Clenching her jaw, she reached down and gently drew the sheet back to expose his face.

Yes, it was her father. Willard Richard Fitzempress. His lips were black, his cheeks sunken. But it was just a shell. She had not been to many funerals in her life, but it had always struck her how claylike a body seemed with nothing animating it. The essence of her father, his soul, had fled.

And yet . . . she sensed a connection to him. Perhaps his body was like a Leering, and it connected her to where his soul had gone. She hoped he would be able to hear her.

His hands had been crossed over his stomach, and she carefully laid her hand on them. It felt as if they were made of stone.

"What can I say?" Sera asked in a hushed whisper. Her voice caught in her throat. Swallowing, she pressed on. Inside, she was rattled. But she would do this. She would make herself do it. "I don't know what to say, Father. That I'm sorry you are gone? That I will miss you? We've been estranged for so many years. Our meetings have been . . . painful. For both of us, I think. I used to look up to you. You were my father, and even though you were strict, I believed you cared about me." The words were starting to gush out, and she let them, even as the tears thickened on her lashes. "You saved my life when I fell out of that tree. Do you remember that day? I was falling so fast. Yet you caught me. You saved me." She bit her lip. "Sometimes I've wondered if you regretted that. You thought I was a threat to you. Competition. You were ambitious. You were always ambitious, although you pretended otherwise. You wanted so badly to rule."

She swallowed again, feeling some confidence replace the misery and sadness. "You broke my heart when you persecuted me, Father. When you believed the lies told to you by others, especially *her*, when you allowed yourself to be deceived by your own self-righteousness and wisdom. She was subtle, wasn't she?" Sera shook her head, remembering the time she'd spent as Lady Corinne's ward. "She twisted you. But you *let* her. You . . . gave in to your darker impulses. In your mind, I'm sure you did the best you could. I don't know what kind of life you led before I was born. I wasn't there to see it. Your brothers . . . the bad example they set. It must have affected you." She sighed again. "But when you lay dying, when you discovered that your time in this second life would soon be over, you chose me to replace you. The girl you wouldn't even accept was your daughter. I think you knew something, there at the end. I think you realized that I wasn't your enemy after all. We're a little too much alike, you and I, although we never spoke of it. We're both stubborn to our core, aren't we? And maybe I needed a father like you to bring out in me my better virtues. If I'd been spoiled or if you'd indulged me, I would not be ready for this moment. I . . . I don't see the throne as a reward or a deserved right. It is breaking my heart again to accept it, to lose what I went to Kingfountain to gain. I wanted so badly to help establish peace between our worlds, but I'm not sure such a thing was ever truly possible. Maybe it was just a fancy. A dream." She let out a ragged breath.

"We've never spoken like this before, have we? So candidly. I never sought to injure you, Father. I hope, one day, you will see that. That you will have mercy. I have always tried to act on my conscience—to do what I thought was best. To be better than you were. Not because I hate you. Not because you never forgave me. But because I can see a better way. So I will try to be a better empress than you were an emperor. And I won't be held hostage to the past any longer."

Sera felt she had said her piece. There was a balm in honesty. She pursed her lips, gazing down the length of the sheet, then wiped her tears on the back of her wrist. Yes, the privy council was anxious that she return and begin her rule. But she'd needed to speak her mind to him.

"Farewell, my lord father," she said at last. "Until we meet again after this life. I hope you will be proud of me then."

Had he heard her little speech? Was he aware of her sentiments? She'd parted a curtain in her soul, and in doing so, it felt as if she'd created a connection between them, however distant. And she felt a throb of approval, love, and peace settle into her. Maybe it was her imagination. Maybe it was just the reassuring presence of the Mysteries. Whatever it was, she accepted it as a treasure.

Sera carefully pulled the sheet back up and covered his face. A stray tear fell and blotted the linen. Mr. Durrant had ventured closer. He now stood at the foot of the bed, gazing at her with a look of sympathy and deep respect.

"To the privy council?" she suggested.

"Yes, of course," he said. Then he tilted his head. "That was very . . . magnanimous of you, Your Highness. And quite touching."

"I would appreciate, Mr. Durrant," Sera answered, "if you would keep the memory of this to yourself."

"Of course," he answered, nodding in agreement. "This was not political theater, nor will it be treated as such. But if you'll permit me to say it, your father could be a bit *proud*. Not in the best sense. You are quite different than he is. And more self-aware than I'd expect from a woman of your young age."

"Thank you, Mr. Durrant. Shall we?"

⌐⌐

Sera addressed the privy council from her father's seat, recounting the events that had led to her marriage and Lord Fitzroy's assassination. It was no small undertaking to relate the intricacies of such a complicated situation, including the role of Lady Corinne and how the prime minister had prepared a warrant for her arrest, but she made it clear that General Montpensier was their enemy and not the people of Kingfountain. Yes, they had rioted, but she believed it was because a master manipulator had riled them. Montpensier had inflamed the baser instincts of the people, their distrust and differences, and had caused the disruption for his own ends—to become the new emperor of his people.

As she told her tale, it became clear from the outraged expressions around the room that her own people's wrath had been inflamed as well. Some of the members of the privy council could hardly remain civil. She was asked pointed questions about her willingness to use the military to retaliate against the enemies of the empire. She was willing, she declared without hesitation, but she would not do so impulsively.

"And how, may I ask?" demanded Lord Tensby, one of the council members, "can we be wise and prudent under such circumstances? Our harbinger, your childhood *friend*, has absconded the realm with a traitor. Lady Lawton has been under investigation these many *months* without the privy council being told. And she was a member of this council, a not-so-secret advisor to the emperor, who is now dead! You bear no blame in this, Your Highness, but certainly Lord Fitzroy should have spoken his mind ere this disaster! She may likely be the cause of his demise."

"Hear, hear!" agreed a few more voices.

"Which brings us to the most pressing matter of state," said Lord Welles authoritatively. "The selection of a new prime minister. Clearly someone from the Ministry of War is needed. We are vulnerable and can depend on General Montpensier pressing the chaos to his advantage. He will strike again through a mirror gate, and without our harbinger, we have no way of knowing which one. I believe that we have three strong candidates for the post, three up-and-coming officers who fought bravely before the armistice. Admiral Ballinger, Admiral Grant, or Admiral Fenwick. You can interview each man, Your Majesty, and choose the one you think best suited for the task. If you would heed counsel, then I shall give mine. Let us take the fight to *their* world. It will be costly. It will be difficult. But we will have the advantage. Any of the admirals, I believe, would be an excellent choice."

"Well said, Lord Welles!" shouted another man.

"I agree wholeheartedly," another added.

There was a self-satisfied air about Lord Welles as he sat back in his seat.

"Would Your Highness like to have them summoned so she may choose?" asked the Minister of Thought.

Sera could see the tide of opinion was turning in favor of Lord Welles's recommendation. Their blood was up. They wanted war, they wanted retribution. Lord Fitzroy had adopted a defensive posture, responding to Kingfountain's attacks as they came. An offensive strategy would require a completely different approach. How many natives of Comoros understood the geography of Kingfountain? She probably knew more than most of them. Hadn't she actually traveled to the various regions?

Sera had to lead the privy council rather than be led by them. "Yes, I would like all three admirals to be brought to Lockhaven immediately," she said, nodding to Lord Welles. A smug smile flashed on his face, and he leaned back, folding his arms.

"Choosing a new lord high admiral is of utmost importance to me," Sera continued. "I will consider each man as a possible candidate."

Lord Welles's look darkened. "You said lord high admiral?"

"Yes. I've already chosen the new prime minister. Someone whom I have worked with for many years. Someone who has earned my loyalty and my trust. Someone who will help organize all our assets, not just our tempests and hurricanes but also our food, our metals, our riches, and even our faith. Someone who can judge and influence the mood of the common people, whom we desperately need and who will bear the brunt of this upcoming conflict." Sera looked around those assembled, seeing the mingled curiosity and fear in their faces. "I name Asriel Durrant as my prime minister."

And no one in the room looked more shocked than he did when she said it.

CHAPTER TWENTY-SIX

EMPRESS

The privy council wouldn't be won over so easily. A convulsion of murmurs and heated resistance followed her announcement. She had anticipated that. Durrant had made enemies, to be sure, but he also had allies. Factions had already started to emerge in the council. She cut short the arguing.

"Enough of this!" Sera said in a forceful, commanding voice. She rose from her seat, knowing she didn't make an intimidating spectacle, but she would compensate in her manner for what she lacked in height.

"But Your Majesty," complained Lord Baxter, "we need the wisdom and expertise of the Ministry of War! You must respect the privy council's judgment."

"Of course you would say that Baxter," said Lord Halifax, an aging man who had managed to maintain his position as Minister of Law for many years. "Surely Law is a more suitable ministry to lead such a conflict. I agree wholeheartedly with Her Majesty's wisdom."

"Please, my lords and ladies!" Sera said even more forcefully, glaring around the room until the council members went silent. Her heart beat fast, but she wasn't nervous. The frenetic energy within the chamber impacted everyone there. "I do respect the wisdom and judgment of the privy council. You serve an important purpose, a check for abuses of power by the sovereign. You have the right to choose the emperor if one has not been named as a successor. That is not the case in this situation. My father clearly named me as his successor, as both his doctors and Mr. Durrant have already assured you. But it is *my* right to choose whom I deem fit to form a government. And I have chosen. You can hardly declare this an abuse of my power. Or reckless either. I know Mr. Durrant. He is wise, eloquent, and capable. I will hear no further arguments in this matter. If I discover someone more capable of fulfilling the role, I will make the change. Now please be seated. I do not intend to replace any members of this privy council at present, save one. Lady Corinne Lawton is hereby barred from this council. Prime Minister, I wish you to sign a warrant for her arrest. Send officers to Pavenham Sky immediately, and have her steward, Master Sewell, arrested and brought to Lockhaven at once. I wish to speak to him and see if he will cooperate willingly."

A triumphant smile flashed on Durrant's mouth. "As you command, Your Majesty. It will be done."

"Lord Welles, I do not know how long the mirror gate closest to Kingfountain will remain open. Lord Fitzroy and hundreds of others will not be returning, so the gate we passed through may yet collapse. I would like the Ministry of War to prepare for an assault on the usurpers. If we allow General Montpensier to consolidate his hold on Kingfountain, he will strike us at his earliest opportunity. I agree that we must act while chaos prevails. For too long we have allowed the general to attack us. The time has come for him to feel the full might and wrath of our empire. Our people have been massacred without mercy. I would hold those who were responsible accountable for their crimes. Prepare our legions for war."

Sera did not like him. But there was no denying his aptitude. Now that Fitzroy was gone, he was the most capable man to direct an assault on the other world. She not only did it for the sake of those whose lives had been so brutally ripped from them, but also to prevent further atrocities, including anything that might happen to Trevon and his family. Part of her still hoped they could bring peace to both worlds and rule them together.

She could see in Welles's eyes that he didn't trust her or believe he'd been forgiven. After he had set her orders in motion, she would begin interviewing the men he had suggested. Hopefully one of them would be ambitious enough to do her will instead of his. She would not make the same mistake Trevon's father had—putting too much trust and care in someone who did not deserve it.

"Of course, Your Majesty," Welles said, dipping his head to her.

Sera sat back down in her chair. "I would like a report on the health of Doctor Creigh. He was an eyewitness to the massacre. When he is capable, I should like him to address the privy council and offer his version of the events. I'm hoping that his injuries have been attended to as I requested?"

"They have been, Your Majesty," said the Minister of Wind. "He was injured severely but not mortally. I will tell him at once of your request."

"Please do," Sera said. She pursed her lips, shifting her gaze to take in the rest of the council. "You are dismissed. Begin preparations for the attack immediately."

⌐⌐

Back in Sera's rooms, Becka helped untie and remove her corset, which eased the aching pressure on her ribs. She stared at the contraption, wondering who had invented it and wishing they'd been flogged. Then Becka helped with the buttons again.

"I never want to wear that thing again," Sera said with disgust. "I wish I could be free to wear what I did in Kingfountain. But we must take things one step at a time."

"The ladies of the empire will thank you, Sera," said Becka with a smile.

"I'm sure they will. Where is the book I had you keep safe? Lord Fitzroy's journal?"

"It's over here." Becka fetched it from a drawer and brought it to Sera, cradling it gently in her arms.

Sera took it from her, settled into one of her chairs, and began to read. She wasn't used to Lord Fitzroy's handwriting, but he had a very stylistic hand. She could hear his voice in her mind as she read his observations, his wisdom. This would be a treasure for his family. A throb of sadness filled her heart. Lady Maren would need to be told. Cettie was probably still on the other side of the mirror gate. Her friend had always held Fitzroy so dear. What had happened to her? Was she a hostage herself? Or could she be part of the plot?

Sera closed her eyes, her emotions churning. So much had changed so swiftly. Was it any wonder she felt a little dizzy from it? What was happening back at Kingfountain? Was Trevon even alive? How she wished she could have brought him home with her. The weight of the responsibilities that were now hers was crushing. But she was determined to bear them, and for as long as her people needed her. She also felt a comparable duty to her husband's family. It was overwhelming.

She took a deep breath and continued to read the journal. It was impressive to see Fitzroy's mind at work. He had been conscientious, deliberate, and his investigation into Lady Corinne's activities was extensive. Sera began to realize how the woman's machinations had affected the whole realm, how many businesses she controlled. Especially businesses that fed the Ministry of War.

She was so engrossed in the journal it was a shock when Becka informed her that the prime minster had arrived. More time had passed than she'd realized.

"You look weary, Your Majesty," he said, looking quite fatigued himself.

"I hope we don't fall back on ceremony," Sera answered, resting the book on her lap. "I've always preferred for you to call me Sera."

"And since I've never liked the name my parents granted at my birth," he said with a sardonic smile, "then you may call me what you will . . . or simply Durrant will do."

"Thank you. I would prefer that."

"I should be the one thanking *you*," he said.

"If I had heeded your advice earlier in my life, I would have made fewer mistakes," Sera said. "But I've learned from them, hopefully. What is that box you're holding?"

It was about the size of a legal document, probably four inches thick. "These, my dear, are the orders waiting for your approval. Requisitions for food, armaments, and soldiery. Writs to freeze the Lawton assets, which are considerable, and confiscate them for the use of the empire. Officers have already been dispatched to fetch Master Sewell. And a letter of condolence to be delivered to Lady Maren and her remaining children."

"And I must sign all these papers without reading them?" Sera asked wearily.

"In a word—yes. But *I* have read them. And made necessary amendments to them. I don't trust Welles and wanted to make sure we weren't committing more power to him than necessary."

"Good. We think alike, then."

"I always thought we did," he replied. "I'm flattered that you chose me. Oh, and I wrote the one to Lady Fitzroy myself."

"Thank you, Durrant. It takes years to build trust and only moments to shatter it. I needed to appoint someone I could trust, someone who would always act in the benefits of my interests and the interests of the people."

"Oh, the people adore you!" He set the beribboned box on the desk near her. "They always have. I'm surprised you can't hear the cheering from the streets up here. The news of your father's demise was grunted at. But your rise to power has lit the imagination of the people like so many Leerings."

Sera tried to stifle the yawn, but her fatigue had caught up with her.

"I know you are tired," Durrant said with sympathy. "But these need to be signed ere you sleep. A slumbering dragon has been awakened, Sera."

"And I imagine the beast needs feeding." Sera sighed. She untied the ribbons and opened the box, seeing an enormous stack of papers. "Fetch me a pen and ink," she asked Becka.

Then she turned and looked at Durrant. "I'm going to give my condolences to Lady Maren in person."

His brow wrinkled. "My dear, you don't have *time*."

"You forget, Durrant. I'm not asking your permission. And I can spend an hour in Fog Willows very easily with this." She tugged open her sleeve, revealing the Tay al-Ard.

Accustomed to the day-night reversal in Kingfountain, Sera had fallen asleep early and awakened early. She was up and dressed before the household servants arrived, and they were shocked to find her ready for the day. Durrant looked refreshed when he joined her for breakfast, which was something of a miracle given what he recounted about his interactions with the various privy council members. Many of them now sought to curry favor with him. From his perspective, the council was evenly divided, some for her and some still against her.

"Give them a chance to come around," Sera told him. "If they don't, then we will begin replacing them."

"Master Sewell arrived during the night," Durrant said. "When would you like to see him? We also need to schedule the coronation ceremony."

"The ceremony can wait," she answered. "I'd like to see Master Sewell immediately."

"Alone?"

"Of course not! Preferably in chains. I imagine he's quite nervous."

"You seek revenge for something he did against you?"

Sera shook her head, setting down her fork. "Far from it. I want to test his allegiance—and to find out what happened to my friend Cettie. Why did Lady Corinne go to her? Why did Cettie help her overrun a mirror-gate portal? Where is she now? The timing of all this is very suspicious."

"Indeed so."

"I also have Lord Fitzroy's journal. He entrusted it to me before he died, and I've been reading it. You'll find it useful in your new role, for he took copious notes about various affairs of state and the investigation into Lady Corinne."

"Naturally, I would be keen to read it," he said, leaning forward with burning interest. "When do you imagine you'll visit Fog Willows? Lady Maren's daughter, I've come to find out, is quite sick."

Sera's brow furrowed. "Anna?" She was doubly glad she'd made the decision to visit. "I was planning to go there this afternoon."

"She's being cared for at Gimmerton Sough. That's the old Harding estate. She fell sick recently."

"Don't the Lawtons own it?" Suspicion bloomed in Sera's heart. Her own father had been poisoned, likely by Lady Corinne. Had she also attacked the Fitzroy family?

Durrant shrugged. "I can find out."

"Please do. I'm finished with breakfast. I'd like to see Master Sewell, please."

"We'll bring him to the study, then, if that suits you?"

"It does. Thank you, Durrant."

After he departed, Sera finished her preparations and then went to the study to await Sewell's arrival. One of the benefits of being empress was the promptness with which her orders were obeyed. Within a quarter hour, Master Sewell had been brought, his wrists in shackles, escorted by a half-dozen uniformed officers.

Master Sewell was unkempt, his normally fastidious uniform was wrinkled, and he looked as if he needed a shave. His eyes were bleary from lack of sleep and intense worry.

When Sera had lived at Pavenham Sky, she had been his prisoner in a way. Their standing with each other had more than reversed.

Sera looked at him shrewdly, keeping her expression guarded—much as Lady Corinne had always done.

"Y-your Majesty," he stammered, bowing his head to her. The officers' stern glances clearly discomfited him.

"Master Sewell," she replied evenly. She cocked her head and looked him in the eye. "Is there anything you wish to tell me?"

His lip twitched. He glanced at his captors worriedly. "I . . . I have reasons to suspect that . . . *ahem* . . . that my service to Lady Lawton has reached an end. No one has heard from her in days. As to her whereabouts, I can only guess. She never told me where she was going."

"That is not very useful information," Sera observed.

He swallowed. "I will try to be more useful, then," he said earnestly. "I was never in her confidence at all, it seems. I was her servant, nothing more. But I have eyes, Your Majesty. She was capable of great cruelty. She toyed with the lives of the upper class. The more privileged they were, the more ruthless she could be. She ruined young women . . . deliberately, without provocation. It was like a game to her." He grimaced. "She would invite them to make confidences to her. And then she'd move against them, crippling their success while adding to Lord Lawton's substantial wealth. She is . . . she is a coldhearted woman. I think she had plans to . . . to remove your maid. She ordered me to keep an eye on her. There was something she'd done that Lady Lawton didn't like. I was afraid for her."

"And yet you did nothing to stop her," Sera said. "You told no one of her machinations, even though they were obviously illegal?"

A furrowed brow revealed the mental torture Sewell was experiencing. "What could I do, Your Majesty?" he said in extreme anxiety. "Who could I have trusted enough to tell? She could make or destroy a family with a glance and a frown. Her position in society was unassailable. And how could I do so without her finding out? For everything I had, I was beholden to her. Yet I feared her. Feared what she would do if she turned her gaze on me next. I tell you, I was just as much a prisoner of Pavenham Sky as you were."

"I believe you, Master Sewell," Sera said, stepping forward. "And I understand from Lord Fitzroy that you were one of his sources, someone who acted for the empire's interests during the investigation."

Sewell paled. "He said he would keep it a secret."

"And he did. I only found out after his death. I brought you to Lockhaven to ensure you hadn't been compromised, and Lord Fitzroy's words and your own testimony have convinced me. There's a place for you here, if you'll take it."

His eyes widened with surprise and the glimmer of hope. "You are too generous, Your Majesty."

"I am generous to those who serve me. Do you know where Cettie was taken? Or anything you've heard your mistress say about her?"

"The Fitzroy's keeper?"

"The same."

"She wrote faithfully to you while you were incarcerated at Pavenham Sky. My mistress used to read her letters. I caught her doing it more than once. Then she'd seal them up again and ask me to send them back. I thought it significant."

Sera relaxed her mouth and gave him a smile. "I think you could still be of use, Master Sewell. At least in terms of helping us piece together Lady Corinne's aims. Your knowledge would be very useful."

He nodded vigorously. "Of course! As I said, she never confided in me, but I did overhear her on several occasions. I think she forgot I was there at times. Rarely did she ever let her guard down. It was after one of her visits to court, several weeks ago. She was after something. Something only your father knew."

"Did she say what?" Sera pressed him.

Master Sewell frowned, straining to remember. "I don't remember the exact words. She muttered it. Something like, 'You will tell me, Richard Fitzempress. I will make you tell me.'"

CHAPTER TWENTY–SEVEN
TERROR

The startled look on Mr. Kinross's face at seeing Sera appear in the middle of the corridor at Fog Willows made her smile. She hoped her surprise visit wouldn't give him a seizure. She'd already tucked the Tay al-Ard back under her sleeve, concealing it once again.

"Hello, Mr. Kinross," she said with a bright smile, "I didn't mean to shock you."

"My dear, Y-your Majesty, welcome . . . I truly bid you welcome to Fog Willows. Did you arrive just now?"

"I did." She gazed up at the walls, savoring memories of the times she'd spent there.

"Did you come by zephyr? I had no notion you were coming."

"It was supposed to be secret, Mr. Kinross. Can you take me to Lady Maren? I'd like to pay my respects in person."

"That is very kind of you, Your Highness. How did you . . . I'm still in shock. Let me tell her you are here. Follow me, please."

Kinross escorted her to the family room where the family had danced in happier days. The estate seemed preternaturally quiet, but then it would. Cettie was gone, who knew where, doing who knew what, Phinia was married, Stephen worked in the mines, and poor Anna was ill. It struck her that Lady Maren was very alone. No doubt Lord Fitzroy's death had struck her hard.

Mr. Kinross went in first. Sera heard a few mumbled words, then he opened the door wider and bowed as she entered.

Lady Maren was crossing from a nearby sofa, her eyes red-rimmed, and a silk handkerchief still clutched in her hand. The two embraced, and Lady Maren's pain and sense of loss seemed to eclipse her own. In many ways, Cettie's family, the parents of her heart, had been like parents to Sera as well. This was the only true family she had.

"You came," Maren said after the embrace, pulling back and looking at her in wonderment.

"Of course I did. I cannot stay long, but I had to come," Sera said. She accepted Maren's hand and followed her back to the sofa.

"The loss of your husband is a bruise that will never heal," Sera said. "I'm bereft at his loss and can only imagine what's happened to your family. But first, how is Anna?" She squeezed Maren's hand.

"Adam Creigh is visiting her right now and trying to recuperate from his wounds. I'm hoping they'll both be back soon. I'm anxious for news. Too many heartaches in too short a time. Joses. Cettie. Brant." She wiped her nose. "Your own father too."

"I'm certain my father was murdered by Lady Corinne," Sera said. "I understand that she came here, Lady Maren. And took Cettie with her. Can you tell me how it happened?"

Lady Maren looked down and then nodded emphatically. "Sometimes it feels like a dream. That I will wake up and all will be back as it was. I'm worried about Cettie. I'm frantic for her. Let me tell you what Lady Corinne said when she came to Fog Willows that day."

The tale she proceeded to tell made Sera's eyes widen with surprise, especially given the way it involved her. The scandal of illegitimacy kept rising like a shadow. Like a worm that continued to live as section after section was cut away. It was difficult being patient during the tale, but she listened, nodding to show her attention, while her mind raced.

"I was with your husband at the end," Sera said. "He entrusted me with his private journal, which I will return to you after my new prime minister has read it. It contains the secrets of his investigation into Lady Corinne. But I assure you, he would have told me if there were any such bad news. We both know he's a man of the strongest integrity. He would never have allowed the marriage to proceed under false grounds. What Lady Corinne told you was a lie."

"I can see that now," Maren agreed. "But at the time, her story felt . . . plausible. Is that the right word? Her words rang with a strange certainty, and Cettie and I were both deceived. As I said, I thought Corinne was taking Cettie to my husband. I fully believed it. Now how I regret not taking matters into my own hands. If Cettie is under the sway of that . . . that cunning woman . . ." Her words trailed off, and she shuddered.

Sera stroked Maren's arm. "I will do my best to find Lady Corinne and Cettie. I wish I could bring you comfort from your grief, but I cannot. My own heart is still grieving. He was one of the best men this empire has produced. I intend to honor him. I don't know how yet, but I will. And I will not give up on Cettie. I cannot."

"Thank you," Maren said, her throat tightening. "It means so much that you came."

~

Three days passed quickly, so much so that it felt as if the skyward arcs of the sun and moon had suddenly begun to accelerate. Sera was not bored in any of the meetings she attended. Problems were presented and solved, and the first massive fleets of sky ships were dispatched through three separate mirror gates. Their orders were to secure the other end and form a series of links where supplies could be brought through to reinforce. Montpensier's forces had tried to resist, and there had been skirmishes but no major battles.

Sera was under no illusions that the conquest would be easy. Quite the opposite. She knew it would be costly in terms of blood and treasure. The thought of so many deaths weighing on her shoulders made her sick inside. Violence begat violence. Would she and Trevon be able to stop it before it spun out of control?

Was he even alive?

On that third day, she was told that Adam Creigh was rested enough to address the privy council. She had reviewed the entirety of Lord Fitzroy's journal, and while she hadn't understood all of it, Durrant had read it too. Many of the details that had confused them were clarified by Fitzroy's chief investigator. It was revealed that Fitzroy's intention of arresting Lady Corinne just following the wedding may have prompted the sudden hastening of Montpensier's plans.

When Adam was ushered into the privy council chamber, the room fell silent out of respect for the man. Sera had known him since their days together at Muirwood Abbey, and he had never looked quite so careworn. He had a cane to help support his weight, and he winced as he shuffled forward. His bloody shirt and jacket had been exchanged for clean garments, but strain had left more lasting wounds. Sera could see worry and fatigue in the concerned lines in his face. The thought of Cettie must be weighing heavily on his mind. The two were still betrothed, and she was stranded on the other world with the archenemy of their people. How well Sera understood. She worried for Trevon in the same way—and she also worried for Cettie. She'd do anything to see her friend reunited with Adam.

Durrant offered the young doctor a chair, but he shook his head, declining it. "As you wish. Members of the privy council, I introduce to you Doctor Adam Creigh, who has graciously agreed to relate his personal account of the events that occurred the day of the empress's wedding. We are grateful he has recovered sufficiently to attend with us. May I remind the council that he served with distinction in the Ministry of War as a ship's surgeon and was instrumental in saving the lives of many of our brave young men. I will also remind you that our empire called on him again to attend to cholera morbus victims in Kingfountain, and I believe he has made some progress in treating its victims and prolonging their lives. While we still do not know the cause, we owe this young man a debt of gratitude."

There followed a sustained applause from the council, and Adam flinched and then flushed. His mouth pressed into a frown, and he shook his head, breathing in and out slowly. He wasn't pleased by the adulation. That much was clear by his expression.

When the noise subsided, Durrant continued, "Doctor Creigh, you may begin."

All became quiet again, and Sera leaned forward in her chair. Adam set his cane against the edge of the council table and pressed his hands there, leaning forward to keep himself steady.

"I am no more deserving of your praise than countless other doctors and surgeons who shared similar responsibilities." He sighed deeply and then turned and faced Sera. "I would also be remiss if I did not thank you, Your Majesty. You saved my life, and each additional day I draw breath is an undeserved gift. Thank you."

Sera nodded to him, wishing he wouldn't be so formal. But then, he always had been.

"I've been asked to relate the events of the night of Lord Fitzroy's assassination. I was not with the wedding party when he was shot. Miss Fitzempress had asked me to remain behind at the castle. Her sensitivity to the Mysteries is impressive. When he was brought to me, I saw that the ball had shattered his elbow, dug a trench down his forearm, and ripped off several of his fingers. It was a painful injury. I believe the shot was intended to kill him, only it did not. Lord Fitzroy may have lost his arm ultimately, due to infection, but that injury alone would not have killed him." He paused, casting his eyes around the room. "There had been some trouble between the guard and the Espion, the king's spy service. Most of the guards had been stationed outside to protect the wedding, leaving the castle vulnerable, but our room was protected by the king's guard. General Montpensier personally attended to the sickroom. I believe he was anxious to know firsthand whether Lord Fitzroy would live or not."

"And why do you suppose that?" Durrant asked.

Adam looked at him. "Because I believe he was disappointed that Lord Fitzroy wasn't already dead. How would one normally react in a situation like that? An innocent man would have been concerned about starting another war. He would have given orders to apprehend the villain. I was in the sickroom, and there was no such talk, no such communication. Montpensier was riveted to Lord Fitzroy's sickbed, and he offered sedatives to help ease his pain. They were all refused, which only agitated the general further. Eventually he was summoned by the king, which relieved me. I had the suspicion that he would have plunged a dagger into Lord Fitzroy's chest if I hadn't been standing in the way."

That remark earned some angry murmurs from the council.

"Lord Fitzroy suffered through the ordeal of the surgery without any pain suppressants of any kind. I don't know how he endured it, but he was very weak and had lost a great deal of blood by the end. He asked to see Miss Fitzempress, and after she was summoned, he charged her with his personal journal and then requested a Gift of Healing." His tone became more somber. "I tried to give him one, but the Mysteries constrained me. I couldn't speak. Miss Fitzempress was chosen to do the Gifting instead, and so she did. It was a sacred experience. One I won't forget."

Adam rubbed his mouth, shifting a bit as if to ease a wave of pain. Then he planted his hands again. "I stayed at Lord Fitzroy's bedside, along with his servant, the Bhikhu Raj Sarin, and four members of the king's guard. It was just before midnight. The city was still rioting in the streets, and the noise floated in from the open balcony window. We heard commotion out in the hall and one of the knights went to investigate. He was shot through the chest. The other guards hurriedly barred the door."

Sera felt the tension in the room grow. She, too, hung on Adam's every word, her imagination filling in the details of the scene. Gripping the armrests of her seat, she stared at him, adding his story to her own memory of the events. When the commotion first started, she was asleep on the sofa, exhausted by the ordeal, and Trevon was writing at his desk.

"The Espion came in through a secret opening in the wall. It swung open and men with pistols and swords started to rush in. We'd all have died right then were it not for Raj Sarin. He flung himself into the midst of them, bringing them down swiftly with nothing but his arms and legs. He pushed them back for a while, but then someone jammed a pistol into his ribs and fired. I saw the bullet come out his back. Still, he fought on, breaking the neck of the man who'd shot him. I was with the knights, trying to hold the door closed. One of our fellows was shot in the face, and each shove pushed us farther back."

The trauma of the event was evident on his face. He clenched his hand into a fist and pressed it against his mouth. Sera could see evidence of the nightmare replaying in his mind.

"There was so much confusion. The door was forced open enough that several arquebus staves were able to be shoved into the room. I was hit by a ball on my arm, and it spun me around. The knights fought back. Raj Sarin managed to bring down all the Espion who came in through that door, although he was shot three more times at close range. I saw him sag to his knees, his face the color of ash. Another man came in through the opening and aimed a pistol at his head. Even though I was injured, I was able to club the man in the head with a water pitcher, rendering him unconscious. I knew Raj Sarin's wounds were fatal. He was bleeding out of his mouth." Adam shook his head, shuddering. "I then went to Lord Fitzroy's bedside and determined to carry him out of harm's way."

The silence in the room was absolute. Sera felt her throat thicken, and she tried to swallow. Tears stung her eyes.

"I knew moving him would cause him more pain, so I apologized. He looked as tranquil as a spring morning. He gripped my hand in his and told me to escape from the balcony. He said there was a lip of stone, only a few inches wide, that I could use to cross from one balcony to the next. He ordered me to get out at once." Adam's voice quavered. He coughed, trying to master his emotions. "I refused. But he hooked his good hand behind my neck and pulled me close so that our foreheads touched. And he ordered me, in the name of the Mysteries, to get to Miss Fitzempress's rooms. He said the Mysteries had already told him that he was going to die. I'd heard the same news myself through the Gifting. I could do nothing but kill myself to try and prevent it. He implored me once more to obey him, for the Mysteries still had work for me to do." He swallowed once more. "Then he kissed my forehead and lay back against the pillows, utterly exhausted."

Adam hung his head low. "His words compelled me. I'd obeyed him in all things before. He . . . he was a father to me. My mentor. My friend. I would have gladly given my life to save his. But I fear he had already made a bargain with the Mysteries to save mine instead. I'll forever bear the guilt of fleeing that awful scene. I slid out onto the balcony just as the door burst open. The final knights were slaughtered. I pressed against the wall, afraid at any moment one of our attackers would look out. But I suppose, in the confusion, they had forgotten about me. They had their quarry trapped on the bed. He was helpless against them."

Sera wiped her eyes, her heart aching.

"I kept as quiet as I could, trying to calm my frantic breath. Then the commotion calmed. I heard a woman's voice, one that I recognized as Lady Corinne's. I didn't hear what she said to Fitzroy, for she spoke too low, and the commotion from the city drowned out her words. But I knew it was her. He said something in reply, although I didn't hear him either. I knew I would die if I stayed there, so I climbed over the balcony, using my boot to feel for the ledge. Although I couldn't see it, I felt it and used it to move away from the balcony." He took a moment to compose himself, and when he spoke again, his voice was steadier. "I had not gone far when I saw them throw Fitzroy's body over the balcony onto the yard below. I believe he was already dead when it happened. There was no struggle. I felt no life radiating from him. There were some guards patrolling the grounds, and they shot the corpse a few times. They laughed as they did so." He breathed in slowly again, his tone revealing that he strained against his growing anger. "They rejoiced in the death of that man. I heard someone say that they would throw him into the river along with the rest of us from Comoros, and they hoisted the body above their heads. By this time, I was halfway across to Miss Fitzempress's rooms. One of the guards down in the garden saw me, and they all began firing at me. That is how I sustained most of my wounds. I would have fallen to my death if not for her."

The reminder of how close they'd come to being killed, to being caught by Lady Corinne, made her cringe. If Trevon had not left the Tay al-Ard behind, she and Adam and Becka would all be dead. At least Corinne's plan had not totally been a success. It was clear now that she had intended to create a cataclysmic disaster in both realms simultaneously. Sera realized that the Mysteries had saved them. A small cylindrical device had been the means of thwarting the woman's plan.

By small and simple means . . . hadn't she read that in one of the tomes?

Adam straightened, his composure restored. "This is my report. I understand you know the rest from Her Majesty's account. Thank you for the opportunity to speak. I hope you do not judge me too harshly."

"Indeed not," said Durrant. "The ordeal you survived would have broken any man. You did yourself credit. Now, best if you continue to recover and fully regain your health."

Adam nodded sagely, but he turned to Sera as the council members began to discuss his story amongst themselves. Sera wanted to ask about Anna, but before she could, Adam leaned forward, his eyes ardent.

"I would beg one thing from you, Your Majesty," he said.

"What is it?" she asked, feeling inclined to grant him anything he desired.

"When I am healed, I request a commission to the Ministry of War that I may continue to help save lives. Grant me an assignment, any you choose, back in Kingfountain. I understand that Cettie is still there." He swallowed. "I wish to find her."

Her respect for him grew. His experience in Kingfountain had wounded him, inside and out, but he would plunge back into the fire to find her friend. She saw the desperate look in his eyes, the pain that gnawed at his soul.

"No, Adam," Sera said, shaking her head. But before Sera could explain her denial, the door to the privy council chamber burst open. It was an officer of Law, his face frantic, his eyes wide with terror.

"What is it, Captain Krupp?" said Lord Halifax in astonishment.

The officer was trembling. "I've come f-from the west. From P-Pavenham Sky."

"Speak man!" said Halifax angrily. The whole mood shifted to concern.

"It's fallen, sir. The m-manor . . . it f-fell."

I toured the devastated area by tempest sky ship. Pavenham Sky did indeed fall, along with all its illustrious gardens, save one. The impact of its crash has convulsed the land in ways unimaginable. Such a loss hasn't happened in decades, and none of the other manors that have fallen were nearly so large as Pavenham Sky. Because it was along the coast, it triggered a quake and a flood that impacted the entire western shore of Comoros. The Ministry of War is not only sending troops to Kingfountain, they are also rescuing thousands who have lost homes and family members. All because a single sky manor dropped like a rock in a pond. When word of this calamity reaches the far expanse of our empire, there will be mass hysteria and fear. It is unavoidable.

If Lady Corinne, who I have no doubt caused this wreckage of human souls, thinks she can cow our new empress, then she is utterly mistaken. The ancients had it correct. Courage consists not of hazarding without fear, but in being resolutely minded in pursuit of a just cause.

—Asriel Durrant, Prime Minister

CETTIE

CHAPTER TWENTY–EIGHT
THE POWER OF MEMORY

"Jump!"

The command was given by the kishion, by her *father*. They stood on the edge of a wall, and he was asking Cettie to leap across to a nearby roof. The fall, a significant one, would shatter her bones. And although she knew the Everoot would heal her, a visceral, primal voice inside her screamed how foolish it would be to make such a leap.

The squirming dread in her stomach was overpowering. The wind tousled her hair and rustled her skirts. The kishion stood there scowling, arms folded, eyes digging into her.

"Why do you hesitate?" he asked angrily.

"Because I'm not certain I can do it," Cettie answered, her mouth dry. Each new day in the poisoner school had brought her to the brink of her abilities. Had it been four days already? She had failed multiple times to do the tasks demanded of her. The teachers continually forced her to face her fears. Grabbing the end of a serpent was probably the hardest thing she'd done, but today's torment—goading her fear of heights—came close. There was no pond beneath her to break her fall this time, only hard, uncaring stones. Much like the kishion's heart.

She had asked him how he'd survived his death at the grotto. But he wouldn't tell her his secrets. Had it something to do with Everoot?

"But *I* am certain that you can. I would not require you to make a jump that was impossible. You're stronger than this."

His words only added to her mental strain. The shelf of roof seemed to shrink farther away the longer she looked at it. Her legs were trembling, and she felt the wind shoving her a bit too hard, making her want to wobble.

"Jump, or I will push you."

She turned to stare at him with a flash of anger. There was no doubt in her mind that he would do it. He was a kishion, a trained killer. And he was her father. This was the man she had seen in her vision, the one who had shot her *real* father, Lord Fitzroy. In the few days they had trained together, he had been merciless in his approach to grind the weakness out of her. Sometimes she earned a curt nod, and it always made her a little angry to know she'd pleased him.

She obeyed him to save Anna's life and the lives of others she loved. If Anna died, she knew someone else she cared for would be targeted next. He'd not mentioned Anna's health to her, but it lingered like a threat over everything she did. But why did she care to please such a man? Why did that even matter? His presence in her life had only caused the bitterest of pain.

"Are you trying to break my neck?" she demanded.

He smirked. "No. I'm trying to strangle your fears. One by one. Fear limits you. It keeps you from becoming who you were meant to be. If you knew, Daughter, that you could not fail, if you were absolutely convinced that you would succeed, what would you *dare* to do?" He reached out a hand and then closed his fingers into a fist. "The world is an orchard with fruit ripe for the taking. The only thing that holds us back is our fear. Fear of what people will think. Fear of what they will say. Fear that it is wrong, only . . . we come to realize that nothing is wrong. People have merely convinced one another to follow certain rules that bind their behavior. Here at this school we must unteach the foolish tenets that have locked and bound your mind. I tell you that you can jump and reach that ledge. I know you can. You don't try because you're afraid of falling. Conquer that fear, Daughter, and you will discover that nothing can truly limit you."

His words did have an effect on her. There was something in his tone that bolstered her confidence. He wasn't trying to harm her. He was training her.

"But I might fall," she said.

He shrugged. "So? What does that matter? You probably won't. Now *jump*." He took a menacing step toward her.

Cettie's whole body trembled. She stopped looking down at the pavers below. She focused on her goal, on the edge of the roof. No, no, this was madness. Why take such a risk?

Then again, a little voice in her head whispered, what did it matter? If the jump did kill her, her torment would be at an end.

He took another step toward her, and she committed to the act. Cettie sprang from the edge of the wall. She instantly realized she had not shoved off strongly enough. The fear turned her insides into liquid—she was going to plummet—but she caught the edge of the roof on her stomach, hitting it hard enough to make her grunt with pain. Her fingers quickly scrabbled at the rounded clay shingles, the edge of the roof scraping against her chest. Her legs dangled below, her feet trying to find something steady she could use to prop herself. There was nothing.

Her elbows pressed down against the tiles, some of which rattled as if they were about to break free. Her stomach was up in her throat, and she gasped and shuddered, trying to keep herself from falling. The instinct of survival was strong, and she instinctively swung her hips to bring a leg up onto the edge. A jolt of energy struck her when her knee made it up, and she felt herself becoming steadier. She grasped one of the tile edges with her fingers and used the leverage to help pull herself up. Then her other knee made it, and she was kneeling, head hanging low, panting for breath.

The crunching sound startled her as her father easily leaped the distance, landing above her. She couldn't resist glaring at him, but she felt a throb of victory that she had made the jump after all.

He reached down to help her up, and she hesitated before taking his hand. Rising to her feet, her knees trembling, she stood on the roof beside him. He then let go of her and stepped up onto the tiles, sure-footed and graceful as a cat. She emulated his walk, but her boots kept jarring the tiles. The air smelled musty on the roof, and she had red dust on her palms from the roof shingles. He reached the apex, the spine, and followed it to another intersection of roof, which was an easy step up. She continued to trail him until they were at last on the highest peak of the estate, the highest point on the grounds. He stood, arms folded again, overlooking the countryside of Genevar.

Cettie joined him, feeling an interesting carefree sensation. She'd never walked rooftops before. Even though she had been the keeper of Fog Willows, she had never dared to explore the estate in such a way. She could only imagine how it would feel to climb the roof of a sky manor. The thought made her giddy.

With his eyes gazing far away, he said, "For many years the poisoner school has been here. There are other compounds like this one, schools that teach different skills." He gave her a brief look and then continued to stare out at the city. "These practices were moved from Pisan because too many people learned of the school. Yes, there is a poisoner school there . . . it's important to keep up appearances . . . but when too many people know a secret, it is a secret no longer. To protect itself, it spread its roots elsewhere. There is so much that people don't know about what we are and what we do. Every kingdom needs people like us, Daughter. To do the filthy things that must be done and cannot be undone."

He sniffed in the breeze. The cooks were hard at work in the kitchen. The scent of the savory meal wafted on the breeze through the chimney. It made her mouth water.

"I watched you at Muirwood," he said, still looking far away. "I watched how they treated you. You were a pariah. You will always be one to them, to those cunning hypocrites who preach mercy and then grind the faces of the poor." His voice was thick with contempt. "You know of what I speak."

Cettie swallowed. "They weren't all that way." And yet he wasn't wrong. Yes, she'd been shunned. She had been ridiculed. They had all studied from the same books, yet so many of the students who'd been born to riches, to cloud manors or estates in Lockhaven, used the Mysteries for personal gain. It was possible to do this. But it wasn't right.

"Of course not," he said, turning to face her. "Look out at Genevar," he said, jerking his head back to the vast city. As she'd observed before, it was so very different from Kingfountain. Although it was a mighty fortress, it wasn't crowded and choked with buildings. There was room for gardens and manors, for orchards and vineyards. It was beautiful, though that couldn't possibly be what he meant. "How many roofs can you see? In the harbor, how many ships? Too many to count. Now imagine this, Daughter. How many millions live on this world? Each one is a person. Each one has hopes and dreams. Isn't it tragic that the vast majority are satisfied living beneath their potential?" He smiled, but it was a sad smile. "As children they imagined themselves growing up to be something better than what their parents were. If they even had parents. But in time, the cruelties of life weighed on them like so many stones. And like water, they follow the path of least opposition. And then they will die, never having achieved a tenth of what they dreamed as children. Life crushes all ambition from them. Only the brave lift up their heads and demand more. And when you make demands of life, it is forced to pay you. Most settle for pauper's wages when they could become kings."

She could see he believed what he said. His tone of voice, the wrinkle in his brow. The stern cold look of a man who'd been beaten down over and over, a man who had gotten up just as many times. A strong curiosity filled her. She longed to know more about him. Yet at the same time, she struggled with her antipathy against him, the man who'd shot her true father while hiding like a coward.

"Where did you come from?" she asked him.

"Do you seek to know me, Daughter?"

"If you'll let me. What made you so hardened?"

"I am from this world," he answered in a low voice. "I served a man, a duke. It doesn't matter where." His face filled with anger, with resentment. "He beat his wife. He tormented his children, made them feel inferior . . . weak. To the world, he presented the trappings of success." He snorted. "When they went to court, he was the epitome of style, sophistication, happiness. His entire family helped create the illusion. But as soon as they went home, he raged at them for their shortcomings, for thoughtless things they had said or done. Or that he had imagined them doing. He was a monster. A selfish, self-important swine. What he did to those children . . ." He sniffed and shook his head. Then he turned and looked her in the eye. "One night, he was raging and hurting his wife. She screamed for help. I thought . . . I thought he was going to kill her. To kill them all. Pity drove me, but hatred too. I went to their room, and I killed him. I strangled him with a piece of cord from the curtains." He frowned at the memory. "His wife . . . accused me. Said I had tried to seduce her and had killed her husband out of contempt. When the officers came for me, I fled, but I was caught. I had a wound on my face from where he had gouged me as I choked him. Justice was swift. They took me to the gallows. My pitiful advocate could do nothing. My words were insignificant compared to the lady's."

He turned around, shoulders bunched. "Rather than lose her wealth or the family's reputation, she sacrificed me instead. She spoke against me, said all sorts of lies. That is what hurt the most. The injustice of it. Surely his corruption was widely known. Yet rather than wrinkle the linen, they chose to hang me for his crimes." He looked at her, his eyes dark and brooding. "I hung. I died. Or . . . they all thought that I did. Before I was taken up the steps to the gallows, I was given a drink to quaff. I didn't realize at the time that it was poison. I was dug free of a common grave while the crows were still picking at the other corpses. And they brought me to Genevar where my name was taken away. Now I am a kishion. And I have had my vengeance."

Cettie couldn't help but pity him for his tragic story. She had experienced her own moments of injustice. Memories of Mrs. Pullman were still raw and bitter to her.

This man had helped injure Fitzroy. He may even have been the one to kill him. She hadn't asked, for fear of the answer. But didn't she carry part of the blame for Fitzroy's death? She was the one who had helped them cross the mirror gate. Had she not played her part, her true father might still be alive. So she deserved, in the end, to die a traitor's death. Maybe that would be the best of all outcomes. But either way, his story moved her hard heart with compassion. Her anger softened, almost against her will. Her hatred began to shrink.

Together they stared at the sky, watching the sun go down. They were still standing there when the gong sounded across the compound.

~~~

"You didn't look very hungry last night," Jevin said as he approached her the next afternoon. They were in the gardens for their lesson. He had been unfailingly kind to her since her arrival. Always ready to explain something she didn't understand. It was a boon that he spoke her own language, unlike the other girls who still tried to befriend her. But

Cettie was attempting to learn Genevese, and she set down the book of grammar she'd been studying before his approach. While she knew magic could help her speak languages, she secretly wished she could find another way to escape, one that didn't involve dependency on a kystrel. And if she did, it would help to know the language of the local people.

"I was a little sore from jumping roof to roof," she admitted, rubbing her stomach.

"Why didn't you see the healers?" he asked with curiosity.

"I don't need to be cured of every ailment," she answered.

"It's not the pain that is troubling you, then," he said, sitting down on a stone wall a short distance from her.

She shook her head no, and he sat there, waiting for her to speak on her own.

Jevin was a very patient listener, which made it easier to tell the tale. "I had a long talk with my . . . father. You know his story?"

Jevin nodded sagely, still saying nothing. His brow wrinkled in concern.

"I don't want to become like him," she said. "I don't think . . . I'm very confident that I don't want to *kill* anyone. That puts me . . . in a difficult situation."

Jevin nodded again, looking at the ground. "You're not the first to have said those words in this place," he said. "And you won't be the last either." He smiled. "I don't think it was *wrong* that he killed the duke. And it wasn't wrong that the duchess had him executed for it. We each have motives for what we do. You'll probably find, as I have, that most people are petty, dishonest, and self-interested by nature. But that does not mean *you* have to be."

Cettie looked at him in concern. "What do you mean?"

"Have you ever heard the tale of Ankarette Tryneowy?"

Cettie frowned and shook her head.

"Her memory has faded over the centuries. She probably wanted it that way. You see, she was a poisoner who served one of the ruling families of Kingfountain. She became known as the queen's poisoner. She used her training . . . the skills she learned at a school like this in Pisan . . . to help *preserve* life. Yes, when someone tried to kill her, she would often kill them instead. But that wasn't her first instinct, and she was exceptionally clever. We're not training you to be a murderess, Cettie."

Her brow furrowed. "What *are* you training me for?" She knew she was to become a hetaera, but she no longer knew what that would entail.

He sighed and folded his hands together. "You're not ready to hear it yet. That will come in time. It depends on how well you adapt to life here. Your possibilities are only limited by your choices. Don't you wonder why we've made you test the limits of your endurance, especially your fears? I mean, jumping across to a rooftop would have been so much easier with a kystrel around your neck."

"But I don't want a kystrel," Cettie said forcefully, partly to counter the swelling urge for one that growled inside her.

"I wasn't suggesting you take one. I was only trying to make you think. If they can banish fear, wouldn't one be useful in such a situation?"

Cettie couldn't deny that it would have helped. "Yes."

"Emotions are what drive us. And they are inextricably linked to memory. Have you noticed this? The stronger the emotion, the more it impresses itself on the clay of our minds. You learned this at the maston school, no doubt, just as I learned it at the sanctuary where I was taught. Your earliest memories of feeling fearful, feeling desolate, are probably the strongest. When you become a hetaera, you will be able to *use* your own memories, your own past emotions, and inflict them on others. You will also be able to draw on the confidence you have gained here at the school. *Those* memories will empower you. Your fears will disable someone else."

Cettie's throat tightened. The ability to do this, to channel the emotions that had once crippled her, become more powerful for them, fascinated her. It made the itch in her mind grow stronger, something she'd experienced before, when handling the kishion's kystrel. "Could you . . . could you show me how it works?"

Jevin shrugged. "If you want."

His eyes began to glow silver.

CHAPTER TWENTY-NINE

KYSTREL

The sight of his glowing eyes made her remember the fear she'd experienced when her father had come for her at Vicar's Close in Muirwood. Part of her wanted to flee. It was a visceral reaction, an instinct that danger was near. Magic had always had its own music for her, and this tune was slightly dissonant and off-key. Still, there was undeniable beauty in the sound—a plaintive cry, a melody that made her want to weep.

"Tell me about the Fells," Jevin said, his eyes shining. "Something you remember. Something that made you afraid."

That was not a difficult request. She had feared the cesspit in the basement of the tenements. She had feared being slapped. Not because of any wrongdoing, but because Miss Charlotte was drunk and angry. But nothing had frightened her as much as the ghosts, particularly one of them. The tall one. Just remembering it brought back the cold shiver from the past. The prickling sensation on the back of her neck, the awareness that it was coming, and then the horror of its eyeless face. She knew what it really was, a Myriad One, but she was loath to reveal that information. Part of her still had a lingering loyalty to the Aldermaston of Muirwood and the training she had received there.

"That's a *strong* memory," Jevin said, nodding.

"You can feel it?" Cettie asked in surprise.

"Yes, my kystrel is like a bridge between us. You were very young. I cannot see what happened to you, but I can feel what was in your heart. Tell me more about this memory."

She didn't want to. She was always quick to drive away memories of that time. He was asking her to indulge in them, to summon them closer and examine them.

"Why?" she asked, her voice quavering.

"Because it has so much power over you," Jevin answered. "When we share a secret, when we share a trouble, its grip on us loosens. You'll see. Tell me."

Cettie's heart was beating frantically now, but she mustered her courage. "I was very young when I first began to sense them. Something inside me opened, and I realized there were . . . ghosts."

"Go on," he encouraged.

She felt sick to her stomach. "They terrified me. As I grew older, I could sense their thoughts. Their menace. They were always nearby, especially one. It was taller than the others. I couldn't see it clearly at first, but I sensed it. Like a shadow in the smoke. The older I got, the more vividly they appeared. The tall one kept coming back, even after I'd been moved to another place, as if it were hunting me."

"Your thoughts were summoning it, I think," Jevin said. "We always summon our fears to ourselves. That is because what we desire most is on the other side of fear. So this being, this entity—your ghost—kept coming for you. What happened when it found you?"

His words sent a whorl of emotions through her. As a young girl, she'd always tried running from it. Always. She'd never wanted to know more about the Myriad One. She'd only wanted it to go away. What did Jevin mean? Was he suggesting that she embrace it?

"When I was little, it . . . it kept trying . . . it wanted to *touch* me."

"Even though it wasn't real. Not a being of flesh."

"Yes. I would surround myself with . . . with the little ones. When they were near, it couldn't reach me."

"You used others to protect yourself. I see."

"It wasn't like that. They were a . . . barrier. But I always knew . . . I knew it would get me. When Fitzroy found me and brought me to Fog Willows, it even found me there."

"Up in a sky manor?"

"Yes. I thought I'd be safe there. But I wasn't." Mrs. Pullman had allowed the monster inside the sky manor. Memories of that awful woman flooded her, making the pain in her heart grow more intense.

"People always disappoint us," Jevin said. "It's sad but true. There are barriers at schools like Muirwood, though. It keeps such things out, but I'm sure it wasn't far away, seeking you out. It could hear you calling to it."

"But why? Why would it pursue me?" Cettie asked in frustration. She had faced it in the woods outside Muirwood. She'd banished it even. How many conversations had she had with Father about it? He'd always reassured her that she was strong, a beacon of light. That was the reason it was attracted to her. But she'd still feared the darkness inside herself. A darkness that was growing now.

Jevin reached out and touched her shoulder. "It was drawn to you because of who you are. Each of us is a mixture of dark and light." He removed his hand and pointed to the moon rising on the horizon. "In each world, there is perfect balance between light and dark. Always moving toward it and then away. You have always embraced the light part of yourself. You've shut out the other half of your nature." He shook his head sadly. "But all is in balance. You cannot deny the whole of who you are."

Part of her believed he was lying. But another part wondered if perhaps there was truth to his words. Life had seemed so clear and structured while she was living the way of the mastons. Now she had lost her bearings.

"So you've summoned your memories," Jevin said. "You've brought back that painful ghost from your past. You're that shivering little girl again, hiding amidst the younger children to protect herself. I can almost see it in my mind. The ghost is coming and reaching for you. And then—"

She felt it happen. Suddenly the fear was gone, almost as if it had been shoved out of her body. There was a tingling sensation inside her, a thrum of power. It was the Mysteries. She was not invoking the power, but she sensed it exuding from the kystrel Jevin wore around his neck. Her fear had been ripped away from her, replaced with a feeling of power, a feeling of confidence.

Cettie gasped at the suddenness of the transformation. Her mind reeled, but she thought she understood how the kystrels' magic worked, and the revelation made her shiver with excitement. "It's like a magnet," she said.

"A what?" Jevin asked in confusion.

"Magnetism . . . it's one of the Mysteries of Wind. I studied it at school. It's difficult to explain, but some iron is charged one way and some is charged another. They either attract each other or repel each other, depending on which direction they face." She rose and began pacing, her mind spinning dizzily. "When you used the kystrel, it turned my fears away. It *repelled* them from me."

Jevin nodded. "I don't know about magnetism, or the Mysteries, but yes, that is how it works. And in the same manner, you can take those emotions, whichever ones you choose, and make them *stick* to someone else."

Cettie nodded in assent. "Yes! This makes perfect sense. It is about repelling and attracting. There must be laws that govern it, of course. Too much distance, and I'll bet the force loses its potency."

Jevin stood as well. "A kystrel works best at close range," he said, nodding. "It is worn near the heart, the seat of the emotions. But its power is directed by the mind."

"Yes, of course," Cettie agreed. Her desire to wear one raged inside her. She was trembling now, not with fear, but with anticipation.

"Don't you see, Cettie?" Jevin said confidently. "You cannot deny part of who you are. Balance is essential in all things. I'm glad we had this chance to talk, but you shouldn't rely on others to inflict their beliefs on you. Even me. Experience is the most important tool you have."

A question struck Cettie's mind, so she asked it. "Why is it that the hetaera are all female?"

"I don't know," Jevin answered with a shrug. "It has always been so. Years ago there was a group . . . the Dochte Mandar . . . who used kystrels to gain power. But it took five men to achieve what one woman could. You are powerful, Cettie, in ways you do not yet understand. More powerful than the other girls studying here. That is why here, at this school, you are treated as nobility. We are all here to serve *you*. Yes, you might get shoved off a roof." He chuckled. "But to break is to be broken. That is an adage from long ago. I wish . . ." His voice trailed off in a sigh. "I wish you'd come to us when you were younger."

He gave her an apologetic smile, as if it were somehow his fault, and then left her. A few moments later, as she stood in the shadows of the trees, she heard the soft notes of his hautboie playing a new and melodic tune. Part of her admired Jevin's wisdom. And his words had made her feel important, respected even.

The urge for a kystrel dwindled inside her. The logical part of her wanted one to study—she wished to learn what it could do, what it was capable of—but another part of her warned all was not as it seemed. This idyllic garden was still full of deadly poison. And her interest in the ways of the hetaera made her feel guilty. The look in Caulton's eyes when she'd shown him the kystrel was unmistakable. He'd been shocked, fearful, and urgent. That part of the Mysteries' power was not to be explored. But why should it not be studied? Why were women more powerful in it?

Could this power be her rightful inheritance?

It gave her much to ponder.

Cettie was unable to fall asleep that night, and tossed and turned on her comfortable bed. That shouldn't have surprised her, but it did. The moon was obnoxiously bright and came in through the slats in the window shutters. She had remained awake long after the compound had fallen silent, as if part of her, unconsciously, understood it was coming back.

Cettie felt the prickle of awareness go down her back as she sensed the Myriad One in the hall. Her ghost. Just as Jevin had warned her, her own thoughts had compelled it. The last time she had confronted this apparition was after taking the Maston Test. The Mysteries had led her outside the boundaries of the abbey to an ancient oak tree with enormous branches that hung so low they brushed the ground. There she had learned its true name and used a maston spell to banish it. Something had happened to her during that experience, something that had awakened powers in her that she had not previously known she possessed. That day, she'd become a harbinger.

Because she was a harbinger, she'd learned Fitzroy was about to die. Why the Medium had chosen to kill such a good man, she didn't understand. She doubted she ever would. Resentment and bitterness always followed that thought. Yet those feelings did not erase the persistent notion that it was *her* fault. She was the one who'd brought his murderer to him. Had that been the goal of the Knowing? Why else would it have sent her the vision, if not to set off this exact progression of events? If it had left her alone, her father would be safe.

Had the Knowing done this to her as some sort of test? The thought filled her with horror, but there was no way to be sure. Either way, she could not help but feel the blame should be shared. That she alone should not bear it all.

Cettie squeezed her eyes shut, but only for a moment. She wouldn't wait for the Myriad One to accost her. Cettie tossed off the blankets and rose from the bed. Where was the maston chain? She had flung it into the corner, hadn't she? At least she would have some protection against it, even if she no longer believed as she once did.

Crossing the small room, she knelt in the corner, searching in the dark for the medallion. Groping yielded nothing. She couldn't see through the shadows, and there wasn't time to light a candle.

She felt the presence of the Myriad One at the door.

Frustrated, she rose and folded her arms over her breasts, determined to stand her ground.

Doors or walls made no difference to such a being. As she stood there, preparing to face the wretched being, a prickle of gooseflesh went up her arms. Her heart began pounding faster despite herself. Within moments, she was a child once more, assailed by the same fears, the same dread. She'd thought she was beyond this . . . she'd thought she was finally safe.

Was she to be tormented by this creature all her life?

At last, little one.

Its voice hissed in her mind as it passed through the door and into view. Oh, she remembered it well. She trembled, but squeezed her hands into fists and braced herself.

What do you want? Cettie demanded. She knew it could hear her thoughts. Then she sensed more of them coming. Not just the tall one, but several others. At least six more.

Why so many? The thought of facing one such being was daunting enough, but there were so many now. Cettie flinched and stepped back, only to strike the wall. She felt helpless, a tiny bird trapped in a cage. Weakness descended on her, ruining the feelings of strength and power she had experienced earlier.

What do you want? she demanded again, trying to summon her will. *You are helpless. You are vulnerable. You knew I would come.*

Cettie's breathing came faster and faster. "Get out," she said aloud. Then in her mind she said, *Banirexpiare.* It was the word of power that had banished this particular creature before.

A sinking feeling wrenched in her gut. Nothing happened.

By what authority do you command me? the tall one sneered. *You have forsaken your oaths. You are and will be a vessel. For all of us. For our queen. It is what you were born to be.*

"I will not," Cettie whispered, shaking her head.

You have no choice. Not anymore.

She felt them converge, joining together as one. Then she felt them ooze into her body. If only she had a kystrel. If only she had the power to repel them. Dizziness washed over her. It wasn't an unpleasant feeling, just a listlessness, a sensation of floating.

And with that feeling came memories that weren't her own. Wars that had been fought in ages past. Champions and heroes, villains and thieves. Worlds collided in her mind, and she felt herself black out from the overwhelming legions of thoughts. It was like being submerged in viscous oil.

When Cettie awoke, she was lying on hard cobblestones outside, cold and shivering in the dawn light.

And she had no memory of the rest of the night.

CHAPTER THIRTY

BETRAYAL

The clear notes of a hautboie began playing in the courtyard, which Cettie could see as she struggled to lift her head. Glancing at her arms, she realized she was wearing a dress she'd never worn before, one from the gallery of dresses. Worry and dread filled her insides. Why couldn't she remember what had happened? Something slithered over her legs, and she realized in horror that she was by the postern door in the wall.

A snake was moving across her body. She crawled away, biting back a scream, and the weight of it plopped off her. As soon as she was calm enough to move, she got to her feet and walked swiftly back to the poisoner garden. She held herself, shivering, and looked back at the wall. The Leering above the doorway was dark.

As she walked, she examined the dress. It was dark blue or violet— the color was difficult to judge in the early light. Colorful ribbons festooned the arms, and a lacy ruff topped the bodice. The boots on her legs felt sturdy and comfortable. She noticed a ring on the littlest finger of her left hand and gazed at it in disbelief. A silver band with a dark sapphire stone. It fit snugly. The disorientation was jarring.

A few images from the night before fluttered through her mind. They were not memories. At least . . . not hers.

Her hair was damp with dew. As she reached the garden, she saw Jevin sitting on the stone bench, playing his instrument. She walked past him, saying nothing, and returned to her room and changed into another dress, one that felt more like her. It took a moment for her to wrench the ring from her finger. She felt she had made an awful mistake the night before, but there was nothing to be done about it. Back in her room, she searched for the maston chain. If she wore it, would it even protect her anymore? She searched the entire room, over and over, until the gong sounded for breakfast. The medallion was gone.

She was grateful the morning meal was eaten in silence. The other girls looked cheerful and eager for the day; she felt as if the sky overhead was full of clouds. An oppressive weight had firmly settled on her. Guilt clashed with anger and despair. As she ate, her mind went to Adam, and she realized with crushing disappointment that he would never want to marry her now. She had broken her maston oaths. She'd succumbed to the Myriad Ones. Just thinking of him caused a stabbing pain in her heart and made the buttered bread and dried fruit inedible.

During combat training, she fought like a woman gone mad. No part of her held back now, and she felt no qualm about injuring the master—even accidentally. She saw the change in his eyes as he defended himself against her attack. Her energy and passion had impressed him. She managed to claw his cheek with her nails and felt a thrill of victory when she saw the blood dripping from her fingers. And then he kicked her in the stomach so hard she couldn't move and had to be dragged to the healing room.

After that training, the girls were brought to the outer courtyard. Archery butts had been arranged, and the students were given bows of various sizes and quivers full of arrows. The instructor was new, a somewhat short man with grizzled hair and beard, very trim and fit. Even though he spoke a language that—by their confused looks—none of them seemed to understand, he demonstrated the proper technique of fitting an arrow to the string, holding up the stock, bringing the fletching back, and releasing it. The girls all struggled, some of them even dropping their arrows while raising the bows.

The kishion watched them from afar, waiting, no doubt, for her to act. After regarding the other girls for a while, she gripped her stock, loaded an arrow, and sent it thudding into the dead center of the target.

The instructor nodded in approval and gestured for the other girls to look at her. Cettie drew another shaft, raised it, and sent it through the inner rings as well. Gasps of surprise came from the other girls, and the thrill of victory helped thaw the icy wedge in her heart. She glanced at the kishion and saw him nod in approval. That unspoken praise had a sour bite to it.

That night, after the sun set and the compound was quiet, the Myriad Ones came for her again. The only warning was the prickling of gooseflesh on her arms. Then her eyes rolled back in her head, and she felt the oily, sickening feeling of them taking over. It was a violation that she detested. But there was no way to stop it. She could not summon power from the Mysteries on her own anymore. A wall separated her from it.

It was a wall too high to climb.

Dawn found her again at the wall of the compound, wearing the same violet gown and boots. The same ring on her finger. It also brought the same melody from the hautboie. Cettie's despair thickened into a clinging, foul sludge. She scrambled to her feet, feeling exhausted. As she approached the garden, she stared at the various poisonous plants and experienced the compelling urge to break off one of the little purple leaves and put it on her tongue.

The melody abruptly ended.

"Cettie?" Jevin called from the shadows.

She had intended to go back to her room, but she stopped mid-step, shivering with chill and disappointment in herself. Turning, she approached him, her head down.

"I told you that you cannot leave the grounds," he said in an admonishing tone.

"I know that," she answered.

"Why do you keep trying, then? The Leerings won't obey you until you have the hetaera's mark."

She squeezed her eyes shut. "I'm not trying to."

Silence. She opened her eyes again and watched him set down the hautboie.

"The last two nights you have tried to leave," Jevin said softly. "*I've seen you.*"

"It wasn't *me*," Cettie said in despair, turning on him. "They're . . . inside me now. The ghosts I told you about. Only it's not just one anymore. There are seven or eight of them. I can't even think when they take over. I can't remember what I did last night. I can't stop them. And I can't stop myself." Tears blurred her sight. "I wish I were dead."

Jevin rose from the bench. "That is not what usually happens," he said, his mouth turning down. "I've not seen anyone react this way before. Are you hurt?"

"No," Cettie said, shaking her head. "I cannot make them go."

"You have an exceptional sensitivity to these things," he said. "Truly, it's remarkable. Can I explain what is happening? Or what I think is happening?"

Cettie had always felt unusual. Different. Why should this place be any different? The feeling of utter loneliness was overpowering. "Yes," she whispered huskily.

"These beings . . . these *ghosts* . . . seek to claim your body to use as their own. Each had a life once. They want to experience it again, using you as a vessel. Even with all its imperfections and ailments, they want to remember living. These beings are very dangerous. They will use you to their own ends."

"You encouraged me to accept them," Cettie said, glaring at him. "To face my fear."

"I did. But I had no idea you'd be this sensitive to their influence. How could I have known? We've learned, over the centuries, that their fits of debauchery are capable of ruining their hosts. Some even go mad. What use is a hetaera who goes insane? None," he said, shaking his head and coming closer. "No use at all. In the past, a hetaera would train with a kystrel and then go to a certain Leering in your old world. There she would brand the hetaera symbol to her shoulder, which would permanently bind a ghost to her body. In a sense, she would give up her identity to become a vessel for a stronger being." Jevin frowned. "Now it is different. The order has found a way to use kystrels to control the ghosts. Now you keep your thoughts, your identity, but you can harness *their* memories, *their* skills. If your ghost could once play a hautboie," he explained, "then you gain that ability. Usually, the bonding has always been one to one. One ghost per person. But you are so powerful, Cettie, that you can contain *seven?*" He chuffed. "I've never heard of the like before."

"What are you saying? That I'm a monster?"

"By the Fountain, of course not! You . . . you are special. You have powers that no hetaera in a generation has ever had."

Cettie felt her heart flutter at his words. She squeezed her eyes shut, trying to ignore the feeling of ambition they'd unleashed inside her. "They want me to free Ereshkigal. Their queen."

Jevin stared at her. "They *told* you this?"

"Yes."

He gave her a strange look.

"What is it?" she demanded.

He was frowning, deep in thought. "That is where Lady Corinne has gone. She's discovered the location of the Leering that has bound Ereshkigal. She's on her way there right now."

Cettie felt a strong sense of certainty. "She won't succeed."

"I can't say whether she will or not. It's been a great secret. One she had to commit murder to learn. I tell you, Cettie, truthfully, that these demons will haunt you and take possession of you every night for the rest of your life unless you bind them to your will. Only with a kystrel can you do this. They cannot pass the Leerings guarding this compound inside *your* body until you have the mark on your shoulder, but they have tried. They want to use you. You must use *them*."

The kystrel would protect her as the chain once had. She was certain of it. She knew she couldn't endure the rest of her life living under the Myriad Ones' thrall, imprisoned at the poisoner school. What if Jevin was wrong, though? What if accepting the kystrel did more harm than good?

"It's your choice," he said with a sigh. "No one can *make* you wear one. It has to be done willingly. But don't consider hurting yourself to be rid of them. To do so would only increase their power over you. I implore you to join us instead. Become one of us. Not as a slave. But as a partner in all that we have. My faith was like yours. Simple. Devoted. I believed in the Fountain and thought it blessed the righteous and harmed the wicked." He smiled sadly and shook his head. "I, too, was disappointed. I was betrayed. But now I have renewed hope. I see the good this order endeavors to do and how it will liberate the poor and the downtrodden from the intrigues of the wealthy and the arrogant. Cettie, this order is the only thing that can save you."

She listened to him, her mind taxed with fatigue. "I will think on it," she promised.

"That is all I ask," Jevin answered, bowing his head to her.

She returned to her room, not bothering to change out of the gown this time. She knelt by the bedstead and offered up a silent prayer. But she didn't believe it would be heard or answered. It was more a declaration of her intent.

Unless you send me a sign, a manifestation that what I have learned is not true, I will join with the hetaera and wear a kystrel. I cannot endure these ghosts any longer. I don't know why you have let them come back to torment me after all these years. I cannot bear it any longer. Why have you forsaken me when I only tried to obey? Show me a sign. Show it to me today. Show me that you care. Or I will join them.

Her fingers locked together, her heart heavy with sorrow. She waited in the stillness, trying to perceive even a flicker of light. Had she deluded herself all these years? Was her faith merely a result of the manipulations of others more powerful than her? Still she waited until her knees ached.

The gong sounded, announcing the time to gather and eat. She wasn't hungry. She wouldn't eat. She would hold vigil one last time, she decided. Give the Mysteries one last chance to reclaim her . . . if the power even wanted her anymore.

She doubted it did.

All that day, she participated in school as usual, ignoring her hunger. She went from one class to the next, silently communicating with the girls, who tried to teach her scraps of Genevese during the short breaks. Still Cettie waited, her mind open, listening for a whisper that bid her be patient. That told her she was cared about.

Nothing. Nothing at all.

As the sun set over the wall of the compound, she walked to where Jevin was playing the hautboie so movingly. Of all the people she had met at the school, she admired him the most. He was a skilled musician, a clever gardener. She respected his self-discipline, how he got up early every day, how attuned he was to the feelings of others, and how he never seemed to look out for himself.

He finished the song as she sat listening attentively.

"Would you like to learn the hautboie?" he asked her with a smile.

"I think I would," she answered. The shadows were stretching on the cobblestones. Dimming the world. "I've made up my mind."

He nodded and said nothing.

"I would like my own kystrel," Cettie said.

"Are you sure about this? We won't compel you."

"No, it's my decision." She pursed her lips, feeling sad but certain. "The Knowing doesn't want me."

Jevin sighed and nodded. "I know how you feel. When I came here . . . those were dark days. It's hard to accept that with such an ideal, no matter how much you give . . . it is never enough. The Knowing is never . . . satisfied. Well, there is another way to attain its power. And you've chosen it. I'm proud of you, Cettie. Well done."

He reached into the pocket of his black jacket and withdrew the small medallion. She recognized the shape, the whorl-like pattern. Picking it up, she let it dangle from the chain and stared at the symbol, the entwining bevels and twists that converged to a single point. She stared at it a long while, intrigued by the mystery of it. Such a small thing to have once made men so afraid.

Cettie slid it around her neck. Immediately, she felt a calm reassurance.

"There," Jevin said with a smile, arching an eyebrow. "How does it feel?"

A sudden insight struck her, something that had nothing to do with the kystrel. She voiced it. "I was engaged to a man back in Comoros. I wish I could have broken it off. To have freed him from me forever." She remembered the parcel she'd asked Becka to deliver. It would be painful for him to get it now. She wondered if there was a way to prevent it from being delivered. Well, a note would have to do. "He's . . . the kind of man who will wait. I wish he didn't have to." Then she recalled Fitzroy telling her about his painful search for the woman he'd loved before Maren. The memory evoked a strange familiarity with her own situation, but something had changed. It no longer caused her pain to think of Fitzroy. Blessed numbness had replaced the awful guilt.

"That's an easy enough matter to solve," Jevin said. He patted her knee. "Why don't you write him a letter. And I will make sure that he gets it."

General Montpensier is a cunning wretch. We made three attacks on the world of Kingfountain, and he has routed two of them. Possibly a third—we haven't heard from Admiral Grant yet. Our sky ships are lumbering back through the mirror gates to shore up our defenses, but Montpensier's fleet has already broken through. It is coming, I fear, directly to the City. He's been preparing for this confrontation for some time. The wedding, the armistice, was only a ploy. He will strike at us with his full force.

The empress, who was crowned this morning in a simple ceremony among the privy council, has commanded the evacuation of the City. The populace will be safe in the floating manors, and zephyrs and tempests are transporting as many of them as possible. Others are fleeing the City in droves. But we don't have enough time. There are simply too many people to move.

—*Asriel Durrant, Prime Minister*

SERA

CHAPTER THIRTY-ONE
THE LEERING OF EMPRESS MAIA

The first time Sera had come to Empress Maia's secret chamber was with a former prime minister, and he had brought her there attempting to intimidate her. Sera's memories of the place were tainted by that interaction. They entered through the room with the placard labeled 117. Beyond it, in the small, nondescript room guarded by two soldiers from the Ministry of War, hung an enormous mirror surrounded with Leerings that kept out anyone who lacked the proper clearance. This time, she passed through the enchanted glass with Durrant in tow, having greeted the captain and lieutenant stationed there.

The stone door guarding the atrium bore the face of the first empress's protector, her bodyguard. The scar on his face, the angry expression set permanently into stone still evoked the menace of the man. Sera gazed at that face, wondering about Maia's life, about the choices she'd faced. She, too, had stood against an attempted invasion, an enemy intent on destroying her beliefs, but what Sera was confronted with was much worse. A war unprecedented in scale. A war she feared might not end.

Sera willed the Leering to open, and the gruff face obeyed her, revealing the pleasant atrium beyond. Just as she remembered, the glow emanating from the Leerings in the ceiling was reminiscent of sunlight. A shallow pool lined with black and white tiles was flanked by couches for comfort. It was a pleasant room, one meant for solitude and quiet, and the power of the Mysteries seemed to emanate from everything within it. But her attention was drawn to the Leering propped on a pedestal beyond the pool.

"The first empress," Durrant said reverently. The Command Leering had, indeed, been given the former empress's visage.

"Yes," Sera answered, glancing at him.

"And she could control all of Lockhaven from here?" he asked.

"She could see out of every Leering in the City," Sera replied. "And from the closest mirror gate. The view out of whichever Leering is chosen is shared in the pool, so we can both see it."

"And you said that with this key," Durrant continued, fishing it from his pocket, "I can use this room as well?"

"Once I've granted you that authority. The key represents delegation. Now place your hand on the Leering."

Durrant's brow wrinkled as he stepped around the pool to approach the Command Leering. His expression was solemn, even stern.

As it should be. She approached the Leering from the other side, but Durrant reached it first. He raised his hand to touch it.

"Take off your glove, please," Sera said.

His eyes met hers. She saw a sheen of sweat on his brow, a look of nervousness. His mouth could not suppress an involuntary frown. But he did as he was bid and removed his glove before touching the Leering. He blinked rapidly, possibly from surprise that nothing had happened.

Sera removed her gloves as well and placed her palm on the other side of the Leering, keeping her eyes fixed on Durrant's as she invoked it.

"Before I grant you authority in this room, Mr. Durrant," Sera said, her voice edged with warning. "I must be certain that you are no enemy. I've trusted you for many years, but I've been deceived before. There is too much at stake now for me to take foolish risks. I also know that our enemies have the power of illusion. They can wear different masks."

"Your Highness, I don't believe that you—"

"Be silent," Sera commanded, and she felt the Leering send a shock of power up his arm to ensure he heeded her. "I abjure you, by the Mysteries, to state your true name. If you lie, even in your heart, this Leering will know, and it will strike you dead. There can be no deception between you and me. It gives me the power to know if you are speaking the truth." Upon inheriting the throne, the Minister of Thought had taught her this function of the Leering.

A dribble of sweat went down the side of his face. His eyes were wide with worry; his jaw trembled slightly. She released the power that had frozen his tongue.

"Now you will answer my questions. State your name. Your *true* name."

The tendons on his hand were taut, as if he were trying to pull his hand away. But he could not. The Medium had seized hold of him and would not let go until Sera released him.

"I am Asriel Durrant," he answered flatly.

She felt a pulse from the Leering, the comforting throb that truth had been spoken.

"Are you in league with General Montpensier in any way?"

His lips pressed together. "I am not, Your Majesty."

"General Montpensier has said that there is a spy in Lockhaven, a person who informs their court. Do you know who that person is?"

He sighed. "I do not, Your Majesty. And after we spoke about this the other day, I have already taken steps to try and discover the spy from Kingfountain. You are doing the right thing by questioning me."

"Have you had any involvement or business dealings with Lady Corinne?"

He shook his head no.

"Say it, Mr. Durrant."

"I apologize. I have not. I have been approached with opportunities by agents who I assumed were in her employ. After your disgrace. I was short on funds at the time, and my prospects were . . . shall we say . . . disadvantaged. I saw the invitations for what they were, an attempt to win my loyalty through bribery. I was . . . tempted. But I have a keen sense of self-interest, and I imagined that yielding to Lady Corinne in any way would put me in her debt. So I refused. They offered, in various guises, several times more. I refused every overture. And this I swear to you. No one save *you* binds my loyalty."

His words pulsed with truth.

"You never told me about the offers from Lady Corinne."

"I did not," Durrant answered. He sniffed. "I hoped that my actions would speak louder than any words. I also remembered what happened to your old governess, Hugilde. And how she was suborned against you." He smirked. "It pleases me to find out I was right about Corinne and her character. But she is far worse than I ever imagined her to be. And that is saying something."

Sera smiled in reply. "Then I give you, Asriel Durrant, my authority to wield the Command Leering on my behalf. You may use this key day or night in service of the empire of Comoros. And I charge you to let no one in this room without my express permission."

"I accept your charge, Your Majesty."

"Please continue to call me Sera."

"I will. It just felt too . . . solemn an occasion for it." He grinned.

Sera released the Leering's hold on him, relieved beyond measure that he had passed her test. He drew his hand away, shaking it as if the Leering had been excessively warm.

"Now let us see how far away our enemies are," Sera said. She placed her hand on the Leering again. So much had changed since she'd struggled to get them to obey her. Life had taught her many lessons, many of them forced on her. When she was younger, she had wanted to do her own will. She'd thought persistence would help her achieve her desire to become the empress. But it had not.

She'd learned submissiveness and self-restraint at Pavenham Sky, two traits she'd observed in Lady Corinne, which had given her greater power and influence. Only Corinne had not used the power wisely or for good purposes. Sera intended to take what she'd learned from Lady Corinne and use it for good purposes.

Even so, it struck Sera that the position she'd always coveted had not been granted to her because of anything she had done, wrong or right. The Mysteries had made her empress.

As Sera invoked the Command Leering once again, ordering it to show her the Leering at the front porch of her home on Kelper Street in the City, the waters of the pool began to ripple. The events she saw were happening at that moment. In the waters of the pool, she saw sky ships rushing up and down from Lockhaven. The evacuation order had been given hours before, and she was pleased to see how promptly it had been obeyed. She began to shift the view from Leering to Leering, from estate to estate, getting a look at all of it. The wealthy families who lived in the sky manors had been outraged by the command to house and shelter the displaced people from below. Sera had no patience to hear the complaints and had refused audience with them. The people were coming, as many as would fit.

Sera shifted her gaze to the Leerings at the gates of the City. The size of the crowds there defied comprehension. Each gate was swollen with people. Some with carts and wagons. Some with their meager possessions strapped to their backs. Children cried. Arguments broke out. She could smell the sweat and taste the fear.

"There are still too many," Durrant said in despair. "We'll never be able to evacuate them all in time."

"We should have started this days ago," Sera said, feeling her heart ache at the scene below.

"We didn't know days ago," Durrant said in frustration. "The general has been biding his time. We are totally unprepared."

Sera's gut wrenched. "Let's see how far away his ships are."

"Agreed. The latest intelligence I have is the fleets will be here by dawn tomorrow. Start with the mirror gate, if you will."

Sera invoked the magic, and the view in the waters changed to the mirror gate she'd traveled through days before. Ships of all shapes and sizes continued to push through. It was truly an armada. The mirror gate had been completely overrun by Montpensier's navy. As she shifted the view, she beheld the extent of the damage. The town there was occupied by foreign soldiers, the wharves clogged with cargo ships. The forces left to guard the mirror gate under Admiral Ballinger had been destroyed. She could see the wreckage of sky ships and sea ships befouling the waters.

"Look!" Durrant said in surprise. A hurricane floated in the sky in the distance, burning. Smoke trailed from its hull as the seabound ships below continued to launch volleys at it. She could hear the shriek of bombs as they arced into the sky and struck the massive sky ship. She saw several men tumble over the sides, falling toward the waves. From such a height, they would die on impact.

"Why is that ship still there?" Sera demanded worriedly. "We can't afford to lose hurricanes. And why didn't he destroy the mirror gate when he realized he was losing!"

Durrant was pacing, his face wrinkled with anger and emotion. "I agree. He left us completely vulnerable by not destroying it. What is Admiral Ballinger doing?" he snarled.

"Losing," Sera answered. "If we've lost our position there, we won't be able to hold the City for long."

Durrant looked at her in shock. "What are you saying, Sera?"

She changed the view, tracking the various Leerings stationed along the coast, from the mirror gate all the way to Lockhaven. There was a long line of ships coming in—supply ships, combat vessels. This was an all-out war, and Kingfountain had brought an invasion force sizable enough to do the job. They were going straight to the seat of Sera's power, to the hub of the wealth of the empire.

He wanted Lockhaven. He would burn the rest.

"We cannot *stay* here," Sera said, shaking her head. "We weren't prepared for this."

"Do you know how many millions are stranded down below?" Durrant said. "You'd abandon them? Leave them to their fate?"

"No, I'm suggesting we draw the fight to us. The wealth is up here, not down below. We will have to face this armada, but let's not do it where there are so many people. The City cannot move. But Lockhaven can."

"But what about the city defenses—the storms that can be summoned?" Durrant said. "It is why you are here, Sera. Why only a Fitzempress can rule. And we've never *tried* moving Lockhaven before. I'm not even sure it can be done."

"That is something we need to know. And yes, I fully intend to invoke the defenses," Sera answered. "But if we can, we must move away from the City. Montpensier is expecting us to defend our capital. He may already have a way of infiltrating. The empire is where *we* are. It isn't the City."

"Where could we go?" Durrant said, seething in frustration. "Across the sea? Will we let the invaders destroy the civilization we've spent centuries building?"

Sera gripped the Leering harder. "No. We're not fleeing. We're going to fight. But we cannot continue to fight the way we did in the past. We have to stop them from coming in. Admiral Ballinger didn't destroy that mirror gate, so we need to. It's too close to the City, and we can't wait for Kingfountain's breach of the covenant to destroy it when Fitzroy's allotted time there expires in a fortnight. Without a convenient place to retreat, Montpensier's navy will be trapped here. Then we use our ships to attack them at night and sink as many as we can."

Durrant rubbed his mouth. "But how will we close the gate? They've already taken the portal, and no doubt the general has left enough ships to defend it."

"We'll use Lockhaven to do it," Sera said. "We will try to move it at night when they cannot see us. By the time Montpensier's fleet arrives at dawn, we'll already be gone. They might be able to shoot down a hurricane. But I don't think they can shoot down a mountain."

CHAPTER THIRTY-TWO

DEFIANCE

The balance of power in the empire was a perpetual dance. Evidence of this was apparent in the taciturn scowls and resistance Sera and Durrant experienced inside the privy council chamber following their visit to the secret room. The council existed to counterbalance any reckless tendencies. And it was clear from the sour expressions in the room that they considered what she wanted to do reckless.

Durrant pitted his will and all his formidable skills of persuasion against the dissenters.

"The longer we debate this course of action," he said, mopping the sweat from his balding temple, "the less chance we have of succeeding. We have seen Montpensier's fleet coming up the coast. There is no time to dither! We still haven't heard from any of Ballinger's men yet regarding their defeat."

"We do not even know if the empress's plan is possible," Lord Welles said. There were many nods in response to his comment. Sera saw that he still had influence, if not power. "Lockhaven has not been moved in over a century. If one of the manors falls, only one, it could devastate the City and its inhabitants. The risk, Prime Minister, is grave. We saw what happened at Pavenham Sky."

Mutters of assent and concern followed the comment.

"There is a risk," Durrant conceded. "I would be lying if I said otherwise. But this happens to be the domain of the Mysteries of Law. Lockhaven was designed to wander. Empress Maia moved the court with her as she visited the various kingdoms under her authority. There are, Lord Welles, bonds and covenants that supersede those of the individual estates. It will move en masse. And surely we should *attempt* it before saying it is impossible."

Some other voices rose in agreement. Sera kept watch on who spoke, trying to determine who was with her and who was against. Clearly Welles was not on her side, but she had the loyalty of the advocates for Law after choosing Durrant as prime minister. The Ministry of Wind . . . if Fitzroy were here, then their allegiance would be fixed as well. But the look on the minister's face told her he was doubtful of her plan. Best not to ask for a commitment from him straightaway. That left . . . the Ministry of Thought. The Aldermaston was fidgeting uncomfortably in his seat. She believed he had no love or loyalty to Welles. His ministry was almost an afterthought to the old prime minister.

"What do you think, Aldermaston?" Sera asked. Though she trusted Durrant to argue in her behalf, he was new and so was she, and the resistance to her plan had been formidable thus far.

All eyes turned to the gray-haired minister. He looked discomfited by the sudden attention. "Excuse me?" he asked, blinking rapidly.

"The empress wishes to know your perspective on the matter," Durrant said, taking her lead. He clasped his hands behind his back, giving the man a probing look. "She has ordered that Lockhaven be moved to the mirror gate during the night. It's already nearly sunset. If we debate until dawn, then the plan will be fruitless."

"I heard the plan, Prime Minister," the Aldermaston replied with a huff of offense. "No need to repeat it on my account."

"I beg your pardon, sir," Durrant said.

The Aldermaston frowned and then cocked his head. "Moving Lockhaven from its position would require a most serious mind. A most deeply committed soul. And, need I add, one that is willing to submit to the will of the Mysteries. Is it not said in the tomes that if one has as much faith as the tiny seed of a water fir, they can say to a mountain, 'Move to yonder place,' and it *will* move? Is this not the principle by which Empress Maia fashioned the Leerings that keep Lockhaven afloat? Would it not take someone of her stature to move this mountain?"

At his words, a hush descended on the council. They all looked to Sera now, and she could see in their eyes the distrust and wariness. She had not done well at Muirwood. She'd always had trouble commanding Leerings back then. And the privy council knew it.

Sera felt a thistle of doubt prick her heart. Who was *she* to think that she could command Lockhaven to move, when a few years ago a Leering would hardly light for her?

"Well said, Aldermaston," Lord Welles concurred. He gave Sera a mocking smile.

A sickening feeling began to creep into Sera's stomach. She felt her own youth and inexperience. These men and women, these people who could ultimately countermand her wishes, were jaded and cynical. They had seen emperors come and go. There was one, Sera had learned about, who had been empress for only nine days during a particularly turbulent episode of civil war. The Minister of Wind was looking at Lord Welles, watching him closely, judging his merits. While they likely would not oust her after such a short reign, if the council heeded Welles's counsel, they would shift their allegiance to his ideas and begin ignoring hers, which would essentially transfer the power of the throne to him.

Hadn't the council begun to heed Fitzroy more than her father?

So Sera had to win their confidence. If she failed in her first attempt at ruling, it would be a disaster. Durrant glanced at Sera, and she saw his brows knit with worry. He, too, could feel the shift in attitude in the room.

"It may be more prudent to await Admiral Ballinger's return," said one of the other officers. "To hear firsthand of his defeat at the mirror gate. A timely delay may be best in such circumstances."

A few of the council members grunted in assent.

Sera felt the sickening feeling worsen. She had to do something. Her own feeling of helplessness, her lack of confidence was spreading. This crisis of confidence had happened to her before while facing the privy council, back when she and her father had been in competition for leadership. Why was it happening again? She'd been so certain her plan would work. Now she saw only the problems with it. The risks.

The uncertainty seemed to spread from person to person, like the cholera morbus.

Durrant rapped his knuckles on the table, hard and commanding. Everyone turned their eyes to him. His jaw quivered, as if he might start shouting. "There . . . is . . . no . . . doubt . . . in my mind," he said in a voice throbbing with passion, his knuckles knocking in time to his words, "that Sera Fitzempress is just such a woman as Empress Marciana Soliven. Maia's wisdom induced her to share her power with her privy council, it led us to this very moment. Well, hear my words, ye members of the privy council. I have known this young woman since she was but a child. I have tutored her and been tutored by her."

As he spoke, Sera felt a rush of warmth fill her. His heartfelt conviction was turning the mood in the room. He was giving her a chance to succeed.

"I have seen her grow from a young woman who struggled to light a Leering to one with complete mastery over the power. I've seen her face persecution with aplomb. She has the most serious mind, the most ardent spirit you will ever encounter. She is more fit for this duty than any who have preceded her in two centuries. I put my trust and my thoughts behind her. Just as each of you should. If you did not believe in her, why did you allow her to lead our people? Well, you might think, she *could* fail. And so she has. I would fear someone who hasn't ever taken a risk and lost. Wisdom comes from experience. The plan may fail. It may succeed. But we will never know unless we *try*."

He planted his palms on the table. Then he turned to Lord Welles. While Durrant's words were meant for everyone in the room, Sera felt they were especially directed at the old prime minister.

"In the end, it is not the critic who must bear the burden of such a heavy decision. No. That duty belongs to the one who wears the crown. The one whose knees shake but do not buckle under the weight of it. Yes, though sometimes our empress will come up short, it is not because of her height or her stature, but because of the awfulness of the task!"

He pushed away from the table, shaking his head. "You see, no real accomplishment comes without error and shortcoming. That is why we have someone who will strive to do great deeds. One who abounds with passion and enthusiasm. One who is devoted to more than personal ambition. One who bears *our* sins on *her* shoulders. One who will either know the triumph of achievement or . . . fail while *daring greatly*. This is what you chose her for, ladies and gentlemen. The least you can do is let her try to budge this hulking bit of rock. And I say that she *can*. I know it. I don't doubt it. And neither should you."

The transformation in the room was palpable. Durrant had won the council over with his impassioned speech. His words had not only quelled their concerns, but they'd calmed Sera's own misgivings.

"Then let us vote," said the Minister of Wind. "Let us vote to support the empress."

His choice of words showed his new allegiance. Sera wanted to grin at her victory. But she'd learned long ago to control her expressions. And she waited in anticipation as the vote happened.

It was unanimously in favor of her plan. Even Lord Welles grudgingly acquiesced.

Sunset. Darkfall. Orders had been given to cease bringing people up from the City. The sky ships were to moor themselves up on the manors. The land-based evacuation would continue for the rest of the night, trying to get as many of the people away from the City as possible.

Sera parted the window curtains and looked outside. Normally Lockhaven shone like a beacon during the night. Some called it the haven moon. But its glory had been muted. As she had ordered, the Light Leerings had all been extinguished. Officers of Law were being sent from manor to manor to enforce the rule, and soldiers from the Ministry of War had been gathered for battle. They would travel in darkness or not at all.

Becka answered a knock on the door, and soon Durrant was standing by the curtain with her.

"I've never seen it so dark," he said, his voice a reverent whisper.

"All must be quiet," Sera said. "When the fleet arrives, we'll be gone."

"We will," Durrant said smugly.

There wasn't much moon in the sky, but she could still see his face. "How long had you been practicing the speech you gave today?"

He pursed his lips. "Several years actually," he replied. "I thought I'd get to use it when you were sixteen. I've always fancied it, though."

"It was a splendid speech. You did well, Durrant. Even I believed it."

"You were its intended recipient. And Lord Welles. I won't forget the look on his face when he caved in. That triumph alone was worth it!"

"Thank you all the same. I needed to hear it at that moment."

He nodded, still gazing out the window. "I thought you might." He turned to her. "Throughout my career, I have been disrespected because I made my abode down below in the City. I could have worked solely in Lockhaven if I'd chosen to. Wealthy families require good advocates to represent their interests. Your mother, for example. But I wanted something more. Not just for personal ambition—mind you, I have plenty of *that* to spare!—but because I saw an opportunity to change the way society had become. I wanted to bridge the gap between. Even though I lived among the poor, I wasn't any less intelligent than the advocates who worked in the sky estates. Less spoiled perhaps. Less vain. But their education wasn't any better than mine. Ever since I was a young man studying at the abbeys, as you did, I discovered how we infect each other with our thoughts."

His expression was solemn. "In my youth, I was ridiculed because of my lack of physical strength. My skill was always with my mind. At first the words smarted, but I became determined not to heed the negative thoughts of others. I would harness what I had learned to better the lives of the people surrounding me. I saw in you a bright prospect. I thought, if I could just harness my life to her star . . . I could really do something!" He turned his head, giving her a serious look. "You are the right choice for empress, Sera. I wasn't trying to flatter you. If you are going to win this war, it will be because you refuse to give up. There will be casualty reports that will sicken and dishearten you. Much will be lost in terms of lives and wealth. On both sides. Once begun, we cannot look back. You cannot flinch. I think you have the mettle for this. Prove me right."

"I will do my best," Sera said, nodding in agreement. She had a dark feeling, a suspicion that once the war began in earnest, it would be difficult to stop. There was much resentment on both sides. But come what may, she was determined to see it through to the end. Her husband was probably a hostage to General Montpensier's Espion.

Durrant glanced back out the window. "I haven't seen any zephyrs come up. I think the last ones are being secured in the landing yards. We'll be ready to depart soon. We should make our way to the Command Leering."

Before leaving the room, Sera reminded Becka to keep the room darkened. She then strode down the inner corridor, which was lit as dimly as her chamber. The Leerings had all been deliberately muted, the curtains were drawn, and inspections from outside revealed that no light could be seen. When they reached the Leering room, her eyes were momentarily blinded by the radiance. She let them adjust and then positioned herself in front of the Leering shaped like Maia.

"It is time," Durrant said, nodding to her.

Drawing upon the confidence she'd felt in the privy council meeting, Sera reached out her hand and touched the Leering, invoking it. She felt the throb of the Mysteries in her heart. There was no longer any worry, no longer any doubt. No hesitation.

In her mind's eye, she pictured the mirror gate she had been to, the high arch nested amidst the sea. *Take us there,* she commanded with her thoughts, visualizing Lockhaven hanging in the sky above the gate.

A shudder rippled up from the stones beneath her, shaking her legs. The queer sensation of movement brought a little tickle to her stomach.

"It's working," Durrant said with a victorious smile.

CHAPTER THIRTY-THREE

BROKEN VEIL

Lockhaven raced against the coming dawn. After Sera had commanded the hovering mountain to move to the mirror gate, it had proceeded on its course without any further direction from her. But she could not control the pace of its flight. She and Durrant left the secret chamber and watched the floating city's progress from the windows of the royal palace. It was steadier than traveling by hurricane or tempest, but there were gentle rocking motions whenever they entered areas where the winds were fiercer.

Still, they were not going quickly enough to ease her worry that they would not reach the mirror gate before the dawn exposed them.

Montpensier's fleet would continue to wreak havoc on her shores, but removing the mirror gate would ultimately cripple his assault. Without an easy way back, without supplies and reinforcements, the force he had sent to invade the empire would be left undefended. Firm in her conviction that she was doing the right thing, she tried to sleep on the couch and gave orders that she was to be awakened immediately if there were any problems.

As she lay on the couch, beneath a blanket Becka had draped over her, her mind went back to the night of her wedding. The night

Montpensier had decided to seize the Argentines' authority for himself. She'd lost track of the number of days that had passed, but she was worried about her husband. Was he imprisoned in his own castle? Had he been executed? Not knowing made her heart ache and worry. Even if she managed to save him and his family, she wasn't sure what the future would look like for them. She was the empress now. Going back to live in Kingfountain was no longer a reasonable option. He was the heir of his own world. She of hers. If she could crush Montpensier quickly, might there still be a chance to co-rule both worlds with Trevon? Or would a bloodbath harden both populaces against the idea of a union? With all the thoughts tangling in her mind, she drifted to sleep.

Becka roused her what felt like minutes later, but she could see bright light streaming in from the curtains. Rubbing her eyes, she sat up.

"The prime minister is here," Becka said, rubbing Sera's shoulder.

"Is it dawn?"

"Yes."

Sera worked out a kink in her shoulder and then rose from the couch. Durrant's eyes were bloodshot. He looked as if he hadn't slept at all during the night.

"What news?" Sera asked him worriedly.

"We're not there yet," Durrant said, an edge in his voice. "Our cartographers suggest we'll be there within the hour, but we'll be fully exposed to daylight. There aren't any ships beneath us at present, but the Leerings at the mirror gate suggest a reserve has been kept to secure the portal. They will see us coming, Sera."

"What options do we have?"

He scrubbed at his scalp. "We can send the sky ships ahead to engage the fleet below. In order to successfully strike at them, we need to go low enough to be within range of their cannons. Reports from the City reveal that the bulk of Kingfountain's fleet is poised to attack

them at dawn. Whatever we do, we must do quickly. But there is . . .
a suggestion."

"I'm ready to hear it," Sera said, squeezing his arm.

"Some of the floating manors, Fog Willows for example, have powerful defenses capable of generating a cloud beneath the manor, concealing it from the sight of those below. I tried myself to summon one,
but was unsuccessful. We thought *you* might give it a try. Not a storm.
Just some clouds to disguise our approach. When it's time to attack
Montpensier's fleet, if you think you could bring more than a drizzle . . .
well, that would be ideal."

"I will do my best," Sera said. She nodded to Becka and then followed Durrant into the dimly lit corridor and hurried to the command
room. There were many people up and about, servants preparing for the
day and soldiers awaiting orders. When they reached the private door,
they found Lord Welles waiting outside. Just the sight of him made Sera
feel a stab of resentment.

"Ah, Your Majesty," he said when he saw them approach. "I wished
to consult with you about attacking the rearguard left to protect the
mirror gate. I believe we can destroy it with an acceptable loss of ships.
I would like your permission to launch the attack now."

"I've discussed this option with her already," Durrant said. "She's
elected to try the other approach first."

"As much as I respect your judgment, Prime Minister, this is a
military engagement, and the Ministry of War should be the first to act,
the first to risk. We don't know what will happen should their cannons
fire volleys at us."

"I imagine any cannon blasts will dislodge boulders, which will
come crashing down on them," Durrant said with a broad smile. "Our
hull is not made of wood, sir."

"Keep your forces at the ready," Sera said, nodding at Durrant to
open the door. "When I'm ready to commit them, the order will be
given."

She saw in Lord Welles's eyes that he wanted her to invite him inside. He had enjoyed the privilege of accessing the command room during his own time as prime minister. To be excluded at such a moment was obviously tormenting him.

"That is all, Lord Welles," Sera said dismissively, pausing at the doorway.

He struggled with his composure a moment, then bowed to her and vacated the hall with an indignant look.

Sera led the way into the command room, and Durrant followed. After the outer door shut behind them and they passed through the mirror frame into the inner sanctum, the prime minister rubbed his ear and shook his head.

"You handled him well," he complimented.

"I don't trust Lord Welles. I don't think I ever will again. We need another commander."

"Changing leadership on the brink of war isn't advisable."

"I know," Sera answered. "I'm just telling you my mind. I'll be watching the officer corps. You do the same. Any news from Admiral Grant yet?"

"None, Sera. It appears none of his ships survived. Not a single zephyr has returned."

Sera scowled at that. Three admirals had been sent into Kingfountain with at least half of the empire's force. All three had failed. This was why Lord Fitzroy had chosen to defend instead of attack. At the time, it had been the right strategy, but Sera knew she could not afford to let Montpensier consolidate his power.

The room was brighter than the dawn sky beyond it. She approached the Command Leering respectfully, then bowed her head as she rested her hand on it. The storm cloud in her imagination surfaced in the pool of water. Durrant pressed his hand opposite hers.

A surge of power thrummed up her arm and through her entire body, several magnitudes stronger than what she had experienced before. The thrum of the power felt like pinpricks of painful awareness.

"Do you feel that, Durrant?" she whispered, eyes opening.

His face was somber. "I do. What's happening?"

The power was so much greater than it had been. The entire citadel nearly hummed with it. Why?

The answer came in a flash. The Leerings in the citadel were responding to the proximity of a greater magic. A magic that went beyond what normally manifested in the physical world, like the literal manifestation of the Deep Fathoms she'd seen while traveling through the mirror gate between Kingfountain and Comoros.

That insight unlocked something inside her mind. It was as if a massive door had hinged open, spilling light into a darkened cave. She squinted against it, in awe of the power that had been unleashed. Then she felt the powerful awareness of another mind. Not the Knowing. No, it was the *presence* of Empress Maia herself. Sera felt tears in her eyes. Something was connecting them, weaving their thoughts together as one.

The information didn't come as words, but as bursts of ideas.

Montpensier's treachery had violated an ancient covenant. Sera could feel the empress's displeasure for what he had done. It was similar to the displeasure she felt that her own society had altered in such a way, with the powerful preying on the weak. The cholera morbus had been but a warning to change. A punishment sent. A reminder given. Now another punishment was coming. A plague of war.

In Sera's mind, she saw clouds gathering in the sky over the mirror gate. She felt Lockhaven tugged toward it, like a whirlpool. The stones seemed to quake under her feet as the speed of the hurtling sky city increased dramatically. Was she summoning this power? No—but yes, in a way she was . . . It was her power, her authority, that had triggered the Leering. Sera thought about tugging her hand away, but she realized she would not be able to. Her hand was fused with the stone, the Mysteries binding the two together.

In the pool of water, she saw the rearguard of Montpensier's fleet. The sailors' mouths parted as they looked up at the sky. There had not been any clouds before, but now the sky was teeming with them, huge billowing monstrous clouds. Cracks of thunder began to ripple, the sound brought to her through the Leerings on the gate. Then a jagged shard of lightning danced across the clouds.

Sera's heart swelled with dread as the storm grew bigger and bigger. Rain began to pelt the crews below. Sera hadn't summoned clouds to enshroud Lockhaven—they were filling the sky above the fleet, drawing all eyes upward. Heavy drops of rain began to plummet, followed by rock-sized pieces of hail. The ocean seethed with the impact, the waves jabbed by the plummeting ice. The storm struck the timbers of the ships, shredded sails, and snapped off the yard arms that held them in place. Some sailors screamed in pain, trying to scamper away and find shelter belowdecks. Others braved the ravaging hail, holding on to ropes or rails to keep upright while the ships rocked beneath them.

The pressure on Sera's mind was intense. She felt herself growing dizzier as the scene unfolded. Then she heard a cry, a shout of warning. The sailors were pointing off in the distance. Lockhaven could be seen on the horizon, advancing toward them. Jagged streams of lightning arced down from the massive rocks. The sight was so daunting it even filled Sera with fear. Mass panic broke out below. Shouts were given, screams to flee that she only understood because of the magic throbbing inside her.

Lockhaven was coming to destroy them.

Sera felt the power swell as the citadel came ever closer to the mirror gate. It was drawn to it, as surely as an iron bar to a magnet. Something would happen when the citadel arrived. She wasn't sure what—

Her thought was answered by the intelligence of Maia, who was still with her, invisible but omnipresent. The mirror gate would shatter, but an opening would form between the worlds. She could see it in her mind—the orange clouds of sunrise on one side, the dark of night on the other. The rift would open in the sky. Large enough even for Lockhaven to pass through. High enough that only a flying craft could reach it. Sera's fleet could pass through, but Montpensier's could not.

"Are . . . you . . . seeing . . . this?" she gasped to Durrant.

His single-word reply was hoarse. "Yes."

The veil between the worlds was breaking.

Lockhaven shook with power. And in the pool, she watched as it continued its approach, all its Leerings blazing brighter than a noon-day sun. As soon as the sky city arrived at the point to which she had commanded it, there was an explosion, a sound of shattering rock. The mirror gate had collapsed. Some of Montpensier's fleet had been in the midst of escaping, and the vessels were crushed beneath the falling stone. Everything caught beneath it was devastated. Only splinters and corpses would remain.

Sera could no longer hold her head up. She was slumped against the pedestal, though her hand was still transfixed to the Leering. She wanted to stop the deaths, but she couldn't, and she wept as she witnessed what was happening in the pool.

"Can you hear me, Durrant?" Sera whispered.

She sensed he had collapsed on the floor and was totally unconscious. Would the same happen to her? Her eyes were shut, her own awareness fading. The thought had no sooner passed through her mind than Sera felt a hand graze her hair—a solid, physical hand.

A voice whispered in her mind.

This you must see. This you must know.

Sera felt the pressure of the palm pressing on her head. In her mind a vision opened. She saw an abbey nestled in a mountainside, surrounded by a huge range of mountains that stretched for miles. It was a small abbey, a little speck of bleached stone against the dark gray rocks.

This is Cruix Abbey. This is where I trapped her.

The perspective shifted, the abbey growing in size until Sera was somehow just outside it. A zephyr bearing the sigil of Pavenham Sky was concealed in the mountains. Knowledge filled her. Lady Corinne was there at that moment. The perspective shifted again, and suddenly Sera was deep inside a vault hidden within the depths of the mountain beneath the abbey. There was a Leering there, one that Maia had made. It was the tomb and prison of Ereshkigal, a being of pure evil. And there, kneeling and weeping before it, sat Lady Corinne, arm outstretched, palm on the Leering.

As Sera saw her, Lady Corinne's head lifted. Their minds were joined for just a moment, and the intensity of the hatred she sensed there shocked Sera to her core.

I see you, Corinne thought, glaring at her savagely.

She cannot unbind the Leering. Only you have the right. She will come for you.

With that warning, Sera's hand was freed from the Command Leering, and the vision collapsed around her, ending with a shriek of frustration from Lady Corinne.

Sera slumped to the ground, darkness smothering her.

Those were the last words she remembered.

She will come for you. She will come for you.

CHAPTER THIRTY-FOUR

SURRENDER

It was a strong smell, a disgusting one, that roused Sera from her state of unconsciousness. As her eyes fluttered open, she realized she was back in her chamber. Becka, Durrant, and the court doctor were gathered at her bedside. The doctor was already capping the vial, removing the foul stench from her nose, and Sera shuddered involuntarily, gagging slightly.

"Her eyes are opening," Durrant said eagerly. His eyes were bright and hopeful.

"Give her a moment, Prime Minister. Your Highness, can you hear me?"

"What was that noxious odor?" Sera asked, struggling to sit up. Her arms and legs felt completely drained, and a wave of dizziness nearly toppled her back down.

"*Hammoniacus* salts, Your Majesty," said the doctor. "Although the odor is powerful, it is harmless."

Sera blinked rapidly. "What day is it?" She looked toward the curtains. They were pulled open, revealing a dark night stippled with stars, along with a strange purple glow. As her vision cleared, she realized what she was looking at—an eye-shaped wreath of clouds emanating sunlight. The rift. It was still open. As she watched, transfixed, a hurricane passed through.

She bolted upright in excitement.

"The rift is still open?"

"It *is*," Durrant said, his voice exuberant. "The mirror gate is shut, but this one—the one *you* opened, Sera—is holding fast. Lockhaven is keeping it open, I think, otherwise it would have shut the moment you passed out."

Sera rubbed her eyes, then looked at her arm. She was still wearing the same gown. "But what day is it? How long have I been unaware?"

"You've been unconscious for the better part of a day," the doctor said. "Some advised it was best to let you rest until you awakened, but the privy council feared you might be incapacitated."

"All blather," Durrant snorted. "What happened to you in that room was beyond anything I've experienced. But the privy council is eager to see you on your feet again. Much has happened during the course of the day. Do you think you can stand?"

"I should like to try," Sera answered. Becka quickly stripped away the bed covers, and the two men retreated a few steps.

"Take my arm," Becka said. Sera did so, wincing as she sat forward with Becka's help. Her stomach made some noisy gurgles, reminding her she had not eaten all day.

"Maybe some juice or tonic," the doctor suggested. "You still look very pale." He was an older man, his bald head fringed with gray hair. She found herself wishing Adam were there instead. But he had left to see to Anna's health. She hoped he'd found her well enough to return her to Fog Willows.

"Some juice, I think," Sera said. Now that her legs were hanging over the edge of the bed, she felt even more wobbly. She held on to Becka until she was ready and then forced herself to rise. She swayed a bit, but her maid was quick to steady her, and then the room felt solid again.

The doctor went to a side table, which had been brought over from across the room for his supplies. He secured a cup and brought it to her. Sera looked at the contents first and then took a sip. It was a mild pear juice, thickened with syrup.

"Should I send word to the privy council that you're on your way?" Durrant asked.

She nodded, then took another sip as she watched the prime minister leave the room to relay the information.

"May I feel your pulse, Your Majesty?" the doctor asked.

"Yes." Sera extended her arm, and the doctor squeezed her wrist with his meaty fingers. Her pulse was throbbing in her temples by this point. She was impatient to get back to the chamber. Her final vision, the one of Lady Corinne at Cruix Abbey, was stark and pressing. A whole day had passed. A day!

"It is strong," the doctor said, releasing her. "I don't see any reason why—"

"Thank you," Sera said, interrupting him, and stood abruptly. Her legs trembled, but she was not going to pass out again. Becka gave her a worried look, but Sera shook her head, indicating she felt fine.

Durrant, who had returned to the room and stood by the door, took her by the arm and escorted her out of the room.

"We'll walk slowly," he suggested.

"Did you see the vision at the end?" she asked him, keeping her voice low. "The one of the abbey?"

"No, Sera. I'll admit that I fainted."

"I thought as much. Empress Maia shared a vision with me. It was of an abbey on the continent . . . Cruix Abbey. I want you to send some armed men in a zephyr there immediately. I want them to secure the abbey. Lady Corinne may still be there. If so, she is to be arrested at once. Then have a tempest and an escort prepared. I'd like to go there myself in the morning."

His eyebrows twisted together with concern. "I don't understand."

"Lady Corinne is at Cruix, or she was when I had that vision. I know what she is after—and she also knows something about me. Durrant, this is of critical importance. That abbey must be secured, and Lady Corinne must be apprehended."

"Of course!" he said, bobbing his head in agreement. "I'll dispatch some men straightaway. What did you see?"

"I will tell you later. What has happened since I fell unconscious?"

"Admiral Grant has returned," said Durrant buoyantly.

"How did he know where to find us?" Sera said in confusion.

"He didn't. He was on the other side of the . . . the portal . . . the sky gate, whatever you want to call it. His foray into Kingfountain was much more successful than that of the other two admirals. He struck initially at Legault and seized the capital. The forces Montpensier left to defend that quarter were inadequate as the duchy of Brythonica is under full revolt. He has spoken to the Duke of Brythonica and one of Prince Trevon's brothers, both of whom went to Legault to meet with the admiral. He negotiated a sort of temporary alliance with them, for we share a common enemy, but when he came back to the mirror gate to help Admiral Ballinger, he found Ballinger dead and the mirror gate heavily guarded. His forces were in a dire situation, cut off in their ability to retreat. And then . . . in his words . . . the sky opened like a flower at dawn, and he could see Lockhaven poised at the other end—" He positively beamed with delight.

Sera had struggled not to interrupt him, but she succumbed to temptation at last. "Trevon's brother? Which one? Is he here?"

"Give me a chance to explain, Sera. Prince Kasdan."

Sera's eyes widened in shock. "He was the one who went missing after the wedding ceremony."

"Yes, the very one," Durrant said. "He explained to Admiral Grant that he was *abducted* by men serving the Duke of Brythonica's daughter, who had come with her for the ceremony. I believe he and the duke's daughter are betrothed?"

"Yes, I think so."

Durrant nodded. "Somehow she knew about Montpensier's plot, or she recognized it in time. After her men abducted him, the two royals concealed themselves and didn't leave with the rest of the family, trusting that Captain Remmer would keep everyone safe. Apparently, that did not happen. The king and queen were executed for crimes against the people."

Sera's stomach lurched, and she looked at Durrant in astonishment. "I cannot believe it!"

Durrant sighed. "Who can be sure what is false and what is confirmed? One thing we know for certain is that a civil war is underway in Kingfountain. Montpensier has been named emperor, and he is quelling the opposition violently."

She dug her fingers into his arm. "What about Prince Trevon?"

"Prince Kasdan does not know his fate. He fears the entire royal family may have been put to death."

She'd feared the same, but it felt worse to hear that Kasdan, Trevon's own brother, believed it.

"Is Kasdan here?"

Durrant shook his head emphatically no. "No, they're not going to put themselves in our hands, even for a conference. People from our empire have been murdered over there with no thought to age or situation. It's been a massacre."

Sera's heart throbbed with fury. Why hadn't Trevon's parents dealt with Montpensier sooner? But the anger immediately gave way to sadness. Dread. His parents were dead, and he might be too.

"Where is Admiral Grant now?" Sera asked.

"He's waiting for you at the privy council. What say you, Your Highness, do we strike an alliance with Brythonica? Do we dare?"

She remembered the Leerings she had seen in the sea caves in Ploemeur. There was some hidden history between the worlds, a secret she didn't understand. But her instincts urged her to trust it.

"I will dare much," Sera said, remembering the words from her vision and Durrant's speech. "I will dare greatly."

The words she had heard from Empress Maia rang in her mind. War was coming. A blight of war.

Admiral Grant was a heavyset man with a blocky face, a thick beard, and a full head of hair. He wore his officer's jacket open at the collar, several of the buttons undone. His eyebrows were very thick and prominent, his nose was a rugged slope, and two creases joined between his eyes, giving him a narrowing look, as if he distrusted everyone and everything around him. They had never met before, but he was one of the men Lord Welles had suggested as the new prime minister. He was younger than Lord Fitzroy had been and had risen through the ranks during the time before the armistice.

He also had the terrible habit of giving her very brief answers.

"And how do you know it was Prince Kasdan you met?" Sera pressed, trying to keep her frustration in check. "And not an imposter."

Admiral Grant gave a curt little shrug. "I don't."

"So this possible alliance may be a deception?" Sera pressed.

"Could be."

Sera frowned. "Tell me what he looked like."

Admiral Grant scratched an eyebrow. "Either he is deceiving us or he isn't, Your Majesty. If he is, then we'll conquer Brythonica too." Blunt. Straightforward.

"Where did you get your information about what happened in Kingfountain?" Sera asked next. "Prince Kasdan wasn't there to witness it."

"He was not," Grant agreed. And then he remained silent.

"Admiral Grant, do I have to peel this onion layer by layer, or are you going to contribute to the conversation?"

The admiral wrinkled his nose and sniffed. "I'm trying to say as little as possible, Your Majesty."

"I can tell that. Why?"

Grant shrugged. His serious blue eyes met hers. "Because there is likely someone on this privy council who is in league with Montpensier. Or someone very near to it. The less I say, the better."

His words caused audible gasps throughout the room. Admiral Grant hooked his thumb in his belt, looking just as unconcerned as he had before. Then the murmuring began, the sidelong looks, the accusatory glares. Sera knew the general had claimed to have a reliable Espion in her court, but she hadn't thought it possible the person could have penetrated so high.

Sera could see the reason he was so circumspect. She smoothed the velvet arm cushion of her chair. "Do you know who it is, Admiral?" she asked in a low voice.

Admiral Grant pursed his lips. "If I did, they wouldn't be in this room right now. Montpensier knew we were coming. He knew which mirror gates each of us would use. We were all ambushed after we crossed." His words caused a sinking feeling in Sera's heart. Was Cettie using her gifts against them now? "I'm awaiting your orders now, Your Majesty. Legault is taken. There are three hurricanes hovering over its capital right now. I don't imagine the general will allow that for long, and I don't have enough soldiers to hold it unless you authorize reinforcements."

"Done," said Sera. "Hold what you've taken, Admiral. Then take some more. The goal is General Montpensier himself, not a particular city." She would never call him emperor, even if he'd found someone else to lead his fleet into battle. She leaned forward. If the spy was truly in the room with them, then she wanted her message to ring in their ears. "You will engage him until he has unconditionally surrendered. Or until he is dead."

Admiral Grant was unmoved by the vehemence in her words. "As you command."

Dawn came once again. It was strange seeing a different sky, always a mirror of her own, through the rift. After nightfall, Durrant had given her a suggestion of what to name it. The idea was inspired by Lord Fitzroy's journal. *Let's call it a Prism Cloud,* he'd suggested. *Look at all the different colors.*

As Sera stared at it, she saw sky ship after sky ship move inside the rift. No one, including Sera herself, knew how long it would remain open.

Montpensier's fleet had started ravaging the City as soon as they realized Lockhaven was missing. But then word had reached them that the closest mirror gate was closed, and they'd scattered to the four winds. Sera's fleet had hammered the remaining forces, tempests and hurricanes hunting down the ships. There were no offers of surrender. No survivors captured.

Sera wore a thick gown and cloak. She'd been told that Cruix was in mountains that were often bedecked with snow. Durrant had found nothing in the tomes to indicate Cruix was any different from the other abbeys situated throughout the realm. Was there something in its history that had been meaningful to Empress Maia? Something lost to the ages, perhaps?

Could this be where Sinia, the Kingfountain Wizr, had been imprisoned?

An escort had been arranged, but Sera had insisted it not be a large one. Though it was not a good time to leave Lockhaven, Durrant would remain behind to act on her behalf in the war effort. She wanted to visit Cruix in person so that she could use the Tay al-Ard, which she'd taken to wearing strapped on her forearm, to return in an instant if need be.

She could not allow Lady Corinne to keep tampering with the Leering that held Ereshkigal.

The door cracked open, and she could hear a familiar voice arguing with the guards stationed there. Adam Creigh. Her quick judgment of the situation indicated that he had been forbidden to see her.

She hurried toward the door.

"Your Majesty," Adam said with obvious relief.

"When did you get back? What is the trouble?" Sera said. The guards looked abashed.

"Just a little disagreement," Adam said, but he did not accuse them of worse. "I just returned from Fog Willows." He reached into his pocket and withdrew a letter. "This had just arrived." His face showed deep concern, even anger. She didn't think she'd ever seen him this agitated. A letter. Who could have written something that had wounded him so deeply?

His next words said it all. "It's from Cettie."

CHAPTER THIRTY–FIVE

LOST

Sera shut the door to her rooms, her already taut nerves thrumming with the potential for new disastrous information. Adam stayed near the entryway, pressing his palm against an end table in a way that would take some of the weight off his leg.

"How are your wounds healing, Adam?" she asked him. She'd taken the letter already, but part of her resisted opening it.

"I'm not a very patient patient," he replied, a quirk of a smile surfacing on his mouth for just an instant. Then it was gone, his brows needling together. He glanced at Becka, who was putting some books away that Sera no longer had need of. "Good morning, Becka. Are you well?"

"I'm quite well," she replied, bowing her head, wiping her hand along the cover of one.

"You came from Fog Willows, you said?" Sera turned the letter over in her hands. "How is the family? How is Lady Maren?"

"Don't you want to read it?"

"I do, but I dread what I will find here. Tell me of the family first."

Adam sighed. His expression became even more grim, if that were possible. "Lady Maren is in mourning, as you can imagine. She did get the message the prime minister sent and was grateful for it. There is an abiding sadness at Fog Willows that wasn't there before."

"I should have sent another letter myself," Sera said, shaking her head. "I will. I still intend to."

"I think it would be appreciated. But not expected. You are very busy."

Sera felt the ache of loss herself. How she had respected Lord Fitzroy! "Were all her children around her? How is Anna?"

Adam nodded. "Anna has been very sick recently, but she appears to be recovering. She was staying at Gimmerton Sough and being treated by the Patchetts' doctor, but I brought her back to Fog Willows with me. She is still very weak. I suspect Lady Corinne may have played a hand in it. The Patchetts are very solicitous about her condition, and they escorted us to Fog Willows in the hopes of seeing a full recovery." He paused, then added, "Cettie's disappearance has struck us all quite hard. The Patchetts were devastated to learn of Lady Corinne's deceits."

"Does Lady Maren have a new keeper yet?" Sera asked.

Adam shook his head. "No, but after that letter, she knows she will need one." His voice quavered with heartache.

She'd put it off long enough. Sera unfolded the letter, not recognizing the design of the seal that had closed it. Upon opening the paper, she immediately recognized Cettie's handwriting. How many letters had she gotten from her friend over the years? She would have known the style anywhere—the slant of the script, the neat scrawl. Just seeing it caused a stab of pain in Sera's heart. The knife went deeper as she started to read.

Mr. Creigh,

I am writing to you to bid you farewell. Forever. I am no longer in a position to accept your proposal of marriage. Things have happened in my life that are irrevocable. I have learned truths that have challenged the very core of who I am. This new knowledge has convinced me that I've been misguided. I believe you are as well. I will not let you suffer bearing the illusion that we can still fulfill the promises we made to each other. We are very different, you and I. While I have fond memories of our friendship, I believe you acted more out of pity than out of a real regard for my feelings. If you were to see me now, you would certainly be disappointed in me, and I wouldn't blame you. This parting is for the best. I have no intention of returning to Fog Willows. Be so kind as to pass along this note, along with my permanent resignation, to Lady Maren Fitzroy.

Knowing what I know now, I could never feel comfortable at that estate again.

Please do not seek me out. That would only be painful for both of us. I do not wish to be found. The empire of Comoros is a wretched place of abject misery. It has allowed the most downtrodden of all to be smashed under the boot of industry. What I suffered in the Fells still sickens me. I cannot go back. I will not go back. I know you are doing what you feel to be right, and that your honor may drive you to seek me out. Again, I implore you to forbear.

I do not ever wish to see you again.

Farewell,

Cettie

Sera closed her eyes, feeling the pain wash over her. Cettie had been her closest friend. She was the strong one. The valiant one. This shouldn't have happened. There was a parcel that Becka had agreed to give to Adam on a special day. Had it been destroyed or confiscated during the usurpation?

Perhaps it was for the best.

"What have they done to her?" she whispered harshly.

"It is her writing . . . but it isn't *her*," Adam said.

The weariness and despair in his voice made Sera's own anguish even keener. The words of the letter echoed in her mind. She turned the paper over, studying it. "There is no indication where she sent it from. How did it arrive at Fog Willows?"

"By zephyr post," Adam replied. "But I don't think she's in our world. It sounds like she's still over *there*."

Sera shook her head. "Maybe she was compelled to write it."

Adam winced. "I don't think so. But I do think she has been deceived. That she is under the power of unscrupulous people. I would like your permission, Your Highness, to travel to Kingfountain and search for her. I've asked you this before, and you did not grant my request. I'm begging you to do so now." He looked at her with firm resolve, with fierce determination.

"Even if you could stand on your own, I wouldn't grant it," Sera said, shaking her head no.

"Please!"

Sera thrust the letter back to him. "Do you understand what is happening, Adam? There is about to be bloodshed on the scale of *nothing* like we've ever seen before. I've unloosed it, but not deliberately. It's not a choice. It's a punishment . . . for us for how we've treated the poor. For them for how they've murdered our people. We may both of us be destroyed before this is through. I cannot send you over there. I may as well just hang you from the gallows here."

The look of pain in his eyes tortured her.

"Please, Sera," he begged. "Let me find her."

"How? We don't have the Cruciger orb anymore. It was stolen, no doubt by Lady Corinne! She was our harbinger, and she's gone. We don't have any way of finding her. And you would be killed." Sera breathed out forcefully. "No. The answer is no."

Adam's face crumpled. "Then I will join the fight. The empire needs surgeons. I can help save lives at least."

Sera closed the distance between them and put her hand on his arm. "No. You have always wanted to be a doctor in the Fells, but I have bigger plans for you. You are going to establish a hospital there. I will see that it is paid for, the arrangements made. You will be in charge of it. I have agents there now."

His shocked look was still tinged with bitterness.

"I will make the arrangements. You have done your duty to the empire a thousand times over. You're not a fleet doctor, Adam. You have always wanted to care for the poor. Well, they are still dying from the cholera morbus. Find a cure for it. Harness your passion for Cettie and do some good in this bloody world." She saw the tears in his eyes, the grief and despair. It made her own voice thicken. "I'm sorry, Adam. I'm so sorry. She's *my* friend too. I mean to find her, and when I do, I will make sure you are the first to know." She paused, her voice full of meaning. "I haven't given up on her yet."

She tried to smile encouragingly. But it was a frail hope to cling to. Cettie wasn't the kind of person who exaggerated her feelings. What she'd written in the letter, she'd meant.

~⸎~

The gray peaks of the distant mountains looked sharp enough to cut through a world. It was a massive range, the shadowed seams still thick with snow that refused to relinquish winter's hold. It was part of the world Sera had never seen, a spinelike mountain range that formed a border between several kingdoms in the empire. Her life had been confined to Lockhaven and Pavenham Sky, and she realized with a pang of regret that she had visited more of Trevon's world than her own. That would change now.

The tempest angled through the narrow crag between two of the largest mountains, and after they passed through it, Cruix Abbey appeared below in a surprising vista that made her gasp in awe. The abbey had been constructed into the cliff face itself, a series of levels and small, squat stone buildings. Even from the heights, Sera could see the trail connecting the abbey to the valley below. They had approached it from behind, and the sky ship had allowed them to bypass the treacherous road.

Smoke from chimneys wafted up from the abbey as the tempest changed its angle and began to descend to the landing yard far below. The thrill of the drop made Sera tighten her grip on the railing. There were soldiers to escort her, half a dozen blue-jacketed dragoons with arquebuses slung over their shoulders. But she neither knew them nor trusted them. She felt for the Tay al-Ard strapped to her forearm, comforted by its nearness. She would not be using the tempest to get back to Lockhaven.

After the ship had landed and the gangplank was lowered, Sera walked down with her escort of soldiers. They were greeted by the captain of Law who had been sent to pursue Lady Corinne the night before.

"Your Highness, welcome to Cruix Abbey."

"Thank you, Captain. Did you find her?"

His frown of disappointment answered her before his words could. "No, Your Majesty. But she was here, masquerading as a pilgrim. Would you like to see the Aldermaston?"

"I would. Take me to him."

"Follow me."

They crossed the small courtyard. The cliffs loomed so high in front of her it felt as if the stones would come crashing down as Pavenham Sky had done. The sun had risen past the vault of the mountains, putting the abbey in its shadow.

Sera had lived in sky manors all her life. Was this what it was like living in the shadow of one? The patches of snow in the heights made her yearn to climb the mountains, to come here as a pilgrim herself. She felt the familiar presence of the Mysteries as she walked deeper into the abbey grounds, sensed the Leerings embedded into the cornice decorations and pillars.

They entered one of the abbey towers, which was warm and fragrant with the smell of pine needles, and the captain brought her to the Aldermaston, who awaited her in his study. She was surprised to find that he wasn't alone.

The Aldermaston of Muirwood was also there, Thomas Abraham, the man she had studied under, the man who had administered the Test for her. Everything about him was familiar and welcome, from his huge gray sideburns to his glasses. The other man, also wearing the cassock of the order, was clean-shaven and had beefy jowls.

"Aldermaston!" Sera said with a brightness she felt.

"Welcome to Cruix, Sera," he replied. "Aldermaston Kearon does not speak your language very well, and he invited me to cross over and lend assistance this afternoon."

"Cross over?" Sera asked, perplexed.

"There are other ways to travel the empire than sky ship," he said. "I think I know why you are here."

Sera turned to the dragoons with her and motioned for them to leave the room. As soon as the door closed behind them, she felt a pulse in her mind, the activation of a Leering. Looking around the room, she tried to discover the source.

"That will prevent anyone from listening in," the Aldermaston said. "You are the empress now and have the right to learn certain Mysteries of Thought."

"Ich vorland zeen," said the other Aldermaston, nodding encouragingly.

"What did he say?" Sera asked.

"He said we will show you. Come with us."

"But Lady Corinne was here, was she not?" Sera pressed. "She came this way?"

"She did," the Aldermaston answered. "She poisoned this man and left him unconscious in his study. Several hours passed before concern for him compelled his steward to open the door. He's lucky to be alive. She has the ability to pass invisibly, we've discovered, so there was no trace of her departure. But she did come here. To this very room. It is the entrance, you see, to the vault inside the mountain."

"Take me there," Sera said.

A floor-to-ceiling picture frame hung on the stone wall behind the desk. The Aldermaston of Muirwood triggered a release on the frame, hidden in the decoration, and pulled on it. A door swung open, revealing a tunnel beyond. The three of them entered the tunnel, which was illuminated by small Leerings set into the rugged walls along the way. The corridor led to a stone door with a Leering set into it.

"Abemfrashe," said the other Aldermaston, and the stone door swung open.

As they approached, Sera felt a growing sense of dread in her heart. The fear was anchored not to the Aldermastons but to the Leering tucked into the darkness that lay ahead. The Leering that hosted Ereshkigal.

"What is this place?" Sera whispered.

"Before we go in, I need to tell you some history that you do not know." The Aldermaston pushed his glasses up higher on his nose. His look was serious, as if he worried what he was about to tell her would cause harm to someone. "Before Empress Maia ruled, she was the daughter of the King of Comoros. A daughter that her father chose to disinherit after he was seduced by a hetaera. What you do not know, Sera, what no one in our generation knows, is that Maia was tricked into becoming a hetaera herself."

Sera gaped at him in astonishment. "What are you saying?"

He held up his hand calmingly. "She was deceived. She did not realize it, but she was already under the thrall of the Myriad Ones. At the time, the ruins of an abbey in Dahomey held a Leering called the Hetaera Leering. It had been cursed, generations ago, so that any woman who accepted its brand on her shoulder would receive a curse. Her kiss became poison. Maia unwittingly sought out this Leering. Someone she'd trusted had taught her to use the Mysteries through a kystrel, even though it was forbidden for women—at that time—to learn. Maia went to the Hetaera Leering seeking answers to a problem facing her kingdom. Her intentions were good, but as I said, she was not herself part of the time. She unwittingly branded herself, and the curse was unleashed again."

He held up a finger. "Maia came to Cruix Abbey and burned it to ash. She killed its Aldermaston. Well, not her exactly, but the being . . . the malevolent spirit inhabiting her. She was racked with guilt for what she had been made to do. After she became the first empress, she rebuilt Cruix Abbey as you now see it. This, you see, is why she made it her life's work to purge the hetaera and the kishion from this world. She had seen firsthand what they were capable of . . . and what their goal was. It's the same thing that you learned taking the Test. The Myriad Ones would raze everything with fire. They would destroy the world."

Sera looked over at the other Aldermaston, who was listening to the conversation and nodded eagerly. Although he didn't speak the language well, he clearly understood what was being spoken.

The Aldermaston said, "Because of Maia's hunt, the hetaera order fled to the world of Kingfountain. There are, I've come to understand, other ways to travel between the worlds besides the mirror gates. The Queen of the Unborn, Ereshkigal, is confined to a Leering inside that chamber." He pointed to the door in front of them. "She was bound by Empress Maia herself after a great struggle. She knew that the Leering could not be bound forever, that there would come a day when people would actively seek to free Ereshkigal. As our world has become more depraved, so has the Leering weakened. Its influence is already apparent. Ereshkigal *wants* to be freed. She *wants* to punish the line of the one who bound her." The Aldermaston looked at her sternly. "You are the one that she seeks, for you are the one who can unbind her. She will use everything you care most deeply about to cajole you into liberating her. To trick you as she did Maia."

The Aldermaston sighed. Sera's heart churned with the awful dilemma. "There is no doubt that Ereshkigal's servants have infiltrated the court of Kingfountain. And now they have recruited General Montpensier to do their bidding. That is the reason they have sought to conquer us. This next war will be unlike any that has been fought before. It is a war that will baptize both of our worlds in blood."

Sera already knew this. The prospect sickened her. "What must we do, Aldermaston?"

His face was grim. "We must win it."

Sera closed her eyes and nodded. *Courage*, she told herself. *We must stand strong.*

"There is one more thing," the Aldermaston said. "Some time ago, you told me that there is a legend in Kingfountain about the Duchess of Brythonica coming here. Do you remember?"

"Of course I do," Sera said. "You said there was nothing. No account of it."

The Aldermaston nodded. "I did say that. I believed it to be true. But I have come to learn, from this Aldermaston," he added, putting his hand on the other man's shoulder, "that there is a record of it here at Cruix Abbey. Lady Sinia came *here*, Sera. It was never to be spoken of. And the information is considered so secret it may only be revealed to the emperor or empress. Not even the prime minister knows, for that role changes too frequently. I was not permitted to know this secret until now."

"What is it?" Sera begged, clutching her hands together.

"Lady Sinia did come here. She came to Cruix Abbey. The record says she cast a mighty spell on this abbey, a spell of protection. But before she departed, she left a warning. She said that in the future, an empress would unbind the Leering. The name of the empress, she said, was the Angelic One. She left the abbey and was never seen again. By anyone."

Sera gazed at him in growing horror. The Angelic One.

Seraphin.

EPILOGUE
FITZROY'S DEATH

All was in chaos, yet Brant Fitzroy felt a surge of calm in his heart. He had known this moment would come. He watched Raj Sarin fight three men at once, all of them Espion. The knife edge of his hand darted forward, a quick kick snapped toward this one's knee or that one's stomach. He broke the arm of one of the men, who'd raised a pistol to shoot the Bhikhu in the face. The shot went wide and gouged the bedpost that Fitzroy was using to prop himself up. The pain from his surgery had not yet subsided, and he breathed in deep gasps.

"We can't hold them!" shouted one of the king's guardsmen, who had been left to protect Fitzroy. A bullet ended his life just moments later.

Another Espion jammed a pistol into Raj Sarin's ribs, and Fitzroy watched the bullet exit the man's back with a spray of blood. Even wounded, Raj Sarin continued to fight, twisting the shooter's neck until it broke. Adam Creigh was at the door, shoving it back as the enemies outside cursed and screamed at them in raw hatred. The barrels of arquebuses snaked in, and more shots were fired. He watched one strike Adam in the arm, spinning him around and dropping him.

This was it. This was the last moment he could act. The defenses were breached, but a final guardsman strained against the door to try to keep it closed. It was an impossible task. Adam managed to make it back to his feet and clubbed one of the Espion with a water pitcher.

With the wooden bedpost still vibrating from the shot that had damaged it, Fitzroy sat down on the bed. His shirt was damp with sweat and speckled with blood. In that swirling moment of violence, he thought of his wife, Maren, of each of his children, including the daughter he had never been able to adopt, Cettie. Their images in his mind were a comfort. He prayed they'd be safe at Fog Willows, knowing that another storm of war was coming. This one would be far worse than the last. It would touch the lives of every man, woman, and child.

Then Adam was at his side, a desperate look on his face. He ducked beneath Fitzroy's good arm and tried to hoist him up.

"To the balcony," Adam panted. "I must get you away. I'm sorry, but this will hurt."

How like the young man . . . still hoping the worst would not happen. "I cannot make it. My death cannot be stopped now." With his good hand, he gripped Adam's and squeezed it hard, palm to palm, skin to skin. "Get yourself out. There's a little ridge of stone, it's not very wide. Use it to cross to another balcony. Get to Sera's rooms."

Adam's eyes widened with anguish. He shook his head no, so Fitzroy squeezed his hand even harder, forcing him to meet his gaze.

"You cannot ask me to forsake you," Adam pleaded. "They will have to kill me before I let them injure you again."

Fitzroy saw the determination in his eyes. Only seconds remained. Fitzroy released his grip and then hooked his hand around Adam's neck, pulling him so close that their foreheads touched. Mind to mind. Heart to heart.

"If you love me, then heed me, Adam. I order you, in the name of the Mysteries, to get out. Go to Miss Sera's rooms. I have known that

I will die, but you . . . you have the capacity to save countless others." Fitzroy's throat thickened. "The Knowing has a work for you to do, young man. Mine is finished. I accept it."

Tears streamed down Adam's face. "How can the Mysteries ask this of me? I . . . I would rather die too."

"I know. But you need to live. You need to live so that countless others can live too. Please, my son. My *faithful* son. Can't I trust you in this?"

The pain of his request hung in the air between them.

"I will do as you ask," Adam answered, lowering his eyes. "I don't understand why. But I will do it."

"Bless you, boy. Bless you." Fitzroy lifted his chin and kissed Adam's forehead. The exhaustion of the moment sapped the rest of his strength, and he swooned.

He felt Adam retreat to the balcony, and moments later the door burst open and a shot ended the last man's life. Fitzroy's dizziness made it difficult to focus. He lifted himself up on his elbow, wanting to face his final moment with courage. There was Raj Sarin on the floor, eyes open, lifeless, a pool of blood spreading beneath him. Faithful to the last. The guardsmen were sprawled around him. One of them was only wounded and groaning. A soldier came in and shot him dead in a stroke of cruel malice.

Fitzroy strained to rise again, using his good arm to prop himself. His other was bandaged crooked, still flaming in pain.

The soldier standing in the doorway with the smoking pistol gazed across the destruction with grim satisfaction on his face. He eyed Fitzroy lying on the bed.

"They're all dead, save him," said the man, stepping aside.

"Leave us," said the woman. Fitzroy recognized her voice. Lady Corinne.

"As you command," said the man before stepping away. Fitzroy felt the tremor of the Mysteries in the air, but it was tainted and throbbing with a fiery rage. The whole palace seemed thick with it. He'd felt it in the crowd earlier, like a savage fury that had been unleashed.

He expected to see Corinne's eyes glow silver. Wasn't that the side effect of using a kystrel? But no, her eyes were normal. She still looked like a lady, dressed in her fashions even though her skirts would drag in the blood on the floor. There was an almost wistful look on her face.

He gazed at her silently. She had won in the end. He'd underestimated her ruthlessness.

"Here we are at last," she said, her voice showing her sense of superiority.

"If you think this ends here, you are gravely mistaken," Fitzroy replied.

She approached him, stepping around the bodies littering the floor as if they were nothing but driftwood. "I've been waiting for this moment for a long time, Brant."

"I imagine you have."

"You still don't understand. You still don't recognize me. But I shouldn't be surprised. People are so easy to deceive."

"What do you mean?" Fitzroy asked. Each second was a gift now. Each painful breath. "What have you done to Cettie?"

"You took her away from *me*, Brant. She was never yours. I brought her to the place where Mrs. Pullman sent me. She's one of us now."

He closed his eyes, the anguish for his child flaring inside him, but then her words registered and caught him up short. "Mrs. Pullman?" He opened his eyes again.

She was near him now. And then he watched as she aged before his eyes. Watched as the cheekbones altered, the eyes changed color, the forehead narrowed. She still wore the same gown—that wasn't an illusion—but everything else had changed. He knew her now, and it slammed into his chest as a battering ram.

"Christina," he said.

"So you recognize me at last," she said, her tone playful. "All these years, Brant. All these years I'd hoped you would recognize me, despite my disguise."

"You haven't *always* been Corinne," Fitzroy said, shaking his head. "She's younger."

"Which made her a more suitable victim," the woman said. "I was her governess first. I went by *Kathryn* then. I helped mold her. Helped her woo Admiral Lawton. All the while I watched you from Pavenham Sky. To see if you'd be faithful to me, as . . . you . . . had promised." She shook her head subtly. "And you weren't. You fell in love with another, just as Jevin said you would. It wasn't cruelty that prompted Maren's shame. It was vengeance."

"Why, Christina?" Fitzroy asked, his heart panging sharply. "Why reveal yourself now? Why didn't you tell me?"

"Oh, and how would that have looked?" she said scornfully. "Would your father have cared any more about me then?"

"Father was dead."

"I know. I killed him."

Fitzroy's eyes flared.

"I'm a poisoner, Brant. And a hetaera. I'm more than the powerless wretch I was. Shuttled away to the Fells. Hidden and concealed. You have no idea what I endured. And I promised myself I would bring all of the sky manors crashing down. Starting with Pavenham Sky. I'm not alone in my quest. And now, with my daughter as an ally, I can accomplish what I set out to do when *you* interfered with my plans. I don't know how you found her in the Fells. But she is my daughter, my flesh and blood. Her father isn't that simpleton you found down below. He was a kishion who trained me in the poisoner school."

"She is good," Fitzroy said. "Her heart is good."

Christina smirked. "So was mine. We can change, Brant. She already is. I just wanted to bid you farewell. Before a hetaera can assume er full power, there is one thing she must do. She must betray someone she loves." A sigh escaped her lips. "That's why I've been waiting to kill you. Until now."

He saw the dagger. He felt it plunge into his breast, into his *heart*. The jolt, the pain, the blinding light. He couldn't breathe.

There were tears in her eyes. Remorse? As his vision blurred, he pitied what she had become. What his own father had driven her to. So many choices spread over so many decades, each one culminating into this moment. How many years had he searched for her in vain? In the end, he'd been hunting her, unwittingly, still. It was over now. He no longer had the strength to fight. Had he taught his children, by his own example, to be better than himself? Each decision, each action, carried so much weight, rippled into the vast eternity of outcomes. Be kind. Be courageous. Be gentle. These were things he'd never learned from his own father. Was his own life enough to break the cycle?

"Farewell, my love," she whispered, kissing his cheek.

And he died realizing that Sera had been truly inspired in her Gifting. Her words whispered in his mind, but it wasn't Sera's voice he heard this time. He felt a peacefulness enwrap him, felt the pain of the mortal coil subside as his heart stopped its struggle to beat.

I Gift you with confidence to know that your deeds will be remembered for generations to come. That your strength and your compassion will inspire the hearts of many yet unborn. Your time in the second life is over. Well done, faithful servant. Your offering has been acceptable.

You will see her face before the end.

AUTHOR'S NOTE

Give me a moment while I dry my eyes. When I was in college at San Jose State, I wrote a novel about the Massacre of St. Bartholomew's Day in Paris in 1572. It was a historical-fiction story about a Jesuit priest who had learned kung fu while on a mission in China, and how he was charged to escort the daughter of a Huguenot spy across France. Throw in some Spanish inquisitors chasing them, and you have the plot in a nutshell of *Tho Death Bar the Way*. While that book will never see the light of day, I've remained interested in that era of history, and some of the surprising details that have stuck with me over the years helped inspire the Harbinger Series.

One of those details had to do with the historical figure Admiral Gaspard de Coligny. He was part of the Huguenots who struggled for religious freedom in France. A marriage took place between a Catholic princess and a Huguenot prince in an effort to end the nightmarish civil wars raging in France during the Reformation. Admiral Coligny was fired at by an assassin. Only, he'd stopped to fix his shoe just as the primitive rifle fired. That little pause spared his life—for a few days—as well as convinced those responsible to instigate the massacre. History swings on small hinges.

I also love the play *Les Misérables* and how Valjean offered to sacrifice his life for the life of Marius, a young revolutionary student who was in love with his adopted daughter, Cosette. History, literature, and music are all big inspirations in my life. Fitzroy is a character whom I have loved and connected with.

There are more secrets to be uncovered as we continue this tale of two worlds. Get ready for the final climax as two powerful civilizations collide. See you again in Book 5 of the Harbinger Series!

ACKNOWLEDGMENTS

When I hatched the idea for the Harbinger Series, I knew I needed five books in order to tell this story. Without the past references, the struggles in Sera's and Cettie's lives, the conflict coming in Book 5 would not be possible. So many people have helped bring this complicated vision to fruition.

To Jason, who believed in Cettie and Sera from the beginning and helped persuade the powers that be to take a risk on an extended saga like this one. His inputs all along the way have been helpful and encouraging. Each book has attempted to raise the stakes, which is his editing mantra and words that I live by.

To Angela, my incredible development editor, who came back from maternity leave just in time to edit this without skipping a beat. A wonderful adventure awaits you in parenthood. (If you knew how much influence she had in these books, you'd leave reviews for her on Amazon as well!)

And to my dedicated first readers who endure the torture of keeping quiet about my latest works: Emily, Isabelle, Shannon, Robin, Travis, Sunil, Sandi, and Dan. Thank you all!

ABOUT THE AUTHOR

Photo © 2016 Mica Sloan

Jeff Wheeler is the *Wall Street Journal* bestselling author of the Kingfountain Series, the Muirwood and Mirrowen novels, and the Harbinger Series. He took an early retirement from his career at Intel in 2014 to write full time. He is a husband, father of five, and devout member of his church. He lives in the Rocky Mountains and is the founder of *Deep Magic: The E-zine of Clean Fantasy and Science Fiction.* Find out more about *Deep Magic* at www.deepmagic.co, and visit Jeff's many worlds at www.jeff-wheeler.com.